The Kakos Realm

Book III:
Death Upon the Fields of Splendor

BY

Christopher D. Schmitz

The Kakos Realm:
Death Upon the Fields of Splendor

Published by Tree Shaker Books

Christopher D Schmitz

PUBLISHED BY TREESHAKER BOOKS
please visit:
http://www.authorchristopherdschmitz.com

For Jason who pestered me for years to keep writing this story and for Adam and Becky who refused to let me write crap and kept making me write better versions of the original Kakos Realm stories.

Christopher D Schmitz

Prologue

Millennia ago, powerful forces drew unbreakable lines; sides were chosen between the two elder powers. But one of the leaders was a liar. From the very beginning, men chose the false words of hay-lale' above the life-giving ones of Yahweh.

Even before the days of mighty Mahalaleel, great-grandson of Seth, the twisted kakos burst into existence—clothed in reality. Supernatural in nature, the basic laws that governed the original reality applied less here. Earth's mankind flocked to this new place where they supposed they had even greater freedom. In reality, they shackled future generations in chains forged of impiety—bondage disguised as freedom.

hay-lale' created other creatures in mockery of man and angel; they permeated his realm of wickedness: where they called home. The ekthro were hay-lale's children, as much as mankind belonged to Yahweh. This domain of altered reality masked and ensnared the hearts and minds of the human race. Corruption spilled over into the realm of Earth and iniquity spread across her lands like a plague. Mankind grew so vile and perverse that it grieved Yahweh—the very God who had given it life. The only option, if He was to fulfill the original plan, was to purge the Earth and sever the link of corruption. Only Noah and his family were spared through the waters of the global flood.

The supernatural gateway joining these worlds, flooded by the waters, barred further passage. Those who had sought respite from the sin-cursed soil of Earth remained trapped in the Kakos. This inescapable place offered no peace of soul. The convicting power of the Spirit which once hovered above the waters was cut off from mankind—reduced to a mere vestigial whispering of the soul.

But, that which is created cannot be so easily forsaken. There had always existed a contract between Yahweh and hay-lale'. Prophecy was written at the dawn of time, and none of hay-lale's creation could deter Yahweh's will. It had been decreed even before the ancient rebellion.

After waters flooded the passage between realms, both human and demon-kind trapped were within hay-lale's creation. Though hay-lale' cared little for the fate of his own kind, Yahweh made provisions for appointed messengers to be sent for his wayward creation.

With hay-lale' absent from the realm, the remaining demon overlords warred amongst themselves, eventually forming a governing body to share in their power base; they created the Gathering in the interest of self-preservation. The council deceived mankind further yet, creating a religion designed to mislead those humans drawn to spiritual introspection. They conceived the Great Lie. Some men's souls yearned for something deeper and a false religion gave them a placebo. The faith honored the fallen creator of this realm: the Luciferian Order came into being.

On Earth, the powers of death and darkness, long harnessed by the Deceiver, was thrown down at the foot of Golgotha. Their submission marked the beginning of the end for Lucifer, the one named hay-lale'. The door to redemption had suddenly been flung wide open to all mankind.

The victory of the cross marked the insertion of the first herald. The chosen angel, Karoz, hurtled through the breach, proclaiming the message of redemption to those trapped inside the forgotten, malevolent lands.

The power of such sacrifice drew men unto the truth. A faithful seed quickly grew into a great flock until the Gathering rose against their immortal, heaven-born enemy. They smote any who pledged devotion to Yahweh and set upon them with the full brunt of their might. Capturing their leader, Karoz, the Gathering eventually drove them out. The remnant scattered like dust in the wind and the under-demons hunted them down until only a small population remained, driven into faraway lands. Living in seclusion, they became only a minimal threat, and one now ruled by fear and self-preservation

They lived, and continue to live, under the cloud of oppression, exiled like some secret cult with a true gnosticism. They possess occluded truth, but remain fearful to violate their mandate against proclamation, too afraid of sharing Karoz's fate. The secret community keeps its traditions and hides the light like a candle battling the wind.

Cautious fear permeates their culture. Any persons who leave are never heard from again. The last such man, Nhoj, clung to his faith, charged with the work Karoz had called them to. He never returned.

Nhoj languished in an eastern dungeon. By faith he healed an injured warrior, a mercenary who had been betrayed and stripped of everything… a warrior marked with destiny.

The fated warrior, a man of renown, possessed great potential in whatever he applied his hand to. But his was just another life shattered and broken by the kakos, like a potter's vase crushed to grog. Nhoj had given him health, but he was brought lower than any thought possible by the trials; Rashnir became the scorn of even the lowest of slaves. Only then was he prepared to meet the final herald of Yahweh's message.

Yahweh's wrath boiled over in the Earth realm as he prepared to pour out his vengeance upon the face of the Earth. But in the midst of the coming retribution, one man slipped through the passage to give witness to those men and women trapped within the realm—people who had never heard the Truth.

Kevin Johnson, with his two bodyguards, the least ranking among Heaven's angels, located the fallen Rashnir. Together, they launched a revolution.

The demonic Gathering, led by the bitter demon beh'-tsah and his dark prophet Absinthium, rise against anything that threatens their power. But even as they plot to seize control of the entire realm and subjugate all its inhabitants, the demons scheme amongst themselves. For eons beh'-tsah' planned to crown himself as the new Lucifer, but long-brewing coup within the ranks of the Gathering delay his dark machinations.

As Yahweh's faithful ones readied themselves to peacefully depart their home in the outlying lands of Grinden, Absinthium roused a war party against his adversaries. They would not be allowed to spread the antithetical message any further. The spread of the Spirit was the only thing the arch-mage had ever seen strike true fear into his master, the dread lord beh-tsah'. The small forces of Spirit-led warriors crushed the Luciferian forces arrayed against them at the quarry of Jand.

The battle was proclaimed a Luciferian victory, a twisted piece of propaganda used to pull more coins into the Order's coffers, though it cost the dark lord of the Gathering more than he had planned and more than he could afford. Claiming to have expelled the renegade threat from their region, the Luciferians continue rallying for more support and tighten their stranglehold on local governments. Broadening their forces and shifting their strengths, they are ever searching for Rashnir's elusive group in order to extract further, deadly retribution.

These second-generation followers of Yahweh understand the importance of their mission; unbelieved by the rest of the realm, only seven years remain according to the prophecy proclaimed by the mysterious travelers from Earth. After that time, the entire land will erupt in flame, destroying itself. The great conflagration will spread, intensifying until it reaches the great gate between the realms. Folding in on itself, it will become a great lake of fire; those left behind will suffer horribly, regardless of their allegiance to Yahweh, the Order, or pursuit of their own lusts.

The Christians, split into three primary groups as they exited Grinden. Kevin's group, the most visible and notorious of these, allowed themselves to be escorted beyond the kingdom of Jand by the wary Luciferian influenced military. Armies from the Nindan government closed off the eastern route, and Kevin settled his encampment on the vertex where four countries joined borders. They waited at the crossroads, praying for direction and guidance as they sought out their next step.

With the armies of Jand and Ninda camping in plain view of the Christians, only Lol and Gleend remained viable options. Kevin, accompanied by many of his friends including Rondhale, Nipanka, Werthen, Rah'-be, and Sil-tarn, await direction. Each of his friends intends to take splinter groups in different paths, spreading their "heresy" like seeds in the wind.

The warrior, Rashnir, leads another group of Christians. Skirting the southern barrens below Grinden, they sneak into the country of Ninda with another team led by his werewolf friend Zeh-Ahbe'.

The third cluster, heading southwest, also skirted the barrens, leaving for the opposite direction. Mirrored on one edge by the Quey forest, the sea buffers them on the other, a corridor of relative safety and substantial concealment. Ersha, Drowdan, Gans, and Thim lead teams west: some destined for the harsh culture of Zipha, others expecting reprisal once the powers that rule Jand discover that the enemy remains within their borders.

Whichever ignorant commander ordered the escort of Kevin's men beyond the borders will face a likely execution. The archmage's order had been to shadow their movements and stall for as long as possible; the Luciferian leader intended to contain them and eventually annihilate whatever threat they posed. Now, any surveillance of their enemies had been thwarted.

War still rages within the Babel heavens, a place known as Paradise, though perhaps glibly. Demonic usurpers contend for beh'-tsah's power and two main groups vie against each other. Still, only beh'-tsah realizes the danger of an unleashed power of the Holy Spirit. He is forced to wage two separate wars, each on different fronts; losing either fight means his undoing, perhaps even the destruction of the Gathering itself and the unlocking of the eldritch fetters that bind the realm together as they allow the demons to harvest its arcane energies.

More than anything else the dark lord of the Gathering desires to dominate his enemies. He wants to flaunt his power before the Most High and parade his accomplishments before even hay-lale'. For now, the demon-lord beh-tsah' can only take pleasure in gloating to his tortured, trophy prisoner.

High above the lower firmament, upon the dusky clouds of the Babble Heavens, the emaciated angel Karoz remains clapped within brazen gyves. Fettered by supernatural chains, he languishes in the dungeons underneath the Lord of the Gathering's throne, deep within the Babel Keep... a place where no holy thing should be forced to visit but where he has remained for millennia.

CHAPTER ONE

"That's just a rumor," the human spat as he leaned across the bounty officer's table, disagreeing with Herang, the charismatic elf who operated it in conjunction with the Order.

"No it's not," the elf insisted. "And I heard that it was Khadron himself riding atop the wooly mammoth. Riding west he was with a full complement of his best Mankran berserkers." Herang hushed his voice when he noticed the barbarian in a troupe nearby.

The Mankran locked eyes with the elf and then continued on his way. Ironically, he was only the third tallest of his hunting party; the other two were something else entirely. The locally renowned company of Nephilim and Phoenix continued through the courtyard at the Temple of Light in pursuit of their next bounty.

"Hogwash!" the human exclaimed.

Herang stepped back in mock offense. "Sheech! Sheech, come tell Jael that I'm right."

A massive humanoid ducked through the doorway and stood up straight. The giant stood nearly ten feet tall. Sheech stretched in the sunlight and nodded. "Herang is right, Jael. I told him the story myself."

Jael waved his words away. "That doesn't make it true! I heard the exact same story in the pub two days ago!"

Sheech leaned over the countertop, daring the diminutive human to challenge him. "I saw it with my own eyes. I was in Paradise on business when I spotted

14

him—the warlord chieftain Khadron the Terrible. His mammoth pulled a giant ark mounted with sleigh rails and his crew of berserkers rode atop of it. I tell you, Khadron was nearly as big as any of my kin."

Jael almost spat with laughter. "A wooly mammoth you say! How did he get a mammoth into Paradise?" He shook his head skeptically, "I think that renowned Anakim constitution failed you—it sounds more like a booze-addled dream than the usual love stories this one tries to convince me of," Jael pointed a mocking thumb to Herang.

"Hey!" Herang protested when a messenger interrupted them, yanking a crate off the rickshaw he'd pulled up to the bounty office.

Jael chuckled and walked away, letting the two get back to work.

"What's this?" Herang asked.

The messenger shrugged. "Dunno—but it came from the Council of Four."

Herang whistled. "Straight from the top." Its contents had to be important if they'd come from the office of the ruling arch-mages.

Sheech cracked the wooden box open and raised an eyebrow. Herang snatched the packing notes and read them.

"New orders," the elf said, taking out a fistful of printed flyers. "These are the highest priority hits ordered by the Luciferian Church."

Sheech looked at the faces drawn on the pages. "These puny humans are more dangerous than vampires?"

"Apparently so," Herang said and began stacking the handbills.

The giant shrugged and began tacking the bounty pages on the top row of the advertisement wall where the elf couldn't reach.

"I don't ask questions or think," Herang said, "I just get paid to organize the hitmen."

***

grr'Shaalg stalked through his underground domicile while making the final preparations for a secret meeting. His brother tyr-aPt, one of ten goblin kings, would soon arrive in Under-Grinden.

He quietly reveled in the fact that his brother was not the real king. tyr-aPt had always only been a mere pawn, a puppet ruler whose strings were pulled only by his devious brother grr'Shaalg.

[Var-shNarr!] snapped grr'Shaalg, [go and retrieve a body for our feast. Speak to no-one.]

[Just *one* body?] The majordomo found the request out of sorts, given his master's ravenous appetite as of late. All goblin rulers leaned towards gluttony.

grr'Shaalg glared back at his minion in response. He had made his command.

Var-shNarr bowed and silently departed the spacious dwelling; his padded feet made a distinct slapping noise against the damp, stone floors as he hurried away. grr'Shaalg had commanded him to silence and Var-shNarr knew better than to break that trust for fear of his life and the lives of his kindred.

grr'Shaalg smiled toothily. He may have become the most powerful goblin to ever exist, he vainly speculated—at least *he would be* by the time his plans came to fruition. Once his plans began unfolding in real time his power would be undisputable.

As Var-shNarr meandered through Under-Grinden's network of tunnels, he saw that clean-up efforts were already well underway. Just days ago, a massive cave-in wrecked a great portion of the new goblin city. Three-quarters of Grinden's Luciferian Temple had collapsed and sunk into the subterranean haven.

Despite the destruction, Under-Grinden still remained an impressive sight: a marvel of underground engineering. Its glorious, massive caverns were dug from deep within the bedrock like a hollow globe and it lay directly underneath the central park at Grinden's center. This was the most ambitious goblinoid project to date.

The immense, stone spire spanning from the floor to the ceiling of the subterranean cavity looked like a jaded butte, like some kind of giant, stone, apple-core. Undoubtedly, the Babble Spire in Briganik had inspired it in part. Around the tower looped Under-Grinden's access to the surface-world where a rocky stairway exited into the surface world's park high above them. The spire also housed the dwellings of the elite. Only the wealthy and affluent members of the goblin hierarchy were permitted domicile space on the core.

Farther towards edges of the orb, the lesser goblins' homes protruded like hives. At odd places in the elliptically shaped walls, huge tunnels opened in different directions. Each connected to the mysterious goblin super-highway.

Var-shNarr arrived at the massive mound of debris when a sentry near the wreckage stopped him. The bodies of dead men were reserved for privileged members of goblin society. Only certain ones had access to the tasty treasures buried in the rubble of the cave-in. The fetid odor of bloating bodies intermingled with the musty air of the cavern and made Var-shNarr's mouth water.

[Halt!] a guard commanded. The sentry grabbed Var-shNarr by the hair and twisted his head around to examine his cheek and neck; he exposed a branded mark that labeled Var-shNarr as grr'Shaalg's slave. [State your business.]

Limbs and parts of human bodies hung limp, peeking out from the stony rubble heap. Arms and faces distended and swelled with the macabre distension of rot and decay. Daring members of the lowest castes had previously rummaged through the rubbish, exposing the bodies. The smallest ones, young folk and children— would be among the tastiest of the buried morsels; they had already been snuck away, hence the need for the sentinels.

[My master wants to eat,] he said matter-of-factly. The sentry released Var-shNarr to his duties.

He dug through the collapsed chantry rubble until his sensitive nose caught the pungent scent of a nearby corpse. He quickly exhumed the cadaver; with much grunting and sweat, he carried it back to his master's hole.

As Var-shNarr returned, lugging the carrion upon his back, he spotted the glimmering armor worn by the troop of royal bodyguards who standing outside the entry. King tyr-aPt had apparently arrived while he was out gathering the meal.

The slave dragged in the body inside and laid it upon his master's table. grr'Shaalg and tyr-aPt had engaged in small talk as they waiting for their feast to arrive and they stopped to look at him while he came. Var-shNarr stood at attention while grr'Shaalg looked the body over.

[Very good,] grr'Shaalg grinned wickedly, pleased with the cadaver positioned haphazardly before him. [A most excellent selection, Var-shNarr,] the goblin praised him. [In fact, I recognize this man; he was once the head priest at the Temple above.]

The shadow ruler grinned as he scanned Frinnig's body with a mischievous eye. [You have been a good servant to me, Var-shNarr, and you know my distaste for potential loose ends. This meeting must remain absolutely secret.] With uncanny speed, grr'Shaalg snatched his surprised servant by the throat and choked the life from him. [Besides, I've always preferred my prey fresh.]

As the light died behind Var-shNarr's eyes, he suddenly understood his master's command to keep silent, also the instruction to recover just one body. His vision blurred fuzzy and then blackened; his spastic struggles ceased.

grr'Shaalg tossed the warm body up next to the cold Luciferian. He and his brother set upon the meal before getting down to business. Their treacherous trade required utmost secrecy lest it ignite a civil war in the goblin realms below the surface.

***

Angry clouds boiled high above the mountains of Briganik. Across the plains of the second firmament, and through the hallways beneath the throne-room of the Lord of the Gathering, a solitary figure stalked the ancient corridors. The cloak-shrouded creature shimmered between the spirit realm and physical reality as needed in order to avoid the posted sentries: an untraceable wraith passing through forbidden places. He was skilled enough to avoid even those piercing gazes of the demons and spirit creatures who could peer into both realities.

The watcher ambled around the bends in the corridor until he exited the demon lord beh'-tsah's compound. His steps brought him to the Grand Stairway where he solidified and appeared as if he was just another faithful Luciferian on a pilgrimage to Paradise... except this pilgrim accessed places others were never allowed to go. Without remorse he violated the privacy of the Gathering, accessing the secret vaults of the overlord's keep.

Grinning, the figure descended the broad, spiral staircase that telescoped upwards and through the Babel Tower. It would eventually bring him to the muddy surface of the abysmal realm wherein he'd been trapped for so long. He paid witness to so many recent events in the Babel Heavens: things that gave him pause for thought and gave him a renewed capacity for hope.

He desperately wanted to reach his destination, but he'd long ago vowed not to use his phenomenal powers and so he remained on foot. At least The Watcher had a long walk to sort out his thoughts.

Despite his conversation with the secret prisoner and the knowledge he'd stolen from the council, he still needed more information. The hidden one needed to seek out the man who claimed to come from Earth, the one whom Yahweh sent.

***

Even despite his perilous circumstances, Kevin wouldn't have chosen any other place or any other situation. Friends surrounded him and he knew he walked in destiny; nothing could be better than that—despite the unique difficulties.

He'd come only recently from Earth, the sister realm. Suddenly snatched up into heaven, he was charged to stand firm against the demonic gathering, enter the realm of Kakos, and lead back those followers of Christ before the realm erupted with fire and judgment.

Such an incredible mission could not be resisted. He'd devoted everything of his prior life to the worship of his God. Kevin lived each day as if his homeland was a mission field, tried to work towards the calling that he knew he'd received. Though he had no idea why he, specifically, had been chosen for this mission; he had no real skills for this, and despite all the men and women to ever exist prior to Kevin Johnson, only *he* had been chosen for this task. Sometimes divine choices thoroughly confused him.

Kevin had no idea as to the Lord's purpose, but he knew better than to question it. He simply accepted the mission and walked the figurative footsteps of Christ out as his guide. Using that as his rule amazing transformations followed; an entire country had started to change.

Not all welcomed the message of redemption, however. Most people, and all ekthro—the direct creations of Lucifer, lived their lives in direct contradiction to the Word. The result was clear, those who'd found hope followed Kevin; everyone else persecuted their burgeoning number. Many had actively risen up to destroy them, even.

Only recently, Kevin's traveling group settled down where four countries' borders met: a literal no-man's land. They'd been evicted from the Kingdom of Jand whose armies encamped just on the horizon as they sought to prevent any reentry.

Luckily, Kevin reflected, the Luciferian King Rutheir died in the invasion against the Christians when they were still near Grinden. The momentary disarray that ensued after his death in battle gave the Christians a small window of opportunity to escape the schemes of the wicked ones colluding against them in Jand. Dividing their numbers, they spread out and left the area before Absinthium and his Luciferian forces could try to contain them again.

The wary military forces of Jand, having seen the supernatural power wielded by their Christian enemies politely, but firmly, escorted them to the border. A Nindan army had come to block access to their country as well; Jand and Ninda often joined interests and it was very probable that the Archmage meddled with *their* politics, too.

Gleend and Lol remained their only two options. Kevin refused to proceed further until he'd prayed about it and felt clearly direction.

Kevin took his seat with those friends and counselors who'd accompanied him. It became his custom to meet with a group of advisors each morning— his job had become too big for any one man.

Rondhale, the bereaved blacksmith, sat closest to Kevin. Rondhale lost his twin brother during the battle in the quarry and he took the loss with great difficulty.

Nipanka sat with a few of his trusted people from Northern Jand. His group in Driscul had grown immensely; nearly half the people in that town joined with Kevin's group as it moved past. Nipanka found the need to appoint his own elders and leader in the same manner that Kevin had done. Thaadim and Erki sat with him, along with their teenage daughter Katerna; also present was Kadoz and Naphta. Their little girls Ezer and Rhabba played nearby with some other children. Kadoz had been radically changed after Rashnir and Zeh-Ahbe' rescued him from a coven of ravenous under-demons.

Werthen sat with the werewolves Rah'-be, and Sil-tarn. He missed the companionship of his friends Rashnir and Zeh-Ahbe' and so he gravitated towards Zeh-Ahbe's kinsmen, an animalistic people that he shared so much in common with. He glanced over his shoulder to check on his ferrets; they romped happily around Ezer and Rhabba's feet chirping happily as the animals were prone to do.

Of course, Kevin's angelic bodyguards were ever present. Jorge and Kyrius were the largest of those who circled the small campfire.

Kevin shared a personal tent with the elf, Dri'Bu and the former Luciferian monk, Minstra. Minstra had also lost someone very close to him and he had nowhere else to go, but he could not seem to accept the Christian message either... as if he was in a state of spiritual shock.

The preacher had grown close to his tent-mates. However, neither were a part of his council except in an occasional, advisory capacity.

As he faced his friends, Kevin's thoughts raced. This task is what God had prepared his life for and he was ready to rise to the challenges.

"My friends," he addressed them, "I am so glad to be with you for whatever little time we still have. I trust that you have all been praying and seeking direction for your teams. We know that we cannot go into Ninda because of their military blockade." Kevin indicated the wall of armored men standing in the distance.

"It is not so much that we *cannot* enter that country; we have little reason to do so. Other teams have already gained access." Kevin held up a tightly bound scroll sent via raven. "Rashnir and Zeh-Ahbe' send their greetings from Ninda. When we passed through Driscul they were just entering the Kantror farm district."

The people in the circle happily smiled and nodded. That their friends, perhaps the two most notorious of their acquaintances, might not make it out of Jand undetected had always been a concern.

Kevin held up another scroll. "More good news," he said, "Drowdan writes that they've encountered no surveillance. He says that they have the buzz of the forest to the north and the sounds of the ocean to the south. They have a perfectly peaceful corridor to travel through which appears untouched by any man or ekthro. They hope to arrive at the southwest edge of the Quey forest in a few days. Then, they too will divide further.

"I have a few general ideas of how we should disperse through the region, but do any of you have specific input that you want to share?"

"We are planning to divide my numbers in half," Nipanka informed them. "Thaadim and Erki will take over the secondary group."

"A wise decision," Kevin assented. Each of the eleven team-leaders retained a few more than one hundred people to each group; Nipanka's workload was greater than any other man's. Kevin agreed that sharing the burden would be smart.

Nipanka continued, "We plan on going into Lol. I think that the people of Driscul will be able to relate to the men and women of the mining communities which dot the countryside. Although, some of our own intend to travel east, cutting across Ninda to reach southeastern Gleend as quickly as possible. We understand that we're committed to a westerly migration, but they want to try and reach their Gleendish loved ones immediately and then make for the Western Gate beyond Nod."

Rah'-be spoke up, "I plan to skirt through the south-eastern Lol and Gleend border and go into Domn."

His kinsman, Sil-tarn looked at him, surprised. It was apparent that he did not know of his friend's plans. Their parting was inevitable, but it had come earlier than expected

"We know almost nothing about Domn," Rah'-be explained. "Even the elf, Dri'Bu, has little knowledge of it beyond the fact that it's a desolate place; such little information passes its borders—not because of hostility but because there seems so little worth drawing people beyond its borders."

Rah'-be continued, "The words that you spoke, Kevin, at the communion and funeral service have burrowed deep within my heart. You said that every human deserves the chance to hear the Gospel message at least once in their lifetime. I fully agree and cannot discount any people who might exist in that country. People of the sparsely populated regions are no less important than the strategic areas you all travel to."

Sil-tarn nodded his head. "You must do as you feel called to do, brother. Not a day will go by that I'll forget to pray for your mission to the men and women of Domn."

"Your goal is noble, and in the Lord's will," Kevin said. "Resistance is everywhere and not everyone will meet with the same measure of success, but you can never know when words or actions might break through and reach someone. Sometimes, when we think that an audience has completely closed their minds and hearts to the Truth, the Holy Spirit will finally bring light to their hearts and minds." Kevin looked sidelong at their prisoner as he spoke; Prock, the Wyvern Rider, leader of Absinthium's now destroyed acolytes, stared daggers of hatred at the leadership council seated around the nearby fire.

His arms remained tied behind a pole firmly planted in the ground. Were it not so, their captive would assuredly try to murder them all.

***

Lightning flashed, cinder and ash blew by and lithe bodies jumped in tandem. Tucking into a rolling maneuver, they stayed below the danger that whizzed just above their heads. Iron shurikens in the shape of a multi-rayed sun zipped above the heads of the black-clad initiates.

They jumped and dodged the bladed projectiles as they pressed onward towards their goal at the center of the field. Absinthium watched over the exercise; it was really more of a culling session, in reality.

Twenty-three men raced through the Fields of Splendor, the grassy field that lay in between the Babel Tower and the Monastery of Light, perched atop the Briganik mountains. These men had been handpicked by the Luciferian prophet to join the ranks of the acolytes. Twenty-seven men had been selected; their numbers would be brutally pruned until only twelve remained. They would replace those who had been lost in the fight at Grinden.

The Battle of Grinden was a momentous loss for the Luciferian Order, though only a handful of individuals even knew that it had gone poorly. Absinthium lost all of his acolytes except for Wynn, the team's explosives expert. The caisson master was now the leader of his acolytes.

Absinthium, along with his remaining acolyte, were able to recover only nine of the deceased members' bodies. The other dead men were lost amongst the wreckage or too ruined to use in their dark magics. Wynn would not miss his rival, the Wyvern Rider.

Surrounding the battlefield where these men trained stood those nine cadaverous bodies. The arch-mage and his remaining servant had performed the necessary necromantic rites to reanimate the corpses of those fallen in battle. Dark servants of the temple had previously stitched up and bolted together those bodies crushed at Grinden under giant stones flung from the heavens.

While the necromantic nine acolytes could be used efficiently and easily, they consumed a great deal of power to maintain and only Absinthium could do it for long. The archmage could only keep them animated properly while they remained in the range of sight, after that they shambled along like any regular zombie. If nearby, Wynn could maintain the nine, but it consumed all of his concentration to do so.

The Acolytes needed to be whole again—they were a critical piece of dark plans already set in motion. Each member of the team filled a special role; each acolyte brought specific talents to the group, and those skillsets were lumped into the collective unit under Absinthium's direction.

Twenty-three men dodged past each other and through the fray, trying to attain their goal: to enter combat and kill their marked opponent without getting killed themselves. The training was grueling and there were specific rules to the deadly game. Candidates were not allowed to hinder each other in their pursuit of their opponent; doing so would fatally disqualify them.

Meandering through the makeshift barricades, stepping in and out of the flickering flame light hurried orc slaves Absinthium had shipped in for their training exercises. Each one nearly human in appearance, they differed from their goblin ekthro in many noticeable ways. The goblins possessed hunched backs, elongated snouts, a slightly chitinous hide, and crooked legs with short bulbous tails; orcs stood straight like men, though maybe more muscled, with green or olive skin, and a mouth like a boar. Some even brandished the beginnings of tusks.

The orcs on the training field each brandished a sword and buckler provided by their keepers. Each was promised their freedom if they could slay one of the acolyte initiates. But it would not matter—none of them were expected to survive.

The real danger of the course was the unexpected: shurikens hurled by the undead acolyte, or a bolt of arcane lightning, or a fireball hurled by Absinthium. Someone would be culled tonight, the mage was sure of it.

Steeling himself, the first initiate locked eyes with his target and taunted him. The orc bellowed and ran headlong into combat. Noticing movement in his peripheral, the initiate sidestepped the orc and rolled under a shuriken as it lodged in the barricade behind him. The orc hurtled a wooden obstacle and brought his sword to bear.

Blocking the blow, the human used the shaft-like moto of his kama to prevent a death-blow and hooked the orc's abdomen with his second hand-held kama. The blade ripped upward and split the creature open as if it were a paper lantern. The orc momentarily shrieked as it quickly vacated black blood and pink viscera upon the ground.

Proudly, the initiate stood, smeared with the blood of his enemy, and prepared to leave the battlefield, his task complete. A rogue orc burst out of the shadows and engaged the surprised initiate who thought he had free access to the battles-edge. The new fight attracted the attention of the necromantic sentinels who created dangerous distractions. One of the undead warriors hurled a caisson into the fray; neither man nor orc gave the spiked box any heed until it detonated, blasting away flesh with shrapnel and charring the victims' bodies with eldritch fire.

Only twenty-two potentials now remained. Absinthium smiled as he flung lightning blasts towards his agile students. Wynn would take over training this new brood in his absence. Absinthium had already informed him that he would be leaving for Jand's Capital City in the morning to install its new ruler. These students would quickly learn, or else they would die.

***

Rashnir and Zeh-Ahbe' walked together while looking for dried firewood. It had become their habit. Their group had made camp near a grove of trees at the crest of a hilltop. Another group of their people remained nearby, practicing their roles and learning their acting parts for a performance written by one of the Grinden believers named Haisauce.

"So, what do you think," Zeh-Ahbe' asked his friend. "Do you think that the people of Ninda will respond like we hope? You should be the expert; you're from this country, aren't you?"

"Well, kinda, but not really," Rashnir replied. "I wouldn't really say this was ever my home. I would more likely say that I put some time in here. I have no idea where I was born or who I was born to; I was orphaned, twice.

"Most of my young life was spent as a servant in a farming district pretty much straight over there." Rashnir pointed eastward to the Nil-Ma farmlands. "I assume that nothing remains there; the Narsh Barbarians came in and razed the entire place. It was pretty much just a fertile delta, one of the smallest districts but most profitable; I've heard it was because Nil-Ma had some demonic reliquary that helped his crops grow and made his animals breed more quickly. The problem was that Mallow, the heir of Nil-Ma who founded it, was a colossal idiot and a jerk. He stepped on a lot of toes in the parliament and sealed his own fate.

"Mallow made enemies on the council, but also screwed up his only long-standing alliances with the farm districts of Teed and Rivalf, the two districts just across the rivers that bordered his land. Both Teed and Rivalf's controlling heirs were women; he tried to seduce them both at the same time. After a couple of years playing his game, Mallow's secret got out and the two ladies realized what he'd done.

"Of course, rather than fight over him, neither wanted him at all, anymore. In fact, neither wanted him alive even, so they combined efforts and legitimized their contract with the Narsh Barbarians."

Zeh-Ahbe' nodded gravely. "Have you ever been back?"

"No, but I've skirted its borders on my travels. Everything was burned, fields, settlements, everything. If there was some kind of reliquary, maybe it was destroyed and that's why everything still remains so barren."

"I can relate to your story," Zeh-Ahbe' said. "My people have no real homeland. Wherever we lay our heads is home to us. The Kil-yaw' have an unforgiving caste system. It saw maybe four or five minor switches or elevations of clans in all of its thousands of years. We had only a minor part, as a lower clan, in the decisions of where we would go next."

"Yeah," Rashnir said. "That's very similar to the typical Nindan. They live in a caste system as well. At the top of the system are the Lords—the heirs to the farm, they own the lands and the crops and pretty much everything; along with the Lords are different businessmen and corporations. Really the only difference is that the corporations don't own the land they work on and don't have a personal voice in the Parliament, but they can certainly influence the Lords' politics in very persuasive ways.

"Both the corporations and the Lords oversee the men and women of their land which includes both freemen and slaves. The freemen can lease land from the local Lord or work in the employ of a corporation or even try and form their own types of enterprise... unless the Lord or a more powerful corporation stops it. Freemen are able to choose their own type of future, and even own slaves or indenture servants to them, like anyone else above them, but they have to pay their duties, taxes, and manage their finances well to avoid becoming indentured themselves.

"The lowest caste has two classes: slaves and indentured servants. Slavery is usually a permanent designation; they are the property of their owners and can be sold or transferred as such. Should one be purchased and set free, the burden is on them to prove their freedom and to retain the proper paperwork as proof. For an indentured servant, the burden is on the owner to hold the paperwork. Usually, once the servant has paid off the debts against him he is freed, but they too often end up in the same situation unless they bank enough money up to enable them to strike out as a freeman."

"So then, our plan," Zeh-Ahbe' continued, "How effective can it be?"

"Well, how effective was the spoken Word for *your* people?"

Zeh-Ahbe' pondered it for a second. "It was fully effective on our lowest caste, it made the next lowest clan give it pause for thought, and the powerful clans dismissed it outright."

"Right," Rashnir said, "The most powerful men and women blind themselves to many things. Even when confronted with truth and real power, they hold too tightly to things they perceive as real power to grasp ahold of anything else."

"But this idea, it is different than a simple spoken message. I think that it is really going to be effective."

"I think so too. The whole concept just kind of dawned on me. Everyone loves entertainment. In Jand, before Harmarty rose to the throne, his father sanctioned an afternoon break for everyone and even hired the players. It greatly helped the morale of the middle and lower classes in Capital City. Part of that whole break was an open forum for entertainers and an acting troop regularly put on shows during that time. The people loved it, but Harmarty shut it down; an open forum for free expression seemed too dangerous for someone as eccentric as he was.

"So, how are we coming on the play, anyway?"

"Almost ready," Zeh-Ahbe' said. "Most people have their parts memorized and they rehearse it even as we travel."

"Good," said Rashnir. "It won't be long before we actually have a chance to present our tale to a group. We will start at one of the small farmsteads closest to a district border. We will be far from any kind of repercussions from the district Lord, should there be any discontent... we are close enough to Jand that our enemies may have influence in the area."

Rashnir paused and looked skyward. Zeh-Ahbe' saw it too. A carrier falcon descended towards their position: one of the Regal Red Tails purchased by their elf friend.

The creature obediently perched nearby and Rashnir retrieved the message. He and his friend clutched their armloads of firewood and brought the bird back to their camp to read the message there.

***

grr'Shaalg and tyr-aPt finished their gluttonous meal and kicked the messy bone fragments and osseous material into a heap at the edge of grr'Shaalg's quarters. He would find a new servant later to remove whatever remained.

Holding up a vial of faintly glowing liquid, grr'Shaalg captivated his brother with his flair for the dramatic. He swirled the liquid around in the corked flask, drawing tyr-aPt's complete attention. The contents seemed to sparkle and glow; it flowed and swished like a medium viscosity liquid but it seemed to fizz as it did so, sparkling and popping like tinder sparks. Truly, it was a whole new element.

[Is that it, brother?] tyr-aPt asked.

[Actually, it is not. This,] grr'Shaalg said, [this is the dominant power behind phase two of my master scheme; it is the mystical nawchash. This is what will remove any barrier in my path to greatness. Of course, I've needed much of it to create the elixir for the first stage.]

[Then on to phase one.]

[Yes, I agree.] grr'Shaalg pocketed the glowing container. He pulled out another cylindrical glass phial. This liquid looked more like swamp water. Dull, dark, and murky its hue paled slight green in color. [*This* is it.]

[You have the capability to mass-produce this stuff?]

[Oh yes,] grr'Shaalg said. [You needn't worry. It's already happening. In fact, I have already chosen my recruits to carry out my plan.]

[And how is it that you are so good at putting your schemes into action without ever leaving a trail to link it to you?] tyr-aPt phrased the question as flattery. He was curious as to the plan and its implementation, but he knew better than to question his brother or say anything that might be viewed as a lack of faith. tyr-aPt the goblin king was smart enough to know that even he could be replaced.

[Simple, really,] he replied. [Some creatures, even some of us goblins, have this foreign concept implanted within us that makes us value the lives of specific friends and family members. Luckily, I was born without this wretched impulse.] tyr-aPt knew exactly what he was talking about; grr'Shaalg had personally arranged for the death of all of their other litter-mates and even his own sow and sire, tyr-aPt had personally assisted him in many of those plans.

grr'Shaalg continued, [Those who are going to be the carriers have received guarantees that the lives of their children will be spared, even rewarded. After delivery, they will drink an entire flask of this serum. They won't make it more than four days before they break down, themselves.]

tyr-aPt grinned. The Luciferians had helped the under-kingdom further their own agenda far more than they could ever know. It was access to their archives and training which gave them the knowledge that grr'Shaalg needed to solidify his control over the entire race. The hidden secrets in their tomes had also revealed snippets of lore that led him to discover the second vial, the one with the mysterious glowing substance.

[Yes, brother, sit back and relax. I have everything under control and well ahead of schedule. Very soon all goblins of the underworld will be united under a common banner—the standard of our own house, and *I will be in control and you just behind me.* Yes…very soon.]

***

Rashnir walked into the camp area. Zeh-Ahbe' followed behind his friend, handing off his stack of firewood for another person to put away.

They caged the falcon just as Jibbin jumped up onto Rashnir's lap.

"What's that?" the little boy asked.

"It's a letter from Kevin," Rashnir explained to his ward. It made him happy to hear the boy finally speaking.

Jibbin had, for a long while, refused to speak at all. His silent phase began right after his parents and siblings were murdered in front of him. That was at the beginning of the Luciferian persecution at Grinden. Rashnir stumbled upon the gang as they assaulted his family and killed them all; only Jibbin had survived. Rashnir promised Jibbin's dying father that he would look after the boy and raise him properly. It wasn't until he faced off against the Dragon Impervious that Rashnir had ever heard Jibbin speak.

Zeh-Ahbe' and Rashnir read the letter together. It was a letter of encouragement. Kevin was optimistic about their plans in Ninda; he really liked their idea about presenting the gospel message as a drama.

The letter also briefly outlined the plans that some of the other ministry teams had made. They all had different paths to travel, but for the meanwhile, many of those roads still ran parallel.

Zeh-Ahbe' and his friend passed the letter around to others for encouragement from their friend and mentor. Every person in the camp had some sort of connection to the preacher who helped open their eyes to the Truth. It comforted and reassured them to read his confident words.

***

Absinthium clung tightly to the back of the griffin that bore him at top speed. Streaking across the sky toward the capital of Jand, he did not notice the lone traveler walking across the harsh Briganik soil. This solitary observer also came from the Temple of Light and had his own agenda—one that would very soon cross the path of the arch-mage and even of the Gathering itself.

CHAPTER TWO

Kevin led his company eastward into Gleend. The opposing Nindan and Jandish armies did not disperse. They would make certain that the infidel cultists had indeed departed their lands before they dared turn back for their capitals.

Looking westward, the preacher could barely see as his friends slipped across the distant horizon, traveling into Lol. On the northern side Kevin could still barely make out Rah'-be's team walking along the border, also heading east on a more distant voyage.

Their goodbyes had been long and officious while they waited between borders, but Kevin understood how hard it would be for many of them in the times to come. He was not usually one for drawn-out goodbyes, but he was patient and could understand how many people needed the formality—he did not have years of ties or the bonds of blood with his flock. Those who were parting knew that they might not see their friends and kinsmen again for many years; it might not be until after death.

Kevin's group, along with a group led by Rondhale, traveled to the town of Sprazik. On his previous journey to Xorst, the capital city of Gleend, Kevin had stayed one night in an inn at Sprazik.

He had originally gone to meet with Gleend's monarch, King Lo-sonom. A man regarded as having a gift of great wisdom and a skilled, but blunt mediator. The king, his two wives, and his brother Havara had all become Christians. Since that trip, Kevin had come to

38

love much about the country and held great expectations. Havara had talked about steering it to become a Christian state that might contend with the Luciferian powers that grew to consume Jand.

Kevin talked with Rondhale as they walked amidst the traveling crowd at a gentle amble. He was excited to return to the same little hostel where he had slept on his last time through Sprazik.

"The Dry Bunk is its name. I came through the area with Havara on my first visit," Kevin explained.

"The food is decent, so were the lodgings, not that we require them, but the staff seemed very receptive to our mission. There was this boy who worked there, a slave actually, who I keep thinking of. He was a Cyclops from the land of Nod."

Rondhale shuddered at the thought, "I have heard of their kind. Wretched folk, the land of Nod is filled with the most frightening types of men. I think that it is chiefly because of fear that civilized men have never prevailed in settling that continent—nobody has tried in hundreds of years."

"You're right, to a degree," Kevin said. "This poor slave cannot even speak; some kind of tongue paralysis has made him mute and it led to the expulsion from his community. That's how he came to be a slave. His family sold him and he was traded around until he wound up in Sprazik."

Kevin continued, "The cyclopeans are apparently born completely normal, but a child's parents will gouge out one eye and fit them with a brace that they crank every day as they grow, pulling the remaining eye towards the center of the head. I imagine that it is extremely painful."

"So I have heard," Rondhale said, "Few people venture to trade with them, if they have the courage, so, we have only a little bit of knowledge of their ways. I've heard that the eye gouging is done in some kind of ceremony to devote the child to some kind of demonic deity, something forbidden even by the Order."

Kevin held up a Luciferian tome that he had acquired before meeting Rashnir. "I have used this book to research a great deal of Luciferian lore. Most of the information is deplorable. It is so skewed and incorrect, but at least it gives me a glimpse of what commoners believe… what their perception of history is. In the very early days of this realm, the cyclopeans were the first high-ranking priests of the Luciferian Order; apparently, there was some sort of major shift in the system when the Gathering was formed."

"The stories say that the cyclopses are cannibals and have their own dark arts, their own kinds of witchcrafts," Rondhale said. "Even the Luciferian Order opposes their cultus. Blood magic is frowned upon—it has too much in common with the vampires. With no civilized influences in the land of Nod, the cyclopeans have been left largely alone in the hopes that they would devour each other.

"A horrible existence. I cannot imagine growing up in such a home." Rondhale wrung his hands, squeezing them as his thoughts turned to the dead. "I couldn't imagine eating anyone, *let alone a brother*."

"Yes, I have heard those same stories, too. I assume that there is so much more to these people than that, though. For my part, I found the mute boy to be quite pleasant."

***

40

Krimko shimmied with glee at his new assignment. After identifying and containing a krist-chin outbreak in the local prison near his station at the monastic college outside of Grinden, he'd earned the favor of the highest mage of his own order: Absinthium. The arch-mage and prophet was ecstatic over Krimko's fervor and actions; the weasel-faced man set fire to the prison, incinerating any vestiges of the dreaded cult. He would not let the potential spread of the faith ripple through the prisoners and he took great pride in his role as the cleanser of Grinden.

The army had uprooted the cancerous sect from their encampment at the quarry. He was ready to do his part to subdue the remainder of these dangerous cultists.

Krimko glanced around as his caravan entered the Nindan parliamentary grounds and smiled. Absinthium had personally commissioned him for this role, sending him as his personal emissary to the Nindan government. His traveling company included the Grinden combat master Jandul, the mercenary Pinchôt, and a few of his chosen men from the mercenary clans, plus a few choice Luciferian monks.

Pinchôt looked both relieved and irked by his inclusion in the cavalcade. He had made it no secret that he loathed his post at Dyule's side; an appointment as the regent's personal bodyguard felt beneath the warrior. This trip was a relief from those duties, at least, but Krimko and the Steward of Grinden had much in common: on the few occasions that they had met, they had gotten along quite well. Perhaps the similarity was what vexed the warrior.

The leader, and only surviving member of the Narsh Barbarians guild, only recently recovered enough to leave the infirmary. Red, raised patches of skin mottled any exposed body parts and painful jagged lines crisscrossed his flesh. Much of his face suffered wounds given to him by the werewolf, Zeh-Ahbe', and he would certainly bear scars all his life. Treatments by Luciferian monks had saved his life.

Dyule was on the political fast track. He was even now being installed as the Minister of Jand as the Luciferian Order restructured the entire kingdom, solidifying the total alliance of church and state. That was the reason that the arch-mage could not greet the parliament himself. Jandish political affairs required all of his attention.

Krimko, Jandul, and Pinchôt left the others to attend to the animals that had brought them. The spacious courtyard was perfectly suited to their needs. Krimko knew that he had little need of protection amongst the Nindans. He had cast a protection spell that would alert him to any danger, but he took the two warriors with him nonetheless.

The Luciferian expected that the meeting would be more of a formality anyway—the archmage had not cleared him to engage in any kind of political deal-making, anyhow. The foreign Parliament would assemble to officially pledge their support to the Luciferian cause, giving the Order a backdoor into their workings and allow for another union of religion and government in the bordering country—something that promised to bring a new flow of wealth to the country.

As the threesome entered the ceremonial building they were greeted officiously by different individuals. None of them had met previously. They were treated respectfully, nonetheless, as if they carried all the weight and authority of the great Absinthium.

Krimko twisted his devious smile into something that seemed more sincere, cloaking himself in an aura of charisma that his tiny frame did not deserve. Pinchôt stayed just close enough to feign interest in his own role as the Luciferian's bodyguard. Jandul shadowed Krimko; the flowing robes of a combat master disguising the fact that, whether armed or not, he would be a dangerous adversary.

A trio of diplomats approached to greet Absinthium's envoy in the antechamber that preceded the parliamentary hall. The foremost of the three wore the most regal vestments and seemed most likely to be a district Lord. Those two flanking him might be sectional rulers of high rank.

Sectional rulers often had important roles in Ninda's parliamentary process. They were allowed to cast votes, although their vote only counted as half when compared to a district Lord. Each Lord was allowed two sectional rulers who might be recruited at the Lord's discretion from any Nindan source except for the slave caste. They were often secretly courted and bribed for their half-vote by other politicians.

"Greetings, Magi-pedagogue. I am Fajill, son of Grist," the Lord introduced himself, identifying his district. "These are my associates, Tat and Parnam." The two sectional rulers bowed regally.

"A pleasure," Krimko replied diplomatically. He merely returned their formality. The Grist district had little influence. If there was a ranking system for the districts of Ninda, the Grist lands would be among the lowest rungs.

"These are my attendants…"

Krimko backpedaled frantically as the men from Grist suddenly snapped. With twitching eyes, a wild-eyed rage overcame them. They lashed out violently at their Luciferian visitors.

In a heartbeat, Pinchôt and Jandul stepped in to defend their ward. As the mercenary drew steel, the combat master slipped his hands to the inner folds of his robes and pulled them out, sheathed in his weapon of choice for close combat.

The t'phar he wore, a ring-like metal band that his hand slipped into, glinted menacingly in the light. On the palm side of the band, small, curved claws that could aid in climbing or gouging deep wounds; from the top of the band protruded three sword-like claws for trapping blades or delivering killing blows. His claws gleamed a faint red, coated in the 'ãbêdâh serum that made the Luciferian weapons able to resist the destructive blades wielded by their krist-chin enemies.

Jandul leapt forward and coated them a brighter red as he ripped open the attackers. Between the rending blows from the t'phar and the precise strikes of Pinchôt's blades, the three Grist assassins didn't have a remote chance of survival.

Several of the other Nindan diplomats ran to the scene as soon as it unfolded. Seconds after it began, the danger was over. Falling over themselves to apologize, the Lords gave their full assurances that they did not sanction any sort of attack. They had never in their history ratified an attack on the parliamentary grounds, and couldn't according to their charter.

Pinchôt examined the bodies of the dead. The pockets of all three were stuffed with some kind of white flower petals. A servant leaned over his shoulder as he examined them.

"Fajill was always chewing on those things," he said. "Everyone always thought that he was on the edge, of his sanity I mean. But whenever he chewed on these, he seemed much worse. Illiac made him crazy, at times."

Jandul sniffed their faint aroma as he crushed them underfoot. "Antigo Vale?" he wondered with a mutter.

Krimko scowled. "It's faint, but it reminds me of the pleasant aroma I noticed the first time I met Absinthium." He waved the silly notions away. "But the Vale has been abandoned for decades."

The Parliament officially convened and heaped apologies upon the Luciferian Order for the unfortunate incident and pledged to give them whatever support the church demanded. Ninda recognized that their fallible political system was minuscule compared to the far-reaching arms of such a benevolent religion.

Krimko smiled. Another country slipped under Absinthium's thrall as the servants cleared away the bodies of the drug-addled attackers.

***

Mar'zal and Bwar stood at the entrance to the great chasm. Walls towered overhead, seeming to stretch to the sky. The path underfoot descended sharply, and any further distance would plunge the two into darkness, hence their hesitation.

Standing tall, Mar'zal held his brow high and noble. The ranking elf on Gleend's advisory council peered warily at the dwarf next to him. Bwar, an Under Dwarf, was his counterpart on the council. They both knew that they would not be seeing any of the humans from the council today.

Together, they served on a group of politicians that advised King Lo-Sonom. The triumvirate of races had operated for generations in unison—but a unity of self-interest, only. The dwarves cared not for the elves, and vice-versa. Neither of the ekthroic races cared for the humans.

Glaring with milky, white eyes, Bwar grunted at the elf. "We might get on with it, anytime you're ready to move." He'd always been surlier than his counterparts, nursing a lifelong grudge.

He gruffed as he lit a lantern to light the way. As a child, he'd been sent to the surface world to serve, and eventually become, a diplomat. Bwar's eyes did not reflect light in a cat-like manner that let him see in the low light of the subterranean realms. He was broken and not like rest of the Under Dwarves. His appointment to the surface world was because of faulty genetics, and everyone knew it.

Mar'zal glanced down at his stocky companion. Neither was happy about the other's presence. They had both received the same invite with instructions that brought them to this place, at this time.

Bwar returned the elf's scowl. Their affairs had crossed more often than they cared for in recent days.

The elf feigned confidence and walked forward, into the darkness, scorning the depth-blind dwarf. Bwar following on his heels, grousing under his breath.

As their eyes adjusted to the lantern light they saw the cast-off debris and garbage that littered the floor of the great rift. The trail was relatively clear; a central path kept fairly uncluttered by various scavengers and by larval skolaxis. The revolting grubs chittered happily. The size of dogs, they would soon mature into the large worms often pressed into service by goblinoids. At this stage, a skolax was harmless, but they would soon metamorphose into a much larger, much more dangerous creature. The giant serpent-insect hybrids moved swiftly on their many jointed legs.

Mar'zal and Bwar continued to pace off a preset distance that they had been given. It took an effort to ignore the creatures that scavenged upon the excrement-coated walls so they kept their heads down.

So far behind them, the entrance to the abyss offered no light. Overhead, the open sky hung above them sandwiched between the canyon walls, but so far above that their path remained completely dark.

High above, the city of Xorst sat upon a rift that split the Gleendish capital with the seemingly infinite chasm. The two citizens of that above-ground world spotted an artificial light in the distance. The illumination shone in the murky dinge and grew stronger as they approached.

Bwar stubbed his foot on something in the dark; it skittered off into the distance, making loud noises as it clattered against the stony floor. The clatter seemed to continue long after it began. What they'd assumed was an echo ebbed into a distinguished sound of its own: a droning, scratching noise, as rhythmic as it was horrid.

The elf and dwarf finally reached the source of the light. Some kind of glowing crystal had been set upon a post. The noise grew louder and they could make out the source's shape as it emerged in the distance. A skolax mounted goblin halted at the shadow's edge.

He hopped down and approached the two, who stood dumbstruck. Neither had known what to expect.

"Your letter," said Mar'zal, "You said that you were..."

"The letter was correct," interrupted the goblin. He wore only a simple loincloth and a purple fez hat. From a fine chain around his neck hung an unadorned metal bar and he spoke the common tongue exceedingly well.

The goblin's grin spread broadly as he confessed, "I am the king of this world."

***

Absinthium sat heavily on a chair in his private quarters in Jand's Capital City. He rubbed his eyes; they were stressed from both boredom and overuse. Political intrigue was a skill in his wheelhouse, but he much preferred real action over pomp and circumstance.

His ceremony had gone well and the local Jandish officials were pleased. Dyule was now the official leader of the kingdom and those minor changes necessary for restructuring as a Luciferian state were underway. The politician's official title was now Minister of Jand. Continuing the monarchy would have only led to problems in the future; with an office of flexible leadership, the arch-mage could easily install whomever he chose should there arise the need.

The arch-mage stroked his creased forehead and rubbed the stress out of his face. He still had a long afternoon and evening. Absinthium needed to receive several reports yet before he contacted his lord and master, beh'-tsah.

Almost playfully, the reclining thirty-third degree Luciferian pointed his toqeph at the far side of the room.

The wizard's staff glowed faintly at the tip as he exercised a minor spell. The qâsam that lay on the table levitated and floated through the air to the theurgist's open palm. It was only with the exercising of raw power that Absinthium found any sort of joy; the pursuit of more, and the maintenance of his power were all that he lived for.

He spat upon the face of the beveled jewel and rubbed the spittle firmly with his thumb. An arcane, glowing cloud seemed to pulse within the seeing stone as it called out for a link.

Krimko answered the call of his master and his shape took form in the inner light of the crystal. His shape appeared as if Absinthium looked at him through the bottom of a glass tumbler.

"I'm sure that I need not remind you, Krimko, that this is a general qâsam. There might be any number of other qâsamai capable of eavesdropping." There had been a recent influx in the mystic stones' availability—and that came hand in hand with certain suspicions. They were otherwise very rare and expensive.

"I am aware of that, Eldest," Krimko replied formally.

"Then tell me what information you have gathered for me."

Krimko explained the brief assassination attempt; Absinthium could have cared less, but he feigned interest as if he didn't suspect any such attempt would take place. Truly, the envoy was just a pawn in the grander game and Absinthium knew that even if Krimko had expired, the end result would be the same. Enough formalities had taken place that Ninda would fall under his control, too.

"The Parliament is at your full disposal. They also provided a report from their northwest border. It appears that their military company sent that way *did* encounter the krist-chins. They were successful at repelling them from the Nindan border."

"Excellent," the arch-mage stated. "Did they have an estimate on their numbers?"

"Yes, they did." Krimko's information seemed to corroborate what had been already reported from the Jandish army. Both accounts confirmed that the group had not yet divided.

Their estimated headcount seemed to reflect the nondivision, but some of the key krist-chin members were conspicuously absent. Absinthium stroked his chin. Despite the heavy losses the enemy *did* suffer at the quarry, he was sure that Rashnir, the lycan clan leader, and other key warriors survived the attack.

"I also have word on their movements. It seems that most of them have migrated into the country of Lol and a smaller group of them have traveled into Gleend. Their revered leader, Kevin, is among the latter group."

"Good, good," Absinthium smiled genuinely this time. *I have plans already for that country.* He was careful not to broadcast that information over the qâsam. "Is there anything else to report?"

"No, sir. I am only waiting for your orders."

"Remain there in Ninda. I may have further use for you in that region."

He relinquished his link upon the magic stone. Its soft glow faded away as the mage wrote a few notes for his records. He looked up to see a goblin messenger darkening his doorway.

***

Long, purposeful strides steadily carried a lone, cloaked figure forwards as it crossed the highlands of Briganik and into the barrens of Lol. Not needing to stop for sleep, he drew nearer his goal with every step. Despite traveling on foot, he would arrive sooner than humanly possible.

***

"I bring an update from my master, grr'Shaalg," the goblin servant rasped in the human tongue. He placed a tightly bound scroll into the Luciferian's hands. He bowed low and made motions to leave.

"Why did your master not come himself," Absinthium inquired.

"I know not. He merely stated that you would be pleased with his report."

Absinthium nodded. There was no real reason that he would have informed his slave as to his comings and goings, but it irked the mage that grr'Shaalg did not elevate a meeting with the Order to his highest priority; it aroused his suspicions, in fact.

He unrolled the document and waved the servant away. His eyes scanned the communiqué and picked out the key points.

The goblin reported that his plans to unite the goblins were effective. Apparently, the subterranean ekthro liked grr'Shaalg's plans for an underground trade federation. The kingdoms desired to join his new organizational structure rather than pay his kingdom duties and tariffs on use.

The mage raised an eyebrow at its claims. He knew firsthand the greed of the goblins; there was more to the situation than grr'Shaalg reported, of that he was sure. They would never band together and allow each other equal access to the subterranean tunnel network. Common goals and ideologies were beyond their ken. If the underground highway had any value at all, they would kill each other over it first. Absinthium knew he would have to keep a closer watch on his shifty goblin minion.

***

"I recognize no being as absolute king of this world," Mar'zal huffed arrogantly.

"Ah, but what you say is the truth," replied the goblin. "As of now, there is none recognized as the absolute king. Even the demons on all their thrones in the Babel Heavens do not wield total control."

"But they will soon," said Bwar, referring to the recent communication he and Mar'zal had both received from Absinthium, chief of the Luciferian Order.

The elf gave him a sharp look. The arch-mage had stressed the consequences of breaking his confidence.

Bwar shrugged. It all seemed like more of the same to him.

"You see, my brethren ekthro, I have a way to topple even the powers of the Gathering."

Bwar gave the under-dweller his full attention, but Mar'zal rolled his eyes. "As if such a thing was even possible," the elf scoffed.

"It is, and I will do it because I am destined to be king—ruler of more than just the under-realm. I will rule *all* and even the demons will bow before me. You will both aid me because I command you to do so; the rewards for allegiance will be great and the punishment for denial will be severe."

The goblin had Bwar's attention. Mar'zal crossed his arms but wasn't leaving.

"We have a common enemy, you see, besides the demons who have sat at the apex of the power chain for too long. Even more than the elves hate the dwarves, we have all been bred with an ingrained hatred of mankind. It is a long-smoldering hatred glowing within every child of hay-lale'. We have tolerated them out of social grace and politics, but the time is coming to unite and destroy them all, every man and woman."

"You give us only hollow promises and speak of things that cannot be done as if it was mere child's play. You are either delusional or you've been sent by an enemy to trap or test us. I will not stay and tolerate your rantings."

Mar'zal turned and walked away. Bwar remained; his eyes were fixated on the goblin and his thoughts consumed by the possibility of his words.

As the elf reached the edge of the false light, the creaking sounds of bowstrings resonated through the darkness all around. In unison, they snapped and the elf crumpled to the ground. Arrows pierced him from every angle.

Bwar growled at the dead elf. "Fool. I never liked him anyway."

"Then you pledge your allegiance?" The goblin's tenor had a threatening undertone.

"You needn't intimidate me. You have my support freely... my King. It's time we pushed all those filthy humans into the chasm."

***

Dri'Bu walked alongside Kevin as the group caught sight of Sprazik in the distance. He and the minister had been deeply engrossed in conversation. Lately, the two, along with Kyrius, had been leafing through Luciferian texts and separating fact from lie as they pulled out what might be helpful or historical.

"So then," Kevin asked Dri'Bu, "you have very little information regarding the Cyclops?"

"Right. In fact, I have very little *trustworthy* information regarding the Land of Nod. There has been so little worth note in that continent that traveling to it made little sense for me. I know many things about Nod, and yet most of the information is unreliable, unprovable, or just plain useless. That is, aside from common knowledge: the vampires live in Nod's mountains and they don't make much noise; they rarely leave their cold halls.

"There are those of my race and other ekthro who used to travel frequently to Nod for the nawchash. That was long ago; they are probably all dead by now. Those who lust for the nawchash seek a different sort of power than I did; I sought ultimate wisdom and knowledge."

"How do you mean, what exactly is the nawchash? I have only seen it referenced in Luciferian manuals as a thing to be avoided, claiming that only through the demonic Gathering should one ever seek true power."

"That's what they told mankind after they formed the Luciferian Religion; it's how they put a stranglehold on the magics of this world. That was in the aftermath of the great flood when wars ravaged the lands and the Gathering formed to preserve the strength of the demons... it was generations later that they finally forbade the nawchash and founded the Order—sometime after they trapped the Dragon Impervious."

"But what *is* the stuff?"

"The nawchash is the source of magic and powers for all rogue mages and wizards that are not a part of the Luciferian Order, for whatever reasons might exist. Ever since the formation of the Order, they made it a point to prevent any other group from offering up any kind of belief, hope, or source of power." Dri'Bu gestured around him to his Christian friends, "Case in point," he said.

Dri'Bu continued, "All manner of rogue wizards and magicians exist, but they keep a low profile. The Temple of Light has its own division that researches reports and suspicious persons; they take care of their own affairs and hunt down and eliminate any kind of religious dissident or nonaligned mage. Their bounty program has always been active."

"I still don't exactly understand what the nawchash is," Kevin admitted. "Like, I know what it does... but what *is it*?"

"It's a consumable substance, a kind of magic fuel, if that helps you understand it. It is harvested from moglobs." The elf saw Kevin's confused look persist. The human was so utterly unfamiliar with his world "A moglob is a small animal that lives in the jungle. The ancient demon aladzoni'a discovered a way to create the nawchash and he vied with the other demon leaders. When they formed the Gathering, they rose up against aladzoni'a and any other threats that they perceived as a challenge to their authority."

"Wow. I thought you said that you didn't know much about Nod."

"Well, there is much more, even, but ancient manuscripts are always of questionable authority. Many of them are full of false information and misleading guidance; it is strange how most unaligned sorcerers pull their primary information from these overtly misleading guides. It's so ironic because they think that following some hidden, secretive texts, they are somehow more authoritative than Luciferian works. The irony is that they are both totally wrong. They all claim to hold the absolute truth but are full of obvious errors and outright lies."

Kevin nodded at the elf's statement. In his home realm, he'd encountered similar things, though, quite in reverse as pseudo authorities tried to dismantle the Truth that he served. Ancient Luciferians and the worshippers of aladzoni'a fought for power and sought to usurp or steal all that was available.

On Earth, opponents of the Logos picked out things that they perceived as errors because of a skewed understanding; what started with faulty reasoning spiraled to vindicate and validate their personal bias against the absolute truth and the love of their own wickedness.

"So then, Dri'Bu, what can you tell me about the Christians who remain in this realm? Do you know where they are?"

Dri'Bu looked sad. "I know how much you desire to know that, and it grieves me that I have no knowledge of their location. Only the Gathering, and I would guess a few high ranking Luciferians, might know. As far as I know, they are not on this continent, but there many places that they could be. They could be on Jeena, Nod, one of the countless islands that surround the main continents, or even in the Babel Heavens.

"I know only a little about their history, how the angel Karoz came and preached the Word to many men and women who followed him. Of course, the Luciferians rose up against them in force and destroyed most of them.

I've heard little of them following that, except for rumors and hints that they still exist, living in exile and in fear. Every few decades, one or two of them surfaces somewhere; the Luciferians capture him or her quickly and nothing more is heard about it."

"Yes, Rashnir said that one of them healed him in the prison beneath Harmarty's castle."

"He told me about it, too. The situation was odd because heretics are usually judged and punished by the church in such short order. I had the impression that Nhoj had been in the dungeon for many years before he prayed for Rashnir's healing."

"I thought the same thing, but I don't see anything odd about it. I see it as a sign of God's providence and love for his people. I think He foreordained Nhoj to be there, knowing that Rashnir would have some critical role to play in His plans for the redemption of His people here."

Dri'Bu nodded. He had not thought of that.

***

The groups led by Rashnir and Zeh-Ahbe' had prepared for their first outreach with planning and prayer. A couple of days ago, they settled on a patch of grass only a short distance near a Nindan village on the borderlands between the districts of Himnp and Kantror.

The village was only a small community of freemen. It was the sort of place that serviced trade and business for local freeman farmers and families who worked by leasing the farm and its crops, even though the deed was actually owned by the district Lord. Villages like this dotted the Nindan countryside at convenient distances between farms.

Similar villages of were common, except for the zones near the Homesteads of the Lords. The Homesteads functioned much like the capital city of any political state. It lay at the historic location of the original Lord and was named accordingly, as was the district, after the founder. Homesteads in Ninda were usually the largest cities and had a great deal of commerce and trade with various offices for different district officials and aides for the district Lords. The Lord usually lived a short distance away from his estate and on his or her private farming lands.

Of course, Homesteads varied in size and style; the smaller and less wealthy districts generally had nondescript Homesteads. Mallow had not placed much emphasis on the Nil-Ma zone and so it was little more than an outpost for paying tributes and rents, minor trade, and shipping. When the Narsh Barbarians razed the lands, they systematically burned everything and sent riders on ahead to notify any freemen who lived on leased lands. Some of those stayed and died in the flames, others fled to the neighboring lands and many became slaves or indentured themselves again unless they had enough hard currency that they could take with them to start a new life.

Today, Rashnir planned a foray into the village under their guise as an acting troupe. Their hopes were that they might spend a couple of days at each village as they passed through in the Nindan districts, giving a dramatic presentation and answering any questions that people might have. With any luck, they could avoid the notice of the Luciferians for quite some time. The Order's influence in Ninda was concrete, but it was never very thorough. Nearly all Nindans had some sort kind of

Luciferian heritage, but temples remained sparse due to the layout of the country. Every Homestead had a temple, but only the larger villages and communities had any sort of building specifically designated for religious functions.

What they had planned, as an experiment, was to perform a small section of the play on the first day. They prayed that the Logos would spread and an even greater crowd might arrive on day two to hear the second half. An acting troupe was always sure to draw a crowd; if they could make the message relatable to the audience, they knew they would touch lives with the message of hope.

Thirty-five of them left their camp to go into the village. The party followed Rashnir and the werewolf Zeh-Ahbe'. Jibbin was also there, sitting on Rashnir's shoulders. The little boy had a part in the first act of the drama; he had so diligently learned his lines and practiced the part of Isaac. The change in the child was amazing; only weeks ago he had been functionally mute and refused to speak a single word, now he was willing to perform a role in a public performance.

Jibbin excitedly buzzed to have an active part in the production and Rashnir was glad to see him so happy. As Isaac, the child had one of the most important parts of the story of Abraham; the production would hopefully reveal to the audience the necessity of a sacrifice to appease God.

Neither Zeh-Ahbe' nor Rashnir had a part to act, but as the leaders, they wanted to be there to speak with people and to introduce the actors.

Through the visit today they hoped to get acquainted with the local folk and to invite people to their first presentation. They would be ready in a couple days and would present a "two-part fantastic drama."

As the Christians closed in on the town's edge, Zeh-Ahbe' sniffed the air. He kept sniffing, in his human form, as they approached. He still had heightened senses compared with any other person. Some odor on the wind gave him apprehension; it was familiar in some way to him, yet he couldn't quite seem to place what it was.

They entered the village outskirts and passed by a variety of shops and kiosks where vendors of all sorts of products and goods peddled their wares. Different kinds of people mingled around them; most of them were easy to pigeonhole by their appearances. Farmers and businessmen dressed distinctly from each other, as did all manner of other folk.

Rashnir and the others were very friendly. They greeted people in the streets and the salesmen at their booths, inviting them all to their production. One woman stopped dead in her tracks when she looked at Rashnir. The ranger locked eyes with her and his steps faltered. Something in the shared gaze spoke to him. He felt certain that she knew who he was, but he also knew that he had never seen her before this day.

His heart sank as he thought of all the different people who might want him dead. Topping the list was the Order and their bounty hunting program.

The woman stood in guarded repose, giving little away in her appearance. Dressed as an adventurer, she wore mostly tanned leather hides and furs. Her golden hair was tied back, further exposing her tanned skin and face.

Rashnir bit his lip and knew it wasn't drawn back for beauty's sake, but to keep her field of vision clear. By her armaments and dress, he guessed that she was perhaps involved with a mercenary group in some way. None of his observations explained why she looked at him so intently.

He immediately felt a connection with her, maybe even a sense of desire. At the back of his thoughts rang a twinge of guilt and thoughts of Kelsa. Accompanying his memory of Kelsa surged an old temptation. Rashnir's mind recalled Absinthium coming to him in a dream— offered him the possibility of resurrecting his lost lover.

Rashnir shook the bad thoughts from his head. He'd long ago accepted the fact that Kelsa was gone forever.

He grimaced, sure that she would approach him as they drew closer. That possibility never materialized. Suddenly, Zeh-Ahbe' planted his feet and held his arms out, halting the group's progression.

Following his eyes, Rashnir saw the reason for the stop. Across the market, a large beast lurked in the shadows between distant buildings. The beast looked like a transformed lycanthrope and it and Zeh-Ahbe' shared their own, knowing gaze.

Rashnir's blood boiled as he slowly peeled Jibbin off of his shoulders. The rest of the troupe mumbled, confused as to why they had stopped. No one else had noticed the creature, and neither had any locals in the streets, luckily.

Zeh-Ahbe' turned to Rashnir, "Stay here with the people. I must go and speak with this one."

Rashnir inferred what his friend had really said: this was a werewolf that Zeh-Ahbe' knew. As he watched Zeh-Ahbe' walk away, Rashnir glanced back at the woman in the streets. She too had noticed the monstrosity in the shadows and had taken action. She slipped behind a small crowd of people and disappeared.

Moments later Rashnir watched Zeh-Ahbe's animated conversation with the beast. It shrunk down to his human form, thankfully, and avoided any panic. The lycans continued talking for another moment and then they both returned to the group.

"Rashnir," said Zeh-Ahbe', "this is Sim-khaw', leader of tribe Zaw-nawb'. I must take him somewhere private and speak with him."

"What's up? Is everything okay?"

"Yes, I think so. He has been looking for me and says that it is urgent."

Sim-khaw' bobbed his head at Zeh-Ahbe's statement.

"I am sorry that I cannot come with you today," he said privately, "But there may yet be hope for Sim-khaw'. But…" he trailed off, "as impossible as it is, he insists that the kil-yaw' needs me, needs the Say-awr, to return."

***

Under the mountains of Arnak, tyr-aPt entertained diplomatic guests sent to his domain by the other goblin kings. The guests seemed happy to be there, which was out of the ordinary for goblins. They normally viewed all others with highly paranoid suspicion.

[I, for one, am honored to be here,] the goblin consul attempted to flatter the king. [King tlaFFr will be most appreciative of the generous gift that you send to his domain.]

The three other goblin diplomats in the chamber nodded and gave their assents, each implying the same sentiment for the kings that they each represented.

The representative of King gid-Orp piped up, [What information can you give us about this plague? Our people are dying in droves and you say that you have got it all worked out. What do you know?]

[I will share everything with you that I know, ffL'iGor,] tyr-aPt replied. [We have a good idea about the origins of this horrible disease. It appears that those locations visited by some of our veterans coming off the recent conflicts have been hit the hardest.] tyr-aPt, along with his brother, had only ascended to their positions because of their skill in telling blatant lies, and this ruse had been carefully planned.

[North of here, near Driscul, goblin kind encountered these krist-chin peoples.] The goblins bobbed their snouts and latched onto the invading cult, rather than laying blame on the dark-dwellers.

Just weeks ago, the Luciferian Order indoctrinated several goblins into its ranks. grr'Shaalg had set his plan in motion, turning these wheels long ago—before the cult had revealed itself.

The goblin leaders knew the true motivation behind the recent Luciferian actions; beh'-tsah and his puppet, Absinthium, wanted the goblins for foot soldiers. Their high rate of reproduction combined with the Luciferians' ability to manipulate the public into ignoring their unchecked growth, would provide beh'-tsah with a massive army, or perhaps a building force.

grr'Shaalg held in his possession a chemical devised by secret apothecaries. They had, of course, been properly silenced. The catalyst ingredient, though, could only be obtained by raiding Luciferian monasteries. grr'Shaalg needed a large quantity of nawchash to manufacture a large enough dose to effectively contaminate the whole goblin population—and access was far easier when they had their own thief in the larders.

In the secret storerooms of monasteries were rows upon rows of stored nawchash, shelved in ages past for some hypothetical reason. They would normally have been secured; the valuable jars were supposed to be secret and hidden in a compound where only those who had passed various tests of loyalty could enter. Over a few days' time, grr'Shaalg's insiders replaced several vials of nawchash with identical ones that were empty but had hairline fractures at the bottom. By the time any Luciferian examined their supposedly safe inventory, all suspicion would fall on an earthquake or weak glassware. None would suspect anything more than a row of leaky vessels.

With the nawchash secured, grr'Shaalg's henchmen poisoned goblin families to make it appear that they had all gotten infected it from the same source: a watering hole that they frequented. With the test successful and those families succumbing to the disease, they moved on to poison the major water sources of the other ten kingdoms, and laid all the blame at the feet of the "toxic krist-chins."

Truly, the magic-based disease was a terror, even though it only affected goblins. It functioned virally and could be easily passed through fluids; it contaminated the offspring of a sow automatically. The chances of an infected male's brood also suffering the affliction were unknown as of yet but it was assumed that they were at about fifty percent.

At first, infected goblins fell ill and felt weak. About two days later, they began to tremble uncontrollably and seep slime out of their pores and anywhere that mucus membranes existed. After two days severe shakes, victims would develop sores and boils all over their bodies, eventually bleeding to death as their innards liquefied and their blood thinned. Those were the results from a direct contamination; the diluted form, picked up from a central water supply, was expected to have the same effect but over a slower timeframe. The poisoned goblins in those nearby kingdoms should experience the same effects over the course of a few weeks, rather than a few days. That would give selected minions enough time to unwittingly travel abroad and spread the contagion.

[Multiple theories exist. If it did not come from these krist-chins, then this infection was perhaps handed down from god himself, the mighty Lucifer, as a wake-up call to our species,] tyr-aPt layered lie upon lie. [As you all know, the first outbreak occurred in my own kingdom and we can trace its origins to certain aqueducts, we don't know exactly where the junk has spread to, for all we know, all goblin-kind could be contaminated by now. We would never know; it does not have any effect on any other creature. It only harms us goblins.

[In a way, we are all lucky that it struck us first, after all, you are all familiar to some degree with my brother, grr'Shaalg. Some of you might know that he is working closely with the magicians of the Luciferian Order and so he has special access to deeper magics and knowledge of arcane things that most do not. It was he who so quickly organized our small number of ekthroic priests to concoct an antidote capable of combating this disease. We take that as a sign that we are on the right path to finding our niche within the Order's new prophecy: a new charge brought forth by the Gathering—and one that includes the creations of Lucifer.]

Several heads nodded. They all knew rumors and had been exposed to the information spies had planted about grr'Shaalg. All goblin speech is somehow laced with at least a pinch of falsehood, and so the diplomats would guess their information was somehow tainted with a tiny mistruth. That mode of thinking would blind them to the larger actuality that his entire statement was wholly false.

In fact, grr'Shaalg used his subservient Luciferian initiates to concoct both massive quantities of antidote potion as well as the poison itself. The cure was designed in such a way that it could never fully remove the root of the problem. Any goblin imbibing the antidote would need to repeatedly take a dose every two days or the disease would flare up again, worse than before. It was the perfect plan to unify his race: grr'Shaalg infected the populace and only *he* had the remedy, a cure that would need re-administration every few days. The loyalty of the kingdoms would become absolute.

None of the others could have believed that their goblin brethren could latch onto genuine faith in the Order's religious tenets—at least none of the high-casted could, anyhow. But, grr'Shaalg had a plan to make that idea more believable: a plan to make even Absinthium believe goblins had unified behind the Luciferian banner. It would be a long time before that ruse could be revealed for what it was.

[I anticipate that this gift of antidote vessels be well received in your home domains, I also hope that not *too many* of your kinsmen and wives will succumb to the disease before they get the remedy.

[My brother is working hard and pressing many servants into the new craft of brewing it to supply enough of the solution to meet the demand and keep our brethren alive. Also, be aware that we have several good leads on the culprits to blame for this. We will need unity more than ever if it turns out that our intelligence is correct. We will have revenge, friends, and we will have it together.]

***

The group Kevin led settled down a short distance from Sprazik, in the cities commons. Their group was simply too large to utilize the local inns. The land was presumably part of the city and would not likely have an owner who would contest their presence.

As they settled down and prepared for a short visit to the community, Kevin felt a strong inner urge welling up within him. In the middle of everything, he slowly sank to his knees and began to pray for his fellow Christians, Rashnir in particular. Others around him followed suit and upheld their leader in whatever burdened had called him to prayer.

***

Absinthium needed accurate information; men had proven to be unreliable as of late. Somewhere in the lines of communication, some overzealous soldiers must have only half-heard his directives after the battle of Grinden. The Jandish soldiers merely escorted their cultist enemies to the country's boundaries and then left them to their own design and patrolled the border to prevent re-entry, though the Luciferian had desired their containment.

That mishap was all in the past—now, he needed surveillance if he hoped to still stem their migratory tide. Without a competent commander to direct and manipulate events in his absence, Absinthium was at the disadvantage of local forces.

He muttered a curse and his black heart seethed hatred for the supernatural force behind the krist-chins' power. *He had to know more.* Rocked back on his knees, Absinthium entered a trance and his eyes rolled back in his head. Smoke from a smoldering bowl of incense curled up and wreathed his head. In a deep bass tone, he chanted a short mantra.

As the moment of dawning seemed to come upon him, he opened his eyes and scried the smoke. Continuing to chant in a barely audible voice, every wisp of smoke and every nuance of its ebb and flow formed a picture within the archmage's mind.

Interjecting his own evil desires through the mental tapestry, Absinthium navigated the stream and flow of time. Events and occurrences interlinked, burgeoning within his brain as he sorted through the divination: things that were and are, events that could be, and occurrences that might never happen. All cluttered up his psyche. He plunged through the vision, pressing on towards the specific knowledge that he sought.

Like spotting the flickering of fireflies on a starless evening, the mage began to map out the locations of his enemies. In particular, he probed deeper, searching for Rashnir. His pride demanded that he destroy or subjugate his enemy… the latter being his preference.

As he flexed his psychic abilities through the veil of smoke, he validated what information he hoped had been correct. The numbers of the krist-chins were slightly smaller than expected, and they'd dispersed close to the Gleend and Lol borders, just as his intelligence suggested. Surprisingly, Rashnir was nowhere to be found. Something obfuscated parts of his eldritch sight.

Irked, Absinthium permeated the vision with his astral probe and pushed his considerable abilities further than he had in a long while. Sweat beaded on his forehead and his muscles tensed. He stretched beyond the limits of even a thirty-third degree Luciferian, but to no avail.

Absinthium sighed and abruptly shrank back, slumping as if he had been relieved of a heavy load. If his probes did not reveal the warrior's location, then he must be dead.

A grin crept across his face and then fell. His hopes of Rashnir's death were not logical. His death should have been revealed in the divination. Worry creased the mage's brow; there were few with the power to shield their entire presence from the psychic plane without disrupting it dramatically. Foremost among them was the ever-present danger to his master's power: the children of the mountain.

Absinthium discarded the notion; Rashnir would never cast his lot in with Lilth and her vampires. While he had no doubt that her brood would love to harness the powers that these krist-chins demonstrated, their foreign doctrines would likely prohibit any kind of union. His master already had plans for keeping his immortal enemies at bay—and they had worked for centuries thus far.

He tapped his finger. It was odd, though, that his enemy was perfectly concealed from him. The more he stewed in the thought, the more it disturbed him.

Still, divination was never a perfect reference. In fact, under *no* circumstance did it ever reveal the *total and complete truth.* But, using knowledge and clever reasoning, a wise mage could usually discern what information he desired to know from the ether.

Absinthium took a deep draught of water to sustain his body. He pulled a thin shoot of herbal stimulant out of a nearby jar and crushed it between his molars. It was similar in many ways to a simple green plant stem, but when crushed, an invigorating and slightly intoxicating chemical seeped out.

The arch-mage blew firmly over the incense bowl and enlivened the smoldering mass. He reclined again into his position and set his mind into the proper state. He would try again to locate his nemesis; perhaps something new would reveal itself in time.

Chapter Three

Kevin relaxed. The overwhelming burden he felt to pray seemed to lift as the evening began. Those who had joined him felt a similar wave of release wash over them.

The camp resumed their preparations and retreated to their personal tents. Kevin and his chosen accomplices would join him on the journey into Sprazik.

His friends gathered together and waited for Kevin. Rondhale, Dri'Bu, Jorge, Minstra, and a few others that had been chosen from the group waited patiently. They seemed an unlikely crew in any other circumstance, especially with Dri'Bu and Minstra's inclusion. The elf had proved himself as a great resource. He was technically not a Christian because he was not created with a soul—similar in some ways to the angels. Minstra, however, was a man of indecision, and a confused former Luciferian monk. Kevin hoped that if Minstra accompanied him and saw the power of God in action, he would eventually be moved to accept the truth for what it really was. Regardless, he was more than a charity case with nowhere else to go; he had cast his lot with the Christians and felt they owed it to Shinna, the old woman, to continue pouring into the reluctant monk who hesitated over points of dogma.

Kevin finally joined his friends and they ambled across the grassy field. The village's edge drew closer and noise from the town became noticeable, although muddled. Somehow, the sounds felt off. Jorge, the one who was the most attuned to that sort of thing, seemed agitated by the seeming wrongness of it.

A pillar of black smoke erupted on the far side of the city and the trumpet split the air. The sounds may have been wrong for a city, but they were accurate for a skirmish. The horn's battle cry went up again and was taken up by another, positioned close to the Christians who stood fixed firmly in place, trying to ascertain what was happening.

The sound of rapid hoof-strikes on hardened earth echoed over the city's edge. A lone horseman galloped in full route; his course would take him directly past the Christians in a matter of seconds.

Another sound rumbled: a dull roar resonating and then revealed itself. Pony-drawn wagons angling for an intercept course on the rider. Accompanying the wagons and pulling ahead of the pack were single horsemen. With lighter loads, they would surely catch the escapee.

As the fleeing horseman rode by in a flash, Kevin and the rider made eye contact. It was Havara! His eyes widened in surprise as they met friendly faces. The prince of Gleend, an acquaintance of Kevin, was in obvious trouble.

It was clear that Havara's pursuit had no qualms about burning an entire village. Volleys of flaming arrows flew through the sky, launched by archers on the war carts dragged by the ponies. Firebrands landed atop the thatched rooftops of Sprazik.

Havara's horse pulled around as he circled back to his Christian friends. The prince's pursuit began taking identifiable shape in the shrinking span between them. Dwarves drove the pony-drawn wagons. The single horses that drew dangerously close were piloted by elves; each one jockeyed with the others to score the killing blow against the brother of Gleend's monarch.

It was clear that Havara could not outrun his pursuit. Finally close enough to see it, his horse looked old and decrepit, not the norm for the prince who had always been so immaculately adorned. The old nag had obviously been the only available beast, indicating his hasty escape. Havara stopped his horse and dropped to the ground amongst his friends.

"I am very glad to see you, my friends. Hopefully, it is not the last thing that we all do," the prince said.

"Not to worry," said Jorge. He tossed aside his over-sized cloak. "None of *us* will die here today. We will protect you"

The elven riders closed the gap as the angel drew an immense blade into existence out of nothingness. The holy sword blazed with a cerulean flame. Jorge spread his wings outward to greet the challengers and then rushed into action.

Spinning like a bladed whirlwind, he dodged the enemies' attacks and simultaneously countered with his own. His fluid motions came like a blur and the angel destroyed the front line of the mounted ekthro. The elves' mounts carried them forward with such incredible momentum that they could not stop until they fell upon the ground split into heaps of flesh and no longer a threat.

With his friends out of immediate danger, Jorge shot off like a flash. A fiery, azure streak followed him as he charged the inbound dwarves at super-human speed, tracing a tail to indicate the angel's path against the incoming dwarven battlewagons. Again, his blue flaming blade divided joint and bone faster than the enemy could react.

Dwarven carriages collapsed in dusty clouds and mounds of debris as Jorge eliminated that threat as well. Yokes of ponies, suddenly separated from their burden, bucked and ran wildly, passing the Christians and fleeing into the distance.

As the angel returned to the group, Havara explained what had transpired.

"We expected the Luciferian's would stir up an attack against us," Havara told Kevin, "but it did not come from them—the humans of the Order never even looked at us crossly. My brother, King Lo-Sonom was meeting with a Luciferian leader in his throne room at a public audience. He boldly proclaimed his faith to the God Yahweh who opposes the Luciferian doctrines; the monk could not even react before the enemy broke the doors down and ekthroic marauders attacked. They killed my brother and the Luciferian, too… and all the others in the hall. I tried to save my family, but Lo-Sonom's wives and children were already dead by the time I got to their home—I barely got out alive, through the laundry systems.

"The assassins included only dwarves and elves. None of the Gleendish humans were amongst them. They pursued me all night and I tried to find rest and shelter here in Sprazik—to find *you, Kevin*, but they tracked me here, and now my fellow humans suffer."

Nipanka drew his own spiritual sword. "Well, let's see if there is anything we can do in their defense."

The others nodded their assents and they entered the town. More horn blasts blew from the far side of Sprazik. Assassins signaled their companions, inquiring for a position. When the call went unanswered, the Christians assumed they must have suspected an unlikely defeat.

Jorge led them through the streets on high alert. Damage to the town was absolute; foundation and walls cracked under the heat of burning structural timber. Flames billowed from rooftops making the sky became a canopy of smoke and soot. In the coming days, nothing would remain but ash. Bodies lay strewn about wherever they had fallen, murdered as the ekthro rampaged in a mad search for Havara.

Kevin sequestered his companions. He pushed through a partially blocked door and entered a deserted storage building which verged on collapse.

Havara stated the obvious, "We will need to find out who is still alive and organize some sort of resistance. First and foremost, we need intelligence."

"First and foremost we will need guidance," Kevin pointed out warmly and pointed skyward. The minister bowed his head and grabbed the hands of those nearest to him. He prayed audibly for provision and protection, for the lost men of Sprazik as well as his Christian companions on the outskirts. As he began, a gentle rain began falling from the sky; it dampened the soot and quenched the flames that fed on the buildings.

The Christians remained in prayer as Jorge ducked through the threshold of the door. Havara, anxious and distracted, found it difficult to focus and watched as the angel spread his wings and leapt skyward.

From his vantage point high above, Jorge could see everything with his eagle-sharp eyes. A relatively small band of trackers and warriors were all that opposed them. They were not prepared for a siege or even a massacre; these assassins were only interested in their quarry, Havara. The biggest weapon oppressing Sprazik had been fear and surprise.

Jorge watched the remaining troops as they left the far side of town, rejoining the rest of their ranks on the town's far outskirts. About thirty strong, they were an odd combination of dwarves and elves.

Last to rejoin the group was an elf who appeared to be their lead tracker. From their body language, he must've told them that Havara had escaped. The lead dwarf seemed startled as the report continued. Jorge grimaced; they must've discovered the Christian group and probably assumed that they'd offered aid. The stocky dwarf's head jerked towards the camp's direction.

Jorge knew that they would soon mobilize with bad intentions. It was up to him to prevent any further damage to the city or his friends. Protecting Kevin and his flock was his divinely appointed task.

The angel shouted a high-pitched call in a heavenly language. Almost instantly Kyrius was in the air and at his side with a flaming sword at the ready. They flew in tandem as wingmates who had flown together for centuries. Their speed and grace surpassed songbirds at play. They flew in and out of each other's flight path, spiraling in randomly arcing patterns.

Ekthroic bowmen indiscriminately let loose with their arrows; none of them could estimate where they might go and arrows flew wide. None hit their marks and in seconds the angels closed the gap between parties. They split their intertwining pattern; each breaking to the outside of the attacker's group, they came in on strafing attack vectors. Swooping down upon their enemies, sapphire flames trailed behind the winged beings like the tails of comets that crissed and crossed paths through the middle of the fray.

Sharper-than razors, the edged blades efficiently tore through the first line of assassins. As they swooped around for a second strike the resolve of the dwarves and elves shattered and they fled for their lives.

Both angels took to the sky and Kyrius peeled off to return to the campsite for help.

Jorge returned to report to Kevin. The threat had been neutralized and there was an immediate need in the town for medical treatment. Kyrius would bring support and soon. Jorge and the others began searching out and tending to the wounded even as more Christians arrived to join their mercy efforts in the town.

***

Night drew on and covered the realm with a blanket of darkness.

Rashnir sat at his campfire with Zeh-Ahbe' and Sim-khaw'. He and Zeh-Ahbe' had diligently listened to the outsider's tale of what had happened in the kil-yaw', the governing council of werewolves, since the excommunication of Zeh-Ahbe's clan.

Sim-khaw' led the lycan tribe Zaw-nawb', which had become the lowest in the pecking order following the Say-awr's departure. When Zeh-Ahbe's tribe chose to follow the way of Christ, they surrendered their powers and werewolf abilities, trading them for an even greater glory.

The Say-awr' had been the lowest caste in the kil-yaw' until they were voted to-ay-baw', a kind of excommunication. Only Sim-khaw' had hesitated in voting against the tribe, condemning his peers as anathema.

Nine of the original eleven tribes remained. Two tribes in the history of the kil-yaw' had been cast off through to-ay-baw' in their long history. While the Say-awr' chose their God over the rule of the kil-yaw', the Shaw-than' had chosen to become servants of the vampires who corrupted them and twisted them to their own means.

"You must return to the kil-yaw'," again pleaded Sim-khaw'.

"You ask the impossible," replied Zeh-Ahbe'. "To-ay-baw' is final and complete. There is no returning to the kil-yaw'. Even if we wanted, we would be attacked for simply drawing too near it."

"But what if I advocate for your return. Perhaps I could convince others on the council to vote for a reinstatement."

"Sehkel-saykel himself said—"

"Sehkel-saykel is dead. Mil-khaw-mah' killed him and now commands the kil-yaw'."

The statement rocked Zeh-Ahbe' back. For many decades the wise, old leader of the Ahee-sthay-tay'-ree-on had guided the kil-yaw'. He had been a respected figurehead by all tribe leaders… except for the bellicose Mil-khaw-mah'.

"Mil-khaw-mah' usurped him. He has ordered all tribes to tsawkhak. Something sinister is happening and the rest of us have been beaten into submission by the stronger tribes. We need the strength of numbers."

"There has not been tsawkhak in three generations," Zeh-Ahbe' pondered the implications. Tsawkhak was a state of constant tribal orgy meant to cause an influx of new offspring. The normal breeding constraints were removed and during tsawkhak each werewolf was ordered to steal additional mates from the local communities; it was only during tsawkhak that outsiders could gain entrance into the primitive, but powerful culture. Historically, it had been used to boost the numbers of troops available for war and domination; the Ahee-sthay-tay'-ree-on had used it only to counter the death toll wreaked on them by a devastating plague so many years ago. "If Mil-khaw-mah' has instituted tsawkhak, then he must intend for carnage."

"Our leaders are divided," said Sim-khaw'. "Some of us want war, some of us don't, but most of us secretly agree that Mil-khaw-mah's leadership will destroy us all. He has violated many of the rules instituted by the temperate Ahee-sthay-tay'-ree-on. Mil-khaw-mah' took the Say-awr' scald and has demoted the weakest from many tribes, many of them from the Zaw-nawb', recreating the lost Say-awr' tribe by forcing others into it, though he has not done the same for the Shaw-than'. Their scald was lost millennia ago."

Zeh-Ahbe' merely bit his lip. It grieved his heart with a kind of patriotic nationalism—but his allegiance to God remained greater.

"Mil-khaw-mah' claims that the Ahee-sthay-tay'-ree-on corrupted the kil-yaw' and that we must return to our vicious roots," Sim-khaw' continued. "We do not know where he is getting the information that he brings to the kil-yaw'; none of us have heard these things that he claims. He also says that the Say-awr' have regained their ability to shapeshift."

"Yes, that part is true—"

"Then why can you not return to the kil-yaw'?"

"Because my people and I would never accept its command over our lives; we respect only Yahweh as our ultimate guide. The kil-yaw' could never accept anything but absolute rule."

"But there are many others, also, who do not agree with Mil-khaw-mah's war-some spirit. Many of our kind wish to see his leadership supplanted."

"No, Sim-khaw', there is more to it than that," said Zeh-Ahbe'. "We have found contentment and peace in the power of God."

The werewolf offered a blank stare in reply. Sim-khaw' could not fathom the concepts Zeh-Ahbe' tried to introduce.

"I will show you what I mean, stay with us a while. Sit and listen to our teachings and beliefs."

Sim-khaw' reluctantly nodded his head, agreeing to a short stay. He came seeking aide to an immediate problem, one that tied into Zeh-Ahbe's roots, but the Say-awr' had found a solution to even greater problems.

***

Several days of chaos had passed in the city of Xorst since the murder of King Lo-Sonom. His gentle way and blatant wisdom had intrigued and inspired many during his lifetime, but his death sparked a new wave of hostility. Citizens reverted back to old grumblings and arguments; racial disputes exploded in every city block. Gleend had always remained a carefully balanced conglomerate of races. Removing the monarchy revealed just how fragile that cohabitation was. The social system crumbled in the absence of any heir apparent.

A Gleendish advisory parliament convened to try coping with the boiling tension. With racial war spilling out in the capital's streets and anarchy running unchecked, most of the local guards walked off—the king was dead and nothing bound the men, elves, and dwarves to service without him. Hard decisions needed to be made. Only the advisory council could quell the unrest.

In truth, they had no true political power. The advisory parliament only advised the king, but with the entire royal line executed, and the country plunged into disarray, they remained the last bastion of a thousand years of peace between elves, dwarves, and men.

Mar'zal, the elven head had disappeared several days ago and so an elf named Elo'misce was called to step into his role. Her people had put her on the council to try and hold her back from acquiring real power. She had been too ambitious, like many of her kind, and parliament was often where dreams went to die.

Before her appointment to the advisory parliament, Elo'misce was governor of an elven town on the east side of the country, Thanda. Her ilk had thought her too aggressive in her rulings against outsiders; certain elves wanted to keep the peace and balance in the racially mixed country.

Elo'misce grinned as she walked into the chamber. Her time had finally come and her enemies had given her the tools to prosper her people, and her own as well

Racial hatred underpinned everything in Gleend. It had wormed its way through elven and dwarven culture for generations with toxic levels of unspoken resentment. It even riddled the council halls.

All signs pointed to one race emerging dominant above the others. Elo'misce wanted nothing more than to expel the other races from the land, or better yet, to slaughter them wholesale and make Gleend an elven nation.

The wry elf took her seat and watched a human and a wrinkly, old dwarf nearly fall to blows. Even now, when the council needed peace and levity to survive, they were at each other's throats, insulting each other and dredging up old disputes.

Elo'misce grinned. Especially now, they had the power and potential to change things, fix the country, create unity—but that was the furthest from what she wanted. She craved blood in the streets. Elo'misce smiled as Bwar, the dwarven head, and Lemant, his human counterpart cursed each other by every thinkable power.

Elo'misce joined the heated debate. "I think that Bwar is right, at least in part," she maneuvered. "For a long time, humans have provided headship over the three races. Perhaps it is time for a change."

Lemant countered her claim, "Mankind wields the throne because it was our ancestors who formed this country, let me remind you. We invited your kinds here to coexist with us in unity; it was ours to begin with and your lands are really only on loan."

The elven politician stared down her nose at him disdainfully. "I believe in our unity," she lied. "For a long while we have cohabited in peace. The wisdom of your ruler, the monarchy that held the balance in check for so many generations, has dissipated. You no longer have any solid excuse to occupy the throne without that bloodline; if it is wisdom that dictates our ruler, why not enthrone a being with a longer lifespan, one that will bring more experience and knowledge to their leadership."

"I know what you would seek to do, Elo'misce," spat Bwar. "You want to put your own rear on that throne and lord above us all. Her claim is only partly relevant. A leader that is too long-lived could easily become a despot, tyrannically lording over us all. The middle ground is best: install a dwarf. We are long-lived and yet still mortal in nature."

Things were breaking down. Humanity had become overlooked entirely. The dwarves and elves already decided one of their kind would rule. The only question was which of the two races? If the brewing cold war was decided by politics, the key would be bending the will of men, the third race... and still, nobody knew the details of the assassination. All witnesses had been murdered!

Elo'misce discounted Bwar's claims and pressed her point further. "The humans have excluded us for as long as they have ruled, treating us as second-class citizens. Even your Luciferian religion has kept us in a lower rank, excluding us because of our heritage and creation."

"That's not even a valid argument," spouted Lemant, "At least not any longer with the recent reforms."

"Maybe," claimed Bwar, "what we need is a mental reform that includes us *all*. Just like your own church has said, 'we should all have an equal part.' In true equality, we should all have a valid claim to the vacant throne!"

The entire council erupted in a cacophony of arguments. Insults and accusations flew across the room at each other. Bwar and his fellow dwarven advisors looked ready to murder their peers. The elves haughty stares and invectives slandered the others in the room. Lemant and his fellow advisors spat barbs at a notable disadvantage.

The council had been given the authority to appoint a new monarch, and judge current affairs. From Lemant's viewpoint, there seemed no way that a human would sit on the throne. Surely a new dynasty would emerge from this room, and there didn't seem a worthy person in the whole lot.

Lemant sat back as the arguments raged around the council hall. His thoughts turned inward as despair took over his thoughts. The only logical course of action was to side with one group or the other and seek a strong alliance that could benefit mankind under their rule.

A firm tap on his shoulder pulled him from his dark revelry. Lemant turned to the messenger who handed him a sealed communication. It carried orders to read at once and directed the messenger to interrupt any kind of closed session to deliver the package.

Lemant dismissed the carrier and hastily unraveled the parchments. His eyes widened at a royal seal affixed to the page. A sense of urgency buzzed in his ears and drowned out the quarrels that flared around him.

The advisor leapt to his feet amidst the council members and proclaimed his findings. "Stay your arguments! I have just received word that Havara has survived the assassination attempt and taken refuge elsewhere!"

Silence shook the hall. The faces of the elves and dwarves fell in disappointment; their contentions for the throne would fall by the wayside as long as Havara lived. None of them looked more upset, however, than Bwar. Lemant narrowed his eyes, immediately expected that the dwarf had some part in the assassination of king Lo-Sonom.

Bwar and Elo'misce traded glances. The sincere look spoke more than volumes of text. That nonverbal communication chilled Lemant to his core as a deep fear for his life twisted in his gut.

The throne had been dangled in front of the other races and revealed how they desired it above all else. Snatching it back so suddenly only fueled the tension between mankind and ekthro. The hall fell eerily silent as the social rifts broadened quietly. A weak voice in the back somewhere motioned to convene the meeting, another one seconded it and hands silently raised to vote. The meeting adjourned under a pall of tension so thick that it had hushed everyone under the threat of a civil war that they all knew loomed on the horizon.

With or without Havara, Gleend teetered on the brink of something new.

***

Mil-khaw-mah' stared down at his humanoid contact. The lycan towered above everyone at all times and rarely resumed his human shape. He viewed humanness as beneath him.

The werewolf bared his fangs as he welcomed the messenger. Mil-khaw-mah' desired power above all else. Acquiring glory through battle and shedding blood were what he excelled at… that was power and he showed his teeth to let the soft-skinned guest know he came at the lycan's pleasure.

Fayge was no ordinary pinkling, however. His hollow eyes and pale skin gave that away. High cheekbones and slicked back dark hair gave him an air of nobility and his neatly trimmed sideburns framed his delicate face. Fayge represented powers that courted the werewolf clans. He came as an envoy from the brood of Lilth.

Mil-khaw-mah' sniffed the air. Of course there would be no fear lingering around the undead. Vampires were powerful, even small ones like this had no reason to fear a mortal creature. His kind had already beaten death.

This vampire smelled unlike the others he had met. Fayge's odor was not archaic, like the dust and old skin smell of the ancient brethren. This one smelled more like the vampiric messenger he'd located in the Tribben Forest some time ago. Mil-khaw-mah' expected that Fayge was a Wendigo. The original vampires, crafted by hay-lale' were limited in their numbers; they would not risk their safety to court one such as Mil-khaw-mah'. The ancient Adamic line would send a created vampire, one who was once a man but seduced by the ageless power: a Wendigo.

"I bring you more information from our spies," Fayge stated.

"Do tell," said the towering werewolf.

"It appears that one of your own has sought out a former colleague of yours."

Mil-khaw-mah' snorted derisively. However, the riddle-speaking vampire had his full attention.

"Sim-khaw' of the Zaw-nawb' has sought out another of the fallen tribes. He currently sits with Zeh-Ahbe' of the to-ay-baw' Say-awr'."

The lupine's blood began to boil. He bit his lip and drew blood as the feeling of betrayal coursed through his engorged veins. The lowest of the tribes, the Say-awr', had been rendered cursed and cast off from the kil-yaw', the ruling body central to the werewolf culture. They were anathema, forever lost.

"Then he must be destroyed, along with the rest of the Zaw-nawb'! Those malcontent subordinates... so afraid of becoming the lowest rank they would seek aid from even the most inferior of the lupine."

"Stow your anger, Mil-khaw-mah'. You must not damage the kil-yaw' any further. Do not forget your end of the bargain; you must restore the kil-yaw' to its origins."

"The other tribes will not be easily persuaded. 'The to-ay-baw' is final and complete,'" the werewolf quoted his one-time mentor and predecessor.

"Then you will force them to understand that the body must be whole."

"Why do you take issue with the Say-awr'?" The werewolf asked, confused and belligerent, "You demand that the Say-awr' be restored but prohibit the original to-ay-baw' clan; you force the creation of a new Say-awr' despite the claims that they have regained their powers. Why do you prohibit the recreation of the Shaw-than' in the same way? It begins to make me feel like I am the one being played; I am moving game pieces but you withhold the strategy from me."

Fayge grinned, showing fangs of his own. "The Shaw-than' are unneeded because they still exist, as you have record of. When the time is right, the to-ay-baw' prohibition will be lifted."

"And the Say-awr'?"

"They must be wholly recreated. We have hesitation about their allegiances and no idea the source of their power. They have chosen to collude with a cult that challenges the power of the Luciferian Order. For reasons that we do not fully know, the leader of the Gathering has spent a great deal of effort trying to destroy them. If he had no other challenges to his power, beh'-tsah might have destroyed them utterly by now.

"For the time being, these krist-chins are too risky to be trusted. They might make good allies in the future if we could find some way to manipulate them—but for now, leave those pieces off the board."

The vampire's mention of manipulation triggered a thought in Mil-khaw-mah's head. Was *he* being manipulated right now, even?

"Why are we reforming the kil-yaw'," he challenged.

"To fulfill your purpose, lupine. You were created for a purpose—everything was... or did you think otherwise?"

"There is no purpose," he snarled.

"Then you do not know your history," Fayge mocked.

"We have the records of the Ahee-sthay-tay'-ree-on."

"Ah yes," the comparatively diminutive creature chided, "the scribes and scholars of the kil-yaw'. But tell me, do you possess the original record?"

"We have kept them since the first! They are authentic!"

"No, you misunderstand me. Do you have the very first records?"

Mil-khaw-mah' paused for thought, then his blood heated again. The vampires must have somehow broken the sanctity of the kil-yaw'. The records kept by the Ahee-sthay-tay'-ree-on were secret and private and stayed only with the kil-yaw'. No outsider could know that the record volumes started at a number higher than one. The numeric sequence began with the number two; none in the kil-yaw' knew about the original, lost tome.

Before the massive beast could seize and interrogate the pompous vampire, Mil-khaw-mah' fell faint. His steps staggered and some mystic power forced his body to revert to its human form.

Fayge firmly stood his ground. His hand outstretched in a typical spellcasting form. The vampire had pulled him out of his lupine form and postured as if it had been child's play.

Mil-khaw-mah' stumbled to his feet. He glowered incredulously at the vampire. Standing there, naked and wet, glistening with the transformation, he still stood as a massive specimen of a man and remained larger than the vampire. The thought to attack him entered his mind but quickly departed; if he had this kind of power and appeared unhindered by the spiritual drain that a spell of that magnitude might take, he must have been more powerful than any regular wendigo.

"Are you calm?" Fayge inquired in a cool tone.

"I am listening," Mil-khaw-mah' said smoothly.

"Good." Inwardly, Fayge sighed with relief. The strain that they spell caused him nearly sent him into torpor—but he was graceful above all else, and there was no need to share that information. Fayge continued, "To understand your purpose, you must know the fullness of your history.

"You should know that there were many records kept prior to the forming of the kil-yaw'. Volume two of your records contains an account of the formation of the kil-yaw'. The Ahee-sthay-tay'-ree-on kept records before that point in a large codex. It just so happens that my people possess this particular book. You are invited to come and examine it at your leisure. It may be important that you can verify its authenticity. Your full cooperation is something we greatly desire, and once you verify its accuracy and examine what it contains, I have no doubt that we will both find the mutual power and glory that our kinds seek in our own ways."

The werewolf met Fayge's hollow gaze. The open invitation intrigued Mil-khaw-mah', though he was more drawn to the possibility of personal glorification than of discovering any lost historical records. He wanted to *be history*, rather than know it.

Their alliance was uneasy, but there were too many temptations and potential benefits for him to avoid leading the kil-yaw' down this path.

"Think about how little you know of your own origins," the vampire said flatly as he departed. Fayge was in desperate need of cooperation, but he revealed none of that. He displayed only confidence and power to the werewolf as he melted into the shadows. That was the language Mil-khaw-mah' spoke and it was what he would understand. He slithered through the night, almost desperate to feed.

***

The days of ceaseless walking brought the nondescript traveler passed Briganik and moved across Lol's harsh terrain on tireless legs. The journey could have been made quicker via other modes of travel that he could certainly access, but he savored the time stewing in his thoughts. He enjoyed the anticipation of the journey. If his hopes came to fruition, he would reverse his condition; he dared not hope or dwell on what might be otherwise.

Day turned to night as he walked… and dusk again to dawn. Several days passed as the landscape on which he trod changed. His mind kept brushing against the one horrid thought, *What if there is no hope for one such as I?* Every time it came, he discarded the notion and focused on his steady strides.

***

Absinthium's legs pumped steadily, bearing him upwards through the grand spire that connected the Order's Monastery of Light to the entrance of Paradise, the demonic Babel Heavens. A jog up through the massive structure would have caused any normal being to pause for rest. The arch-mage had earlier cast an invigoration spell that supplied him with limitless physical energy as long as he remained focused on the spell.

As he finally burst through the final entry to Paradise, he was once more reminded of the war that raged for possession of the Babel Heavens. It had been a constant state, to some degree, ever since the departure of hay-lale'. This most recent conflict had arisen from within the Gathering itself, as it often did. The untimely coup split the ranks of Gathering and divided his master's attention just as the krist-chin threat began to rise before them.

A heavy contingent of beh'-tsah's troops guarded the Paradise entrance which remained the most convenient access point between the upper and lower firmaments. Absinthium, no stranger to the demonic lands, snapped his fingers and sequestered a gang of mixed ekthro troops and a ghostly white horse to take him safely to beh'-tsah's castle, the meeting hall of the demonic council. As the dread lord's most trusted servant it was foolish to travel exposed in Paradise; beh'-tsah's enemies would too willingly assassinate him.

They neared beh'-tsah's fortress and the archmage's bodyguards peeled off as the mage pulled his pale steed ahead, speeding to his master's fortress. The immense, black curtain wall towered over the landscape. Crafted from eldritch, black iron and seated atop the realm's leylines, it had been wrought from a single piece by its creator. Everything about the stronghold reeked of power and strength.

As he approached the blocked entry the barbed portcullis raised in greeting. Absinthium rode through a passage where the dismal light of Paradise bled through the murder holes above him, just as boiling oil might if he'd been an enemy. The arch-mage loved everything about this place.

The metal grate clattered noisily behind him and the Luciferian dismounted. Hitching his beast to a nearby post, he sought out his demon master.

Stalking through the dingy halls, he passed the throne room and walked into the antechamber where he often awaited his master's commands. He did not feel the presence of the dark lord as he waited, kneeling on the cobblestone floor of the chamber. The dark Lord of the Gathering usually hovered somewhere nearby in an ethereal form, undetectable to the human eye, and on guard to protect his seat of power. In that state he could siphon the power from the spiritual leylines that threaded together the magic of the realm, translating the sinful nature of mankind into raw power.

In his spirit form, beh'-tsah harvested the energy unto himself; essentially filling his being with a type of fuel to power his magic. Despite the invisibility to humans and most humanoid ekthro, most creatures could still sense the aura of tangible evil that the demon over-lord exuded. That sense of ominous power chilled even Absinthium at every meeting; only beh'-tsah could cause such a tingle of dread in his spinal cord.

A demonic scullion entered the room and groveled for attention. The wretched demon looked wasted and emaciated, clearly a servant of the lowest ranks of their kind. It amused Absinthium to know that even a human being could contend with many demon's power.

"The dark lord bids you locate him in the dining hall," the loathsome creature groaned.

Absinthium silently rose and strode through the compound. He knew his way around the facility better than many of those beasts that lived within.

He found beh'-tsah feasting at a fully spread table. The buffet stretched across the entire room. Delicacies steamed and leaked fluids upon various parts of the table, though many of the diverse dishes that had been heaped upon it were considered revolting or even anathema to some races and cultures.

Absinthium approached his master. The demon over-lord remained seated in a massive chair, three times the size of what an ordinary man might require. Even seated, the dark lord towered above his prophet.

beh'-tsah had fed and grown upon the bitterness and sins of mankind, becoming a terrible sight to behold. His purple veined wings draped behind him like a cape and he consumed the prepared dish before him, his canine mouth loudly crunched the bones of whatever creature he ate.

He finally finished ingesting the roasted creature and rose on lion-like haunches to greet his loyal servant. His blackened hide contrasted the shimmering crimson loincloth that hung from his waist; the dragon-scale garment contained the undying spirit of meh'-red, the previous Lord of the Gathering. The only part of his boar-like hide that was colored other than a dusky charcoal gray was the diagonal scar that ran across the demon's muscular chest. The ivory colored wound was mostly covered by a newly acquired chest plate assembled from human bones.

Absinthium fingered his wizard's stave as he studied beh'-tsah's new armor. He had almost lost his toqeph in the same battle where his master had received the mark. The angel, Jorge, had actually cut his master. These krist-chins' supernatural weapons were unlike anything they'd ever seen and could even physically affect beh'-tsah as he sat high above in the Babel Heavens.

"You noticed my new breast piece," the demon bragged.

Absinthium nodded. Bloody pulp and ligaments still clung to the skeletal structures splattering the ivory framework with red taint. Many of the bones were still fresh and the smell of cracked ossein permeated the air as the pungent marrow scent leaked forth.

"While you were away setting Dyule up as puppet ruler of Jand, another krist-chin followed in Nhoj's footsteps. He was preaching to anyone who would listen and we quickly snatched him up."

"Let us hope that this doesn't become a common occurrence. We would not want those two groups joining forces. Perhaps we should take further precautions."

"It would be prudent," the demon intoned. "I fear that they are somehow being inspired by the power of the Holy Spirit. He must be quenched. Our enemy has unleashed a terrible foe, but one that we have all but expelled once before."

Absinthium nodded as beh'-tsah's bovine tail swished in annoyance. "I assume that he has been dealt with?"

"I would not be dining were it not so," beh'-tsah said flatly.

The mage nodded glumly. He had hoped to deal with the case personally; Absinthium took great joy in tormenting heretics.

"The battle for paradise is consuming more and more of my attention as it reaches a climax. I find myself increasingly placing this duty to destroy all krist'chins upon you.

"The coup within the Gathering was expected, if not ill-timed. However, it was the resurgence of this rogue cult that has proven to be the major encumbrance to our grand plans. For all its danger, the coup could have been a good thing; it ousted my enemies and will allow for new allegiances to be forged: bonds that will not grow cold yet for some time."

"The battle goes well then, or poorly? What do you require, master?"

"I want you to destroy this threat, this cancer that disturbs my campaign for total control! I want these krist'chins destroyed. I give the task wholly over to you to manage this malignancy."

The demon surged with anger. An appearance of another would-be missionary from the long-dormant sect must have disturbed him greatly—more than he let on. If Karoz's disciples began mustering enough courage to leave their home and preach, then it would require more effort to contain them. That would mean more energy wasted by beh'-tsah to merely maintain his current position.

"Whatever your instructions are, I will follow." Absinthium bowed low.

The overlord smiled broadly.

"The quick strike against tah'av'aw's fortress went as planned," beh'-tsah shifted gears. "I had directed makh'al'o'' keth to annihilate all of his resources immediately following the uprising; his decision to cast his lot with the dissenters was impulsive and typical. His forces remained unaware of the coup and makh'al'o'keth's army caught them unprepared.

"The instigator, peh'-shah, is holed up in kah'-as's lair, I assume. Most of peh'-shah's army has been scattered. kah'-as has the most strength and best defenses; raw-tsakh' is besieging those defenses even now, but it will likely prove an extended campaign.

"There are other forces, too, jealous demons who the dissidents persuaded to aide them in besieging my home. Those have been recalled and now reinforce the army gathered at gay'-ooth's castle. The combined armies of zaw'lal' and gaw'law' have engaged them."

Absinthium nodded. The Order maintained a carefully balanced relationship with the demon lords of Paradise. "Those Luciferian mage's with devotions to certain demonic masters have been informed of the changes within the Gathering. They have been commanded to either choose a new allegiance when the Gathering reforms or join their lords at their castles in Paradise to suffer the consequences of war."

"Yes," the demon purred, "a small number of those with true loyalty ascended the tower, opting to join their masters." beh'tsah fingered the chitinous breast piece that he wore, picking at little bits of human flesh that clung to the bones. Those who chose poorly were immediately seized by my forces at the tower's portal.

"Because this has flared into all-out war, everyone has courted the remaining demon lords—those not on the council. Those who remain on my side of the battle, of course, have no proven loyalty; their best chance for garnering the most power or even forming their own eventual coup exists with my continued reign."

The mage nodded knowingly, "The war in Paradise cannot be ignored because it could dethrone you, but if I fail to control this krist-chin threat, then all will be for naught."

"And we cannot ignore the ever-looming threat that Lilth and her brood pose. With the Gathering breaking, they might take advantage of its momentary weakness and spread their own brand of taint. Even now her agents have been seen at work."

"I will see to it that the Order hires more hunters and keeps those threats manageable." The demon ripped another body apart at the table and began to devour it as his minion explained his plans. "My new acolytes are nearly ready. Rebuilding my corps of elite warrior mages will let me replicate my efforts on a larger scale. It will take some time to season them properly, but they will be of great use."

"Good," beh'-tsah said. "You will need them in the days to come. Once they are functioning cohesively I want you taking charge of the entire anti-krist-chin operation on the first firmament. This war consumes too much of my attention and I cannot afford to divide my efforts. You will head up my campaign against the threat; exaporeh'·omahee will keep watch on the activities of the undead and report back to you.

"For the most part, because the recent skirmish left Grinden's population in such shambles, the krist·chins have been significantly villainized. Continue those measures and slander them as you prod along the Order's revival.

The demon seized an immense, writhing viper from his dining table, "I have such plans—machinations that even you do not know about."

Absinthium did not quite fully understand his master's meaning.

The demon bit the serpent's head off and it ceased struggling. Blood splattered to the floor as its body uncurled from beh'-tsah's forearm and fell limp.

Chapter Four

Nineteen men now remained. They stood stark and bare, standing at attention as Absinthium inspected them. He examined their naked bodies closely for signs of wounds and scars. Surviving this long without incurring some sort of wound proved impossible; they had run rigorous gauntlets and engaged in deadly exercises. He looked them over, but less as a measure how many wounds each had taken and instead searched for signs of proficiency at mending their wounds via dark rituals and potions. Each potential acolyte was responsible for healing his own defects.

The scarred and rough crew of disciplined hopefuls appeared in better condition than Absinthium had hoped for. Since the last inspection, only three of them had died. Pink, fresh scars showed the mage that their survival had not been for a lack of trying on Wynn's part. Absinthium smiled with satisfaction; these men were tough and had proven it by their very survival.

His Acolyte roster had room for only eleven of the nineteen who had survived tonight's test. Wynn held the top Acolyte spot and Absinthium himself was always the thirteenth member. He barked an order and the team equipped themselves for a new training exercise.

Silently, they filed out to the training grounds. What used to be a verdant field behind the Monastery of Light had become a blasted patch of dirt pocked with craters and broken turf. They assumed an obedient posture, waiting for instructions for whatever this next session required.

Absinthium wandered into their collective number as he muttered a simple spell. As the orb atop his toqeph radiated a sphere of arcane power, a supernatural darkness gathered overhead. Knitting together, the boiling, inky mass grew into a dome of shadows that enveloped the men.

The privacy screen helped Absinthium obscure his actions from the rest of the Luciferian Order. None of the three other Arch Mages on the Council of Four realized that he had built his own private assassin group.

Absinthium regarded his peers as imbeciles and trusted that his magic was far superior. For years he had operated within the Order with complete impunity. His magic abilities far exceeded those of his peers Eroschit and Bellitahs, and to be compared with Mesler would be a joke, the old Battle Mage could hardly be considered a Mage ranking wizard in any discipline other than combat.

As the dome of darkness completed, the mystic envelope of shadow sealed against the ground and simulated a nighttime environment. Absinthium wanted to cut the numbers of acolyte potentials to a maximum of seventeen. Whether from wounds or from exhaustion, at least two of these men would die today.

They formed two groups to face oncoming hordes of attackers. Wynn knew best what it meant to be an acolyte and he led the nine men that he considered best suited for his team. Casualties would probably come from the secondary group.

Absinthium stepped beyond the dome of darkness and to the slave pens where armed warriors waited with weapons reclaimed from past hordes. He perched himself on a rock with a good vantage point and nodded to one of his master's demon scullions who unlocked the gate and sent in the waves of opposition.

The culling would now begin.

***

Kevin left Nipanka's company, bidding him good journey, urging him to return to the original plan: to voyage to the mining communities of Lol. The preacher couldn't shake the sense that some terrible ill would befall them if they did not break company as soon as possible.

He bit his lip. If the Spirit had shown him anything over the years, it had been that this was one of the ways He communicated.

Turning to the matters at hand Kevin seated himself on a short wooden stool in the town square where his Christian brethren surrounded him. Havara stood next to him and an angel flanked each person. The Christians had moved directly into the main body of the village where the buildings could offer more protection.

Kevin glanced across the area, eyes lingering on the buildings damaged by the mixed-race invasion. A distinct resentment for the nonhuman species stirred in the local people.

Sadness hovered over the preacher's heart. He planned to preach a message this evening to the remaining people of Sprazik and the people had been inspired by Havara's claim that they would hear the message King Lo-sonom died believing. Kevin's mind kept turning to the grief in his heart; during relief efforts to help repair the community he had found the dead body of the young, mute cyclops who so intrigued him.

Havara turned aside to speak with to his local subjects. He detailed assignments for keeping watch and answered a myriad of questions from the people. Fear gripped them tightly. No one knew if another attack would come again—nor how soon.

The messenger they'd sent back to Xorst to announce that Havara had survived the assassination attempt had not returned. Hopefully, Havara's human allies were able to stave off any further attacks; a second, blatant coup would likely provide a cause for the humans to band together over. Even if Havara died it might give them something to rally around. If elves and dwarves killed the prince and took the throne they might not succeed in keeping it.

None of the humans noticed as a tall, cowled figure meandered into their midst. The shrouded visitor had come such a long distance. He slipped easily through the crowd with a nimbleness that defied his size.

The two angels noticed him, however. They jumped forward, wings flared wide and swords brandished to protect the two important figureheads behind them. The sudden movement made those nearby recoil with surprise. Only the cloaked traveler failed to flinch.

"What are you doing here," demanded Jorge, weapon at the ready.

"Please, please," the figure begged as he pulled back his hood. The handsome traveler dropped to one knee. "I come with peace." He brushed long strands of his umber hair away from his fair-skinned face. Apart from his somber, grayed eyes, he looked just like one of the angels.

Kyrius took a defensive position in front of Kevin and Havara as Jorge approached the visitor.

Jorge put the blade of his holy sword right next to the newcomer's head. The stranger did not withdraw even as the righteous, blue flame-light bathed his face. The light, which normally revealed the blighted true forms of demonic beings, turned up surprisingly little. His fair skin fell slightly ashen under the holy light and a brown patch of decay festered on his chin and brow.

"What is your name, demon?" Jorge commanded.

"My name is ekerithia." He spread his palms outward in desperation. "But I do not consider myself one of *them*. I must know, is there any hope for me? Please, I want to repent."

***

Absinthium ran out of orcs. Every single one of them had fallen to the serrated edges of his trainees' kamas. They regrouped to their two clusters, taking advantage of the momentary rest between waves.

The archmage observed the scene before him. Corpses and body parts scattered the field; his acolytes had been drenched in sweat and blood. Flames flared in spots belching acrid smoke, wheezing and snapping as each spat tiny embers into the air like glittering confetti.

At the edge of the dome, necromantically animated bodies of previous Acolytes stood like pillars at the edge of the darkness. They functioned as scribes, keeping statistics on each of the warriors. Only eleven of them could be chosen.

Larger than the orcs that they had just faced, the next wave consisted mostly of ogres and even a few trolls. Absinthium gave the signal and the creatures rushed in under the cover of darkness, each brandishing various devices of war and howling guttural battle-cries.

A concussive thunderclap tore up brown sod and cleaved flesh and joint as a wave of alchemical fury erupted. Wynn's group cleared a whole flank and darted into the smoldering region to clean up any survivors while expanding their protection buffer.

The other team expended the last of their projectile weapons and rushed into the fray pairing into five groups of two. Only teamwork and martial skill would keep them from casualties.

Wynn's troops fanned out in an elliptical formation. His teammates also worked in two-man groups, the foremost warrior kept up defenses for his rear partner who concentrated on spell casting. Any enemies nearby fell by the blade and the next tier of adversaries fell to a variety of spells.

Absinthium watched the events unfold from afar and through the eyes of his undead helpers. Wynn's team advanced and broadened their effective range as the trainees' prowess annihilated their foes; fireballs and lightning bolts blasted forth to take down the deadly creatures.

With Wynn's group performing so well, the enemies shifted its focus to the other team. The secondary team became hard pressed by the added attention. Their defense started crumbling under the onslaught as their enemies piled up against them.

In desperation, one of the initiates stepped back and drew upon dark power. He cast a spell that erupted in a burst of wind, flinging bodies in every direction like a hot typhoon. It was a clever move but scattered both friend and foe alike across the field. The situation should never have progressed as far as it did.

Amidst the tumult, hopeful acolytes picked themselves up from the dirt and rushed to regroup against the charging ekthro. Their positioning had improved despite the battering blast of the gale.

The slowest acolyte to reach the rally point was swept off his feet beneath the blows of a massive troll. In a flash, the troll pinned him down with a massive, calloused foot and smashed him like an egg with its jagged, stone club.

Watching his partner perish, the next closest acolyte tried to flee. The troll cackled gleefully and gave chase, encouraged by the possibility of easy prey. The acolyte grinned. He'd goaded the beast and leapt towards a nearby wooden structure and used his legs to spring back, ricocheting back at the surprised troll. Turning, he brought his claw-like kamas to bear and lodged them deep within the monster's chest.

The troll shrieked as it toppled and the brave fighter raked the edged hooks through unresistant flesh, delivering mortal wounds.

He reached into his gear pouch but struggled with a snagged belt. He needed to use a vial of caustic chemicals on the body. Without some kind of acid or fire, the troll would eventually regenerate and he would have to battle a smarter, tougher version of the creature. He momentarily diverted his attention and rummaged through his belt pouches.

Two nearby ogres hung back, deviously plotting their attacks. They took advantage of the acolyte's momentary distraction and cast tangles of razor-wire at him.

The acolyte saw their movement from the corner of his eye. He dodged the first one but jumped directly into the path of the second nest. The metal, ball-like devices at the ends of the tangled wire netting reeled in rapidly and the razor meshwork contracted, dismembering the human where he lay helplessly tangled.

With the rest of the Acolytes surviving the next few minutes, Absinthium recalled the remaining ekthro. If he waited any longer, more acolyte potentials than necessary might fall, several already suffered substantial wounds that needed immediate attention.

Absinthium shook out his enchanted haversack and muttered a spell. The sigil branded sack, a necromantic item of his own design, shimmied like a flag in a stiff wind. A supernatural vortex pulled at the molecules of the animated undead. The former acolytes evaporated, breaking into dust that the bag sucked up and held. The sigil on the filled bag gleamed like filigree.

The archmage returned to the acolytes' barracks to pour over the training records and notes that he'd taken. Tonight he would decide who made the final cut and who would be put in reserve.

Absinthium glanced at the six coffin-like boxes. Lights of a design and pattern that mystified even him blinked in reply. He knew very little about how they worked or what forces powered them. He didn't need to understand how it worked, though; he had witnessed the devices' capabilities and infinite power supply when collecting these boxes from the sparsely populated country of Domn. Inside the chambers had been six inhabitants of the old-world country where they'd been placed into stasis prior to the country's descent into a war-torn wasteland. The arch-mage would use them now to hold the remaining six Acolyte potentials as reserve units.

The spell caster grinned, reliving an old victory in his mind. He'd long ago taken these from *his generation's* Eldar Darkshield before the mysterious demon from the box raised up another priest to crown as his avatar.

He tallied the scores and made some critical judgments. He circled eleven names with a grin. Now came the critical planning stage of his new team's first *real* mission.

Absinthium reached for a dedicated qâsam stone. After a few moments spent calling, grr'Shaalg's image came into view through the qâsam's crystalline facets.

"My Acolyte roster has been refilled, grr'Shaalg. Our forces will be on the move again very soon and I have need of you for my plans. Be prepared for my call to action."

***

The Christians in Ninda made a second trip into the village to give their presentation. Their encounter with Sim-khaw' had delayed them a couple of days. In retrospect, the actors for the play were relieved to get a few extra days of practice, though Rashnir was sure that they would have done well without any extra rehearsals.

Many of the Christians took those extra days to find their way into the city and speak with the locals. The people of Schworick began noticing there was something different about these travelers; they seemed happier than most other visitors: some kind of deep-seated joy.

Rashnir and Zeh-Ahbe' spent much of their time speaking with Sim-khaw'. Those men and women who went into the village were cautioned against sharing any outright anti-Luciferian sentiments. That fact would be revealed during their drama. They'd been given a tight window of opportunity and it was best not to spoil it.

With Rashnir in the lead. the group entered Schworick's limits again. Zeh-Ahbe' accompanied him with Sim-khaw' in reluctant tow. The lycan's brain seemed hardwired against many Christian values. He lacked the ability to understand those same things his new companions—even the Say-awr' ones—believed. Nonetheless, they encouraged the tribal leader to accompany them and witness the tenets of their faith as they lived them out firsthand.

The acting troupe and a few others from the camp followed their lead. In an effort to attract as big a crowd as they could when they presented their drama, Rashnir played a simple tune on his lyre and the actors sang along. People peered out of doorways and waved to the group.

"Come and see our drama," one would say as the rest sang, and, "Follow us to see the act," they invited others.

Rashnir smiled as he strummed the stringed instrument. It had been a gift from the angel, Kyrius, given to him at their parting after the events in Grinden. Another, however, had given the gift of musical talent to him; Kelsa had taught him how to play, the basic fingerings for the easy chords. He smiled and played as he reminisced the late nights they spent together and her whimsical idea that he must learn to make music.

You must have more talents than just killing people, she once said to him. *And besides, the man that I marry must be able to play me my favorite song at our wedding.*

His revelry fell apart and his fond memory evaporated like vapor. Rashnir's misstep was bad enough that he had to restart, but he did not let on to his friends that he'd spotted trouble. He'd locked eyes again with the woman that he noticed the last time they'd come to town. The company resumed the merry tune, oblivious to his apprehension.

Rashnir sidestepped out of his group as they passed him by. He could catch up with the rest of them at the location they had picked for the drama. Something strong connected him to this woman and he felt compelled to find it out.

The attention of the crowd remained on the acting troupe. The woman, however, fixed her gaze on Rashnir. Hesitantly the Christian warrior walked over to where she stood.

"What is your name?" he asked her.

"My name is Ly'Orra," she said. She wore a similar outfit as in her last appearance. She would be hard to spot in the wild. Well camouflaged in her myriad shades of brown, tanned leather and tufted furs were complimented by her tawny hair and bronzed skin. Emerald eyes revealed an inner, jaded edge that burned fierce with iron will.

Ly'Orra leaned on her tall staff as she spoke, though Rashnir noticed various weapons held fast by her baldric. "I believe that I know who you are, but enlighten me anyway."

"My name is Rashnir," the warrior bowed to greet her formally.

At the deepest part of his bow, she swung her staff in a swift upper-cutting motion, squarely striking Rashnir in the jaw and knocking him off his feet. He crashed to his back, shocked and betrayed by his own emotions.

"Just as I thought," said Ly'Orra. "I have heard stories of your deeds, but you don't have any recollection of mine. *I am famous among my people*," she hissed. "I have followed you through story for many years, though I thought your legacy long crippled by the sins of your past." Ly'Orra baited him with the reference to the false story of him betraying his former commander and best friend, Rogis.

Rashnir's eyes narrowed, but he kept his composure. The famous Ranger had been more than just a figurehead and mentor to him; Rogis was his lover's father. When the wicked King Harmarty framed Rashnir for the murder it had nearly destroyed all hope he'd ever dared to gain.

"Among the people of Zipha, I am renowned. In my recent wanderings, I heard a rumor that you had risen from the ashes of despair and joined forces with a dangerous sect of heretics." Ly'Orra glanced towards the nearby troupe.

Surprised, Rashnir raised his eyebrows at her comment. He was unaware of free people living in Zipha. The country bordered Jand in the west and suffered cruelly under the bands of slavers. He pointed to his friends as they rounded a bend in the road and exited view. "Do they really look dangerous?"

Ly'Orra pulled a dagger from her hip and threw it; the blade buried itself in the soil a handbreadth from Rashnir's leg. She asked coyly, "Did I look dangerous when you first saw me?"

"What do you want, Ly'Orra," Rashnir asked.

She laughed as the warrior pulled himself to his feet. "I want to kill you," she said, "But fairly." Ly'Orra jumped and delivered a fierce kick.

Rashnir deflected it with his palms as he maneuvered away.

The Christian ducked under a strong swipe of her battle-staff. It might have knocked his teeth out had it connected. Rashnir backpedaled to get out of her range. He did not want to hurt her, neither did he want to draw his sword and startle the townsfolk with the flaming blade.

Ly'Orra pursued him and he dodged her blows. Tumbling past a kiosk, he heard the vendor who ran it chuckle about the situation as if it might've been expected. "Looks like one of them visitors made Ly'Orra mad."

She cornered him and rapped him across the body with her staff. The stinging blow made him turn to defend himself. She swung and struck again with her wooden weapon. Rashnir juked and ducked the assaults as best he could, not able to convince himself yet that he needed to strike his attacker.

Ly'Orra lunged with a stabbing maneuver that would have knocked the wind from his lungs. He slipped the blow and purposefully fell upon the outthrust staff with all of his weight, trapping the pole and cracking it with his force.

Undeterred, she dropped the pole and drew her blade. The steel curved subtly with a certain feminine appeal, though Rashnir knew its edge was just as deadly.

She slashed with the blade forcing Rashnir to dive for cover behind an old market-stand someone had abandoned in the alley. His opponent jumped to the serving area of another nearby booth and pulled a long blow tube from her sash.

"Why do you want to kill me?" he asked, bobbing and weaving to throw off her aim.

She blew forcibly into the pipe as Rashnir grabbed an old barrel lid. A swarm of small, poisoned darts lodged themselves in the makeshift shield with a loud *thwap*. Ly'Orra shouted and jumped from her position, leaping in for a killing blow.

He tossed the lid to the side and rolled away from her attack. Jumping to his feet, he sprinted away from the battle with the crazy woman.

Ly'Orra screamed in frustration as he escaped. The scoffing and laughter of the onlookers nipped at Rashnir's pride as he fled the alley, but that meant little to him as the woman pursued him through the street.

"Coward," she screamed. "Stand and fight!"

Repeating himself, Rashnir yelled over his shoulder, "Why do you want me dead?"

"For the glory! For the renown!" She yelped her answers between puffing, tired breaths.

Rashnir ducked around another corner and into an alley. A towering pile of packing crates blocked his path. He could never scale the unstable heap in time.

She rounded the corner and Rashnir threw a crate at her. Her sword lodged in the soft wood. The warrior yanked the crate backward to throw it to aside but her longsword held fast.

Ly'Orra pulled two shorter blades, one from each thigh, and pressed the attack.

Rashnir tried reaching for another crate but yanked his hand back just before Ly'Orra's bladed stroke could sever it.

Out of options, Rashnir finally drew upon the Lord's strength and called a flaming blade to his hands. Blue flames blazed with other-worldly glory as his defensive parry burned through both of her assassin's knives at their hilts.

Without losing a stride, Ly'Orra punched him in the side of the face. The weighted dagger pommel added enough momentum to make it hurt. As he reeled from the blow, a quick leg swipe knocked Rashnir flat on his back again.

She seized the opportunity and snatched her sword, still caught in the crate nearby. Ly'Orra kicked the wooden box from the blade and turned to deliver a final strike.

Rashnir deflected the blow with his own flaming blade. Shards of Ly'Orra's weapon flew off like shrapnel; she tried to strike again. Each of Rashnir's ripostes whittled her weapon down further until she stood over him grasping only a useless handle.

She pointed down at him, fuming with rage. "This is not over," she said with an accusatory tone. Ly'Orra dropped her broken weapon in the dirt and glared at him as he climbed to his feet again.

With a disgusted scowl, she turned and departed.

***

Jorge and Kyrius kept a close watch on their prisoner. They detained the supernatural being who proved a mystery to them. ekerithia had come willingly and seemed to have no intention of causing harm—and that puzzled them most of all. Still, they took no chances with him.

Blades at the ready, they questioned ekerithia further. The holy glow they emitted bathed their captive in a revealing light.

"Why does your appearance not fully transform under the holy light of the blade," Jorge questioned. His interrogation had been demanding and ekerithia's answers were as forthright as possible.

"I do not understand the question."

"Your appearance… the discerning power of the Holy Spirit."

His blank stare revealed ekerithia's ignorance on the matter.

Jorge got closer. Grabbing him, he pressed the flat of his blade almost against ekerithia's skin. "Why do you not transform fully into your true state, demon?"

"I have always been just as I am," ekerithia replied. "Only as I am."

"Well, not always," commented Kyrius as Jorge relinquished his hold.

ekerithia sighed, forlorn, "No, you are right… not always." He thoughtfully fingered the slight blemish on his face. "But since that moment so long ago, that moment when hay-lale' deceived me and this mark formed. I have gone these last several thousand years hating that moment—regretting the decision that I made. I admit he played on my jealousy and persuaded my heart, but for a moment."

The angels looked at the figure that had once been one of their own like a brother. While the glory of the Lord rested nowhere on him, neither did that foul, spiritual aura that typically wafted off from the demonic hordes.

"I heard of the redemption of mankind. Men have been brought back into the fold of God. Tell me," ekerithia pleaded. "And what of the angels?"

Kyrius looked at the creature. He knew what ekerithia dared to hope.

"Has our creator made a way for us? Is there some recourse available, some way to repent and recant?

"I have not been twisted and corrupted to the extent of the rest of hay-lale's fallen host. My heart is not blackened from wicked deeds like the rest. My fall has been the object of an ever-present regret; a mere moment that has haunted me for millennia. My deeds should speak well of me."

Jorge bit his lip, "Though you may have abstained from committing wicked acts since that time, ekerithia, your heart is still black. I think you know that you cling to a false hope. We were created with a purpose, and that very specifically, as tools of our Lord. He did not make provision for our redemption as he did for His children. *They* were made in His likeness.. with many choices in their lifetime, each one an opportunity to obey and reveal His glory in some way or to respond to it. You know how that is not so for us. It never was.

"You stood among our ranks and rejoiced with us when He set the cornerstone of the Earth in place. You were there when we sang the praises at the beginning. You were created with the knowledge and abilities to serve Him as designed, and yet *you* chose to leave that behind."

Ekerithia's eyes fixed on the ground, forlorn. "But I was malcontent. It was those deceitful words, whispered like kind counsel… *the poisoned words of hay-lale'*."

"But you *knew* the Truth. For a time at the beginning, He was the only light in the heavens; it was only ever His glory that lit our first abode," said Jorge.

A long silence passed between them. ekerithia refused to make eye contact.

"Then am I to be damned for my first mistake?"

Jorge wordlessly worked his mouth. All three of them knew it was more than a mistake—even angels made those. This had been sin.

Kyrius interjected, "You are tainted. Perhaps you cannot see... you do not think like one of us anymore." He added quieter, "You are not one of us anymore."

ekerithia looked from angel to angel, comparing each one to himself.

"You think like a man, you no longer use the wisdom that we were made with," Kyrius continued.

"Explain."

"You think like a human, resentful of your condition—though your fallen condition is only *your* fault. You refuse to accept your actions as your own. You hide behind your anger and resentment over consequences and hold to a false hope that everything will somehow be fine in the end... hoping that the consequences will just fade away. Those are all very human thoughts and contrary to the laws of Heaven.

"This is what Jorge has been trying to tell you: we are not men, stop thinking like one. We love our Master, but the way that we show Him is through our obedience; we choose to show Him in every moment of every day." Kyrius chuffed, "And we have it so much easier than these humans: *we* witnessed most of creation, *we* have intimately known our God. As tools, however, if we choose to go our own way then we become useless to our Master, broken and lost."

"And what! He cannot fix us? Of course, He has that power, so why won't He," ekerithia ranted.

"But why *should* He? You have spurned His love and refused Him. Worse, hay-lale's kind has systematically worked to drag mankind further into the pit since the fall."

"But not me, *personally*!" ekerithia's words echoed in his own ears. Even *he* heard the human, childlike whine of them.

Jorge spoke more softly than normal, "Maybe not, but the refusal to act in accordance with His wishes, which are to redeem mankind, only benefits the cause of death and darkness."

Kyrius put into understandable terms, "You have changed, ekerithia—perhaps less physically, but you have. Your decision was a final one. When either a good or wicked man's choices result in his own death, he changes. His essence no longer resides in the body that his family will bury… but it carries on in another form. He cannot return to his body—sinner or saint, his choice was a final one and his soul goes to judgment, just like every other creature. Your decision, too, has changed your very being from one state to the next. There is no return, only judgment, and one void of the mercy that He shows to his true children."

ekerithia stared off into emptiness. A somber look shaded his face as realization sunk in. His old fears had been correct: ekerithia was beyond redemption, but worse, his mind had been distorted. The angels were right, his thought processes had somehow fractured, and he no longer possessed the wisdom of the Lord.

For a moment he glimpsed that wisdom again through the angels' insight. He saw himself from their point of view. All of the spirit beings in the Host of Heaven were created with both great intellect and with great moral responsibility, when he had faltered, his mind shifted… no longer Christocentric. ekerithia realized that all his thoughts from that moment onward were consumed only with himself, his own needs, and his own plight. Selfishness ruled him and he saw no remedy. ekerithia's mind had been overthrown by sin.

Staring at his feet, his hopes dashed, ekerithia asked, "Will you kill me now?"

Jorge looked ready to affirm that, but his friend interjected. "No," said Kyrius. "You only have the here and now to live for, and you know that. You might try and take what comfort that you may while you still have the ability to do so."

"Thank you," ekerithia nodded his head soberly—his fallen mind working like a clock, suddenly wound up. "I know that this is worth nothing to you, but I give you an oath that I will not lead men astray with the enticements of sin, like the rest of my kindred."

Jorge acknowledged his statement, bobbing his head in affirmation. His body language clearly indicated skepticism of the demon's vow.

"I need some time to think, to gather my thoughts. Before I go, would it possible to speak with this man from Earth, with Kevin?"

"He is preaching to the townspeople right now, a very receptive audience. He displays his love for Christ by doing His work, bearing His message," said Jorge. "It's almost ironic."

"I think that their passion and zeal is why hay-lale' hated them so much," mused ekerithia as he scanned the distant group of humans. "They do such simple things, but it demonstrates love for Him beyond what any of us were ever capable of."

***

Jandul shadowed Krimko as he wandered the halls of their accommodations. The Nindan Parliament had appointed them an elaborately furnished guest house for personal use for as long as Absinthium required his servants' presence in Ninda.

Krimko snatched a rock from the pavement and hurled it at a bird. The sinister Luciferian grew bored. He had amused himself for a while by torturing small animals, but there were no more to be found.

Walking into the courtyard, he found his bodyguards engaged in some sort of gambling game. There wasn't a sober man among them. Jandul frowned in disapproval; these guardsmen were all that remained of the mercenaries' guild members after the incident at Grinden which toppled the Narsh Barbarians guild and disbanded the Rogis' Rangers faction.

Empty liquor crates and empty flagons cluttered the landscaped garden floors. The drunken, disheveled men didn't care about their surroundings. Aesthetics meant nothing to them at this point.

Krimko approached the inebriated throng, looking for some kind of entertainment. One man stood and leaned heavily on a mossy retaining wall, urinating. After a long drunken groan, he turned back to the players. Jandul rolled his eyes when he saw that it was Pinchôt. The warrior was drunk and it was barely past mid-day.

With little to entertain the mercenaries who had accompanied the Luciferians they naturally passed their time by drinking and gambling. The intoxicated warrior fell back into his empty seat at the table and resumed the game with his men. The contest was unfamiliar to Krimko, who had spent most of his young adult life on monastery grounds with the Order.

Pinchôt dealt three thin wooden tiles from the pile to everyone at the table. Working in teams, they shouted over each other, trying to agree on how much to bet and whether or not to play or fold. The table talk nearly resulted in a scrum.

The players finally placed bets and each player tossed one wooden chit to the table, face up, along with his wager. The object was to have the highest score without breaking the number on the table; each time a bet was made that number changed by a player adding a new tile to the pot. Players could only play two tiles at the end, and they could drop their third tile face down if they paid a double ante. Point values of the pieces varied and a few of them had negative values. The two-person teams added their scores together and winners split the pot.

Jandul stood by patiently as Krimko watched the game unfold. Pinchôt and his partner lost several hands in a row. The warrior cursed relentlessly and guzzled another drink. More hands passed, but Krimko didn't see Pinchôt win a single one.

Frustrated, Pinchôt jumped to his feet in a flurry of expletives. Pointing an accusatory finger and cussing out his partner, he pocketed his diminished stack of coins and stumbled away hotheadedly. As he staggering drunkenly away, the rest of the players mocked and derided Pinchôt's luckless partner.

Pinchôt meandered past Krimko and Jandul. He muttered something about not being able to find another good partner.

Krimko watched him pass by. Finally, he decided to follow. Jandul stayed back. He was not fond of Krimko and now that he had found some form of entertainment, that being his intentions on Pinchôt, Jandul felt that his babysitting duties had ended.

The diminutive Luciferian professor caught up with the irascible drunkard. Pinchôt still rambled aloud to nobody in particular. He ranted on about his best partner who was now dead.

"Tell me," pestered Krimko, who trailed on Pinchôt's heels, "what do you mean?"

The drunk looked over his shoulder and engaged Krimko in conversation as he wandered. "Th' only good teammate I ever had," he griped, "got kilt by them krist-chins." Pinchôt spat a curse, and then took a deep draught from the flagon in his fist.

"Grirrg was the onliest one I ever worked good with. If'n it weren't for Rashnir and his liddle friends, we could've taken em all on—an we woulda won, too!"

"Tell me what happened at Grinden," said Krimko. "Jandul doesn't talk much and there are few who survived the ordeal. Those who fled won't admit it by talking about it."

"Yeah, fer sure," he said. Pinchôt was so drunk, he would have told a mortal enemy intimate details.

He started with his hatred for the traitor, Rashnir, and briefly described his own rise within the ranks of the Rangers under Jaker's command. With many slurred adjectives, he recounted how King Rutheir appointed him to the Narsh Barbarians and how he and Grirrg, his second in command, worked exceedingly well together in combat situations.

"I hadta drag myself out of that quarry on my own. Ferryman picked me up by the Rashet's landing, charged me extra fer bleedin on his boat." Pinchôt traced his scars with a forefinger. "Mauled by a werewolf. I practically bled to death in tha' pit. I woulda, too, but my hate made me strong nuff to inch my way back ta Grinden."

Pinchôt raised the bottle to his mouth again, drowning the memory of pain. He spat words so spiteful that his voice twisted with malice, "My *hate* made me strong. One day I will kill Rashnir *and* his friends."

Hate was a strong motivator. But whether sober or not, it was hard to discern Pinchôt's true reasons. The once-barbarian swirled his drink and sniffed it. The hate may have been a mask for Pinchôt's disappointment. He had seen King Rutheir's plans: a violent campaign of forcible expansion. The mercenary king planned to take over Zipha under the guise of revenge for years of the abduction and enslavement of his people. Ninda and Gleend could be easily conquered through the same political mouth flapping that currently strangled its people. Screep would fall if they skirted the edge of Briganik without tipping their hand too early—and the Screepans were already accustomed to living under the governance of the ruling castes of anakim. Lol would join his ranks willingly rather than fight. Domn was mostly a wasteland and the few diehard settlements remaining would easily fall. Beej and Mankra were tough, but an extended campaign could prevail—especially with the rest of the countries already under his rule. But they could never take Briganik unless the Order let them.

Absinthium would certainly give it to a strong king with his commitment to institutionalize Luciferianism and enforce its rule upon the land... effectively unifying them all.

Pinchôt spat as he felt the resentment turn his stomach sour. Rutheir's plans were good—and all for naught. He'd lost more than his partner that day, he lost hope.

Krimko stood nearby, taking in Pinchôt's tale. "Hate made me strong," he repeated, tracing a scar with his finger and taking another swig of toxic brew. The warrior lurched and stumbled towards the wall where they had paused. Pinchôt wretched all over it, gagging and spitting vomit against the partition.

"He should have been like a brother to me," Pinchôt declared, his voice full of confused emotion.

Krimko gave him a quizzical look. He had no basis for understanding the drunkard's statements about the traitorous ranger.

"He was my hero," he whispered hoarsely. A tear mingled with the slobber that had soused the side of his face. "Why'd he hafta do that... back when we were rangers..." Pinchôt trailed off. He paused for a second, deep in thought, then fell to his knees and heaved the remaining contents of his guts into the basin holding a potted plant.

When he stood, Krimko asked, "Feeling better, now?"

Pinchôt took another swig off of his bottle. He swished the booze around in his mouth and spat the fluid onto the potted shrubbery washing the taste of bile away. He took one more gulp, this one to settle his stomach, and replied, "Yes. Much."

They wandered deeper into their guest house.

"You know," said Krimko as Pinchôt slumped against the hallway wall, "in the Luciferian Order, we catalog very many mystic devices, enchanted artifacts and such. There is one that I know of, in particular, one that you might be interested in."

The hung-over warrior raised an eyebrow. He wiped the drool from his chin, "I'm listenin. I'm always lookin fer new toys."

"The Khay-hee is no mere toy. It is a priceless device that can give you back your most trusted partner, Grirrg. Would that be valuable to you?"

"Abs-lootley," he slurred. "Whadda I gotta pay for it, or do I hafta devote myself to the Order or sumthin?"

Pinchôt practically nodded off; he would probably pass out soon and the conversation would end. In this stage, as he drifted off amid the spinning, reeling fog in his mind, a sense of bonding connected the two with mutual understanding.

"No cost. I will give it to you. It is mine to do with as I please. I gave it away once, already," Krimko smirked, "But... the owner has outgrown it. He has no real benefit from it any longer."

"Great," Pinchôt smiled wryly in his drunken stupor, prying his eyes open with great effort. He drowsily gave the Luciferian a thumbs-up. His head bobbed, tilted back down, and his chest slumped. Pinchôt was no longer conscious.

***

Absinthium sent the mental query across the aether streams, making psychic contact. He found his mark and forced his words into his target's mind.

A shrieking noise screeched deep within Krimko's brain, filling it utterly. He finally fell to his knees and clutched his skull as the pain in his head intensified; words echoed in the lobe behind his eyeballs. His hands trembled with a migraine and he laid on the ground to keep from blacking out entirely.

"Y-yes, my master," Krimko sub-vocalized, recognizing he'd been summoned by a powerful entity.

"Contact me via your secure qâsam," Absinthium contacted him. "I await your call."

The mage broke the link so that Krimko would be released from the intense pain that accompanied this form of communication. Most untrained monks could not tolerate psychic conversation for long. Too much of that type of exposure could destroy an untrained mind, literally fusing parts of the cerebrum while liquefying others.

Krimko shook off the agony and stumbled to his feet again, feeling as if someone had just struck his head with a log. The blinding light behind his eyes receded. He wiped away the thin stream of blood that leaked from his nostrils and scampered back to his room in order to use his seeing stone.

***

Absinthium commanded his minion through the magic seeing stone. Only minutes had passed before his secure qâsam called to him. His subordinate probably still suffered the minor effects of psychic shock but had managed the call anyway. Krimko continued to impress the arch-mage: he had placed his superior's desires above his own immediate needs.

"Plans are being set in motion, Krimko. You are a critical piece of my plans and I require action now."

"Command me, Highest Arch-Mage." Krimko pressed a finger against his nostril to stop the trickle of blood.

"You must meet with the Nindan Parliament. Do it immediately. I require troops from the Lords. Their response will show their true support of the Luciferian cause."

"Yes, Arch-Mage."

"Send these troops to the Adumarr district. My agent will meet them at the Adumarr Homestead."

"Do you require our presence there as well?" Krimko asked, wondering about his entire company.

"No," Absinthium said. "After this foray, your presence in Ninda will no longer be required. You may return to Jand. I know that Dyule is nervous whenever his favorite bodyguard is absent.

"I will be sending Zilke to you. He should arrive in a few days' time to take over the Church's work in Ninda. The Order's presence in that country has fallen decrepit these last few decades... I can see that now. Just bear in mind that I may call on you again at any moment; I am in constant need of those whom I can count upon."

The mage's image faded from view leaving Krimko alone and holding a darkened, empty jewel.

Krimko placed the gem on a dedicated stand in the corner of his room. He analyzed what he knew of recent events and compared them with the request for military support.

He could only guess that a strike against the krist-chins was about to take place. Reports had said they may have gone into Gleend and the northern Adumarr district was a good launch point for any kind of attack.

The decision to replace him with Zilke made sense from any perspective. Krimko thoughtfully tapped his chin. Zilke was a member of the Devotion discipline; his training would make him a prove the best choice for bolstering the religion. Krimko and Absinthium both belonged to the Scholastic discipline and were generally better administrators and usually more comfortable within the monastery than the community.

In any event, Krimko would be freed up to revitalize Pinchôt's friend before the carcass became overly desiccated. A wicked grin spread across his face. More than the idea of helping a friend, Krimko enjoyed the idea of reclaiming the Khay-hee from its current proprietor.

***

Light pulsed from the crystal. Normally only a dull glow, it shone brightly in the subterranean caverns, illuminating the goblin that it quested for.

grr'Shaalg sat in his stone chair, brooding. He'd begun to feel sour about his dealings with the Luciferians. He knew that it would be a costly alliance, but never would he have risen so quickly to power if it were not for the information that he pilfered from the Order or their assistance in dethroning the under-realm's ruling predecessor. He had plenty of warriors, but he did not want to give up more goblin troops so readily for another creature's ambitions, it went against his selfish and prideful nature.

The qâsam continued to pulsate. Finally, the agitated goblin rose and responded to his communication stone. The arch-mage would not be happy if he delayed answering.

Absinthium's dark eyes seemed to pierce the goblin's mind. "I require troops." He commanded without hesitation, "Send a battalion as far north under Ninda as possible. More forces wait in the Adumarr district. Show me where the nearest access point is to your network; I will be sending you one of my Acolytes."

Placing the crystal on a parchment map of his main underground passageways, he gave the mage the coordinates for the best access point. Goblin tunnels and caverns were often rerouted or collapsed, but many main reinforced thoroughfares existed that could be counted on to be reliable routes.

The mage's image faded and grr'Shaalg's quarters fell black with the sudden lack of light. Absinthium's demands were absolute and the goblin had no choice but to obey them.

Despite his disdain for the situation, grr'Shaalg knew he needed to stay compliant... at least for now. He had brokered this deal with the devious arch-mage from the beginning, and now he was called upon yet again to supply the Order with a resource that he owned: cheap military support.

Soon, very soon, the goblins minions would be limitless, but for the meanwhile, casualties would likely come from his own ranks. grr'Shaalg was ever a realist; he realized that his only value to the Luciferians had been for foot-soldiers and shock troops.

Like a bubbling cauldron of tasty erfwin, the underhanded goblin's plans simmered on the fires of subterfuge. When the moment was right he would spring his plans for ascension. He slouched on his secret throne. One day he would dominate the land and lord over Absinthium... even the demonic Gathering! But, that day was not today, and for now grr'Shaalg acquiesced to the Luciferian mage's demands, drew up the order, and sent it to his military commanders.

CHAPTER FIVE

Zeh-Ahbe' opened the drama with an announcement to the crowd that had gathered around. Entertainment always proved a welcome respite from the toil of local agriculture. The lycan had never been a man of social importance and so there was little chance that he might be recognized by anyone in the crowd, and even then, not likely associated with the supposedly dangerous cult element.

Jibbin leaned up against Rashnir who sat on the edge of the area nearest to the acting troupe. He tried to stay obscure enough that he wouldn't be noticed. Despite his recent female troubles he wanted to stay on hand in case any kind of problem with Luciferians—he might otherwise keep his distance for the sake of the mission. Behind the main body of the crowd, he spotted Ly'Orra slip past like an animal stalking her prey. She gave Rashnir a glaring stare as she meandered out of sight.

Rashnir sighed. She definitely knew his location.

"What you are about to witness," Zeh-Ahbe' said in his best theatrical voice, "is the first half of our story. It is a true account, occurring long ago and in a land far away, even further than the land of Nod."

Zeh-Ahbe' bowed and stepped to the side as two of the players came on stage. Yavim and Yarrow took their places. They two were an actual married couple, and both quite old.

Yavim played the part of Abram/Abraham and Yarrow played Sarai/Sarah. They sat and talked idly about their lives, how they had followed the will of their God in all things. Behind them was an open tent, set up as a prop.

"My dear Sarai, who will inherit all of our possessions when we die? Our God has told me that I will have as many descendants as there are stars in the sky."

"Oh, Abram," she said, "You are ninety years old, and I am far too old to conceive. Perhaps you misheard what God told you."

Haisauce, another actor, spoke from offstage. He bellowed through a large horn to make his booming voice sound even louder. "I am your God and I have not misspoken." His deep, bass voice thundered enough to yank the crowd's attention into focus. "Your name shall now be Sarah, and yours shall be Abraham, which means 'father of many.' Your own wife will bear you an heir and through your line will I create my people. They will be my people and I will be their God. This is my promise to you."

When he was done speaking, Yavim and Yarrow got to their feet and went to the far side of the stage making a break from the previous scene. They spoke once again, mentioning that ten years had passed since their names had been changed. Yarrow went into the tent, out of sight and three men came into the scene.

Shardrim, Wiik, and Finartion were the actors' names. They wandered closer to Abraham hurried to greet them. "Please, do not pass by your servant." He invited them to sit and promised them that he would feed them and make them comfortable.

"Thank you," said Shardrim. "And, where is your wife, Sarah?"

"Sarah? She is in the tent," he replied. Yarrow could be seen leaning out through the tent flaps, clearly eavesdropping.

"You have recognized your Lord," said Finartion. "We bring a message from your God. About one year from now, Sarah will conceive and bear you a child."

Sarah began to laugh, then quickly covered her mouth with her hands and slipped back into hiding.

"Why do you laugh?" Finartion called to her.

"I did not laugh," she denied his claim from inside the tent, slowly peeking out so she was visible to the audience.

"But you did laugh. I know even your thoughts."

"But how should I bear Abraham a son? I am nearly ninety years old; I am much too old."

"Nothing is too difficult for your Lord. You will bear a son for Abraham, my chosen vessel, at the appointed time."

Finartion turned to Abraham and told him, "We must go now. I will not hide my actions from you; you are destined to be a great and mighty nation.

"There is great wickedness in the nearby cities. I must go there and judge them. I will destroy the evil cities; the prayers and pleas of their victims have risen to God above and I must destroy their wickedness."

Yavim and Yarrow went back into the tent as the three men departed. Then, another scene change and Jibbin ran onto the set.

"Father, father," he yelled and ran up to give Abraham a hug.

"Oh, Isaac," he said. "I thank God every day for you since your birth. Now, come, it is time for sleeping."

Once all of the actors were inside the tent, Haisauce spoke again through the horn. "Abraham...Abraham, wake up."

Abraham came out of the tent and called out, "Here I am, Lord."

"Abraham, do you love me?"

"Of course, my God." Yavim did an excellent job, speaking to no one in particular as if he were really conversing with some invisible, supernatural being.

"What would you give me to prove your love... your ultimate love?"

"You know my heart, Lord. I would give you anything. I love you *above all*."

"I want you to give me your son, Isaac, who you waited for and who you love beyond measure."

"Of course, my God. He is yours. I consecrate him for you; he will carry out our covenant... and all of his descendants after him."

"No, Abraham. In the morning, you will take your only son and go to the land of Moriah. You will offer him to me as a burnt sacrifice on a mountain where I direct you."

Silent moments passed. Abraham's jaw agape, his eyes welled up as he looked at the tent beside him and sunk to his knees.

The crowd hushed slightly. They had become familiar with these sorts of dictates and bloody sacrifices under the oppression of the Gathering.

"My Lord?" His voice nearly cracked.

"Only with the ultimate sacrifice can your ultimate love be proven."

Yavim bent over. His face on the ground, he wept for a few moments until Yarrow opened the tent flap and stepped out.

"Have you been out here all night?" she asked.

Rising to his feet, he went over to her. Pulling her close, he hugged her tight.

"What is it, Abraham?"

He whispered into her ear. An extremely pained look of disbelief passed across the actress' face. He continued to whisper in her ear until it turned into a look of resignation.

Letting go, he called out to the boy. "Isaac. Isaac, come out here."

"Here I am," cried Jibbin as he jumped out of the tent.

Rashnir watched him. He proved undaunted by the crowd of people that had seated themselves around the area to watch the production. Rashnir smiled proudly at the little boy's courage.

"Isaac, we must go on a journey."

"Is it far?"

"No, not terribly so. We must go to sacrifice to our God. You remember what I always say about God?"

"Our sacrifices prove our loyalty?"

"Yes, my son. That is it; to obey the eternal laws we must shed blood; that is what has always been required to prove our allegiance to Him."

"Shall I get a lamb, father?"

He hugged the boy. "No, Isaac, God will provide a sacrifice."

Yarrow ran and hugged the boy tightly. As she squeezed him, Yavim picked up a bundle of sticks from beside the tent.

She relinquished Jibbin and disappeared behind the tent. Yavim and Jibbin wandered to the edge of the set. As they did so, the stagehands quickly collapsed the tent and put down two potted, scrubby trees in place of it.

Pointing towards the shrubs, Abraham said, "We will worship God over there."

Rashnir glanced at the crowd. Many of the people followed the tale closely. The language used thus far had been vague enough to include God Yahweh as the deity if not some member of the Gathering's pseudo-pantheon. Many similarities existed between the account of this story and demonic sacrifice traded for blessings. Nindans, especially, understand the tale; many Luciferian priests performed ceremonies to ensure demonic blessing on farmlands, ceremonies that often required the blood of a child. Regardless of familiarity, that did not make such a sacrifice easy.

The two actors approached center stage again, coming back to where they started. Yavim laid the bundle of sticks down on the ground. Drawing his knife, he cut the cord that bound them and then laid them out.

"Isaac, my beloved son, do you love God?"

"With all of my life."

"Isaac, God commanded me to sacrifice *you*."

"Daddy?"

"Son, do you love our God?"

Isaac hugged Abraham. He repeated, "Our sacrifices prove our loyalty."

"My son," he embraced him back, then scooped him into his arms and laid him upon the sticks.

Yavim raised the dagger high above his head. He closed his tearful eyes and tensed to strike. The crowd stiffened.

"Abraham, Abraham! Wait," bellowed Haisauce. "Here I am! Do not sacrifice your son. I have tested you and see that you would not withhold even your only son from me. You have proven your love.

"Because you were willing to bless me with your sacrifice, I will bless you eternally and multiply you. Your seed will possess the gate of our enemies."

A stagehand shooed a lamb through the potted brush.

"See, Abraham, I *have* provided a sacrifice."

Rashnir noticed several moist eyes. He assumed that some of those who seemed most deeply moved by the story may have been folks who underwent the similar, Luciferian rituals, but did not receive as merciful of a benediction from the deity commanding the rite.

***

Kevin wandered back towards his tent where it stood pitched in the market square. He meandered through the rest of his brethren's dwellings. Joy bounced his steps and he hummed a tune as he came back from ministering to the townsfolk. During his presentation of the Gospel message, Havara told his personal faith story; it sparked such an interest that whatever remained of the village pledged to seek this savior for themselves.

It made him smile to know that even those who couldn't come to grips with the concept of conversion had sworn to search out their beliefs. Even the non-proselytes devoted themselves to upholding those who did.

In the back of his mind, Kevin's thoughts turned towards his intense curiosity about the sudden visitor in their midst. The angels had immediately viewed the creature as a threat and carted him off for interrogation.

As his thoughts hovered over the issue, Kevin spotted Kyrius coming to greet him. The angel had his usual smile on his face and Kevin returned one in kind. Kyrius's smile quelled any worries that the preacher might have held about their visitor.

"It has been a success," Kevin informed him of the preaching outreach.

"I know," the angel replied. "I can feel their rejoicing in my spirit."

"Then… you have news of your own?"

"Yes. Jorge and I have interrogated this demon. He has provided us with a detailed history of himself. He is… something of an anomaly."

"How so?"

"Well, ekerithia was once a rather powerful angel, certainly more powerful than me or Jorge, probably even moreso than any of those who rule over the Gathering— at least at the time of the fall. We don't exactly know who is a member of that council at this point, demonic alliances being what they are; according to Dri'bu, there seemed to be a coup forming about the time we entered the kakos.

"Anyhow, before the fall ekerithia was seated above beh'-tsah. Things change, though—and the odd thing is how ekerithia has changed so very little.

"He possesses very few of those traits common to other demons, such as the ugliness that they inherited. He still resembles one of our kind. Even under the holy light of the Logos, one could barely discern the difference. His appearance did not corrupt, except for a vacant look in his eyes and a mark upon his face. He claims to have abstained from all sin and destruction since the fall; he even claims to be remorseful for it."

"Wow. That is odd for a demon."

Kyrius nodded. "I can understand his position, though. Angels are not automatons. Lucifer courted a great many of us during his insurrection. Some were harder to sway than others… some couldn't be moved at all, but I imagine that some of those who gave in to his persuasions immediately wished that they had resisted."

Kevin asked, "As did ekerithia?"

"According to his story, yes. Since then, he has wandered the lands for millennia, alone, resenting that decision each and every day. He foreswore corrupting God's children and so he has waited and watched… looking for an opportunity."

"Waiting for what?"

"For knowledge—either of judgment or to redemption. He is a little obsessed with the subject in fact. He remembers the promise of the Logos: of Christ's redeeming grace. Most demons have forgotten about it or else completely discounted the promises of the Logos. ekerithia has, for thousands of years, clung to a false hope."

"So what are we to do with him?"

"There is a certain nobility left within him. We plan to release him; he promised to keep away from tempting and corrupting men."

Kevin tapped his chin thoughtfully, wondering about the trustworthiness of a fallen angel.

"If he hasn't acquired a taste for it by now," Kyrius offered, "I don't know that he'd suddenly develop it now."

"Would it be possible for me to speak with him, do you think?"

"Yes. In fact, he requested it."

Kevin nodded. He followed Kyrius' leading down the city street to the place where Jorge detained the fallen creature. Kevin shuddered; though the night was still warm, it felt like the temperature dipped slightly as they drew near.

A small campfire lit the place where Jorge guarded ekerithia. Jorge stood and the other sat in a patient, cross-legged position. Kyrius and the preacher moved to the fire and Kevin sat opposite the flames from their guest while Kyrius stood a step behind his friend.

For a few moments, neither said anything but merely studied each other as the fire popped and the flames danced. At last, ekerithia smiled wryly.

"You asked to speak with me." Kevin leaned forward.

He nodded. "I wonder if you might carry a message for me. It would seem appropriate since you are the Lord's appointed messenger for this plane."

"A message?"

"Yes. Just a simple thing, really."

Kevin raised an eyebrow.

"I wish…" he hung his head low as his words trailed off. Long hair obscured his face, but the others could feel his emotions breaking. "Will you tell our Lord that I am truly sorry? I know that it will not matter, but this is my one request. I am sure that it will appear to be the *least selfish act* that I will have committed by the time the end arrives."

"I will," Kevin said. "And what will become of you?"

"Well, I am sure that you can deduce my fate. In the meantime, there is just one thing that I want to experience in the last few years left to me, and I will

settle for whatever false version of it I can accomplish."
The creature stood to his feet.

"What is that?"

"I will obey the long-denied exhortations of my
soul. I will stop resisting that powerful urge I have battled
for so long. The seed that hay-lale' planted within me
before your ancestors were cast from the garden will
finally blossom."

"Seed?"

"The great desire. The driving passion within all
of my kind." His skin seemed to pale further as he made
his proclamation, ekerithia's voice took on a kind of
harmonic taint and his eyes fully clouded with inky black.
I will become a god."

As he uttered those words, a sound like metal
wind chimes tinkled. Feathers fell from under his cloak,
metallic and heavy, yet somehow supernaturally supple.
The shed feathers clinked as they slid down his backside,
detaching slowly from his wings, creating the notes to a
musical lament for the lost one.

ekerithia glanced at his feet where a growing pool
of feathers accumulated around him like autumn leaves.
He looked to Kevin with a glint of terror in his eyes.
Then a hardened resolve took them over.

"It has begun, then." He turned to depart.

"Wait, ekerithia." Kevin stopped him. "Can *you*
do *me* a favor, now? Do you know where the Christian
remnant is?"

"Yes. I know a great deal about them. It was, of
course, a major interest of mine, for many years. But I
always knew that they could not help me."

"Where are they?" Kevin spoke full of excitement
at the prospect.

"I do not think that it is in my best interests to divulge all of my information, so freely. I have my own plans to think about, now. What I will tell you, is that not even I would go where they are, and even the demons of the Gathering must act with caution when walking into that place."

"What? You won't tell me anything else?"

"Only that I shall hold to my earlier promise. I will rise above in this realm, as a god, and yet I will not lead mankind further astray." He turned to Jorge and Kyrius. "Keep him alive, former brothers. He carries an important message for me."

With that, ekerithia turned and walked away into the darkness, withdrawing from the flickering light for good. Feathers trailed behind him as the last vestiges of apparent glory fled.

***

Rashnir froze in his tracks. He'd only led his team of actors half-way into Schworick for their final act when he spotted trouble dead ahead. Three women barred the path to the village. At the forefront of the trio stood Ly'Orra with her weapons drawn; two other women, similarly clad, stood by her side.

Zeh-Ahbe' flashed Rashnir a look of warning. He measuredly nodded his head, acknowledging the danger. He stepped out from the group and bobbed his head towards the village, indicating that they should continue on without him.

The werewolf led his group of comrades towards the village by a different path. Paying them little attention, the warrior women watched them go with relative disinterest. Rashnir waited until they were beyond reach before he stepped towards the women who wanted him dead.

He stood little chance of surviving an attack out in the open without drawing upon the Logos' power. The warrior did not feel that the timing was right for that quite yet... he did not want to jeopardize today's drama and preaching by using such an obvious weapon so soon.

Off to the side of the road sprouted a thick grove of trees that shaded the grounds of an old cemetery. He angled towards it as he walked towards his opponents.

They matched his vector, maintaining eye contact. Rashnir suddenly broke rank and fled for the cover of the grave markers as the women sprinted towards him in order to intercept.

Rashnir leapt headlong over the wrought iron fence which cordoned off the burial grounds. Ducking into a roll, he came up on his feet and slipped behind a large cenotaph just in time to avoid the two arrows. The missiles clattered against the monuments erected in honor the dead and buried elsewhere.

He checked the inscription of the stone he hid behind as he called out. "Three versus one is not very honorable, Ly'Orra." Rashnir glanced around him, all of the tombs and headstones here were cenotaphs: headstones that honored the departed but were not buried here. His focus shifted to the grove: they were all ephay trees.

The warrior dove behind a different marker, but no missiles flew by. His words must have struck her pride. Peeking out, Rashnir spotted the three women approaching slowly and cautiously.

Launching into a run, Rashnir headed for the trees. He might be able to use the ephay defensively... or the carnivorous trees might kill him. His hope was that he could stalemate his opposition and force them to reason with him.

His pursuit followed closely. They stopped at the edge of the shade cast by the trees. Rashnir, raised in the region, was also familiar with the deadly plants. He jumped across the undergrowth and landed only on spots where the light reached.

Ephay trees were typically planted as a form of disposal for communities; sometimes people planted them to eliminate waste and garbage. They were deadly and especially efficient at consuming men and other creatures. It was likely that a plague had ravaged this village several decades ago—perhaps the cemetery was empty because these trees had disposed of the bodies and contained the contagion.

Rashnir hopped deeper into the protective buffer—keeping well within the shafts of light that split the canopy.

Ephay trees were quasi-sentient and shared a kind of a hive mind as the undergrowth below them connected and interwove to form a nervous system. The creep, as it was called, functioned as a kind of that the trees used to sense, or "taste" things and determine if something was edible or not. A kind of lichen that grew around the juglan protected the ephay's fruit and helped spread the creep from fallen seeds as they baited the trees' primary food source.

The fruit had highly addictive, pain-killing and psychotropic properties. Creep grew upon the fruit and could be felt by the tree's sensory organs. Veins intertwined beneath the sod to connect each tree, linking into the hive mind and sending nutrients and support—digested creatures—where it was needed.

Vines of varying sizes hung about the branches. Prehensile and quick, each one brandished a sharp, clasping orifice attached to each end. The trees could strike almost anywhere with their appendages.

Rashnir's foot faltered and a whip-like tendril lashed for the spot on the creep where his foot touched the shade. He yanked his foot back into the light before the tree could snatch him.

The only safety on the creep was in patches of light where the leaves were knit thick enough to fully shade the ground. Bright light temporarily "blinded" those spots on the creep, rendering them insensitive so long as a person didn't stay for too long.

Rashnir stood in a patch of illuminated creep, debating which way to go next. Glancing over his shoulder, he saw one of the female warriors nock another arrow. Ly'Orra pushed the woman's bow down. Apparently, she wanted the honor and glory of this kill.

The ladies followed Rashnir, leaping into the sparse patches of sunlight to pursue their prey. Overhead, the vines hanging from the gnarled wood began to quiver and twitch. Sensing prey around them they trembled in anticipation of a meal. The Ziphan warriors observed the restless liana and noticed a bird flit through the shade and pierce a fruit cluster with its needle-like beak; a vine shot out and engulfed the creature before trailing to the ground.

Ly'Orra glared spitefully at Rashnir as she tried to navigate a safe path towards him. Her quarry jumped to another space keeping a tree trunk between them. Other than her cursing and the grunts and groans of physical exertion, the wooded coppice remained silent as a tomb.

"Stand and fight me, if there is any honor left in you!"

Rashnir turned to size up Ly'Orra. The spaces available dwindled significantly. He feared he might be forced to do exactly as she demanded and fight her. Her accomplices attempted to flank him on both sides. If they got around him, they could close in and trap him.

One of the ladies tried to jump across a large patch of shady creep. She stumbled, barely clearing the darkest part of the creep and landed in a shady zone. A green tendril reached for her ankle. The warrior woman pulled her leg away at the last moment and the vine slapped at the undergrowth in vain.

Rashnir broke a sweat. He would run out of options quickly. No more safe places remained where he could move without leading into an intercept course with one of Ly'Orra's friends. He turned back to find Ly'Orra moving to block his only escape lane. He grimaced and altered course, heading towards a larger illuminated area. He would be forced to fight her.

The women tightened their formation around him, leaving no doubt that the battle would happen. Ly'Orra leapt to the lit zone nearest where Rashnir stood. The illuminated glen created a perfect arena in the center of the small woods.

Rashnir readied himself as the amazon flipped over the patch of sensory undergrowth that separated them. The remaining two women readied their bows to ensure the appropriate outcome. Rashnir backpedaled, trying to persuade the woman one last time.

"Come on, Ly'Orra. Isn't there any alternative?"

She drew another rapier from the sheath strapped to her thigh and advanced on him. She moved lithe, like a cat, and steered him back towards the creep.

"Of course there's an alternative. You could kill me and my friends will sing songs of my glorious, honorable life and untimely demise. But," she sneered, "I hardly think that you will emerge victorious, *not now*."

Rashnir held his hand in a grasping position. The Logos slowly materialized in his ready grip, blazing with its cool azure.

"Ly'Orra," he sighed, "I had truly hoped we could be sensible. Haven't you learned anything since our last encounter?"

"Of course I've learned," she snapped at him while bringing her blades down to bear. They met with a sizzling flash of red heat and an eldritch crackle.

The edges of her blades did not yield to his holy sword. They clashed and locked as the friction between supernatural forces caused the bound weapons to spit sparks and hiss menacingly. She pressed him backward, trying to knock him onto the creep. Rashnir spotted the flask peeking out from her open hip-pouch; the glass had been etched with a Luciferian stamp.

"So you *have* learned something," he quipped.

The 'ãbêdâh greased weapons began to heat up as the cerulean flames licked around them. The weapon protection serum could not stand up to the holy power of the Logos indefinitely. The magic serum had been devised by the dread demon beh'-tsah. His Luciferian worshippers used it, as well as anyone who would pay for the stuff. The weapon worked in the short term. Many of Rashnir's friends had fallen to them in Grinden when the magically imbued blades were first brought to bear.

He scowled at the red sheen upon her weapons. Ultimately, however, the dark power would fail, just like its designer's evil ambitions.

Sensing the give in her weapon, Rashnir tensed under the woman's increasing pressure to debase him, hoping her blades would snap. Just before the weapons' heat became unbearable, Ly'Orra exerted a final thrust and pushed him towards the creep. Rashnir twisted under the expected push and somersaulted sidelong over her thigh, using the flat of his hand to slap the bottom of her purse. Her vial of 'ābêdâh solution sailed through the air just as he rolled to his feet.

Ly'Orra whirled around to see her opponent retrieving the glass container. She roared in frustration, pointing her blade point in his direction.

Rashnir fingered the jar's Luciferian emblem thoughtfully. The reddish serum glinted in the light beams as he uncorked the stuff and swirled the viscous ooze around within; a cloying scent wafted out from the flask.

"Where did you get this," he demanded. "How did you know about it?"

"Word travels fast," she retorted. "Nobody thought the stories were true. You wield a dangerous power, cultist, but I will take you down before you can destroy the realm with the taint of your flames." She lunged and traded blows with Rashnir, parrying and maneuvering him through the lit sections of creep.

Rashnir riposted her blows and sidestepped her advance whenever she overextended herself. He still had no desire to strike a killing blow. Ly'Orra's rage felt more misled than hateful.

She looked up from her exposed flank. Regret traced her face—reproach and anger with herself for allowing her form to break in such a way that her enemy could have killed her. She locked eyes with Rashnir and knew that he could've killed her had he chosen to.

Rather than strike, Rashnir threw the wicked ampoule into a shady section of creep. Vines snapped outward like hungry snakes, the fastest of them engulfed the bottle whole before retracting into the tree limbs.

A stern look set Ly'Orra's face like flint. She charged for Rashnir again. Her thrusts and cuts were calculated and well planned. Rashnir kept up with defensive maneuvers, staying away from the deadly, edged fury.

His ears buzzed with distraction. The corner of his eyes picked up subtle movements rustling in the trees.

With lightning speed, the rustling turned to a full offensive action as mouthed vines struck and entangled one of Ly'Orra's accomplices. The woman howled as the tendrils' ends bit into her flesh.

Ly'Orra dropped her guard and screamed for her friend, "Ri'Aqua!" she screamed her name. The woman had remained in the same spot for too long and her own shadow had finally awoken the creep beneath her feet.

Rashnir's heroic tendencies kicked in and he jumped into action. The fallen ranger delivered a sweeping maneuver to Ly'Orra's feet, knocking her to the ground where she could neither harm him or become ensnared herself—at least not immediately. He snatched Ly'Orra's blades and threw one at the green, tangled knot as it struggled to hoist the amazonian woman off of the verdant floor. The twirling brand severed the carnivorous vines and they recoiled as more lashed out to seize the meal. The second blade cleaved the new vines that just begun to reach for her, buying her a few seconds of reprieve.

Swinging his own sword high above his head, and spinning as he went, Rashnir sprinted across the active creep towards the injured woman. Insatiate vines snapped at him like a scourge, but each was met with the incomparably sharp edge of the Logos as it shredded them like a mill.

Under the umbrella of his graceful cuts, Rashnir shielded Ri'Aqua. With his free hand, he scooped her up and held her fast to his side before continuing to move to another sun-laden section of undergrowth.

Depositing her there in momentary safety, the warrior leaped to another safe zone, and then quickly ran away. Without enemies blocking his path, he found an easy exit route through the deadly copse of ravenous timber.

Not allowing the Amazonians a chance to regroup and try again, he withdrew as fast as he could and slipped back into the village, leaving his pursuers far behind.

***

Werthen looked back. Behind him rumbled a small cart laden with children. They laughed as it bumped and jostled along. The donkey-drawn wagon shook as it crossed the harsh and rocky terrain. The fiercest swings made the children laugh and smile as if it were a game; the ferreter worried, though. They were far from anywhere to find replacement parts if a carriage broke.

He thanked God for the animals that his missionary team rode upon—they'd come by them quite miraculously, in fact. As they traveled west across the harsh lands of Lol, their feet had become sore and their backs weary. As they pressed on, they spotted the first mining village in their path. Oddly, however, the entire village proved deserted.

Werthen sent his friend and bodyguard, Vil-yay, to scout the town for danger before moving in. Vil-yay had been appointed to Werthen by his leader Zeh-Ahbe', the leader of Vil-yay's lycan tribe. The werewolf proved quite adept and Werthen knew Vil-yay's loyalty was unquestionable.

Upon returning from his survey, Vil-yay reported that the place was eerily deserted. The food and stock of the place hadn't even expired. The entire place felt off... as if all the residents of the village had suddenly vanished. Mines and shops had been left neat and tidy, as though the owners might return to use them at any moment. Fortunately for Werthen and his group, they'd noticed the large ranch at one edge of the abandoned community. Perhaps the livestock had been the luckiest. All fences and animals still remained, although the animals were in desperate need of tending.

Feeling safe enough, the Christians took over the community for a few days, enjoying the slight sense of normalcy that came with operating a non-hostile settlement. With no clues as to the previous residents' whereabouts, they finally took the animals, resupplied themselves, and continued their journey.

Still, the cause for the vacant village remained a mystery. It niggled at the back of Werthen's mind as they crossed the plains of Lol, even if the collective beasts of burden eased their struggles and generally improved morale.

With the traveling made easier, they traversed the parched turf and rock-strewn soil with much better speed.

According to a hand-sketched map supplied by Dri'Bu, they would draw near another mining community shortly.

A few hours passed and the deep grooves of the rutted earth leveled significantly; the carts no longer threw the children like ragdolls. Without the complaining of the stressed wagon tack, the arid landscape took on a peaceable quiet.

Werthen noticed that the roads widen; the ground felt harder, better packed and well used. A solid dust-cake had formed. It sloughed most of the gravel off to the side making a more comfortable trail for the feet unshoed creatures.

Consulting his map again, Werthen located the town of Granik. He flipped the reverse side and read the elf's brief notes about it. The walled town boasted two primary industries: mining and metalwork. Granik's metal bricks were often sold to tradesmen across the region and ingots bearing their stamp often passed through Grinden.

Long ago, the lure of easy riches drew many people to Granik when someone discovered precious jewels in the mines below the rocky, hillside city. As always, the riches petered out. Many of those folk, once made wealthy from initial discoveries, eventually found themselves poor and digging ore in the company mines for menial wages or smelting metals in the allied smithies.

In the distance, dark fumes belched from the hillside. Werthen and his companions assumed the foundries were in full production. They hoped to arrive within a soon, given their current pace.

On the approach, the travelers passed several run-down offshoots of the town—outlier communities made up of run down shanties and dilapidated outbuildings. Burned out granaries populated the landscape. Vil-yay sniffed the air, catching familiar human scents. They looked abandoned, but some kind of premonition hung onto the lycan's senses. Something didn't seem right.

Werthen slowed the company to a halt so he could examine a snarled dome of metal jutting up from the wreckage near the side of the road. It wasn't the twisted network of metal that caught his eye but the human hand that protruded from the structure. A palm lay upward in defeat.

He dismounted and approached the tangle of fused steel. Vil-yay joined Werthen as he approached the crude containment cell.

"What do you think," the lycan asked, "maybe criminals?"

"It's impossible to tell," Werthen replied. "Cultures vary so much, even across such short distances. Whatever their story, someone put this prisoner in there intentionally and doesn't want them ever released."

Werthen's mind turned briefly to Rashnir as he looked at the prisoner's limp hand. The famous ranger's fate had been similar, though without bars, and his redemption proved a rallying point for those drawn out of Grinden.

Through the odd shaped openings of the heavy metal cage, they noticed there were two men within. Nearly incapacitated, both appeared battered and bruised, staring at their visitors with sunken, fatigued eyes. One looked old with willowy hair and skinny limbs, the other man seemed younger and stronger—even through the emptiness in his eyes the spark of an internal fire glinted from the dark. A pile of gear, apparently belonging to these prisoners, lay stacked just beyond their reach on the far side of the enclosure.

The old man, his wrist hanging out of the enclosure, twitched and groaned as the Christians' shadows fell across him. The afternoon heat felt almost unbearable as it made the air shimmer. It distorted the appearance of the city on the horizon as it reflected off the white tinted gravel scattered across the landscape.

Meeting Werthen's gaze the younger man spoke. "Welcome to Low-Town. I hope, for your sake, that you don't intend to stay."

CHAPTER SIX

Jibbin scanned the audience. The child stood on his tiptoes, searching for his friend and guardian, Rashnir. The drama was about to continue, culminating in the revelation that the story was true and that all of human history in hay-lale's lands had been based on lies.

Zeh-Ahbe' affectionately messed the boy's hair up. "He'll be ok. I'm sure of it."

"I know. He will be ok." Jibbin convinced himself as he sank back the flats of his feet, but his eyes continued hunting for Rashnir.

An audience had arrived and the stage was assembled. Zeh-Ahbe' went to the middle of the stage, like a ringmaster, and announced his players. At the furthest reaches of the modest crowd, Rashnir popped in to view and Zeh-Ahbe' waved to Jibbin.

The little boy hopped up and down so he could see over the crowd. He waved to Rashnir who flashed a smile in return before slipping out of sight again. Jibbin settled down, his mind finally set at ease. It would have been hard for him to perform with any uncertainty for his friend's fate. Jibbin had already lost his entire family, murdered before his very eyes; Rashnir had been the one who saved him from the same fate and the boy might not prove capable of another loss.

Using his best theatrical voice, the sometimes werewolf addressed the crowd. "When last we performed, you saw the first installment of our drama: the nearly tragic story of Isaac and his parents Abraham and Sarah. That is only the beginning of the saga, and much takes place between our story today and yesterday's tale.

"In those years in between, we find that God did indeed keep his promise to his faithful servant Abraham. Abraham's children multiplied and became a nation in their own right. Some of them were loyal and followed the God of their ancestors; others spurned him and were left to their devices and paths which led to their enslavement and destruction."

Zeh-Ahbe's gaze swept over the audience. They had quieted so all could hear. Many of them looked familiar from the previous performance. Zeh-Ahbe' thought the men and women in the audience had a kind of yearning hollowness fixed deep in their eyes as they looked at him—something he felt achingly familiar with. He could sense their souls crying out for hope, but there was only blackness as they tried to reconcile their Luciferian beliefs with their past experiences and faulty theology.

"If I had weeks to stand before you," Zeh-Ahbe' said, "I would tell you about the things God did to display his love to… the people he made a covenant with." He had wanted to say "his creation," but that would have been too clear of a signal to his audience. As it was used commonly, *God* could have meant any sort of supernatural deity or creature of great power; it might have been merely a figurative device or could have indicated an unknown a demonic power.

There were many stories involving alternate deities commonly told as entertainment or even accounts told as a matter of the historical record whereby the god in question was a demon; supernatural creatures had been known to make pacts with men and their offspring and use their powers to condemn or bless. All of mankind, though, knew that Yahweh was the Creator and that Lucifer was the crafter of ekthro.

Zeh-Ahbe' made sure to choose his words carefully. He didn't want to alienate the audience before he'd given a chance for revelation. The God he referenced would be made clear in the course of the presentation.

With a smile, Zeh-Ahbe' continued. He gave more background information as the actors assumed their places behind him and prepared for the story to truly begin.

***

Rashnir stood before the arched door of the lavish, little building. Immaculately furnished, even the door seemed to radiate an opulent glow giving it an aura of wealth and success. Someone had propped open the ebony stained hardwood door to allow the gentle breeze to circulate. The Luciferian building was tiny compared to the temples in larger communities but was one of the larger buildings in the farming community. Still, its appointments made it impressive. Rashnir stepped through the door and into the foyer.

Two hallways branched away from the entry, one led to the offices of the Luciferian appointee who oversaw the diminutive temple. The other was stocked with the moneyboxes and idol booths for Luciferian worship and supplication. The smell of incense and unwashed bodies wafted from that section, but that was not where his interest laid; he went the other direction.

Moving silently, he passed the head office. Briefly peering inside, Rashnir spotted a wicker basket filled with fruit. It had been placed in a shaft of light.

It doesn't surprise me, he thought. *The leader here must be like every other Luciferian priest I've met.* He shook his head at the sight: a basket of ephay fruit. The crooked clergymen who operated here were probably selling the addictive fruit to the local addicts on the side.

Rashnir found a place to hide next to a support pillar and slinked into the shadows. He felt certain of two things: that he could find answers how Ly'Orra had procured the vial of 'ãbêdâh, and that she wouldn't be looking for him in the Luciferian cathedral.

He waited in obscurity, praying that the ranking cleric would return to his office soon. The sound of footsteps and private chatter echoed in the hallway. It increased in volume and tone as a pair of speakers drew nearer.

Seconds later Rashnir could understand what they were saying. It was small talk, mostly, something about the local crop production. The footsteps stopped and one voice, the temple master most likely, told the other person, probably a parishioner, that his office was a mess and he would need a private moment to tidy up. Rashnir heard the unmistakable sounds of wicker being drug across stone tile, and then the rector invited the voice in to chat with his ephay fruit hidden.

Rashnir waited patiently for the parishioner to depart. He wanted to question the temple master. It would be important for him to gauge their watchfulness in case they'd prepared an attack on a Christian group. The warrior wouldn't have thought it likely before, but the presence of 'ãbêdâh meant he shouldn't discount the possibility.

His mind began to wander away from its primary focus. It snapped to attention as crisp and purposeful steps clapped against the tiled floor. There were several boots, and their steps sounded urgent in their pace.

They grew almost loud as they approached and the priest's conversation ceased. He, too, had likely heard the arrival.

The footsteps stopped outside his door and Rashnir heard her speak. "Pheema," Ly'Orra demanded. "I need to speak with you, immediately."

Rashnir's heart jumped at her voice. She could conceivably initiate the massacre of his people if they had the alchemical means to rise up against them and catch them unprepared.

Pheema, the priest, excused his friend so that they could have a private conversation. His nondescript footsteps drifted away as they carried the parishioner beyond the main hallway.

"Yes, my dear," Pheema inquired. "How can I serve you?"

"I require more of the potion that you carry," she demanded.

"What? Why? Are there krist-chins here?"

The priest had sounded worried—fearful even. He had no idea that the group was nearby and that meant that they were safe, for the moment. Rashnir breathed a sigh of relief from behind the structural support where he rested and prayed that his enemy wouldn't feel compelled to hurt his friends in order to get to him.

Ly'Orra paused. "No," she lied. "But I require more of the serum, immediately. There is a foreign krist-chin that I must kill. I will hunt him to the ends of the earth for slighting my honor."

Rashnir smiled, comfortable with that sentence. It was only him that she sought, and only to preserve her odd sense of honor; she did not hate all krist-chins, just him.

Pheema pried, "Where is the bottle I just sold to you?"

"I lost it in the ephay grove and the creep swallowed it."

"Well," he smacked his lips and gave her an implicative laugh. "Had I known you were prone to dabbling with such pleasures I would have made you a good deal on a sack of ephay fruit." His tone dripped with innuendo, "Then you wouldn't have had to risk your pretty little self in the deadly woods."

Rashnir could hear him drag the basket of ephay fruit out of hiding.

"Enough, you slimy little man. I don't need your rotten fruit. Where can I find the ʻābêdâh?"

Pheema sighed. "A runner from the monastery near Grinden is dropping off cases of at all the temples within his reach. I have some left, but it will cost you, of course. It will cost you double since you need it so badly. After all, I do have limited supply. Of course," his voice took on a lascivious tone again, "I'm always willing to negotiate a deal—maybe you'd want to trade for the pleasure of your company?"

Voices stopped and Rashnir only heard sounds of a man choking. Rashnir grinned, assumed that Ly'Orra was strangling the suggestive priest. *Too bad she's trying to kill me—I kind of like this woman*, he thought.

"I will pay your double fee," she spat, "and you will give me a *double dose*."

A gagging noise: it sounded like an affirmative.

The man cursed and gasped for breath. "Why do you want to kill him so badly?"

"You understand nothing about honor. You prey on the weak."

"Hey! Everyone's got to make a living," Pheema wheezed.

"Not everyone gets to live," retorted an unfamiliar voice, under her breath.

"It is not your place to speak, Shi'Nala." Ly'Orra's voice carried a venomous taint.

"Oh, please," she said in a catty voice. "Your role is to burn out in a blaze of glory so your sister can rise from your ashes and retain the throne. I hardly think it fair to *her* if you kill this man. He would be far better suited as kingly breeding stock judging by his prowess and actions."

"Your opinion has been previously noted," Ly'Orra growled. "But it is *my own* Pawar—and only I will endure it. You can tell my sister I died in the flames of glory: *that is your place*. You will be a servant forever. My place is to transcend," she snapped.

Silence reigned for a moment. The doomed warrior princess' point had obviously been taken.

The clinking of glass against glass tinkled in the room. "Your 'âbêdâh," said Pheema with a raspy voice. The thunking sound of a coin purse dropping on the desk signaled the departure of Ly'Orra, Shi'Nala, and Ri'Aqua. They left in the same manner as they had come.

***

"Father," said Jibbin who remained in character, "why must we sacrifice this lamb?"

The little boy held a lead rope tied around a small sheep. He addressed Yavim who played the part of his father in the second act. They were already into the drama and the audience had seen the story of a father and son that traveled to the city of Jerusalem so that they could give a sacrifice to the God of their forefathers, the God of Abraham.

Jibbin hugged the lamb. "But I love him. I don't want to kill him."

"I know, child, but sacrifice is never easy. Our sacrifices, though, prove our love and loyalty to our God, and He will watch over us and take care of us—even in sorrow. The traditional sacrifice of the lamb only foreshadows what will one day take place for all people, a final sacrifice made for everyone. It will be so powerful that we will never need to shed more blood to appease God."

A few men in the audience stroked their chins thoughtfully at the premise.

"Now, keep a hold of that animal. We are coming into town and we don't want to lose him before we make it to the altar."

"Yes, father."

They walked to the other side of the stage where the other actors clustered together to make a crowd that argued with itself. Yavim pulled one of them aside.

"What is happening here?," he inquired.

"The temple leaders have captured him."

Yavim stood on his tiptoes to peer over the crowd. "*Him*? But he's a prophet and a teacher. He has only helped others and never profited by it."

"Exactly. He makes the temple rulers look bad in comparison."

"So they would just kill him outright?"

"I guess so," the actor replied, and then he turned back to the clamor of the crowd.

An armored man pushed a half-stripped actor across the stage. The man stumbled and fell to the soil. Dramatically, the warrior took a prop whip and began to hit the man; the fake whip, made of cloth and soaked with watered-down animal blood, streaked the actor's skin with bloody residue. Finartion, the actor playing the part of Jesus, screamed as each stroke lashed him.

The group of actors followed the warrior with who flogged the prophet and surrounded him. Only one woman hung back. She fell to her knees in tears, reaching out to Finartion, as if longing for him.

Above the heads of the rancorous crowd, the whip rose and fell. Yavim grabbed Jibbin and turned his head away. The woman, played by Yarrow, wailed and cried out, "My son! My, son..."

Overseeing the drama from the edge of the stage, Zeh-Ahbe' noticed a spindly looking man at the back of the crowd. Something seemed distinctly wrong with him and warning stirred in Zeh-Ahbe's spirit. He quietly slipped away to investigate.

Yavim hugged Jibbin. "Quickly, go over there," he pointed stage left. "I will find you shortly." The little boy obeyed, lamb in tow.

A black-cloaked actor snuck onto the stage. He wore a fair porcelain mask under his hood. The figure joined in the mocking and incited any of the relatively quiet ones to yell louder. As he compelled them they barked suggestions like, "Hit him again!" and "Nail him to a tree!"

At that last shout, the crowd dispersed enough for Finartion to be visible. The warrior shoved him the ground and onto a beam that had been laid there earlier by stagehands. Finartion's hands were tied to the beam and spikes hammered into the wood with the illusion of being nailed through his hands and feet.

They dropped the base of the vertical beam into a post-hole they'd dug earlier. When they raised the wood so that it seated in the hole and stood erect the cross was clearly visible, and with Finartion hanging upon it. Yarrow cried, now prostrate.

With the cross made clearly visible, the man whom Zeh-Ahbe' shuddered and twitched violently. He fell to the ground and screamed obscenities, tearing his clothes as he shrieked.

Zeh-Ahbe' grabbed the man and shook him. A hollow ached stewed at the pit of his gut and his spirit knew what was wrong with the man. "Come out of him, demon."

"Not the rood!" The man shrieked, "The power of the High One is here…"

"I belong to a power greater than yours. Leave this man alone!"

Only visible to Zeh-Ahbe', the under-demon leapt out of the man like a shadow separating from its owner. It snatched Zeh-Ahbe' by the throat, trying to strangle him—only corporeal enough to harm its enemies.

Giving a wide enough berth, the crowd watched with raised eyebrows as he wrestled with the spirit being. They could not see the invisible monster, their eyes were not opened to that realm and the demon refused to reveal himself. Only the Christians and the demon's victim could see the emaciated, sore-covered figure that fought with Zeh-Ahbe'.

"In the name of Jesus," he yelled as he kicked the demon out of its grasp. It fell to the dirt and scampered away like a wounded animal, screeching.

The monster's piercing wail echoed through the streets. Its piercing, vile voice reached the audience's ears with painful intensity.

Zeh-Ahbe's voice rose above the shrill sound, "By the power of the Son of the Living God I bind you to silence!" The noise immediately ceased and an uncanny stillness fell over the crowd.

The once-possessed man looked up at Zeh-Ahbe' who extended a hand. He took it and the Christian pulled the spindly man to his feet.

"You are free from its control, now. Watch, and rest," he pointed to the stage area. The actors had not lost their places. "This play shows the source of a power that lets humans resist and usurp even the demons." The audience turned as one with rapt interest.

Onstage, Jesus hung on the cross. The crowd gave him distance; the warrior guarded him against interference, warning others to stay back until the messiah had suffered and died. Seemingly invisible, the black-clad figure passed by the guard and personally taunted the Christ.

"If you are the Messiah, the Son of the one true God, then use your power to come down from there. Save yourself," he taunted.

"I will not. The love I have for my people holds me here."

"Prove your power. Rescue yourself and rule over this world with your power, if you truly can. Release yourself from your pain and bonds and I will give it *all* to you."

Christ looked down at him. "You fool, demon."

The black-clad figure hissed. He ripped away his fair mask and pulled back his hood. Underneath the facade was another mask, a hideous and twisted visage.

"I and my Father, Yahweh, are one. I choose to make this sacrifice for my beloved children. I understand the true power of sacrifice and my blood will eternally redeem and empower my followers.

"Depart from me, foul hay-lale', wicked Lucifer. You will only deceive my children for a while longer. Your days are numbered."

"*Yours* are numbered, Holy God." The demon exited the scene.

Jesus looked skyward. "It is finished," he proclaimed. Then, he hung his head in death for a few moments.

The actors solemnly came and lowered the cross, unbinding Finartion and draping a cloth over him. They carried him off-stage.

Jibbin came running back on stage holding only a simple length of rope. "Father! Father! I am so sorry. I lost the lamb."

"Don't worry, my son. Another sacrifice has been provided for us. And look, there is the lamb now." Yavim pointed as Finartion walked back on stage, wearing a royal robe.

The actors who had previously beaten him approached and bowed down at his feet. "Death cannot hold me. My power is even greater than the grave."

Zeh-Ahbe' stood in front of the crowd. He'd never given such a petition to friends or strangers. He submitted to his fear only enough that he closed his eyes as he spoke, explaining the important message behind the drama they had just witnessed. "This is the truth," he said. "You have witnessed the story of Christ and also seen an unplanned display of his power.

"We are Christians, the enemies of the demons and the Luciferian Order, hated because who choose to return the love that God has shown us. If we are unwelcome here, we will move on and not bring His message of hope to your village. But, if you *desire to hear* how *you too* can become one of us, then we will gladly share His holy Word of redemption with you."

Zeh-Ahbe' finished his appeal and opened his eyes. A crowd of about one hundred people had pressed in around him and the stage crew.

***

Rondhale, the blacksmith, walked east. His brethren surrounded him as he followed an intricately sketched map provided by Dri'Bu. Raz-aphf, one of the Say-awr', accompanied him, keeping in close proximity at all times. The converted werewolves each took their roles as protectors very seriously.

Several of Zeh-Ahbe's tribemates were sent along with the one-time metal worker for protection; Kevin had his angelic escorts to watch over the other nearby group. Gleend had suddenly become a dangerous place that seemed to teeter on the brink of civil war with racial tensions stretched to breaking. Only a few of the Say-awr' remained with Kevin because of that brewing disquiet.

The Christians had left Kevin and the rest of their friends after helping them set up an encampment in Sprazik. Rondhale followed Havara's advice and stayed well below the capital city; Xorst had fallen into complete disarray and there would be little that the Christians could do there until Havara had reclaimed political power on behalf of his family. Staying south of the city, they traveled east towards Vigna, after that they intended to go further towards the town of Dant. Kevin and Havara planned to tackle Xorst after they finished their work in Sprazik. The long-term safety of Rondhale's team relied on Kevin and Havara's success in Xorst.

"In the clan, everyone is a brother or sister," Raz-aphf said as they rode. The lanyard around his neck swayed with the movement of his mount. A tooled piece of obsidian hung from the straps.

Rondhale grinned. "That must be nice—to have so many siblings."

They rode in silence for a few moments longer. "One of my brothers carved this for me," Raz-aphf said, taking the totem from around his neck. "He was one of those we lost at the Grinden quarry."

The blacksmith nodded his head solemnly as his friend's horse moved closer. Raz-aphf held out his hand and thrust the necklace upon Rondhale.

"Now *we* are brothers," Raz-aphf said with a half-grin.

Rondhale returned the half-smile and nodded his appreciation. He knew better than to refuse such a gift.

Raz-aphf and Rondhale spoke about many things on the road and Rondhale's respect for the werewolf only grew. He and his kin had already shown insurmountable loyalty to whatever cause their people committed themselves to. Raz-aphf had clearly committed to his new friend's well-being. Rondhale appreciated that; life had seemingly grown very dark in the days since his twin brother's death. He glanced at his companion and touched the item hanging around his neck. Raz-aphf was family.

The trail meandered southward as the craggy Drindak canyons split the horizon and the two shared stories from their previous life before Kevin had convinced them of Truth. Light-hearted, humorous stories helped pass the time along the roads. Not much traffic crossed the caravan's path and any that did made sure to keep heads down and avoid direct eye contact. With racial tensions brewing country-wide, travelers minded their own business.

Rondhale watched a group of dwarves pass and then cracked and massaged his knuckles. He reminisced and finished his story, "my brother was so angry with me that he chased me into the barn. I don't even remember why he was mad, but I ran as fast as I could. I got into the haymow where we kept the feed and bales for my father's cattle. Jhonnic was so upset that he threw a pitchfork at me and speared me straight through."

Both Rondhale and Raz-aphf laughed hard. Rondhale pulled up his tunic to show off the faint scars that still marred his abdomen. Rondhale chuckled and wiped away the moisture at the corner of his eye. "Brotherly love," he chuckled.

"The tines missed anything that might be vital and didn't chip any bones. They just pinned me to the bundles of hay I was standing against.

"My brother just stopped, dead in his tracks, staring at me in disbelief. Of course, neither of us could believe what he had just done. He froze and I thought I was gonna die. I tell ya, he said to stay put, and that he was going to get our mother, but when he ran off, I thought he went to hide for fear of what she would do to him." Rondhale laughed again, telling stories brought release and relieved his troubled emotions.

"And my mother, when they finally got back, you should have seen her tear into Jhonnic," he smiled. Family had obviously been important to him. "She didn't even pay attention to me...there I am, run through and bleeding, and my mother is beating my brother with a switch." He laughed until he sighed; a glisten came to his eyes. "Anyway... good memories."

Raz-aphf smiled too. It was not so much the story that he found amusing, but the way his friend told it that made the whole incident funny. "I truly wish I had been able to meet your brother sooner. I had only spoken with him in passing while we were all at Grinden."

"Yes. I wish that too. He would have liked you."

The werewolf started to speak but then held up his hands for silence. Raz-aphf sniffed at the air.

"What is it?"

"Smoke," he replied soberly. Raz-aphf quickened his pace and pulled ahead of the rest of their company to scout ahead. Rondhale halted the caravan of their people and then caught up, matching him stride for stride until they came to the top of a gentle rise. A grassy expanse spread out before them.

Below the crest of the ridge where they stood lay the village of Vigna. Its buildings and structures blazed angrily, belching black smoke skyward. Its citizens fled like ants in the distance, running from some unknown threat. Many of them headed directly towards the Christians' position upon the road beyond the hillocks.

It took only moments for the situation to become clear—why the citizens fled rather than quelled the fires. The fleeing refugees were pursued, chased by forces that began emerging from the burning city, readily giving pursuit even as they set the rest of the town ablaze.

"It's like Sprazik all over again," whispered Rondhale.

Raz-aphf nodded his assent.

Rondhale and Raz-aphf whirled their horses around and rushed back towards their caravan while shouting orders. The Christians, already witness to one recent massacre, quickly pushed together any carts, wagons, or bulky gear that they had brought to form a barrier on the apex of the slope. There was no way that they could all find enough protection behind the makeshift blockade, let alone offer sufficient aid to those who fled.

Rondhale grabbed a young man he knew he could trust. "Robear, do as I ask you, and quickly. Take half of our people and stand below us—be visible. Form a line about twenty meters from our barricade, here." He pointed.

"But what about…"

Rondhale cut him off. "There is no time to discuss it. Just trust me, and pray that those below make it to you in time. As the villagers start to get close, protect them. Send some of our own with them to continue their retreat and leave some to defend the stragglers. Remember, we don't need any heroes! This is a tactical retreat."

"Yes, sir," Robear said, and then ran to make sure his men were informed and prepared.

Moments later, Rondhale and Robear each had the large group of Christians briefed and ready: one group on the east and one on the west. As the harried villagers approached, the Christians beckoned them onward and hurried them into their fold for protection.

A hail of arrows, fired by elven pursuit, crippled many of the humans. The casualties were easily overrun by the swiftly moving ekthro. The oppressors showed no mercy, savagely murdering any they caught up to. Dwarven arsonists finally finished igniting the remnants of Vigna, mounted their pony drawn wagons and barreled away from the burning town. They shouted battle cries, not wanting to be left out of the hunt.

The fastest of the fleeing humans came to the top of the hill and collapsed in relief, thinking that a contingent of human soldiers had been sent to protect them. There wasn't time to break the news to them. Another wave of men and women followed close behind them; the ekthroic butchers came in fast.

Shouting and beckoning, the Christians urged the people to hurry faster but did not break their line for the sake of their defensive formation. The Christians from Robear's wall of men broke into clusters and retreated with the passing Vignans, running alongside to protect the weary and weak.

The pursuing ekthro watched the fleeing group disappear over the ridge of the rising slope, unable to see Robear and the defenders escorting the refugees into their protection. Bloodthirsty elves hollered and hastened their pace to close the gap, not wanting to let any get away. If they scattered over the ridge they would be harder to round up. No matter how much glee the ekthro took in the slayings, this was a massacre and not sport.

Jostling, pony-drawn carts caught up and nearly passed its elven counterparts who charged on foot. The groups unified and caught sight of their quarry. They split to either side of the wagon walls that were stacked with supplies and rushed around the short, makeshift wall enveloping it.

The combined forces of wicked ekthro bore down on the line. Raz-aphf, and his eleven Say-awr' pack-mates who had accompanied Rondhale, tensed for the right moment. They lay prone behind the makeshift barricade, lying in wait.

Robear's defenders dispersed and scattered as the dwarven war-carts drew ahead of the elven runners. The fleet-footed warriors guarded the backs of the Vignans and took a wider route that looped back towards the barricade, drawing out and splitting up the quickest of the aggressors. They diverted the dwarves' attention while splitting the raiders into smaller parties and buying the Vignans a little more time.

Frothing with exertion, the ponies that pulled the carts glistened with sweat and threw flecks of spittle as they galloped madly with their stout, frenzied drivers in tow. Battle-lust had taken over the bearded soldiers; their beady eyes and murderously blithe faces twisted into awkward impressions of the human blueprint that they hounded with such fervor.

Dwarven assailants picked their marks and targeted the bands of humans that they deemed the slowest or weakest. Doughty warriors tensed in anticipation of their next kills as they rode in the beds of the battle-ready rickshaws with readied weapons. Most carried axes and others brandished a shortened variety of halberd. Many had already been splattered with blood and effluence from prey harvested down the slope.

The ponies' nearly trampled their targets but the Christian protectors turned just in time to face the dangers that fell upon them. Azure flames flashed and shining, double-edged swords materialized the instant before the ekthro entered the fray. The flashes of holy light panicked the sweaty ponies and they reared up, jarring the dwarven fighters and skidding the battle-carts into wild fishtails.

Dwarves tumbled from the wagons, heads knocked into complete disarray. Many drivers flew from their seats and well over their chargers. The battle-ready ekthro in their attack positions fell stunned to the ground, unprepared for such a reversal of events.

As the individual Christians and Vignans saw what happened, they altered course and attacked the battle-wagons, striking with whatever weapons they carried and could find. Carriages tipped over, becoming traps as the defenders flanked the dwarves from all sides, lunging at the disoriented attackers and cutting loose the yoked beasts.

Wild ponies ran in every direction, cutting off the elves who skidded to a halt in the rear-guard as their over-zealous compatriots were plunged into chaos. Some elves held back and sheathed their blades. The others continued the mad charge forward as their ranged fighters planted their feet and readied their bows.

They could make strategic shots and pick off much of their prey from a safe distance. A ranged threat should have given the dwarves a chance to regroup and assert their melee superiority over such wearied humans.

As the elven archers reached for their quivers, their pointed ears twitched with the sounds of shrill howling. They turned just in time to spot the hulking werewolves of tribe Say-awr' sneaking past a flaming, dwarven cart with uncanny speed and falling upon them.

With the raw strength and ferocity of their lupine forms, Raz-aphf and his clansmen ripped through the flank of the ekthroic forces, gutting them completely. Any of the marauders who had earlier intended to burn Vigna off of the map shrieked with terror as they recognized their doom. Even the quickest elven sprinter couldn't outrun the lycan warriors.

Brilliant flaming arcs of blue separated dwarven joint from limb and the hulking white behemoths of muscle and fang easily disposed of the elven contingent. None of the ekthro could escape from the Christians and none of them had anticipated such powerful weapons that so easily broke their own.

Despite the fatigue, Vignans mopped up the stragglers and the Christians tended to the wounded.

Raz-aphf joined Rondhale at the crest of the ridge as the former blacksmith looked out over the scene. The village was in flames and the grassy hillside painted with splotches of crimson. Below them, just beyond the reach of any attack, stood the elven commander of the destroyed ekthroic contingent.

The elf and the Christian leader locked eyes. She stood there, also surveying the scene and making her own deductions. With reigns in hand, she mounted her horse and galloped away into the distance.

***

Bwar sat in the circle of firelight. His shadow stretched and danced, playing with the deeper darkness and flickering against the shadows at the light's edge. He felt comfortable enough deep underground but the current state of political affairs had him on edge, more so than the chittering noises coming from the semi-larval skolaxis around his position.

The goblin to which he had pledged his allegiance, grr'Shaalg the shadow king, sat nearby. From what he had learned of him, the goblin's brother was tyr-aPt, one of the ten ruling kings of the deep race.

Their meeting had just wrapped up. Bwar was flustered over the failure to assassinate his victims. Discord brewed in Gleend, just as engineered, but all did not go precisely as planned. Without removing the human element the Dwarves could never gain the authority that they truly wanted.

"The royal line was supposed to be destroyed," the dwarf lamented.

"I fail to see how that is my fault, or my problem," grr'Shaalg stated flatly.

"But it was you who said that we must keep the peace with the elves."

"I said nothing of the sort. I said that you must cooperate with them to destroy the humans. Evict mankind not just from Gleend, but from all of known reality. Once they are all dead, by all means, kill the elves. I don't care."

"The dwarves could have done it better. You should have left surface dwellers out of it; you could have just lent me some of *your* troops as support. There was no need to get Elo'misce involved, too."

"You say that, but your results have proven otherwise. Your ruffians failed to assassinate the king's brother. Since that time, Elo'misce has proved very eager to extinguish the light of humanity. Had you succeeded in your task, you would have had the perfect political opportunity to elevate *yourself* to the throne, with *any* amount of diligence and political maneuvering. This is your fault and yours alone.

"As for my lending military support, that will come in the future. My forces under Gleend are currently on a large-scale assignment. You will become aware of their movements very soon.

"Be aware, Bwar, that there are many other players in this grand game. Far more than just us. Some of them will be just as eager to destroy *you* as you are *them*."

The dwarf spat a curse, "Elo'misce."

"If you become less than *completely* useful to me, I will send you to greet Mar'zal on my behalf. Perhaps *he* could enlighten you as to my disposition."

Bwar swallowed the lump in this throat. "Understood," he said muttered gruffly. It was clear to him that political wrangling would never accomplish the required tasks. The only option was to join Elo'misce and completely fracture the political makeup of the country they shared. They would either eliminate the humans who lived in it or join Mar'zal whose corpse likely incubated a brood of skolaxis larva.

It chaffed the dwarf's pride to unify with an elf, but he had a clear precedent to do so. He could always kill her later. In fact, he planned to.

Bwar left the ring of flame light, returning to his place in Xorst. His directives had been made clear to him.

As soon as Bwar departed, the goblin sent his guards away. He opened the amulet at his neck and contacted his brother.

***

Werthen moved his company of people well off of the road and into the dying shade supplied by the shanties near the road. The air was no cooler there, but at least the hot sun overhead and the glare from the gravel underfoot couldn't as easily scorch those under his care. Soon after midday, the sun would finally begin to dim in intensity but they needed to respite until then.

The ferreter crouched down in the heat, looking for a resting place near the wrought iron cages of what the prisoners within had referred to as "Low-Town." Vil-yay rummaged through the detainees' equipment and supplies looking for any clues as to their identities.

Wiping away the beading sweat, the two captives watched as Werthen sifted through their belongings. The harsh sun had long since scorched their skin and darkened their skin.

Werthen was respectful and cautious with their items, but couldn't just open their cage. If these men were criminals, the public would not look kindly on the Christians for releasing them.

"I see that you have some Say-awr' among your numbers," noted the younger man. Vil-yay set down the knapsack he rifled through. His face revealed his surprise. The captive pointed at Vil-yay's tattoos which designated his status within the tribe; not many people outside of the Kil-yaw' could read what they meant.

Werthen sized up the man. He sat hunched and looked uncomfortable, but a spark smoldering deep within his eyes showed that his spirit was not defeated—perhaps no imprisonment could. His almost-bald head was full of stubble. It had been shaved fairly recently. His shirt was off in a vain attempt to offset the intense heat.

Tanned dark and covered in tattoos, a nasty looking scar on his belly ripped through his torso with a shot of milky-white, scarred flesh more prominent than any of his tattoos, revealing where he had once been ripped open.

"We will gladly tell you all about ourselves," Werthen said, "but first, satisfy our curiosity, who are you?" He was unsure if he could believe their claims, and so Vil-yay continued investigating as he tilted his ear.

The old man groaned and trembled. Werthen poured a cup of water from his canteen. Accepting the cup, the younger prisoner cradled his comrades' head and poured a dribble onto the defeated man's cracked lips.

"I have been given many titles in my life. I am the Untamed Mankran, the Raider of Ziphan Slave Dens, Hunter of Wendigo, and the Desired of Ly'Neesa."

At the mention his Mankran birthright, Werthen deduced his name from stories he had heard. "You are Shimza the Greater?"

"No... yes. But it is just Shimza, now." He fingered the scar that webbed its way across his abdominal muscles. "I have not been back to Jand since I acquired this mark. I lost my previous partner, my brother, a few years ago. Since then, nothing has paid as well as the Monastery of Light's bounty on the wendigo or their masters."

The older man sipped on the water cup, barely regaining consciousness. Shimza helped regulate his drinking when the water slopped down his chin.

"This is Fixxer, my partner."

Fixxer coughed, "Pleased t'meet ya. Don't listen to a word he says," he wheezed. "You should never trust a man from Mankra." The old man chided.

"Tell me why you are confined to this cell?"

Shimza pointed at the city in the distance. It towered over them upon a nearby plateau. "High-Town," he said, "it's been overrun by the wendigo."

Werthen's blank look revealed that he wasn't familiar with the term. His werewolf friend explained. "The wendigo are vampires, the brood of Lilth. Long have they been the enemies of the Kil-yaw'," said Vil-yay. "There are two kinds of vampire. The more powerful of the two are the elder vampires, the original creation of Lucifer; they were the first of all ekthro to be created. When Lucifer first began crafting living beings, he tried to recreate what Yahweh had made, only modified and perfected—but they were lifeless. Their strengths were greatly amplified beyond all men; this made the vampires very powerful, and the Gathering still fears them and they spend much effort guarding against Lilth's threat.

"The wendigo are the second sort of vampire, those that were once human and traded their soul for immortality and power. Elders can sire as many wendigo as would give up their mortality, but the elder vampires are rare and limited in number. Their elders, created by Lucifer himself, are the most powerful. They even have limited abilities to access the natural, magic leylines. All vampires must feed on the nephesh of man, the life-blood, to compensate for their soullessness: that initial, motivating breath of Yahweh-God that sustains us. The elders were created without it and the created wendigo choose to relinquish their claim on it."

"You seem quite well informed," commented Shimza.

Vil-yay pulled a sleeve back from his forearm, revealing a few more tattoos. The caged warrior raised an eyebrow. "You are a mythos-keeper," he read the werewolf's designation within his tribe. "I see by your marks that you are also an accomplished warrior."

"I once might have been. But even the strongest of us Say-awr' were regarded as lower than the weakest of other tribes. These signs mean nothing to us anymore. The Say-awr' have left the Kil-yaw'."

The old man raised an eyebrow at the statement. "Nonetheless, you could come in handy to our cause," said Fixxer. "We intend to clean out that nest of undead vermin." He nodded towards High-Town. "They're up to something in there. I don't care so much what they're doing as long as we get our bounty, and the chance to test out some of my new inventions. We will certainly cut you into our profits for any... assistance." The old man rattled the wrought iron.

"We care little for profits," said Werthen, "but we can certainly release you."

"Well, *we care*," the old man piped.

"Really," Shimza disagreed with him. "You were thinking about profits when we were turning free those workers and organizing a rebellion in the slave quarters?"

Fixxer scowled. "Means to an end," he tried to downplay his empathy. "Besides, some things are just plain right to do."

Werthen smiled. "We can help you in more ways than one, I think. Let me tell you about *our* mission, now. I think that we could certainly benefit from each other and reclaim Granik High-Town together."

***

Against the dim backdrop of candlelight, grr'Shaalg contacted his brother, the king in name only. The qâsam glowed faintly in his hands as he activated it and waited for a response.

After a short while, just before his patience dissipated, tyr-aPt responded to the call. The subterranean ruler held the communicator at arm's length as he bowed to his master.

[Report to me,] grr'Shaalg commanded.

[Yes, brother,] intoned the king. [Your chosen envoy is performing well. Griq'nnr is a capable and adept creature. He has already toured seven of the other nine kingdoms and brought them relief from the anthrofusis virus.]

[Excellent,] a grin crept across his twisted face. [Then I expect that a growing number of the faithful are finding their way to the path?]

[Absolutely. Griq'nnr's nawchash-empowered toqeph is quite impressive. The signs and wonders he performs would have convinced some of them even if they didn't have ulterior motives. Many pledge faithful allegiance to the new doctrines that he brings. There have been other goblins with arcane skill, but he seems to be especially powerful when it comes to the magic arts.]

grr'Shaalg bobbed his head. [I handpicked him for this assignment. He was one of those initial goblins trained by Zilke, the dead priest's plaything. It should come as no surprise that Griq'nnr excels, considering his genetics.]

[He is one of yours?] asked tyr-aPt. His voice conveyed surprise. [I thought we had decided not to let our situation repeat itself.]

[That had always been the plan. Other than this one, I have devoured all of my other progeny at birth. This one eluded me for many years and I did not know he existed until he had already made his own name. It wasn't until after I assigned him to Zilke's clique of trainees that I learned of his heritage. By the time I discovered it, much training had already been invested into him. I thought it wasteful at that point to do the obvious.]

Looking skeptical, grr'Shaalg assured tyr-aPt, [Should the need arise, I could consume him any time that I want. And you would do well to remember that; the same applies to you, brother.]

Through the seeing stone, tyr-aPt bowed his head in submission. Neither addressed whether or not Griq'nnr knew his lineage. [Your plan truly is genius,] he said, shifting the mood.

[I know it is. I will soon reach the pinnacle: become the most powerful being in existence. Not even the combined power of the demonic overlords and their hordes will able to stop the unified forces of swarming goblins… not when I am through with them. Goblins shall rule in the depths, across the surface, and atop the heights of Paradise.

[Even now Griq'nnr trades the katadoolu serum, respite from the anthrofusis symptoms, for the allegiance of our brethren masses. He sets up places of Luciferian worship and installs goblin shamans to lead the ceremonies. The shamans, meanwhile, proliferate our plague while manufacturing the katadoolu. Every two or three days the anthrofusis will flare up without refreshed administration.

[The kings of the land will no longer be deified by their subjects. And if kings are no longer looked at as minor gods, then it will be easier to tear men away, to unify them behind one flag: Luciferianism.

[Of course, Absinthium wants this… and we will bide our time until the perfect opportunity strikes. We will plan for that right moment. Once we have allied ourselves with enough of brother races we will spring our trap: the xenocide of mankind. We will unite the ekthro and overthrow mankind, leaving only the children of Lucifer's true heritage. Using both religion and addiction we will conquer even our allies.

[Once the numbers of man have diminished, the magic leylines will grow weak and brittle and the power of the demons will fail.]

[Won't Griq'nnr and our shamans need the leylines?]

grr'Shaalg responded with a cock-eyed grin. His brother didn't always keep up on the details so he was glad he'd tracked him. [We will have stockpiled all available sources of the rare nawchash and equipped our forces with it. Goblin kind will rise above all; *my fist* will shatter the gathering and *my falchion* will slay my enemies. I—and my allies—we will sit in the thrones of Babel. You and I, brother, *we will rule*.]

[Truly you are the Shadow King, grr'Shaalg. Our kingdom would have long ago faltered under Nvv-Fryyg's reign had it not been for your devious mind.]

[I am aware,] he bragged. grr'Shaalg boasted openly to his brother because there was no other being he could do so with. The goblin's pride compelled him to gloat about his plans, and he could not do so to any other. No other creature could be guaranteed to maintain the Shadow King's confidence.

[Now, I must go.] grr'Shaalg looked away from the stone. [Absinthium's qâsam is calling. Something is happening. Some kind of major operation is underway, one that temporarily requires a heavy amount of our warriors.]

[The krist-chin threat?] tyr-aPt asked. But grr'Shaalg did not answer him. Instead, he severed the connection and retrieved his other, pulsating jewel.

Slightly distorted, the archmage's grim face appeared within the facets of the gem. "Gather the troops that you promised to prepare," he commanded. "It is time."

***

Rashnir sat in a cluster of folks near a smoldering campfire. He led a discussion with the new converts from Schworick. As he directed the flow of the question and answer period, he noticed his werewolf friend also engaged in an intense conversation across the way. Zeh-Ahbe' tried to enlighten Sim-khaw', but every time they spoke, it seemed something drove them further apart than ever. They could barely find common ground on the basic definition of terms, as if they no longer spoke the same language.

Focused on his own talk, Rashnir remained unaware of the lycans' conversation. The converted warrior explained to them what it meant to be Christ-like in the face of a world dedicated to their destruction.

"What it means to me," he said, "is simply following the master. I am a pretty simple man. Many of you know my history—tales of my former life. To be a great warrior you must train a great deal. When I trained, I copied my teacher's movements and followed his instructions. That is how it is for *us, too.*

"As we follow the instructions of our Lord and follow in what He did, try to be like Him, we will eventually train our lives to resemble *His.* This is the process He called sanctification; it means no longer being

184

like the rest of the realm and like other people but instead being more like Jesus."

Rashnir continued speaking, answering individual questions to the best of his knowledge and ability. While he did so, he kept a wary eye on his friend. As his session wound to a close, Sim-khaw' walked away, looking disappointed, upset even.

Zeh-Ahbe' met up with Rashnir when Yavim took over, offering a new perspective from his personal life.

Jibbin chased another boy, playing in the grass just beyond the collection of adults. As soon as Rashnir was away from the crowd the child immediately pounced on the ranger. Rashnir warrior scooped him up and absent-mindedly swung him around, entertaining the child while he carried a conversation with his friend.

"I don't know what it is, why I can't get through to him," Zeh-Ahbe' lamented.

"Don't take the blame for this yourself," cautioned Rashnir. "Faith and understanding are decisions that only he can make."

Zeh-Ahbe' grimaced. "I think that Sim-khaw' has great motivation, but a wrong perspective. I can only admire that he acts in the interest of his whole tribe, even the entire Kil-yaw', in his effort to discover the root of our power. That interest in power, though, is still holding him back. He pursues the truth too broadly; he cannot see that it is found in a person, Christ, and not merely some totem or thing to be acquired and used."

"He is pursuing the power and not the person of Christ?"

"Exactly," sighed Zeh-Ahbe'. "I am afraid that we continually run into the same walls. If he cannot come to grips with the Truth soon, I fear that he will give up and harden his heart to it."

Their conversation halted as Rashnir did a double-take towards the town of Schworick.

Zeh-Ahbe' turned to search out whatever held his friend's attention so raptly.

Rashnir set Jibbin on the ground. "Go find Haisauce," he told him. Jibbin stubbornly stood his ground for a moment. "Now," said Rashnir, "I will be alright, but I need you to go. Stay with him until I come get you."

The little boy ran off through the clusters of adults, pausing to look back apprehensively. The child hated abandoning his guardian. Though he knew Rashnir was more than capable, Jibbin's fear that he would lose another family ran deep.

Three women, all dressed as professional warriors, walked towards the Christians' campground. Their faces were hard and fearless as they approached; their attention seemed fixed upon Rashnir and their hands flexed around drawn weapons as they met his gaze. There was no hiding, and running did not seem to a wise option.

Slowly and reluctantly, Rashnir walked out to meet them. Zeh-Ahbe' caught up and flanked him, inviting himself along. "Woman trouble?" he jokingly asked.

"Big time."

The women, whose names he had learned were Ly'Orra, Ri'Aqua, and Shi'Nala, each held swords in practiced grips. They were well prepared for a fight if one presented itself.

Zeh-Ahbe' sniffed and wrinkled his nose as the two parties closed upon each other. He asked, "'Ãbêdâh?"

Rashnir nodded. "Yup, and that's gonna make things tough. If she wants a fight, right here and now, I am afraid I may have to kill her." He frowned at the comment. He really did hate being forced to take lives— that was the past he'd left behind when Kevin showed him the meaning of Truth. Rashnir prayed silently as the distance between the parties shrank to nothing.

The five people came together, but blades did not clash. Shi'Nala placed a hand on Ly'Orra and stayed her comments. Shi'Nala stepped into the foreground as Ly'Orra scowled at her.

"Rashnir of Grinden," she queried, "may we have a word with you?"

He was almost dumbfounded. Rashnir expected more unprovoked and random attacks, not pleas for a rational conversation. "By all means," he guessed by Ly'Orra's grimace that this woman was not her friend. "My ears are open, Shi'Nala."

Shi'Nala's eyebrows rose with unguarded surprise. She had no idea where he might have heard her name. He had only recently discovered that information by eavesdropping in the temple.

"My companions and I do not see eye to eye on all things. One thing, in particular, are the interests of Ly'Orra's sister, Queen Ly'Neesa. I am Shi'Nala," she formally introduced herself, "Executor to the Queen. I represent a limited extension of her power and will."

"Queen of where?" inquired Zeh-Ahbe'. "I am not familiar with your people."

"Nor I," added Rashnir.

"We Ziphans," she said plainly, "have been ruled by a queen ever since our inception. The first queen, Ly'Mara, founded our country with other warrior women who based its structure on honor and the rule of female superiority."

"Zipha? I've never heard of there being a free people living in Zipha."

"We are a remote group," Shi'Nala told him, "the people of the treetops. We claim ancestral ownership of the country; it was ours to begin with and we still own it. It does not belong to the trolls and ogres who abuse the land and harvest mankind for slave labor. They are a curse from fates long past."

"Fate?"

"Yes, Fate. It is the predestined outcome of every event, a very god in its own right."

"I think that you have a skewed sense of theology."

"I am not here to debate semantics with you, Rashnir," interjected Shi'Nala. "I come with a request on behalf of my queen."

Ly'Orra exhaled loudly, interjecting her displeasure at the conversation. Shi'Nala glared at her.

"So there are free people in Zipha," interrupted Zeh-Ahbe'. He could hardly believe it. Having traveled abroad, he had never imagined anything other than trolls and ogres inside its boundaries.

"We live constantly on guard from the threat of our neighbors. It is our belief that we are being tested by fate. Once, our borders could barely contain our people, but that was millennia ago. Over the years, we kept losing a battle of attrition against the trolls that attacked our defenses. As time went on and our people wore down, we began to realize that fate had predestinated for us the state we are in now. We also believe that we are on the cusp of a new takeover, that our warrior women will overtake the threats and that Zipha will again be a strong nation."

"You had a request," Rashnir commented, not paying particular attention to the sales pitch for a Ziphan vacation.

"Yes, I do. I have watched you through our last few encounters. In addition to your martial prowess, you have demonstrated honor and nobility. For my part, I have been instructed to seek out honorable mates for Queen Ly'Neesa, in addition to supervising her sister."

This time, it was Rashnir's eyebrows that rose in surprise. "I am being asked to marry the queen?"

"Marry? What a silly idea. No, you may be chosen as a candidate for breeding stock. You, along with other qualified candidates, will be selected by the Queen or her noblewomen for breeding and romantic purposes. You will be given a salary, citizenship almost equal to a noblewoman's, and enjoy all of the pleasures that such a duty entails."

Rashnir rocked back on his heels at the reality of the suggestion. Zeh-Ahbe' put a firm hand on his shoulder. "My friend, do not even entertain the thought. The end of your path does not lie in Zipha."

He looked his companion in the eye. Zeh-Ahbe' was right, of course. That road could not coexist with his calling and the Lord's leading.

"I apologize, but I must decline," Rashnir agreed. "What you ask of me would tear me away from my path and purpose. Please, let me tell you what I have come to believe—the thing that now guides my life."

"No," said Ly'Orra as she stepped forward. "Let me tell you something. My destiny lays standing over your corpse. I will complete my Pawar; I will keep my honor and I will have your death."

"Pawar?"

"It is our sacred tradition that keeps our lines of succession free from entanglements," Ri'Aqua explained. "After the firstborn of the queen reaches a healthy, safe age of breeding, the others within the immediate royal line pursue the Pawar: the pursuit of glory and death in battle, seeking a name amongst the stars and accumulating glory until their fate takes them. They seek out and conquer as many notable warriors as possible in personal combat until..."

"Until?" Zeh-Ahbe' pressed.

"Until fate happens... the inevitable."

"I think," Shi'Nala slid in coyly, "that Ly'Orra might desire you for herself and that is why she seethes so. She wants to destroy you because she could never have you for herself, except in battle."

Ly'Orra's jaw dropped agape as she turned to the other woman. She levied a harsh slap across Shi'Nala's face. The Queen's executor took the full brunt of the blow as if she had expected it—even deserved it.

Shi'Nala did not retaliate; there was no need. In the end, Shi'Nala would live, return to Zipha, and bear children. Ly'Orra would not. Shi'Nala smiled even as her cheek glowed red from the strike.

"You are my next mark, Rashnir," said the doomed warrior. "My chosen bard has already begun composing the next verse of my Pawar."

Ri'Aqua nodded at the comment.

By now, a crowd had begun to form behind Rashnir and Zeh-Ahbe'. The curious onlookers had formed a semi-circle as they tried to make sense of angry woman and the murderous situation.

"She *will* kill you," Shi'Nala said matter-of-factly, "unless you choose my option. Come to us. You can be a boon to the people of Zipha and father many prosperous and successful daughters."

Ly'Orra shoved Shi'Nala. "Do not force my hand. His mind is made up, as is mine. He is next in my Pawar."

"If that is how it must be, Ly'Orra," said Rashnir. "Shall we go to blows right here?"

She addressed the situation, took in the crowd. It was full of children and beginning to press in on all sides. This was not an optimal field of combat.

"No. I will not fight you again today. But beware; I will strike when the opportunity suits me."

"Well it had better be soon," interrupted Shi'Nala as she rubbed her sore cheek. "I, and your queen, await the completion of your Pawar."

She scowled back at the executor. She was still a noble with amplified rights due her station, but Ly'Orra was still royalty, at least until her honorable death.

"We *will* meet again in combat." Ly'Orra turned and left. Her counterparts followed suit.

Shocked, Rashnir stood next to Zeh-Ahbe'. Neither knew quite what to make of the situation. Within a matter of moments, one woman had tempted him greatly and another delivered a death warrant. They could only look at each other and laugh.

CHAPTER SEVEN

Cool humidity permeated the subterranean blackness. Night would soon fall, reflected the arch-mage, but he would not be above ground to witness it.

Two of his new acolytes deposited a rack upon the earthen floor of the staging area. A powerful, important relic hung upon it.

The damp air seemed to crackle as Absinthium neared the artifact that he'd brought with from the Monastery of Light. He caressed the reptilian-scaled garment, a potent gift from his demonic master, the Dark Lord of the Gathering.

Crimson scales glistened in the pale alchemical lights that illuminated the cavern—they wouldn't risk discovery by drilling opening vent holes for torches. Absinthium savored the power he felt as he caressed the garment, but he would not don the mantle just yet. When the time was right, he would put it on; the mantle was only brought out for the most taxing encounters.

His magical shroud was a cache of great power and supernatural energies. The totem was made from a patch of hide that had been torn from the great dragon meh'-red, the shapeshifted demon who led the Gathering before his master beh-tsah'. Imbued with a heavy dose of nawchash, the armored mantle was a separate, temporary power source should the mage need to tap into it. He rarely required it, but the arch-mage had learned to over prepare for this specific enemy.

Absinthium leaned his toqeph staff against the rack where he'd mounted the shimmering mantle of power. His gaze scanned the rows and rows of 'ābêdâh vials neatly arranged in glimmering stacks. The Luciferian's grin widened; his attack could soon begin.

***

Shimza dropped a handful of dried mushrooms into his pot and reconstituted them and took a bite of jerky from the supplies in his pack. He and his partner, Fixxer, tried to regain as much health as quickly as possible. They had already explained as much as possible about the bloodthirsty threats prowling the area to the Christians who they had taken refuge with.

Darkness would come relatively soon. The small remnant of a local population had already taken shelter in the mix of shanties and rundown shelters that dotted Low-Town.

Since freeing the wendigo hunters, Werthen and his group had discovered that there was more to Low-Town than initially appeared. Once the visiting group finally settled down and seemed to pose no threat, the people of Low-Town came out of hiding. Seeing the vampire hunters walking among the Christians dared the townsfolk to hope again.

Werthen and Vil-yay discovered a great deal about the people. The bulk of the remaining community came from socially unwanted segments: the elderly, the non-influential, the poor, and those who opposed the new regime that recently assumed control of Granik. They proved themselves generous despite having so little to offer; they availed themselves to the Christians, nonetheless.

As dusk drew near, most of them, including Shimza, had been brought up to date on who the Christians were and what they believed. Some of the folks joined their ranks. The more stubborn and skeptical challenged the Christians to free Granik High-Town and prove that their God was truly all-powerful.

Werthen gave thought and prayer to the issue before responding. "We have an interest in reaching the people of this country. Every person alive is entitled to hear this message of hope; it should be a basic human right. There are souls in bondage trapped in High-Town. I am unsure yet what we will be able to do, but we will attempt *something*. I must pray about it further."

Night crept closer and Werthen appointed a watch detail at the wendigo hunters' insistence. The vampires would not be happy that the Christians had released Shimza and Fixxer who had been placed in the cell to die as an example to the downtrodden folks of Granik. Their message: resistance would not be tolerated, went unheeded.

Before the shadows crept too long Shimza and Fixxer met with Werthen and Vil-yay in their tent. The Christian leaders needed more information about the exact happenings inside the city. There was little they could do without specific details.

"We've been inside the walled city," said Shimza, indicating Granik's High-Town. "We also interviewed many of the folks in High-Town before our eviction."

"We discovered a lot of odd things," interrupted Fixxer. "This isn't like any of the other vampire nests we've cleared out before. Granik is more than just some random feeding zone or ghoul nest; there's a grand scheme here… a more sinister purpose.

"For instance, all of the mills and foundries shut down, commercially anyhow. They aren't exporting anything anymore, as far as metals go. The foundries run, but they are only making beams and mining tools as if they've ramped up excavations without pulling out any resources. The economy is destroyed but nobody inside cares. Anybody whose complained has been kicked down to Low-Town, or killed."

"The whole place seems to have shut down and closed itself off from the rest of the world," continued Shimza. "*They are digging for something*, and nothing else matters to them. The wendigo control all of High-Town. Anyone left whose not been enthralled has likely become one their ghouls."

"Ghouls?"

"People who have not been offered the false-life… the option of becoming a vampire. They are instead held in reserve as dedicated blood donors, addicted to the euphoria that it causes when the creatures feed. Ghouls, in every way, are the slaves of the elders and of the wendigo."

Werthen furrowed his brow, trying to unravel the mystery. "What could they be digging for? Precious metals?"

"No. Vampires have no need for riches; that is not a path that they follow for control or influence. Whatever it is they seek, it must be powerful and it must have been buried here for thousands of years before the miners became aware of it."

"So what can we do, then?"

"We can only prepare, *for now*," said Fixxer. "We will need to develop a solid plan of attack. Whatever is happening in Granik, it can't bode well for humankind."

***

The watcher stood on the hillside observing Kevin as he walked through the encampment with his angelic bodyguards. They'd just returned from trying to converse with their uncooperative prisoner, the forgotten acolyte. It seemed pointless and showing him kindness proved ineffective; Luciferian hearts were like a stone.

ekerithia's powers of observation were immense; for thousands of years, he had done nothing but travel and observe life from a distance. He sensed what was about to happen—could feel the tremors of coming doom he'd guessed would come since before he left his tower. ekerithia could hardly fathom how his former brothers could not foresee the threat. It was easy to spot the creeping, southern army as it weaved snake-like through the shadows, finding places to crouch and strike from the dark.

Desire welled up within him; ekerithia wanted to fly to the preacher, to warn him of the danger he was in. Instead, he did what he'd always done. He stood... and watched. There was too much danger involved. Risks were too high. The fallen angel didn't have any special compassion for Kevin nestled deep within in his hardened heart, but ekerithia needed the preacher to live so that he could further his own goals before the realm crumbled and expired. Of all of Kevin's warnings, ekerithia took that one most seriously.

With a scowl, he stood and bore witness. If this battle went poorly it might necessitate changes to his plans. Already the Gathering had split, warring with itself, but the Christian threat had given the demonic council tunnel vision, of sorts. After tonight he would need a new diversion to distract the Gathering.

ekerithia set his jaw and tried again to convince himself he didn't care about the fate of Kevin. He knew that the preacher was doomed.

Unless...he thought with a grin... *there are others in this realm.*

***

Kevin walked flanked by his bodyguards and confidants. His efforts to reach the Wyvern Rider had been, thus far, fruitless. Nevertheless, Kevin had frequently gone down to speak to the prisoner, showing him every kindness.

Each exchange had gone as the last. Prock sat and endured the preacher's attempts to speak with him—only glowering as if the man had tried to break him with his compassion. The acolyte barely even acknowledged the other man. Unreachable, almost catatonic, he seemed like he was plotting, waiting for the right moment.

Prock remained tied to a post in the ground; he had been humiliated, dethroned and demeaned by his prey. After every visit from the Christian leader, Prock tried to loosen his bonds with renewed vigor. The ropes, tied by the larger of the angels, never budged. The Acolyte could only stare daggers at Kevin's back as he returned to his business.

"What do you think might reach him?" Kevin asked Jorge and Kyrius as they wandered through the middle of their encampment spread across Sprazik's marketplace.

"I fear that he may be too far gone," said Jorge.

Kevin looked to Kyrius, the more optimistic of the two. He wanted to hope that he could have an impact on their prisoner.

"I might have to agree," said the other angel. "He may be hardening his heart to such a degree that he could never receive the Truth, no matter what evidence is presented."

The preacher sighed and nodded. They continued walking in silence. He respected their opinions, but Kevin wasn't ready to give just yet. He certainly didn't have a backup plan for dealing with the dangerous warrior but he couldn't stomach his execution.

In tandem, Jorge and Kyrius stopped suddenly. They looked about frantic and worried. Their keen eyes darted this way and that with defensive body language and wings flared out in alarm.

"What is it?" asked Kevin.

"There. Look," Kyrius pointed to the horizon and Jorge turned his head.

Kevin could barely make out ekerithia on the horizon. The fallen angel stood in the distance. "He looks sad," Kevin commented.

Suddenly, the air seemed to shimmer and the ground rumbled, shifting slightly below them. Patches of earth fell away all around them; earth cracked and chasms split open. Screams echoed through the village as goblins poured out of the fissures and wielded falchions. The subterranean warriors and cut down the innocent all across Sprazik, terrorizing people with blades while others plummeted to an unknown future.

With burning swords Jorge and Kyrius leaped into the fray, charging in opposite directions. They cut swaths through the attacking goblins and the chaos quickly blotted them out from sight.

Jorge glanced back as Minstra, the Luciferian battle monk Kevin had invested so much time into since

Grinden, charged towards the preacher. Minstra planted himself in front of his friend and took a combat stance.

A woman shrieked nearby as she clutched her child. The cry pierced Kevin's heart and overwhelmed his emotions. The preacher dropped to his knees to pray for his people. Minstra watched his mentor take a helpless form and tightened his gut—pledging himself to the man's protection.

Dusky goblins swarmed through the village like secret shadows, bearing all manner of tattoos and markings, colored and branded differently. Sounds of the battle reverberated off the remaining buildings and the reek of ãbêdâh permeated the air. Explosions erupted and nearby structures burst into flames.

The azure blades of the Christians sprang into existence, shining like valiant beacons. They strobed and flared as they defended against the attackers with skillful defense; they were only slightly hindered by the surprise assault.

Jorge streaked through the streets at supernatural speed. Few enemies gave him pause as he cut through the offense. The angel paused to look back through his swath of destruction and find Kevin.

Goblins rushed for the earth-man. Minstra whirled and kicked, cracking gobbling skulls with his feet or the nunchaku he'd trained within the Order. A surge of ekthro rushed forward—too many for the monk to handle alone and the preacher kneeled in prayer! Any goblin that made it past the monk and grew too close to the preacher fell in spasms, overcome with a pustule-inducing blight. More than his monk friend, the man was protected by supernatural forces. The angel rounded a corner and dashed out of sight.

Kyrius cut through a blanket of opposing ekthro and whirled to take stock of the situation. Goblins continued spewing from their holes in the ground. Some of them rode upon massive, worm-like creatures; many didn't carry the typical falchion that goblin warriors typically wielded. Kyrius suddenly understood why.

A group of stalwart Christians stood back to back with flaming, blue swords blazing brightly. The cadaverous remains of scores of goblins lay at their feet. Kyrius screamed for them to scatter, but it was too late. A suicidal goblin ran towards them as archers fired flaming arrows at him and the wooden cask strapped to his back.

The Christians' eyes widened as they comprehended the situation. A split second later the detonation vaporized everything in the vicinity. Nothing remained of them, the light of their swords permanently snuffed.

Kyrius screamed in agony as blood from friend and foe splattered across his chin. All over the village, his friends began falling under the onslaught.

***

Bre's sharp eyes were drawn to the fire the moment the first spark caught fuel and leapt into life. The elf silenced his two companions. "You see it?" He pointed. "There are figures, darker than shadows, advancing on Sprazik."

The two other elven scouts stared into the night, neither agreeing nor discounting their kinsman. Despite his unspoken status as an outsider, Bre outranked them for good reason. He'd honed his skills in Lars, the last Gleendish town before the wastelands began, and came from a stronger, sturdier breed of elves. He and his kin spent most of their lives in the wilds, far from the comforts of the urban, developed areas—just as fair and handsome, but more accustomed to the sorts of perils that honed their renowned scouting skills.

"We've got to get closer to the city," Bre urged them.

His two compatriots grudgingly followed as they advanced on Sprazik. In their eyes, 'city' couldn't even be used for any but their own home, Xorst.

A bright flash, like ball lightning, cracked the sky. Buildings suddenly erupted in flame. The three sprinted towards the town.

"Stay here," Bre commanded the two lesser scouts. "Watch the road," he cursed between breaths. "War or weather regardless, we can not lose our quarry! I'm going to climb that silo."

The two elves sank into the grove of trees nearest the highway as Bre scaled a rickety ladder and climbed the derelict grain silo looking for a better vantage point to search out their mark. They absolutely could not let him slip away.

***

Flames spat cinder and ash into the air lighting the night sky with the glow of raw pain. Subterranean explosions kept opening new holes. Entire buildings sank below the soil as the goblins destroyed both their enemies and their own without distinguishing between the two.

Kyrius took charge of a group of Christian warriors and directed them as they pushed the goblins from their vicinity. The angel wielded his blade deftly and his warriors stepping into the flow with him.

Suddenly, his flank ripped open with a swath of eldritch flame. The force of the blast smashed him against the walls of a shredded building. He grabbed his gut to stop the bleeding and used his other hand, trembling hand to pull out the deeply lodged shrapnel.

Kyrius gasped as he watched the others fall under the serrated kamas of the acolytes—a familiar threat reborn. In warrior-mages' midst, the archmage led their charge. His mantle glimmered blood-red in the flame light. His footsteps crackled, vibrating with unholy power.

The angel lunged for the Luciferian leader, ricocheting off of the first three acolytes in his way, striking a blow at each. The assassins skillfully deflected each attack as they parried defensively—but none of them was the angel's target.

Absinthium met Kyrius head on wielding his staff as a weapon. The old man's prowess was unbelievable and he traded strikes with the angel. The air shook with power as the two blocked and thrust.

Absinthium batted away an azure strike and spun his toqeph like a windmill, breaking the wounded angel's defense wide open. The spin chained into a second blow as the gnarled end of his staff delivered a wicked uppercut to Kyrius' chin, staggering the heavenly warrior backward. Absinthium crouched low to the ground and thrust with his staff, screaming a magic trigger word.

Kyrius stumbled backwards, too shocked to comprehend his plight. A colossal burst of energy struck him in the chest. He felt his feet leave the ground. A tempest of arcane power slammed into him hard enough to blast him clear of the village. Just before his vision blurred and blinked out, he saw the burning rooftops of Sprazik; he saw Kevin below, shielded in prayer and his protector, Minstra struggling to keep pace with the influx of new enemies. far below, a large group of men marched on the town from the south—the Nindan border. His limp body rocketed clear through an empty silo near the barn at the towns' edge. He burst clear through with a cloud of splinters, and then he saw nothing but black.

***

Havara, rightful king of Gleend, huddled alongside his people. Already weary and wounded from his previous pursuit, he and three other countrymen had fought their way clear of the thickest battle.

They crept through an alleyway and broke into a building through its rear door. Havara entered last, seeing everyone inside safely. Women, children, and those men he'd fought with looked to him for hope, but he had no idea what to do—his brother had always been the wise one. Havara felt torn between the faces of the helpless who pleading for protection and his sense of duty which urged him to fly into battle and help beat back their assailants.

Pacing the length of the dark floor his face twisted in consternation. The men, all citizens of Gleend, joined him. "King Havara, what do we do? We must protect these people," one blurted out.

"But what about the others out there," another disagreed. Blood from a gash on his cheek slicked his grizzled beard. "We could better protect them by ending this madness with our own swords!"

Havara glanced back and forth between the two. A third warrior, the youngest of the three, hesitated to speak. "Speak man," Havara commanded him, "it might be your last chance before we all die. What seems best to you?"

"We stay or we fight, either choice puts us in peril. *You,* you are the last king of Gleend if we fail. Our

203

people, *our race*, needs you. Your countrymen need you to survive this battle. *You* must flee! It's not an act of cowardice, but the mandate of your office."

The King looked at the young man. He certainly had logic on his side, but it was the option he liked the least. "I need a moment." Havara paced the floor of the building. The air felt deathly still on the inside, yet the walls reverberated with the cacophony of a battle all around. Every eye stayed fixed upon him, but his own were squeezed tight; he prayed desperately for an answer.

With a crack, the front door burst open, breaking apart as falchion wielding goblins poured inside. Women shrieked in terror; the first two men charged forward, bellowing their battle cries. The younger adviser turned to Havara. "Flee!" he screamed, pushing the king to his feet.

Havara ducked out the rear. Pride soured his heart, but duty demanded his survival.

Sprinting as stealthily as possible he skirted the fray. Havara found an old gelding trapped with its reigns tangled in a snarl of thorny bracken. Half-starved, it had probably been tied to this post since before the first attack on Sprazik—before Kevin arrived to help set things in order. He untied the weary beast and swung a leg over the animal's back.

***

Absinthium watched the angel trail a streak of flame and vapor as he rocketed away. He pointed to targets and sent his minions to kill the weakest and most helpless first.

The arch mage's favorite weapon was demoralization. He stood on his toes and searched for his target.

Grinning, he spotted the preacher towards the center of the collapsing village. He caught the eye of the monk. They locked eyes and he recognized the monk as one of the two who had thwarted him at the quarry by Grinden.

He snarled with rage so ferocious that the monk flinched. Minstra's resolve crumbled as he did a double take between the prayer-shielded leader and the brutal spell caster.

Minstra took a step back, began shrinking away from the gaze of the archmage.

Absinthium's dread eyes pierced the defector and pleasure welled up within his heart. The monk didn't stand a chance—his heart had already faltered and they both knew it. If the monk stayed, he *would* die by Absinthium's hand.

***

Jorge swung his sword and ripped through the segmented carapace of the giant skolax that harried his dwindling number of friends. Blue-grey effluence splattered across the burnt soil; the insectoid creature shrieked as it thrashed its last.

The beast's driver leapt at Jorge from its position. The goblin didn't make it to the ground alive as Dri'Bu gutted the tunnel-dweller midair.

Kevin's elven friend moved fluidly, working in tandem with the angel as if they were one. Dri'Bu demonstrated the skill wielded by the elven elders. His age did not slow his combat prowess in the least. With a dagger in one hand and a saber in the other, he became a flurry of blades.

"We've got to fall back!" Dri'Bu shouted to Jorge as he effortlessly dismembered a wave of snarling enemies. "Our losses are too great!"

The angel knew it also. This was not a battle that the enemy needed to fight. The Luciferians skewered them with attrition, whittling away at the Christian forces, trying to damage and demoralize them.

A shrieking goblin charger sprinted towards the elf and angel. Dri'bu threw his dagger at the ekthro and sliced the creature's leather harness. The confused goblin charged forwards even as his explosive barrel fell to the ground and rolled towards the goblin firing squad who kept their flaming arrows nocked.

With one fluid motion, Dri'bu cleaved the sprinting goblin's head from the body, pulled his dagger free, and thrust its blade into a broken barrel of pitch near his feet. He raked the flammable edge across Jorge's sword, igniting the dagger, and chucked the firebrand at the tumbling barrel before his enemy's headless body hit the ground.

The barrel detonated and leveled a cadre of goblin archers with a short-lived blossom of deadly fire. A moment later, the bodies sank into the sands as a new portal opened and more enemies leaped forth.

In the darkness beyond the new wave of goblins, the blue swords of their people flashed and flared as they battled the enemy. Too often cerulean blades winked out of existence, overwhelmed by the scale of the sneak attack.

Jorge watched the former Luciferian monk, Minstra, flee for his life. Fear motivated him to escape the battle. The Christian's eternal confidence, however, doomed the rest of them to stay. So caught up in the battle, they did not think of the implications of such heavy losses.

"Retreat!" the angel bellowed the order. This was neither the proper place nor time for this battle. There could be no positive outcome for them. Screams echoed from the edges of the city as the Nindan army finally encroached upon them, violating the sovereign borders to cut down those who fled.

The horizon flashed with white-hot brilliance, trailed by a sonic boom. A geyser of pure energy shot into the air, trailing a spiraling plume of smoke behind the flailing comet. Jorge's angelic eyes identified Kyrius's body flung like a shooting star as it arced across the sky.

"Kevin!" Jorge gasped in alarm.

The angel and the elf sprinted headlong through the fray, dodging and counterattacking as necessary. A chasm fell open before them, belching alchemical smoke and falchion wielding goblins. The sooty ekthro swamped them, pressing in around their sides to stall them.

Out of the pit crawled another immense skolax driven by a familiar looking goblin. Seated on the creature was a cloaked, hooded man: an acolyte. His face looked the same as their hostage, wearing the typical acolyte appointments with an additional bag slung over his shoulder.

Jorge's anger welled up within him. A broad stroke of his massive, flaming sword cleared the forward path, dismembering any foes in front of him. Before the angel could charge ahead and engage the Luciferian fiend, more acolytes leaped from the cavity below and engaged him on all sides. Their black cloaks flapped as they brandished serrated kamas; the stench of death rolled off of them and the little flesh that was visible below their hoods looked pallid and necrotic.

The undead acolytes engaged the angelic warrior and the elf as one. The others followed after the necromancer who animated the bodies. They attempted killing blows against the skilled elf but concentrated mostly on grappling the angel, keeping him from taking flight.

"The prisoner!" shouted Dri'Bu as the skolax writhed its way through the street and away from them.

"Forget the Wyvern Rider. We need to evacuate—find Kevin and get out of here!"

***

"It's him! I'd recognize him anywhere," urged the taller elf scout, noting the royal gauntlets that the approaching rider wore.

A man on an old horse galloped straight for the pass they were guarding. The beast looked ready to die on its own feet.

"You're right," the shorter elf said. He glanced at the treetops where Bre's body had been flung when the silo exploded. "More glory for us!"

The pointy-eared scouts leapt into the road, firing their bows. The animal trilled and shrieked as it pitched forward, launching its royal rider almost to their feet as they hurried to nock their next arrows.

Havara crumpled to the ground, rolling violently. One leg snapped, breaking with an ugly, wet noise. The monarch growled like a bear and pushed through the blinding pain. He rolled to his good leg and smashed an armored gauntlet into the jaw of the shorter elf, sending his arrow into the distance while the shooter toppled into the grass.

Dropping his bow, the taller elf swung his fists at the wounded prey. The first punch connected and knocked Havara back a step.

Havara anticipated the second blow and dropped his head. The elf's fist impacted against the top of Havara's skull at the hardest part. Elven knucklebones shattered. The King launched forward, trying to tackle his opponent.

The tall elf kicked his legs back and wrapped his arms around the human's waist. Havara roared despite the agony that burned in his busted leg; he gritted his teeth and charged forward, feeling every movement as bone grinded against bone like two pieces of pumice.

Havara and the elf rolled through a ditch and crashed into a tree, the elf took the full force of the impact. Havara collapsed to one side while the tree held the elf secure; a broken branch punctured through the elven scout, hanging him in place like some kind of morbid scarecrow.

Just in time to see the shorter elf, chin bloodied and nose broken, Havara raised his hands and barely blocked a kick to the face. He staggered to his feet and locked arms with his opponent. They struggled momentarily before both of them stumbled over the edge of the deep, rocky ravine which hemmed the road at the far side.

***

The skolax crawled at a brisk pace. Though the angel and elf pressed their assailants back, the mounted enemies maintained a space cushion at all times. The distance remained just enough so that Wynn could maintain control of the undead fighters that stalled the angel, keeping him from gaining enough momentum to tear huge swaths through their forces.

Wynn glanced at the nearby sight, diverting only a fragment of his attention so that he maintained control of the animated acolytes. The sight made him smirk and intensified his bloodlust.

Tied to a stake and undisturbed sat his former superior and rival. Prock, the Wyvern Rider, former leader of the acolytes, was tied to a pole in the dirt like some common criminal. Wynn and Prock's eyes met, a glimmer of hope flickered in the captive's eyes.

Wynn sneered at his fallen comrade. It might've looked like a rescue mission, but Wynn had no intention of losing his new place as the acolyte's leader. He had no ties of loyalty, only his mission and selfish ambitions. Not even the ties of blood held sway over him—as Absinthium had demanded.

Prock struggled against his bonds as the skolax continued unabated. He bit the gag that kept him from casting spells or speaking. Prock shook against the ropes and realized his brother had no intention to free him.

Wynn rode further away and his former brother screamed through his muzzle, "*WYYYYYNN!*" His betrayal was final and complete. Prock shuddered and seethed with hatred. It rolled off of him in frigid waves.

Tied to his post, he momentarily locked eyes with the besieged angel. Prock struggled against his fetters to no avail and screamed in frustration, "RAARRGH!"

Absinthium strolled confidently through the destruction. Flames raged all around him. The only krist-chins in the immediate vicinity were those who felt drawn to the center of the town, undoubtedly on a fool's errand to rescue their doomed leader.

Those stupid enough to stand their ground would face the same fate as their mentor. Kevin, however, would not be granted as swift of a death as his underlings were receiving. The mage grinned as he half-dreamed of torturing his adversary.

A young warrior entertaining delusions of grandeur charged the Luciferian. Holding his blazing, cerulean blade in high guard, he burst through the line and ran to strike down the mage. Absinthium effortlessly sidestepped the Christian. He swung his staff around with such force and power, that it bashed through the boy's skull, tossing him off his feet like a rag doll. Absinthium chuckled mirthfully.

Of the few werewolves that remained in this encampment, most had already been dispatched by goblin zealots and their explosive barrels. The last of them leapt over a pile of debris. He roared in defiance, fur slicked red by the blood of his enemies. The lycan leveled its animal gaze at Absinthium and charged.

The archmage grabbed a nearby casket and shook off the fleshy detritus which had once been a kamikaze goblin that never reached its target. With supernaturally enhanced strength, he flung the barrel of explosives at his pursuit and followed it up with a simple fireball.

The werewolf took the full brunt of the cask's detonation just under his chest. The powerful lycan stopped and stood tall. His eyes suddenly turned vacant with shock and he looked down at his body. What little remained of him was mostly flame darkened bones that his lupine body had previously been attached to. Meat had been blasted away and nothing remained below his smoldering chest. He grunted and took one more step before collapsing in a charred, dead heap.

Two of his new acolyte's flanked Absinthium. The rest of his crew dispersed through the village, preying upon any remaining krist-chin people and the residents of Sprazik who had entertained them. The mage strode confidently and unchallenged. His goal was finally within his grasp.

***

Jorge struggled against the constant oppressors as he chased after the skolax and its riders. Dri'Bu was similarly entangled behind him by two of the necrotic wights. Another five vied against the angel, never tiring and never letting the angel find an escape vector or get up to speed.

The skolax skittered through a nearby street. A familiar block yawned open before them where the ground split, pocked by chasms and holes that had opened all around.

Jorge struggled against his foes. Only a short distance away, Kevin knelt in prayer. The preacher seemed to glow faintly as if a heavenly aura shielded him from outside harm.

The angel screamed a warning to him. A kama-wielding wight strode forward, intent on seizing the preacher. As Kevin concentrated in fervent prayer, the glow that encompassed him pulsed with an expansion; the undead acolyte stepped into the light and collapsed under its protective power. The necromancy which animated the corpse dissipated.

A second corptic acolyte tried in vain to tackle Kevin. He suffered the same fate and buckled under the heaviness of Shekinah light that wreathed the preacher who clutched the leather-bound bible to his chest.

Through the air, a loud, wicked voice echoed. Jorge saw Absinthium striding through an open route. Not even glancing at Kevin, the mage locked his gaze on the angel who had battled him at the Grinden quarry. Absinthium's booming voice beckoned his scattered acolytes, calling them to converge.

The dragon-scale mantle glowed as if it flickered with internal flames. Absinthium made his intent clear as he tightened his gauntlets and snarled at the angel. As he closed the gap, the air crackled with magic. The ground vibrated with supernatural energy, pebbles strewn about the cracked cobblestone rattled and hovered several inches above the ground.

Jorge knocked back the wighted acolytes with a devastating roundhouse cleave; his opponents broke and shattered into dust as they fell. Like a sandstorm, they blew on the fell wind, sucked back inside the leather satchel that Wynn carried.

Dri'Bu cried with surprise. His assailants, too, were sucked up like a sandstorm. A wave of goblins rushed him from the shadows and the elf disappeared under the mass of goblin oppression.

Only Jorge and Kevin remained in the center of town. Absinthium barred the angel's path, standing between the angel and his ward. He could not rescue his friend without first facing the wizard. As they stared each other down, more cloaked acolytes arrived. They surrounded and contained Kevin while Absinthium snarled in defiance.

The mage lunged, expertly whirling his staff. Absinthium and Jorge clashed in an epic duel. Magically energized and empowered far beyond human capabilities, meh-red's mantle gave Absinthium the edge he needed to contend with the angel.

As their battle raged amidst the chaos, the last acolyte arrived. Surrounding Kevin, they began to chant. Worry built up within Jorge's gut; the distraction was enough to loosen his defenses. Absinthium feinted and parried in one smooth maneuver. Finding an open target, the wizard screamed his trigger word and blasted the angel with a magic ball of energy. The force-beam shot from his fingers and slammed the angel across the battlefield.

Jorge's body smashed into a stone wall, shattering it. He cried out in pain and surprise as the wall crashed down around him.

The angel's howl distracted the preacher momentarily. Kevin's eyes blinked wide open in a moment of worry.

"*No!*" screamed Jorge from the smoking pile of rubble. He vainly stretched a defeated hand towards his friend.

Time seemed to move in slow motion as the ground beneath the Acolytes fell away. They dropped straight down into the caverns below, taking the preacher with them, enveloped by darkness.

Absinthium disappeared with them. The air still shimmered and crackled with raw energy as the hidden mage brewed a powerful spell.

Jorge shook off the masonry and clambered to the edge of the hole; Kevin was down there! Deep resonant words boomed through the air like thunder and the hole shot magma forth, like a geyser.

All around, the ground quaked and any remaining goblins leaped down the holes from which they'd launched the attack. The booming incantation crescendoed with a roar that rattled the ground as some arcane earthquake shook the soil.

Jorge sprinted and took flight on his injured wings. His spirit comprehended the words of the spell. He knew that doom approached. He raced above the streets as fast as he could manage. The angel swooped down and scooped the battered elf up and into his arms.

He flew above the heads and weapons of the enemies that surrounded the borders. The goblins had fled but the Nindans who closed off any retreat had blockaded the perimeter. They vainly launched arrows at the angel as he climbed for altitude. They didn't seem to heed the ground's tenuous rumbling and refused to break the net that prevented any escape—they would not risk angering the archmage.

The angel soared above, well out of the danger zone, as a deafening crash thundered behind him. Its mighty roar sucked out all other sounds and pulled the night air towards the epicenter of the void. A split second later, the entire village crushed into the ground as if flattened by some giant, invisible fist, pulled downward by the evil powers of the realm. Nothing escaped its annihilation. Only a heated crater remained where the village of Sprazik once stood.

Nothing remained. The bodies of goblins, Nindans, Gleendans, and Christians alike were smashed to atoms.

Jorge landed and collapsed in a nearby grassy meadow, leaking blood from his wounds across blades of grass. Dri'Bu still drew breath. He lay injured and unconscious, appeared as if he would live provided he wasn't bleeding internally. Unsure if any of the others survived, the angel groaned with frustration and pain. His heart-wrenching cry ripped through the witchy air and echoed across the night-chilled moors.

The angel had failed in his most important task: to keep Kevin safe and he felt his defeat in the fiber of his being.

No stars were visible in the inky sky. The night was as black as possible.

Chapter Eight

Rashnir jumped out of bed with a gasp. A sheet of cold sweat sheathed his skin. His skin rippled with goose-flesh as the blast of cool air hit him and the hair at the back of his neck prickled. His heart ached… something was very wrong.

He stepped through his loose tent flap. Zeh-Ahbe's gentle snores behind him proved that it was still early morning.

Staring long and hard into the distance, a cold seed of dread had taken root in Rashnir's gut. The sun had barely crested at the horizon, but its rays came with no sense of hope. This day the morning light brought Rashnir a feeling of evil. This was not a morning; it was merely a well-lit phase of night.

The warrior retrieved his musical instrument from his tent and walked to a nearby fire pit. He sat down on an old stump and stirred the waning coals, stoking them to life. Rashnir got the fire going again.

Rashnir gently strummed the strings as he prayed. With eyes closed his fingers intuitively pressed the frets making a worshipful song as he pressed forward in prayer. His guts ached with the feeling of spiritual tension; he could not shake that feeling that something evil hung around—and he had no control in the matter. Something somewhere was very, very wrong.

He arpeggiated two more chords and then one by one all of his strings snapped.

***

Walls of the craggy passage he explored were bathed in shadows and barely lit by the hole that yawned open above him. It didn't matter. ekerithia didn't need light to see, anyhow. The more distance he kept from the ancient Deep Well far below and from the western gate, the more powerful his created body was.

Peering through the dark, he reached through the shadows and retrieved a tattered, damaged tome. It was the thing that he required in the absence of any hope for redemption—his ticket to Plan B.

Detecting voices, he clutched the book to his chest and slipped into the greater darkness. Now, more than ever, secrecy was paramount. He couldn't be discovered so early and let his plans unravel.

ekerithia kicked over a pile of corpses, both human and goblin, and slid through the crack that their bodies had obstructed. Writhing through the fissure as if his body was made of smoke, he squirmed his way further into the depths, below the goblins network of tunnels, below the labyrinth that the overreaching ekthro presumed they could use it to further their own ends.

The fallen angel needed to travel quickly and without observation. To do that, he would have to delve deeper still and walk through the heart of Tartarus with this book that was such a critical key to his plan. All that he needed now was for Lilth to uphold her end of a hypothetical bargain struck eons ago.

ekerithia went deeper. He slid further into darkness.

***

Dannrick fluffed the plush blanket that hung draped across his impotent legs. He could smell the pungent, soured aroma of the kaboshalged stewing in the nearby kitchen. For almost longer than Dannrick could remember he had been confined to his chair. It had been specially fitted with rolling feet shaped like upside-down goblets. Perfectly spherical bearings had been inset into their bottoms so that the chair could be easily pushed about from behind.

Despite the fact that his legs had not worked in years, he could still enjoy many pleasures of life, things such as the delicacies that his wife cooked for him. The kaboshalged was a traditional Luciferian feast of lamb or kid boiled in the milk of its birth mother; that which meant to give it life became the medium of its death.

He grinned when he saw his son walking up the driveway. It had been several years since his last visit. Dannrick took much pride in his son's position with the Order. He and his wife had always been devout, raised their only son according to the doctrines and traditions of their faith.

Without knocking, Krimko walked through the front door of the spacious home. His father beamed with joy at his appearance. Krimko had not been by to visit since his mother's funeral.

Sniffing the air, Krimko commented, "Good. You have something to eat."

Dannrick called to his son, "Come! Sit! It has been a long time since you have visited. Tell me, how has the Order kept you busy? I heard that you were single-handedly responsible for putting down a rebellion at a temple prison."

The Luciferian professor glared at his father with beady little eyes. He did not hide his disdain for the corpulent cripple. He and his father had so rarely seen eye to eye, even before the injury, which Krimko secretly knew he'd been responsible for. Ever since that day he'd expected everyone to dote upon each of his requests.

Krimko glanced at his mother in the kitchen. She'd waited on him hand and foot right up until her death—and then afterward when her body had been animated.

"I cannot stay long," Krimko replied. Dishes clattered as he shuffled through the cupboards searching for the family's finest dishware. He poured himself a bowl full of clumpy, white-hued kaboshalged. "I am really only passing through."

Krimko grabbed the sides of the large stockpot, intending to take it off of the high flame. The heated handles burned his fingers, and he let fly with a string of expletives.

"Here, don't trouble yourself with that busy work. Let your mother do that. Marith!" yelled Dannrick. "Come, Krimko. Tell me what's been happening."

Marith bustled out of a nearby room and went straight to the kitchen, sensing Dannrick's desire. She grabbed the hot pot with her bare hands and took it off the flaming stove. Marith set the container on a countertop and addressed her son.

Krimko stared at her for a moment. She looked bored, even for a corpse. "Mother," he said with a nod.

"Come, come!" Dannrick called again. "Your mother is such tiresome company. Come in here and tell me what has been happening abroad. It gets so lonesome here, sometimes."

"It's about to get worse, Father," he said with disinterest. Krimko jammed his hands into his mother's abdomen. Her pale, sallow body gave no resistance as Krimko grabbed ahold and ripped out the magical device nestled within her ribcage. He wondered if she felt relief at the loss of necrotic animation that forced her into continued service to such an oaf.

Marith's body crumpled into a heap without the artifact empowering her body. The device resembled a metal crustacean inset with a teardrop-pearl that seemed to pulse with mystic energy.

From his chair, Dannrick screamed, "No! No! Put it back! What will I do without her? Who will care for me?"

Krimko regarded him for a second. "I was worried about that once before when Mother died the first time. I put the Khay-hee in her so that she could continue minding after you; there was no way *I* wanted to be bothered with the task. But I no longer care, and I require the device for something else."

"Well what about me?" shrieked Dannrick. "What am I supposed to do? I have no one else to feed me, to empty my bedpan, to move me." He shook his chair with anger and it skittered a little ways across the floor in a random direction.

"Like I said, I don't care."

He dropped the Khay-hee into the haversack that he'd slung around his shoulders. He topped off his bowl with simmered kaboshalged and took it with him. Stepping over his mother's cadaver, he gave his father a mock salute and let the door slam shut loudly behind him.

The fat man screamed in anger, easily audible through the open windows. Dannrick sounded more like a child throwing a tantrum than the venerable figure of wisdom he'd always claimed to be.

Krimko knew that Dannrick would eventually wither away, likely taunted by the odor of the rotting kaboshalged. He grinned as the sounds of Dannrick's cursing faded with the distance and he left his father's house behind for the final time.

He licked his fingers, enjoying the last stew his mother would ever make. Krimko scraped his bowl clean and tossed it into a nearby bush at the end of the driveway. He had always loved her kaboshalged.

***

The distance stretched long as the watcher descended even further and stepped nimbly through the dark of Tartarus. The cold clink of chains and stone echoed through the supernatural darkness. The air was void.

He'd flown through the cavernous dungeon at top speed, barely a glimmer in the air. No doubt, ekerithia appeared like a mere mirage to the denizens of such advanced depths. Even *he* could not see here unassisted.

Just a few steps ahead, the ascending stairway rose, barely visible in the dim illumination provided by the light orb he'd brought. ekerithia's toes nudged and rattled a chain in his path, eliciting a groan from a nearby captive.

The orbs he carried had been a parting concession at a long-ago meeting with Lilth when she'd approached his outpost for palaver. They would undoubtedly come in handy, especially considering exactly what was trapped within the one. Holding the glassine sphere to his face, ekerithia peered into the source of the light. A human soul swirled within the vortex of turmoil and spiritual aether. This was no ordinary sphere, trapping the disembodied soul of some random child of Lilth. This entity had not volunteered and needed to be broken to be useful; despite that, it was infinitely valuable.

Long had the vampire queen watched over the soul inside his orb. Lilth's seers had tipped her off to this particular destiny and so she had spent considerable resources and bent every rule of magic in order to seize the spirit before it escaped to the judgment halls beyond the western gate.

"I know your origins, little one," ekerithia whispered. His quiet voice boomed across the subterranean emptiness as he addressed the captive. "You are my bargaining chip and my prisoner, for now. But, if you not be required, you will be my princess. Perhaps *you* will be the key. And then..." ekerithia held his face and the glowing orb near the face of a nearby captive—an angelic creature chained to the perfectly hewn wall; the prisoner squinted against the light and shielded his grimy face with shackled hands. "And then, brothers, then hope will come again!"

The demon slipped the source of illumination within his cloak and silenced it as he paced up the steps. He placed it in a leather sack of dust and ashes. It clinked against another, similar orb before the two baubles settled into the fine silt that kept them silent. Behind him, a moaning cry of hope arose in the dark, starting small, and spreading to all those chained below the depths of creation.

***

"No, all of them," Werthen insisted to Jaylen who he'd put in charge. "You need to take the caravan west as soon as the sun rises. Any of the people from Low-Town are welcome to go with you, believer or not."

The night had fallen uneventfully, but a fell, starless sky unscrolled across the heavens. Certainly, tomorrow would bring pain and blood.

"But wouldn't that be dangerous, to allow nonbelievers so close to us?"

"Don't forget, Jaylen, it wasn't so long ago that *you* were a nonbeliever, too."

The young man nodded. That was what Werthen loved about Jaylen, he was thoroughly analytical. Jaylen could be more than a leader; he was a good manager, too.

Vil-yay piped in, "Have faith. It won't take long for them to see your faith lived out before they want to join you in it."

Werthen nodded. "Besides, it is our duty to protect them. We released Shimza and Fixxer. That already implicates us as far as High Town will be concerned. We're going to look like reinforcements to an enemy faction. And High Town is probably watching us even now." Werthen glanced at Shimza who stood near the door. Every muscle of the warrior's body remained tense.

Shimza nodded from his post where he monitored the walls of High Town through a collapsible scope. Darkness closed around the walls and an aura of evil wafted out from the vampires' city like a mist—palpable enough to choke a person. "Given the size of your group, there's no way that you can have come here unnoticed."

"We're responsible for these people, Jaylen. Even though we didn't know what we were doing when we released the vampire hunters, anybody left in Low Town is going to pay a price for letting us do it." Werthen paused, "Despite it all, I would have probably released them again, anyway, if I had to choose all over again."

Jaylen nodded, "Okay. I will lead them. But what about you?"

"Only a few of us will stay," Werthen replied, grasping for words. They still hadn't formed a concrete plan. "A small group has a better chance of avoiding detection. We will get in and do our best to free whatever people seek it, or hinder the vampires' plans as best as possible."

"Heh," Fixxer chortled, "That's assuming that we last until dawn. Things'll only be able to feed in the dark. Feeding in daylight turns their stomachs."

Shimza shook his head. "I still don't think that they'll attack tonight. We won't see anything more than a scout if anything. Lilth's children are calculating. Cold. They won't come down just yet, not until they've assessed our new allies' strengths."

"We'll be well away tomorrow morning," Jaylen promised. "We will pray for your success," he said heavy-heartedly.

"For now," Werthen stated, "We pray for time... and an early dawn."

***

Dyule paced around the garrison headquarters as if his appointment was beneath him. Every furnishing appeared to upset Jand's newly ordained king.

Pinchôt grimaced at the foppish air that he'd suddenly adopted. The former ranger rolled his eyes knowing that Dyule was doomed to follow in Harmarty's self-indulgent ways.

Krimko shot Pinchôt a sly glance as Dyule prattled about, trying to find a seat that didn't offend his royal buttocks. Pinchôt had never disguised his disdain for the bureaucrat turned king. He couldn't quite understand why the last son of the great Rogis had fawned so greatly over Pinchôt.

"Do you suddenly find Grinden so disagreeable?" Pinchôt scowled at the royal popinjay.

Dyule finally found a chair and sat, feigning contentedness at the seat. "Quite contrary, my dear friend. The only thing that I find disagreeable about my humble beginnings is the fact that this madman, Rashnir, still draws breath."

"I've no love lost for him, either," Pinchôt started.

"Was it *your* father who was murdered by this brigand? I thought not! Why is this man not delivered to my dungeon for torture?"

"We've captured several of these anti-Luciferians," Krimko interjected with a giggle, reminding himself of their doomed fate. "Many of Rashnir's loved ones burned alive in the prison fire before the krist-chins fled."

"And that justifies it? My entire family burned at Rashnir's first betrayal! I can never be sated until that scum becomes my personal object of torture! I want him, and I want him alive!" Flecks of white spittle flew from Dyule's lips as he ranted.

"And how will you hold this one in your prison?" Pinchôt stated the obvious. "He's escaped the royal dungeon before, and that was *before* he had these mystic powers. He'll just cut his way out with that magic blade of his."

"I said alive, not intact," Dyule spat. He wiped the drool leakage from his lip. "Cut his arms off if need be!"

"Is this obsession really the wisest use of Jand's resources?" Pinchôt crossed his arms in disgust.

"*Are you suddenly a sympathizer?* This man is single-handedly responsible for the deaths of my entire family and the last two monarchs... and you think it wise to leave him on the loose? Rashnir is the Scourge of Grinden! More than just the murders he has gutted the Grinden district's population and economy! Now *you*, my most trusted bodyguard and friend come to his aid?"

Krimko stepped between Dyule and Pinchôt. The fighter's wild eyes betrayed the fact that he was about to assassinate the new king himself.

"That's not what Pinchôt is saying, my King. I think he's getting at a new idea that I've been mulling over, myself. Perhaps the best way to expunge this threat from memory is to offer a bounty on all known krist-chins. On top of that, perhaps you should form a special group whose sole mission is to extract your revenge upon this dangerous sect."

Dyule gave him an intrigued look, suddenly calmed by the idea. Pinchôt also glanced at the Luciferian, curiosity written upon his face as well.

"Let me explain. We know that these cultists regard each other as family, like brothers and sisters— adopted by their god, as if such a thing were possible," he scoffed. "Rashnir has claimed a new family, a large family with many members you can use as pawns for your revenge. Keep avenging your cause. Let us form an elite unit, a group of specialists who will systematically destroy whatever pockets krist-chin cultists arise."

"And you will bring me Rashnir, alive!" Dyule demanded.

"Eventually, yes. That is our ultimate goal. But this team will hunt down these dissidents wherever they are uncovered until they can find and bring him to justice."

"I like this idea," Dyule pondered aloud, tapping his fingertips against each other.

"I knew you would. In fact, I've already started putting together such a team to anticipate you. But," Krimko gave Pinchôt a sidelong glance, "You would need to free your servants present to this endeavor."

The king hesitated and glanced at his two favorite escorts. Reluctance scrawled across his forehead as he thought it over.

"You have Zilke. He can take over as your primary Luciferian advisor. He's quite agreeable, for a goblin—very humanized due to his upbringing. And you have plenty of military support to pick a new bodyguard from."

Pinchôt interjected his own thoughts. "You cannot cage an eagle and expect him to remain a good a hunter. I am a hunter; release me to extract your vengeance."

Dyule finally nodded. "So be it. Burn my enemies alive; my resources are yours for the efforts. Bring me the skins of krist-chins and send the word. I will hang curtains in the royal palace made from my enemies."

The king stood and shook the dust off his feet. "Form your krist-chin death-squad; just bring me Rashnir," he stated flatly as he left the garrison.

Pinchôt stood there, flabbergasted. He couldn't figure out how Krimko had gotten Dyule to release him from his service. Obviously, the king's hatred of Rashnir was stronger than his insane attachment to the hunter.

"Come," Krimko slapped him on the back, shaking him from his bewilderment. "Welcome to the Death-Squad. I have something to show you."

***

Rashnir leaned closer to the fire as it popped and hissed near his feet. "You're still missing the point, Sim-khaw'." He squinted and rubbed his eyes when the smoke singed away what little moisture remained in them. Rashnir hadn't slept much, haunted by something he couldn't seem to identify.

"Why do you say this?" the werewolf argued from his human form. He nodded to Zeh-Ahbe' who sat next to him. "He can change into this greater form. He has evolved, somehow. Obviously, I believe in whatever power or god that can cause this. I wholeheartedly accept that! But whenever I transform, I am still just Sim-khaw', leader of the Zaw-nawb'."

"My friend," Zeh-Ahbe' spoke honestly, "It is only the power that you are seeking. Yahweh does not release blessings to you because you do not truly commit to Him. It is an issue of the heart, not mind."

"My heart is true! I will take the scald and endure the trials of any deity that can empower me as he does you. I will pay any price!"

"But *there is no price*... You are not seeking Him," Rashnir stressed. "You are merely seeking the *power*. God is a person, and He is jealous for hearts; He does not care about payment or duty."

Sim-khaw' screwed up his face in confusion. "Explain."

"Let's say that you developed a friendship with a kinsman who did not have much, but you had plenty to spare. This kinsman asks to borrow an item from you and so you give it to him. He later asks for another and another. You comply because this is your friend. You later ask him to mind your fire while you go hunt, but he refuses. What do you say?"

"He is no friend; he is a parasite and the worst of kinsmen. I want my items back because he was untrue!"

"And that is exactly what is happening here. You are asking for something from God, and yet you an untrue friend. You are merely asking to receive *His things.*"

"This is futile." Sim-khaw' stood to his feet and paced a few steps in either direction. "How does this help the Kil-yaw'?"

"It's not about the Kil-yaw'," Zeh-Ahbe' stated. "This is about *you.* This is about a personal god wanting to know you. He did not come for the Kil-yaw', He came for *you.* Just you. The man you are and were before taking the scald and joining the clan."

Sim-khaw' fidgeted. He seemed like he wanted to say something, but then closed his mouth and shifted topics. Separating his identity from the community he'd been raised within was difficult and uncomfortable. "Where will you take your group next?"

Rashnir had been talking about moving their people soon. The longer they lingered in any particular area, the greater the chance that Luciferians would come against them… or of wearing out their welcome.

"I'm not really sure, just yet."

"Well," Sim-khaw' growled, "You certainly tend to garner a lot of interest." His joints began to pop and groan as he let his lycan form expand his humanoid body. Sinew and muscle stretched until he transformed into a bulging hulk, shaggy with coarse wolf hair that hung lank and oily.

Zeh-Ahbe' and Rashnir both stood to scan the horizon.

"I see them," Rashnir sighed.

"Them?" Zeh-Ahbe' asked.

Rashnir pointed in the opposite direction that the werewolves were looking. Camouflaged in a grove of scrub brush the three female assassins monitored Rashnir's activities.

Zeh-Ahbe' turned his friend's head and pointed in the opposite direction. In the far distance, barely discernable, one lone, cloaked figure stood in the open— the tall, cloaked figure looked like Jorge of Kyrius but made both lycans' hair bristle. Something deep within Rashnir knotted his guts with an ill omen. That feeling of dread that had kept him from sleep deep into the previous night reawakened in the pit of his stomach.

***

Nothing moved on the landscape except for smoky bursts of sand that blasted across the wastes surrounding High Town. Werthen and Vil-yay crept through the rocky goat paths that Shimza and Fixxer led them along.

"How much further?" Vil-yay asked, skirting a skeletal copse of dead bracken.

"Not much. This trail meanders up to the rear walls. Looks like there used to be some pasture land back there before the grass burned up and the town shut down. The only goats left around here now are fertilizer." Fixxer kicked a desiccated heap to emphasize his point. Flies abandoned the remains and buzzed in a swarming flurry for a second before dissipating.

"And you're *sure* it's unguarded?"

"Why would any part be guarded?" Shimza gave them a wry look. "It's the most boring part of the town, and the least glamorous."

Werthen asked in confusion, "But isn't that a reason to guard it?" He scanned the walls again, as he had all day while following. They had hoped to avoid detection in the confusion of their people's withdrawal. Of course, if they *were* being watched, that would further improve the Christians chances of leaving unmolested and it would make sure their certain deaths meant something.

Fixxer muttered solemnly, "One would think so, but you have to understand vampires. Lilth and her kind are all about status: they thrive on adoration and addiction. My guess is that anyone left in town besides the mining proles will have been turned... become a ghoul by now. They are slaves to the feeding... being chosen to donate blood to their lords. It's an honor to serve the elder Adamic or wendigo masters. Ghouls desperately crave a master's acceptance; they *need* to become a Wendigo. Their blood feels like it boils at the thought that they won't be chosen. It's emotional anguish for them.

"Still, menial tasks and posts abhor them. Ghouls want to stay as close to the prestige as possible as they look for ways to draw their master's accolades. And yet, in the end, they become the foot soldiers of their lords, doing exactly what they hate in hopes to gain what they love."

Ahead, a wall had crumbled and broken. What had once been the livestock gate lay decimated; a tall pile of broken stones barred their path. It rose almost as tall as the city walls.

"I think your door is broken," Werthen said.

"Nope, it's just how we left it," Shimza said.

"*Exactly* how we left it." Fixxer turned a dismembered figure over with his foot and noted the face. "He's got skin still, the Wendigo haven't been out here. Likely they got ghouls scavenging for em too. They haven't been out this way since the earlier revolt."

Shimza whispered, indicating to keep as quiet as possible as they got closer. "We're going over the pile. I don't think we'll be seen... and it's stealthier than knocking on the front door."

The four climbed swiftly and quietly over the rubble heap and inside the walls. Most of the stones were hand-hewn: debris pulled from the mines. Within, more piles of fragmented dross filled the grounds.

"Sure are a whole lot more of these." Shimza caught Vil-yay's look. "The mines have run out of room to dump the waste with such hurried excavation... This way."

Shimza led them through the maze of rubbish and then through a labyrinth of derelict shanties. Soon they walked in shadows that had grown long.

The hunters scowled as they glanced at the skyline. Moving silently took too long and the journey up the slope to High-Town had stretched out into the afternoon. The sun crept towards the horizon more quickly than any of them cared for.

They quickened their pace through Granik's ghetto. Distant clanging sounds echoed across the town as the foundries rolled out new tools.

"What are we looking for?" Werthen dared a whisper.

"I marked the shack where they held us and stowed our gear when we were captured during an earlier uprising. We have to find it." Shimza scanned the nearby buildings, mostly livestock shacks.

Vil-yay looked up at the sky. "But it's getting dark. Won't that increase our chances of encountering enemies?"

Mangled bodies of slaves lay in random locations as they drove deeper into High-Town. Flesh had been ripped from them, leaving only skeletal remains wearing tattered tissue and, occasionally, shackles.

"We were likely to find em no matter what. But yeah, we better hurry. They keep their slaves nearby and we don't wanna meet a Wendigo unarmed. They like fresh meat much better."

"And an elder... an Adamic vampire?" Vil-yay gave Shimza a skeptical look.

Shimza looked at the smaller man as if he might stand a chance. "You're Say-awr, right?"

"Yes."

"Then never." Shimza pointed to a crumbling shack. "There it is." A long chalk scribbling painted the corner of one nearby building. "I doubt any Say-awr could stand long against an elder. Maybe you could take an unsuspecting wendigo... if you were lucky."

They crept up to the wall and peered through the casements. Wrought iron bars crisscrossed the windows. The small building appeared unoccupied.

Like wraiths, the four stole inside silently. Shimza immediately began rifling through a pile of gear that lay in the middle of the room. He and Fixxer started reclaiming all the things they'd lost.

Suddenly the door burst open.

A gray, hairless man stepped inside. He carried a gnawed-on human arm and blood dripped from his distended mouth. Hissing a shrill scream, the monster brandished his knife-like claws. The ashen undead charged forward.

"Wendigo!" Shimza snapped. He dove under the monster's lightning quick slash and frantically searched for any ready weapon around the room.

The wendigo leaped for the bounty hunter, but slammed to the floor in a cloud of splinters—snatched midair by a nine-foot, hulking mass of fur and muscle. Tiny sigils shined like silver sheen as the lycan's muscles rippled.

Before it could react, Vil-yay seized the surprised vampire with both hands and smashed him down upon his up-thrust knee, breaking the fiend in two. Sick mud splattered from two writhing halves of their attacker and Vil-yay dropped them to the floor before the filth leaked the stuff everywhere.

Crawling frantically, the cadaveresque entity tried to scramble away as Shimza found a wooden stake within the pile. "Got it! Don't let that thing get away."

Vil-yay snatched the torso section as it tried scrambling for the door, clearly outmatched. He dug his razor-sharp claws into the chest cavity and yanked his grip wide; muddy gore flung everywhere. With a distinct thump, a glass orb clattered against the wooden sub-flooring.

"Say-awr, huh?" Shimza gave Vil-yay a surprised but approving nod.

"Don't judge us by what you think you know. We broke from the Kil-yaw' and pursued a greater calling. Now, we serve a higher power."

The bounty hunters merely nodded.

"Quick, let me show you this." Fixxer showed them that the shredded body pieces of the Wendigo still twitched. Evil magics within them called out to each other, trying to reform. "This is a new Wendigo. His human body is still dying, so he wasn't very powerful... at least not yet. These things normally look like normal people instead of revenants, animated corpses: those are the vampire's foot soldiers. When the turning process is completed, the vamp's guts turn to dust. Stinkin things bleed sand."

"And what's this?" Werthen asked, tapping the orb. It seemed to glow with an internal, electric mist. It shimmered in tandem with the scattered body parts pulsing.

"The captured soul of a dead man. Gotta break it to really kill a wendigo, otherwise, they'll just get back up in a few hours." Fixxer stomped on the orb as hard as he could. Nothing happened. He bent down and stabbed the thing with a dagger he'd retrieved from the pile. The orb seemed impervious. "Now watch."

Shimza took his stake and easily pierced the orb. The wooden tip popped it like a knife through a soap bubble. The rattling stopped. "Only certain kinds of trees work. The bright ones: trees from good forests. Ancient lore says the trees from the earth realm alone can pierce their souls. These orbs reside where the man's heart once was."

Vil-yay looked at Werthen. "Kevin spoke of trees and animals that came over here from Earth. If Yahweh created them, perhaps they have greater power here in this realm?"

Shimza nodded. "Perhaps. It might be a good theory... if I believed in your god."

Fixxer prattled about excitedly as he rummaged in the pile. Shimza continued explaining the situation. "If there are new wendigo here, then there are definitely elder vampires here. Only the Adamic line can make new wendigo... although wendigo can create ghouls and revenants."

The old inventor procured a large metal and wood contraption. "I think we're almost ready to set out." He swung the large, metal barrel of the device around as if pointing it at imaginary foes.

"What is that thing?"

Fixxer grinned ear to ear maniacally. "Alchemical boom-stick. I call it The Arbalist!"

***

Something reached through the darkness and tagged his head, jarring it against a jagged stone and opening a fresh cut. Blood seeped through the preacher's bindings and down onto the body of the writhing skolax.

Kevin didn't know how long he'd been traveling. He couldn't see anything except the dull, silver shine of his captors' eyes.

Wracked by pain, the aches in his body were nothing compared to the turmoil rooted in his gut. Cuts and bruises couldn't compare to the uncertainty of what might happen to him next.

He spat out the dirt and grime from his bloody mouth. His tongue, raw from biting it while his transport jostled him, had swollen between his cheeks.

You never said it was going to be like this, Lord!

Kevin's angry mind sunk with a moment of self-pity. Sorrow took his heart for a moment before he seized it and brought it back from the brink. *I knew this could happen. Torture and death doesn't change the nature of God.*

He sighed and closed his eyes against the painful dark, remembering happier times. After so much time in hay-lale's fallen realm, his previous life seemed abstract as he conjured up memories of his life before. Family, friends, and life, in general, had seemed so normal before, but now it felt so foreign.

Kevin's mind couldn't seem to make sense of it. It argued that one of those two lives had been a dream. His flesh lied to him, Kevin knew. They were both very real. He just wished that he could see a glimmer of light to give him hope.

The musty air tasted foul and fetid and the chattering of his kidnappers sounded like an orcish dialect. Kevin needed *something* to relieve his restless mind.

Time stretched forever long in the violent darkness. Then, a faint light glowed nearby. A hot, red sickle shone as a Luciferian acolyte's kama neared the preacher's face. The sparse illumination revealed little about the assassin except for his displeasure at the captive's consciousness.

Tied where he was, Kevin could not resist as the acolyte unstopped a flask and poured the vile, thick fluid into his mouth. Squeezing Kevin's lips so that he couldn't spew it out, he punched the preacher in the stomach. Kevin gagged as he reflexively swallowed.

It only took seconds for the elixir to numb Kevin's mind. Moments later, his mind reeled in the blackness and he fell unconscious.

***

Pinchôt stood slack-jawed before the mountain of a man who had once been his partner. Grirrg stood motionless and breathless while Pinchôt circled him, noting the paled flesh and stitched skin where he'd been sliced open in battle by Rashnir's friends, Werthen and Rondhale.

The barbarian stood straight and tall. He was naked except for a crude loincloth and a few pieces of odd armor that appeared either bolted on or grafted into his flesh. An odd contraption clung to his chest, encasing the breastbone of his torso with dark machinations. It looked like legs of a golden crab caging his heart.

Despite the modifications, there was no mistaking the identity of this celebrated warrior.

"Is it really you?" Pinchôt stared in wonder.

"It is I," Grirrg replied with automaton disinterest.

"We've done our best to preserve his flesh," Krimko noted, fingering a section of the barbarian's back where some other man's skin had been stretched across and pinned over the wound. "Parts of the decay were irreversible but we've done our best to restore him to a fully functional state."

"Functional?"

"Well yes. Grirrg is dead, but he's not gone." Krimko glanced upwards at the behemoth's empty eyes. "He's lost his emotions, parts of his 'personality.' But his memories, skills, and talents are all still there… inside. You will find him as reliable a partner as you ever had. But perhaps more of a tool than a friend." The Luciferian retrieved a wooden crate from nearby and opened it to Pinchôt. "His soul might be gone, but most of him... the important parts still remain."

Bent low, Krimko dragged out a heavy war-hammer. His pair of prized hammers had been Grirrg's favorite weapons. He had wielded one up until the day he died in the quarry battle. The Luciferian had somehow acquired the spare.

Pinchôt took it by the handle; further amazed by the gift Krimko had given him. "Truly, you are the friend I've lost since Grinden." He rummaged through the crate filled with various weapons and personal effects from the Narsh Barbarian armory that would help make Grirrg battle ready.

"There is more," Krimko stated, producing a small bottle from his pocket. It was filled with a glittering, metallic looking unction that emanated a peculiar power. It radiated energy like the air near a lightning strike. "This is a spare vial of nawchash. Quickly, take it. Hide it on your person. It is too valuable to see daylight where any random spirit or demon might glimpse it or any seer might discern what it is and seek to steal it."

Pinchôt promptly pocketed the potion. The warning was so grave that it overwhelmed his curiosity.

"Let me show you this marvelous device, invented long ago in a foreign land. This, my friend, is called the Khay-hee." Krimko walked around Grirrg, who stood tall and motionless, a passive weapon waiting to be activated.

Light glinted off the device's encasement as Pinchôt examined it. The artifact appeared to have been fused into the barbarian's body. A steel medallion poked through his sternum where a glassine, shimmering jewel was mounted; metallic tubes sprouted off of the artifact like segmented legs attached to an arachnid body. Pinchôt laid his finger on the tubes; they pulsed with the gentle hum of internal movement.

"They are filled with 'ãbêdâh serum," Krimko grinned ear to ear with a devious smirk. "It courses through Grirrg's veins!"

A slow, knowing smile pulled at the corner of Pinchôt's lips. "I have made him a literal juggernaut." Pinchôt placed the war hammer into Grirrg's massive hand.

The barbarian turned and looked at Pinchôt. His hollow, vacant eyes burned cold and empty, yet as fully ready for battle as he'd ever been.

"How soon before we are ready to start tracking down rebels?"

"We've just got to pick a few additional men and gather supplies," Krimko stated. "I've already had some provisions and weapons prepared with an executive order from Dyule."

Pinchôt smiled deviously. "Then let's go hunting."

***

The day drew late and, despite Rashnir's premonitions, no ill fate had befallen them. He and Zeh-Ahbe' monitored the camp for hazards all day. Despite her threats, Ly'Orra and her companions remained out of sight; they appeared to have left, possibly gathering information and formulating a strategy for future strikes.

In the distance, the other danger lingered. The watcher remained on the crest of the hilltop. Building a fire, the pseudo-angelic figure waited.

Rashnir watched the cloaked creature with an unsettled heart. Something about him was not right, and the warrior's soul buzzed with a warning that burned deep inside his chest. A spiritual heaviness fell on him whenever Rashnir checked on him from afar.

"What have you decided," Zeh-Ahbe' asked him.

Rashnir sighed, wishing he knew something, anything, about the thing lurking on the horizon. "We should go out and confront this entity."

Zeh-Ahbe' nodded. "It's better to face him in the daylight than in the dark, should things go ill."

"Exactly. Let me make arrangements for Jibbin with others... just in case." His silence spoke enough. Whatever the creature on the hill was, they agreed that it was not human, and assumed it might be some kind of demon, though it did not carry itself like the minor fiends that they'd faced so far.

"I will have Sim-khaw' watch us from the distance. His senses will be the best; he can, perhaps, give the group an advanced warning if this turns out hostile or launches an attack on our people."

Rashnir nodded his approval. Minutes later, he and Zeh-Ahbe' strode up the hill's approach. The hooded figure stood to greet them. In fact, it appeared as if he'd been waiting for them to do exactly this.

"My name is EXERITHIA," he stated cordially. "I didn't want to alarm you and your group, so I thought it best to wait in the distance."

The two Christians returned the demonic creature's look with a skeptical glance. They still kept their distance, remembering their Grinden battle with beh'-tsah.

"I would answer any questions that you have, but there is too little time. Your friend is grave danger."

Careful not to touch it, he reached inside his cloak and procured a thick tome, bound in heavy burlap cloths, Kevin's Bible. It hung from the ropes ekerithia had tied around it as a handle.

"I hope that this is sufficient evidence to prove my words."

"What?" Rashnir's face fell aghast with dread. The doom seated in the pit of his stomach roared back to life, amplified a thousand times. "How did you get this?"

"I found it in the goblin tunnels under Sprazik, or what is left of Sprazik. The entire town has been annihilated by the Luciferian Order. They captured your friend ...my friend."

"Kevin would never befriend a demon," Rashnir snapped, snatching the book away from the demon.

"Life is more than our mere alliances," ekerithia replied. "Life is made up of our choices, and I chose to put my friendship in his hands. *He must live.* He has made a promise to me, one that he must survive if he is to accomplish it."

"But you're a demon," Zeh-Ahbe' stated as if some reminder was needed.

"And I often wish it were not so; and to his credit, Kevin made this promise to me *before* I became as I am now."

The fair-skinned demon shifted gears, controlling the conversation and not wanting to have to explain how that change came to pass.

"There is something that you should all know, the world of demons, and their precious Babel, is not as unified as you believe. I say this in strictest confidence, assuming that you, Kevin's most trusted friends, are as trustworthy as he.

The strongholds of the Gathering will soon come falling down.
The destruction will come sooner rather than later."

Rashnir bit his lip and nodded. Something in his spirit confirmed the truth of the entity's story. "Tell us what happened."

Briefly, ekerithia summarized the events of the Sprazik attack and his assumptions that they would transport Kevin to beh'-tsah, the chief of the Gathering. They would bring Kevin to Babel.

"First, they will take him through the underground labyrinth, a vast network of tunnels crafted before the first men set foot in this realm. They will ascend the tower at the Temple of Light and carry your friend to their central stronghold. Likely, they will take him to the demon's feasting table."

Rashnir bit his lower lip in consternation. He couldn't imagine trusting a demon, but the longer he held onto his friend's Bible, the heavier it seemed to weigh. Everything within urged him to fly at once and rescue his friend and mentor. Rashnir knew that his mind would debate his heart over and over, even win the argument and insist that he remain with the people he'd been commissioned to lead. But he also knew that his heart had already decided on a course of action.

Everything within him urged the ranger to rescue his lost friend.

Chapter Nine

Absinthium's nostrils burned as the acrid smoke bit at the tissue walls. Tears ran down his cheeks and the wizard's eyelids fluttered but he did not pull his head away from the bowl of smoldering embers. Pushing through the white-hot pain in his senses, he found the silver cord that he searched for.

Grasping the power he sought, he mixed it with the dark fuel of his demon-master and plunged into a hazy vision, discerning the future. His spell would not show him exactly what he *wanted* to see as much as it would reveal what he *needed* to see to achieve victory.

Sweat poured from his physical body, but Absinthium paid it no mind. The more he recognized it, the more it translated through the smoke he scryed, giving everyone a liquid-like appearance.

The arch-mage stood with arms crossed, powerful. A liquefied version of the dark lord towered nearby, cowing Rashnir, that once-cursed warrior. The environment surprised him; they were in Babel, at the spire's gate. With that realization, everything else suddenly became more real and the vision seized the mage's full consciousness.

"Get out of here!" the werewolf coughed and spluttered, spitting through the bloody drool that gurgled up from within.

Rashnir stared at his friend, panicked. Kevin lay on the ground just behind the two warriors. Freshly cut manacles still clung to the preacher's limp wrists. "Run, Zeh-Ahbe', I'll hold them off!"

Looming above them, the demon laughed at the impotent courage of his captured mortals. Nothing could save them and Absinthium could nearly taste the victory.

"Go!" Zeh-Ahbe' charged at the monster even as blood sputtered from the gaping wound in his midsection.

The werewolf staggered and lurched as he closed the gap. Snarling, beh'-tsah sliced Zeh-Ahbe's feet from under him and stomped the lycan into the ground, breaking him open with a sickly, cracking and squishing sound.

Bellowing with victory, the Dark Lord of the Gathering charged towards the remaining humans. Spitting fire and flaring his wings wide, beh'-tsah slammed into the ranger, bringing his blade crashing to the ground with enough force to split a mountain. Flames erupted with volcanic fury and the ground shook, but it was the point of an azure blade piercing through his master's spine that lodged in Absinthium's terror-stricken eyes.

Wounded and bloodied, Rashnir stumbled from under the lurching fiend. Absinthium screamed as beh'-tsah slumped to his side while the ranger triumphantly severed the demon's head. That dreaded blue flame melted beh'-tsah's skull to slag, evaporating it like mist—no spell existed that could revive him from such a condition!

The vision began to fade and Absinthium shook with hatred. Fear burned through his veins. Even as the supernatural sight darkened he watched the ranger and preacher descend the spire and escape the clutches of the

Gathering. Soon, he saw only smoke, then the inside of his closed eyelids.

Absinthium vomited the last remaining fluids from his stomach and discarded his sweat-soaked robes before smashing the incense to the floor. He chugged from a jar of water to replenish his body before dehydration set in.

Terror lodged deep in his chest. He had to stop this vision from coming to pass. The Arch-Mage saw not victory but defeat in his vision. Rashnir would kill his master unless he intervened.

The ranger had to be stopped by any means possible. Existence's most dangerous warrior was scheduled by fate to destroy the mighty beh'-tsah. A trap had to be laid, and the perfect bait already languished in his master's dungeon.

***

Trailed by four of her advisors, Elo'misce ducked below a damp, rotting beam. Darkness enveloped the elves and the fetid smell of decomposing wood filled their nostrils. This mining shaft had obviously been abandoned for a long time and for good reasons.

Pressing through the blackness and towards the sound of trickling water, they finally arrived at their appointment. A faint glow lit the center of a large, rough-hewn chamber. Someone had cobbled together a makeshift chair at the center by the light. A single goblin sat alone in the middle of the luminous halo.

Elo'misce and her men walked into the light. A cracking rumble briefly trembled from within the shadows as the ground shifted minutely. "Is this location safe?"

"It is less safe than usual," a new goblin voice spoke from the darkness.

"Who are you?" Elo'misce demanded.

The quick sounds of bowstrings snapping sprung up all around and the goblin on the chair fell over dead, pierced from every side. The elves recoiled in surprise. Without harming any of the elves, the under-dwellers' display made it abundantly clear: the goblins could kill them on a whim.

"I am the reason you have come to power, Elo'misce. It was I who decided Mar'zal was unworthy. I am the true king and engineer behind everything happening in Gleend." grr'Shaalg stepped into the light and seated himself on the chair. He kicked his feet up on the dead creature's body, nonchalantly using him as a footstool. "He was disposable, and a demonstration was needed for you to know the gravity of your situation. I present you with a choice. This same bargain was struck with Bwar after Mar'zal refused."

Elo'misce glanced at her men. She couldn't read any of their stony expressions… not in this low light. "I'm listening," she flatly stated.

"My forces are already on the move," grr'Shaalg said.

She gave him a cold, inquisitive stare.

"I know what it is that you want: a nation without human influence. I am poised to give that to you, to tip the scales of this civil war in your favor."

"What I want is the total supremacy of the Elven Empire," Elo'misce clarified.

"Of course," grr'Shaalg leaned back upon the simple throne. "And eradicating the humans is the first stage of that grand plan. I envision a new Gleend emerging from the ashes of this war that I've engineered."

The elf gave him a wry look.

"Yes, it was my plan all along. I used the Luciferians to stoke the fire of malcontent, arranged for the assassination of the royal line, and organized the ekthroic cleansing teams who now patrol the lands, eliminating humans. You see, in the new Gleend, the Elven race will control the dirt above ground, and the dwarves will return below ground to the halls they once prized before we cast them out into the sun."

"And the goblins? Surely you cannot dictate to the other under-kingdoms such terms: force them to surrender the subterranean territory below Gleend."

Squinting at her, grr'Shaalg replied, "I *AM*, the goblin empire. My every word is law and my plans become reality. I am the Shadow King and I rule all in the firmament below your feet."

"I'm sorry," Elo'misce offered a terse, political apology. "I didn't mean that you lacked the authority. I wondered where you would send your own kind. Where will the goblins relocate to; why would they surrender the area?"

"I have loftier goals than the dirt above or below Gleend," grr'Shaalg retorted. "This is merely one phase in a larger plot against higher kingdoms."

Elo'misce nodded, seeming to accept his vague answer for what it was. "How will you ensure that we will retain this land? Dwarves have become accustomed to life under the skies; many of them may want to occupy *both* realms."

The goblin snapped his claws and two smaller whelps pranced into the flame light. They carried a long parchment that they quickly unrolled and held perpendicular to the ground, displaying a detailed cartography of Gleend's borders and landmarks.

"You see your beloved country, yes? The lands crawl with the bearded oafs," grr'Shaalg taunted. "What if there was a way to eradicate nearly all of them in one swift maneuver?"

"Wipe them out. Genocide. Yes," she cocked an inquisitive eyebrow, "our people would rejoice if someone did such an act, but that kind of campaign could never be waged in the short-term. It could never happen; they are as vigilant as the elves are suspicious."

"You're not thinking deviously enough," grr'Shaalg clacked his talons against the arm of his chair.

"Our alchemists have tried poisons and diseases. The dwarven constitution is too hardy."

The goblin lifted off his throne and stepped in front of the map. "Do you not know the history of the Drindak Canyons? I thought the longevity of the elves would surely lead to a longer memory of their lands and historical deeds."

Elo'misce gave him a severe look to hide her confusion.

"Surely the sheer, vertical cliffs of the canyon walls should be a clue. Most of Gleend rests upon the edge of a knife. The crust of the land at these marked points is suspended upon giant support pillars. I have seen them myself. These circled points on the map are the substructures that were altered millennia ago when the canyon was formed—part of an argument between powers far older and greater than yours or mine.

"With the proper leverage and power, large tracts of land can be dropped vertically, collapsing upon everything inside the crust, entombing all within."

A malicious spark lit behind Elo'misce's eyes. "Yes," she planned aloud. Return the dwarves to their home realm; honor them at a gathering in their native tract. Collect them in one central location to pay tribute and then crush them all with minimal surface displacement."

The insatiable elf turned to her peers. They all nodded in agreement, just as eager for such a plan as she.

"Do we have an agreement, Elo'misce?"

"Yes," she nodded vigorously. "If you can deliver on such a plan, then we will ally with you."

"Excellent," grr'Shaalg clapped his scaly hands together. Blades glinted in the dark as goblin assassins seized all of Elo'misce's peers. The elven consort stood rigidly, not provoking their captors.

"My lady?" one asked, pleading for intervention.

Elo'misce looked from his eyes to grr'Shaalg's. "What is this, Shadow King?"

"Surely you understand the need for security and secrecy," grr'Shaalg cooed. "We cannot have any potential loose ends."

The elven diplomat looked back at her men and understood. grr'Shaalg was right, the need for secrecy was too great. She trusted her four men—but she her appointment had been relatively new… she did not *know* these men.

"We will treat them as we treat all of our prisoners," grr'Shaalg promised her, giving her a glimmer of hope for her comrades.

Elo'misce nodded. She turned on her heels and walked towards the cave's exit, refusing eye contact with her people. Ultimately, she knew that *they were all* expendable in the face of a lofty notion like the eradication of both humans and dwarves in her country.

"We will send someone to contact you in the near future," grr'Shaalg called after her through the dark. "...my lady."

As the shadows ebbed at the mouth of the cave, the bloodcurdling shrieks of her captured elves barely reached the tips of her ears. She dusted the subterranean grime from her fine, diplomatic garb and left for Xorst.

With the burgeoning light, her feet found fresh resolve and renewed strength. Under Elo'misce's guidance and solid elven leadership, Gleend would be purged.

***

As suddenly as ekerithia had come into their presence, he melted away, leaving Rashnir and Zeh-Ahbe' with the incredible burden of knowledge regarding Kevin's fate. Their leader would be brutally murdered if they did not somehow intervene.

Rashnir hurried back and began stuffing supplies into his pack. He flung a cloak around his shoulders as if he might depart at any moment. Kicking open his tent flap in such a hurry, he matched Zeh-Ahbe' pace for pace.

"Don't try to stop me," Rashnir told the werewolf. "I'm going to rescue him."

"Don't *you* try to stop *me*," Zeh-Ahbe' retorted. A similar travel pack hung from his shoulders as well. "Somebody must stay here to lead the people."

"I'm going. I've already made arrangements."

Zeh-Ahbe' feigned a hurt ego. "Well not with me? I thought I'd be the most qualified. Didn't that even cross your mind?"

"As if I doubted you could be convinced to stay behind. This is Kevin, after all."

The duo walked through the camp with an intent purpose. The rest of their company watched them, understanding some great task lay before them, but unaware what it was.

"You don't think that we're just being played, do you, Rashnir?"

He stopped mid-stride and gave it a moment's thought. "It's possible. It's very possible. But something in my gut tells me that this ekerithia creature is telling the truth… at least in regard to Kevin: he's on his way to Babel."

"Then what's our plan?"

"Plan? Storm the gates of Babel and rip it from the sky if we have to—they have Kevin!" Rashnir bit his lip and grew more reasonable. "I don't know. There is no plan, but it's a long way to Briganik—I'm sure something will come to me before then. We'll see if we can get some horses as soon as possible."

Rashnir ducked inside a tent and Zeh-Ahbe' followed him. Jibbin sat on the floor with two other children. They stacked blocks into towers and tipped them over with squeals of delight.

The warrior scooped the child up as he laughed. Rashnir squeezed him in a tight hug. "I've got to go away for a few days, Jibbin. I don't know when I will be back."

"Why must you go?"

"Some nasty, bad guys have kidnapped Kevin."

"Kevin?" Jibbin snuggled in against Rashnir's neck, squeezing against him. "No! You've got to save him," he exclaimed. "You're Rashnir. Nothing can stop you."

"I certainly hope so." He swept back a mop of Jibbin's tousled hair and gave the boy a kiss on his forehead. "Be good. Mind Haisauce; he'll watch you until I return."

The child stood at the tent's entry and watched as Rashnir and Zeh-Ahbe' hastened to the edge of the encampment.

Sim-khaw' stood in their path. "You're leaving? Something that distant creature said has upset you?"

"A friend needs our help," Rashnir said.

"Then let me accompany you," Sim-khaw' insisted.

Rashnir and Zeh-Ahbe' traded hesitant looks. "We will only be gone a couple days," the Ranger promised.

"But you will need assistance. Surely, you will need all that you can get."

"Yes, but I'm sorry, Sim-khaw'. It is a matter of some secrecy and stealth. We really cannot take you with us. I'd really hoped to spend more time with you so we could answer all of your questions... to show you everything that you need to help you believe, but this is a matter of life and death to our friend."

"Please, stay until we return," Zeh-Ahbe' called as he walked backwards. "Can you do that?"

Sim-khaw' grimaced reluctantly, but he eventually nodded curtly.

Zeh-Ahbe' and Rashnir strode west, into the night. They left behind a village of friends and one bewildered werewolf.

***

From his perch on a tree limb, Elo'wiind seethed anger, spitting curses between stating data for his subordinate to record. Watching the Vignan humans and their interloping rescuers through a telescopic lens was almost too much for the elven general.

"Bring me my qâsam!" he barked to the lieutenant that stood behind him. "My sister must hear of this."

"Right away." The lieutenant stuffed his list into a deep pocket and leapt thirty feet to the ground where he snatched his superior's satchel. He returned to his place a few moments later where they spied their enemy from the broad branch.

Elo'wiind rummaged through the bag and pulled out a fistful of plush velvet. Unwrapping the heavy fabric, he exposed the seeing stone to the air and activated the gem. Only recently acquired, it had been his prized possession. Qâsamai were so rare, and he had gotten such a good price on the stones that he had to lie about its price to allay suspicions that he had stolen or killed for it.

After several unanswered attempts, the qâsam crystal finally linked to its mate.

"Elo'misce, what took you?" the general vented his frustrations with a rhetorical question.

"I have been rather preoccupied," Elo'misce stated blandly. "If you have called me, things either went very well or disastrously so."

"A route. A complete and total route," he cursed in the eleven black tongue. "The Vignans were rescued

255

by these antiluciferian heretics. They did not even number many, but they wielded a terrible power. Mostly, it was those headstrong dwarves that brought our downfall.

"The invaders wielded blades of flame and have formed an alliance with the werewolf clans. The beasts were massive, larger than my memory of them—it must be the Kaw-bade' clan."

"Calm yourself, brother. There is no army under the open sky that can defeat a properly prepared host of warrior elves. Continue monitoring the enemy; I will send you reinforcements, supplies, and a means to defeat them.

"Now tell me, Elo'wiind. What of the dwarven contingent that accompanied you?"

"Nothing. Completely destroyed. The idiots rushed ahead and ignored all sense of strategy. They broke ranks and found themselves inside the mouth of a dragon. Not one remains alive."

Elo'misce spat a curse. "I must find a way to spin this somehow to our advantage on the council floor. We will need proof, however. Capture either a Vignan or a krist-chin to validate your report or Bwar will publicly skewer us, politically."

Elo'wiind nodded his agreement and soothed the qâsam, quieting the signal. He wrapped the cloth back around the device and returned to his duties.

Very far away, a goblin worker grinned. The light waned from his spying qâsam. He let it sleep after a successful eavesdrop. His superiors would be pleased with the information he'd gleaned.

**

256

"I can feel their eyes on us," Raz-aphf said to Rondhale.

The blacksmith nodded, squinting against the acrid smoke that bit his eyes. Granik continued to smolder; blackened structures stood as if weary fighters, dreading another wave of battle.

"So much death and loss," Rondhale whispered under his breath as he surveyed the damaged village. He wrung his hands and thought of his brother.

The breeze held a deathly hallow and the sharp tang of smoke filled the air; Rondhale rubbed the soot taint from his nose. "How can you see or smell any of them?"

"I don't see or smell any of the attackers. I can *feel* them, though. Intuition. *They are there.*" Raz-aphf pointed to the distant trees. Elves are relentless when their pride is damaged.

The two turned back towards town. They had saved what they could.

"At least all the fires are out," he told Raz-aphf as they walked to the town's center where the Christians had planted their group. The only remaining well was there.

"That may be what worries me," Raz-aphf replied.

Rondhale shot him a quizzical look.

"The people. Look at them."

All around the streets of Vigna sat weary, soot-smeared residents. Their clothes were tattered and their eyes sank deeply... devoid of hope. They lay scattered like ragdolls dropped by some capricious child.

"We have to do something," Rondhale agreed, walking adjacent to the lengthy line of Vignans waiting their turn at the central well. Water had become the most necessary supply.

"Well, that's what we do," the werewolf quipped. "We bring hope and help."

With a sudden snap, the heavy, iron dowel in the well-house broke in two. The halves of the rod fell with their chains, clattering against the stone-reinforced walls and splashing into the water below.

The peoples' resolve snapped as well. Dejected, the residents responded in their own ways. Some wandered away; others merely sat and slumped over, waiting for either a miracle or death to take them. Those who remained in line looked more like a funeral procession than anything else.

"I have something that can repair this," Rondhale said. "Vignans!" he called out. "I am a blacksmith—I can fix this! Nobody will stay thirsty." He jogged to where he kept his personal belongings and retrieved a long package.

Unwrapping the parcel near the well, he brandished a long war hammer, the weapon that had killed his brother months earlier. The hammer's staff was made of a metal alloy, making it lighter and stronger than other, more common metals.

Raz-aphf eyed Rondhale as the blacksmith sized up the pole against the housing unit. It fit perfectly.

Rondhale returned the screwed up look. "I don't know why I kept it. It may have been morose, but it's exactly what we needed."

The lycan nodded. "It's perfect. Can you let it go, though?"

"Of course," he replied, affixing a new chain and bucket. "Now let's get these people some water." Rondhale paused, "And hope."

"That's exactly what's needed."

***

Krimko slipped inside the door, not bothering to knock. He never knocked. Announcing himself wasn't in his nature, he felt it beneath him. Krimko also secretly hoped to catch his contacts in situations that forced their loyalty to him and was always on the lookout for such scenarios.

Zilke placidly looked up from behind a desk. Hidden around a musty corner in the cellar office, the room was perfectly suited to goblins. Zilke's face didn't indicate surprise, but perhaps resentment. Krimko could never quite tell, goblins were hard for humans to read.

The sly Luciferian placed a heavy stack of parchments on the desk. "I'm here to instruct you on your new duties. You are being promoted to an advisory capacity." Krimko did his best to hide any shades of resentment in his voice; thousands of years of religious, xenological discrimination was hard to give up so quickly. "You are essentially taking over my previous role while I advance to a more intriguing office."

Zilke returned a steely stare. "I will aspire to the example you set," he said while leafing through the regulatory guidelines that Krimko had drawn up for him.

"The duties of your office will be quite simple," he started saying, indicating the papers. A faint pulsing light in the corner of the office interrupted the ranking mage.

Krimko arched a curious eyebrow. "You possess a qâsam? Answer it."

"It is a personal artifact. The call is likely of a private nature."

"My goblin language skills are rusty, albeit serviceable." The human kept his beady eyes locked on the goblin.

Zilke met his gaze for an uneasy moment and then retrieved the qâsam. After activating it, another goblin revealed himself through the stone. They all looked the same to Krimko

[Report,] Zilke said in his native tongue.

[Insurrection, my priest. I was told to inform you so that you can have the rogue cultists in Gleend tracked.]

[Krist-chins in Gleend? Where?] Zilke glanced away from the qâsam and to his superior. Krimko's full attention was on the stone.

[The town of Vigna. Krist-chins have taken it and fortified it against the elven and dwarven forces that are set against it. Human hostages are plentiful. Perhaps you can pass this information up the chain of command. Also, there has been sightings of heretics just south of the Gleendish border southwest of Vigna; Ninda hasn't committed any forces against it and it might be some time before they are even aware.]

[It is done.] Zilke assured him and severed the link. He turned to address Krimko, but the mage was pacing in deep thought.

"Yes, yes. This is perfect," he muttered to himself. Krimko had forgotten any notions of possible disloyalty. "The team can be made ready on short notice. Not only will Gleendish relations be furthered, but we can wipe out a nest of heretics and test my team under real battle conditions."

He paced and muttered for a few more moments. Finally, he stopped and turned to Zilke. "You have my instructions," he confirmed with one hand on the door.

"Yes," Zilke replied, gesturing to the sheaf of writings. "I am quite capable."

"Good. May Lucifer guide you," Krimko said flatly. "I have bigger things to accomplish."

***

Elo'misce looked up as her doorman rapped the distinct "urgent" pattern on her entrance. The wooden aperture swung open and her informant stepped inside. The elf looked saddle-worn as if he'd ridden long and hard to reach her. Even slicked by sweat and dust of the road he was fair and handsome with hazel, far-seeing eyes; he fit her exact preferences.

Her eyes twinkled as she bid him in. The gateman closed the door behind them and the rider greedily poured himself a cup of water from the pitcher on her table.

"What news," she demanded.

"Sprazik," he sputtered between gulps. "It's destroyed!"

"That news is a week old," she chided.

"No! *It was besieged again!* I reported previously how Havara had hidden there after fleeing Xorst. His allies from Grinden protected him when they arrived, but now the city is gone!"

"Disappeared? Like magically invisible?"

"No! Razed, obliterated. Havara's friends, these Krist-chins, have powerful enemies. An Arch-Mage arrived with his own army, plus a contingent of Jandish and Nindan soldiers."

Elo'misce turned to hide her surprise and work through her thoughts. "The Luciferians have a genocidal hatred of these Krist-chins," she muttered. "It must be more severe than even the racial divisions in Gleend."

"The battle was like none I've ever seen. The magics wielded by both sides literally destroyed the landscape. Nothing more remains at Sprazik but a smoking, charred crater. All flesh inside the city was disintegrated when it erupted. The most important part of my news is that Havara is dead—he was in the city."

She turned to her rugged spy. "Have you heard rumors that Havara had become one of these Krist-chins?"

Elo'misce was already sure of his answer. Perhaps she valued his opinion, but more likely, she subconsciously wanted to extend the conversation with her handsome asset.

He recognized her intent and the tips of his ears flushed when he nodded. "Yes. Everyone has heard that. His brother, Lo-Sonom, made a proclamation that he and his wives had each changed allegiance to this God of the Humans. It is logical that Havara joined them."

Elo'misce nodded. "It's true then, either in fact or by popular belief. Have the doorman get me my attaché." She quickly drew up a note and sealed it with her signet ring; she had her servant dispatch a messenger to the Temple of Light.

"This is excellent news," she told her spy. "You shall be rewarded greatly in my new empire." Elo'misce snapped her fingers and three elvish guards seized the informant and shackled him.

"What is the meaning of this," he demanded, shaking violently in his chains.

"It's just a safety precaution," she assured him. "I must detain you for a few days to make sure there are no information leaks. She shuddered to think of how the goblin shadow-king used alternative methods.

"Don't worry," she assured him, gently tracing his cheekbone with her forefinger. "I promised you a reward in due time and you have proved yourself as a valuable asset." The elven politician smiled at him and licked her upper lip. "I promise you will enjoy your stay."

Elo'misce turned to her guards and warned them. "Do not damage him. Detain him in my personal guest quarters. There is much to do immediately with this information, but I will come later to further... interrogate, our valued countryman..." She winked and trailed off, searching for a name.

"Bre," he inserted for her while relaxed against his captors. "Bre. Scout First-Class of Lars."

Elo'misce nodded. "I will see you as soon as my schedule clears, Bre of Lars."

***

Havara awoke with a wheezing cough as if dust lined his esophagus. "Water," he croaked through his thirst. The word felt like a blade unsheathing from his throat. With fuzzy vision, he scanned his surroundings.

He lay in a pile of rags near a small campfire; a wooden splint had been tied around his broken leg. He'd lived, so he surmised that friends must have found him. Then an elf stepped into view. Havara jumped to his good leg and fell over as his strength gave out.

"Havara! It's me, Dri'Bu," The elf called out as he ran to the King's side. He was no young elf, but the first elves defied all aging. Dri'Bu offered him a jug.

Havara rolled over and gladly accepted the water. He sucked it in, coughing and spluttering, soaking his tattered clothes. He didn't care.

"I suppose you probably can't recognize me," Dri'Bu chuckled waving the tatters of his once-fine robes. "Got news for you. You don't look so good either."

Water dribbled down his chin and Havara finally caught his breath. He looked up at the elf in surprise.

Purple and gray bruises swelled and marred his fair features. A large patch of Dri'Bu's light hair had been burnt away. "How long've I been out?"

"We found you a couple days ago in the ravine with a dead elven tracker."

"Did we stop em?" he asked weakly. "Sprazik? My people—are they…"

Dri'Bu only grimaced.

Havara shared a moment of silence with him. "Who else survived? Surely it's more than just you and I."

"Define 'survive.'" Jorge stepped near. The angel stooped over another bundle of bedding, changing the bandages of his patient.

Havara hadn't noticed Kyrius lying there until now. Again, he wondered aloud, "Kevin?"

Jorge shook his head negative. A grimace spoke volumes to the angel's pain. "Absinthium has taken him."

"And Kyrius?"

"Still unconscious," replied Dri'Bu. "But I think he will survive."

Havara struggled to his feet again. He tested the weight on his damaged leg and wished he hadn't, but he just couldn't stay seated. "There're still four of us. What are we going to do about Kevin?"

"Correction," Dri'Bu said, handing him another flask of water. "There's *maybe* two and a half of us at best."

"But what will they do to him?"

Jorge stood gazing into the horizon. Arms crossed, he set his jaw.

"They will likely torture him," Dri'Bu answered flatly. "There is no value in forcing him to recant, as if that could happen. Kevin has wounded the pride of Gathering, so there will be few options. Perhaps torture to gain their revenge? But eventually, *they will kill him*." The elf caught Jorge's rigid posture at the words and tried to soften the blow. "But for now he's likely in the dungeons of the Babel Keep: the largest fortress at the center of the land above the clouds. The demon will want to flaunt his kill… use Kevin's capture to demoralize his opponents."

Havara reached for a long stick near the firewood pile. He leaned on the staff and limped a few steps. "How do I get there?" he asked.

Dri'Bu laughed. "Go west, past the hills and into the Briganik Mountains. Enter the Luciferian Temple of Light and pay the toll to ascend the Grand Staircase which will bring you to a land they call 'Paradise.' Follow the signs like any other Luciferian Pilgrim would and you'll eventually find the Babel Keep. It's the main castle where they claim the mighty hay-lale' once held court."

Havara nodded and grit his teeth. Taking two more steps he paused for breath. "West it is, then."

"Dri'Bu," Jorge stepped over. "Stay with these two until they are well enough to travel, then find Rashnir's group; they are south in Ninda." The angel put a heavy hand on the old elf's shoulder. "You are a most excellent person. I see no reason why the Most High One would not grant your request for a soul. No created being can fathom the mind of God, but had I the ability, I would certainly meet your desire. You are certainly more than any ekthro."

The elf looked up into the angel's eyes. "You're coming back. You'll make it back—I'm sure of it."

Jorge helped the pained Havara back to his bed. "Tell Kyrius to remain strong in my absence. Don't let him follow me after he eventually wakes... one of us must go to uphold our duty and I'm glad to be the one to do it." Jorge bent over the other angel and kissed him. "Goodbye, brother."

"Wait," Dri'Bu called. He tossed Jorge a wad of rags from his own bedding pile. "Tell anyone you meet on you travels that you are a wandering anakim on pilgrimage. If anyone asks, tell them you are mendicant worshipper from the house of Horpah. They are the poorest of the anakim; outcasts and beggars, nobody pays them any mind. Above all else, don't show anyone your hands or feet. All children of Anak have six digits on hand and foot."

The elf pulled a few metal coins from his pocket. "Give the warden this. It should more than pay the toll at the Grand Stair. And keep your cover if you want to find Kevin alive."

Jorge gripped Dri'Bu in a half-hug and accepted the money.

"If God truly hears my prayers, they are all for your safety," the elf said emotionally.

"God hears them, my friend," Jorge said as he departed. "*I* pray that He answers them."

***

With boots kicked up on the table of the mead house, Jaker tipped his head back and quaffed the dark, house ale. Smoke wreathed the empty table he operated from. Empty chairs were turned out, inviting potential clients to pull up and contract with him.

He'd set up a small mercenary trade on the furthest east parts of Briganik. Mostly, he and the remnant of Rogis' Rangers figured they would work rescue operations on behalf of family members whose loved ones had been abducted and whisked away into Zipha by orcs and trolls.

Five of his most trusted comrades remained with him since he broke with his friends after the debacle in Grinden. Each of them had set up an operation in different saloons across the town, networking together to find more contracts and employment. So far, only a handful of jobs had come their way.

Something inside of him compelled Jaker to stay with his former comrade Rashnir after the battle at Grinden Quarry, but Jaker couldn't quite commit to his level of belief.

No, that wasn't it. Deep down, Jaker saw religious commitment as a threat to his personal freedom.

With business slow, the portly, bald bartender ambled over to Jaker's table. His sweaty jowls shook as he walked. "Ya know," he leaned against the sturdy table, "I heard that the Temple's looking for mercenary work."

"I never took you for a church man, Puget," Jaker took another gulp of ale.

"I never had much sense for it," Puget remarked, "but business has been slow. I figure it's not beyond me to sacrifice a few coins in shik-kore's coffer and say a prayer if it puts more gold in mine."

Jaker raised his glass in mock worship, "Well, if religion is a business, no better place to pay homage than at the priest's house."

"Well said. But go see the edict for yourself. There is some serious coin to be had if you can hunt for bounty."

"I'll do that." Jaker tossed a coin onto the table and departed.

Across town, he found the modest, local Luciferian temple. He ducked inside and scowled skeptically at the carved depictions of the various deities of the Gathering.

Jaker found the public address board and located a large, written notice. The poster claimed large bounties for proof of execution of any known, "religious dissidents of the dangerous krist-chin cult." Even larger bounties were offered for live delivery.

He peeled back the carefully pinned, mass-produced leaflets which plastered the board. Some were for specific persons such as "Rashnir the Ranger" or "Kevin of Earth." Underneath the flyers, old bills remained which promised bounties and provided information on recent vampiric activity.

Apparently, the Order has given my friend's a higher precedent than even those lifeless blood suckers.

"It's just over here," a priest interrupted Jaker's thoughts. The Luciferian escorted a gang of young, wild-eyed ruffians. "Here it is," the priest budged in front of Jaker.

"This is the poster. It outlines the terms and conditions of bounties. Now, you should know that krist-chin hunting can be very dangerous, albeit very profitable. You are aware of their flaming, magic swords, correct? Might I suggest that you purchase some 'ãbêdâh serum from the temple before you depart? It's the only thing that can shield you from their weapons."

Jaker stepped back as the priest explained the best way to equip for and kill a krist-chin. The former ranger shook his head incredulously; Kevin's influence had spread across the continent. Jaker anticipated that he'd probably not seen the last of his friends from Grinden.

***

Bwar's stubby legs ached. He'd run as fast as he could to make the appointment at the council advisors' library. He walked through the corridors until he found the appropriate place.

The dwarven advisor passed two meandering Luciferian priests who discussed politics: a man and a goblin initiate who walked with an authority that seemed to surpass his low rank within the Order. The goblin excused himself and peeled away as the human priest continued towards the exit.

Crumpling up the papyrus scrap with his instructions, Bwar arrived on time. He scanned the racks of political annuls and spotted Elo'misce. His elvish counterpart stood waiting, holding her own scrap of paper.

Bwar ambled over to her as she slipped the note into her pocket. "Waiting for someone?"

Elo'misce scowled at Bwar and ignored him.

"What does your note say?" he accused.

"What note," she denied.

"I'm guessing it only says the words 'Shadow King' and a time."

She eyed him suspiciously.

"And I bet the time is now."

Elo'misce turned. She seemed about to start a nasty exchange when the goblin priest Bwar had earlier passed snuck into their midst. The goblin clacked his jaws to get their attention.

"I have your orders," the goblin hissed. They start with an explicit demand that you both cooperate to unify Gleend against the humans."

The dwarf and elf both rolled their eyes. They acquiesced to the command, but neither seemed happy to do it.

"The machine has been started. It is your duty to keep it rolling. You will both be rewarded with your own kingdoms once the Shadow King has revealed himself."

"What do you mean," Bwar growled.

"See for yourself," the goblin pointed to the window.

Bwar and Elo'misce stepped to the portal that overlooked the courtyard below. A raucous crowd of dwarves and elves had gathered along with a few other, rarer ekthroic brothers. At the head of the throng stumbled Lemant, their human counterpart to the Gleendish advisory council. His wrists were tied behind his back and a rag bound his mouth.

An elf shouted above the crowd, condemning the human for imagined atrocities including preferential, racial treatment, racial oppression, thievery, and even the assassination of King Losonom in order to succeed him on the throne.

"Kill him!" the crowd howled. A dwarf procured a heavy miner's rope. A noose already tied the far end. An elf tossed it over a tree limb.

Lemant tried to run from the crowd but was rebuffed at every turn. The horde pressed forward.

"There! In the window!" one voice shouted. The crowd quieted to a dull roar as they turned their attention to the advisors in the windows.

A glint of hope dared to enter Lemant's panicked face as he recognized the advisors above. He pleaded for them to intervene with his eyes.

Elo'misce turned to the goblin. He nodded his assent.

Staring into Lemant's eyes, Bwar turned his thumb downward. The crowd cheered. Elo'misce turned her wrist and did likewise. The crowd lost all sense of itself and forced his head in the noose.

The human priest Bwar had passed earlier in the hall stumbled through the open arch which led into the buzzing courtyard. Himself a human, the fear of an all-out race war plastered across his face. "This is madness! Give this man due process!" he shouted them down.

"Kill the humans!" a gruff dwarven voice bellowed. A hundred mixed voices agreed as they seized the priest and tore his limbs from his body before jerking Lemant from the ground and strangling him with his own weight.

Lemant kicked and struggled as if it could save his life. A nearby dwarf tore a branch from the tree and clubbed the advisor until he stilled and the blows split his softer parts open, spilling the human's insides onto the ground.

The mob reached fever pitch and spilled beyond the courtyard, screaming demands that all humans die. Voices of terror rang out across Xorst—human voices.

Like a murderous smoke, the crowd dispersed. Elo'misce turned back to the library, but the goblin was gone.

"It has begun," Bwar said with a giddy tone. "At long last, my people will rise again, and it all starts with the fall of humanity."

Chapter Ten

Across from the hunters, the man with a weasel-face fidgeted excitedly. He strutted into the Temple of Light's central commons area and approached the canopied bounty claims kiosk. Krimko grinned as he displayed the dismembered forearms of his victims.

Krimko dropped the bundle of limbs onto the tally officer's table with a sickening thud. The former ranger, Pinchôt, brought up the flank of the elite bounty hunting cadre tailed by a scarred behemoth of a man. Grirrg's expression remained blank while he followed. Jandul, the combat monk, reluctantly kept pace with them.

The Luciferian diplomatically hid his surprise at the sight of an elf working the station. Krimko nodded as the ekthro counted the body parts

"Wonderful! So glad to see the fruits of your labor have paid off, my friends." Herang, the elf made small talk, asking about their exploits as he checked the authenticity of the cross-shaped, sword-like markings upon each arm to verify they were not forgeries. Krimko became keenly aware, mid-discussion, that Herang spoke more for the audience of the crowd surrounding them.

"I can see that you adequately prepared for taking your bounties by coating your weapons and shields in 'ābêdâh serum. Did you know that members of our registered bounty-hunting roster get a discount on that potion which is an *absolute necessity for hunting krist-chins*? You also get the earliest alerts and first opportunity on exclusive contracts, including suspected krist-chin movements." Herang pitched them like a snake-oil salesman and he'd certainly gained the ear of those meandering around the group in the market square.

Krimko shot a questioning look to his comrades. Jandul only grimaced. He'd not been sorry to see their assignments keep the team beyond the immediate reach of the Order's central hub; he resented the insincere commercialism so prevalent at the Temple of Light. The church was a business—one that mankind had embraced over the last couple centuries.

Herang practically cajoled Jandul. "I can see you're skeptical. And I can understand since there is a small registration fee." He intentionally dropped a tray of coins slightly higher than necessary so that they clinked dramatically for full effect. "Here are your earnings for just these bounties. We can just take the fee out of here." He slid the flat of his hand into the pile and pushed just a few coins away from the primary pile. Krimko, no stranger to chicanery, noticed they were a heavier denomination and equaled almost half their earnings.

About to decline the offer, Krimko stopped short when the elf continued. "And if you agree today, I will give you a free qâsam!"

Krimko blinked. Qâsam seeing gems were well known to be extremely scarce and highly valuable. The ears of others seemed bent to the conversation as well. "What is it linked to?"

"To The Order's department of intelligence," Herang replied. "It's how we send out any new bounties and pertinent information about the krist-chin threat."

"But qâsamai are so expensive," Krimko countered. "And rare."

"It just goes to show you how committed The Order is to stomping out this threat." His words hung in the air, tantalizing them with opportunity.

Krimko shot Pinchôt a glance. Pinchôt shrugged indifferently, perhaps with mild curiosity. "Show us more about this 'intelligence department.'"

A broad grin spread across Herang's face. "Certainly. Sheech! Come and man the table; I'm giving a tour."

Sheech, a lumbering son of Anak ducked through the door of the nearby building and handed Herang a qâsam before he turned to mind the booth. He stood taller than even the massive Grirrg by at least a full head.

Herang led them away from the shade of the pergola and towards an exterior wall; it had been plastered with flyers and leaflets. Bounty sheets promised payouts for krist-chins. Some of the bills were generic; some of them bore illustrated prints of key members in the Grinden cult.

Krimko squinted maliciously at a mass-produced rendering of Kevin. Bitter to his core, he spat at the likeness.

Opening the entry and motioning for them to follow, Herang led them through a few stony, rust colored corridors and into a room buzzing with activity. Luciferian monks hovered about, performing various tasks such as scrying, communicating with others via qâsam, and marking movements and suspected incursions upon a large map. Most of them appeared to be Adherents of the Order which meant they held at least nine ranks, although none of them wore any visible indicators of a chosen discipline. The distinct lack of such emblems seemed to indicate the possibility that the Order had developed a new one.

Darkened slate walls listed bulletin points. Large headings were scrawled in chalk at the top of the giant boards. Some boards recorded information pertinent to the tracking of krist-chins, some itemized information regarding Lilth's brood, and others yet listed generic anti-Luciferian occurrences that needed dealing with.

A curtain parted across the room and a stumpy man who could have been Krimko's brother stepped in. He stopped short and locked eyes with the short Luciferian from Grinden. They recognized the kindred, cruel spirits within each other. Holding a few leaves of loose papyrus, the man stepped back the way he had come, seeing that the room wasn't currently secure.

"What's in there?" Pinchôt pointed at the curtain.

"This room is for lower-sensitivity assignments and information. The other one is more highly confidential," Herang replied.

The elf walked them through the chamber, using it as a selling tool to solidify the deal. At the far side of the room, a large rack rested. It boasted many numbered cubbies built into it.

"I assume, then, that we have a deal," Herang said. "Nobody ever gets this far and backs out after seeing our operation." He motioned grandly to the nearby slate-list which listed a number for the corresponding qâsam in the cubby-rack. The list proudly displayed the title of "Honorable Hunters." Each number followed with a team name and a column for recorded kills, using different symbols for types of prey. Very few confirmed kills were marked with the krist-chin sign. "What name shall I add as your operative team name?"

The typically silent barbarian opened his half-closed eyes, suddenly lucid as something in his personality clicked on. "Deathsquad." He hissed, and then he relaxed back into his normal repose.

Optimistically trading glances, even Jandul gave a benign shrug of approval. Krimko sneered deviously.

The title was hokey and over the top. Pinchôt looked at his peers and didn't see any disagreement.

"'Deathsquad' it is."

The elf nodded. "Wonderful!" He dragged a shaft of chalk over the leaderboard and drew their name just below the highest ranked team, a crew calling themselves Nephilim and Phoenix.

Herang smiled with a deceptive elven smile that had proven impossible to read for most other species. "I'm sure that we have some very interesting information and specific missions that you may be interested in."

***

[Mighty tyr-aPt,] the pustuous bRraphf prostrated himself before the goblin king's throne, [we bring you this token gift of gold and slaves.] The majordomo of the qrn'Ke kingdom motioned grandly to the chained line of dwarves; each slave had been hobbled at the heel tendon, but still maintained strong upper bodies. The slaves each held a small box of treasure.

grr'Shaalg watched approvingly from the shadows. King qrn'Ke had even come. Visiting another king outside of war-time was an unprecedented act and boded well for the devious shadow ruler. He understood the king's motives as he stared at qrn'Ke's swollen goiter. It had webbed with mucus and leakage.

[He has seen firsthand the effects of anthrofusis,] grr'Shaalg mused. Time was too urgent a concern for qrn'Ke to trust the antidote for the goblin disease would be delivered in time. The devious grr'Shaalg knew how *he* would act in bRraphf's position. He would have distributed the katadoolu to as many of his loyal peers as possible, but he would not have gotten it to qrn'Ke before the sickness took full hold—and then it would have been the bRraphf kingdom.

grr'Shaalg smiled. That was probably the exact reason that the king traveled to his neighbor's kingdom for a chat. He expected each of the other eight kings to do likewise, and grr'Shaalg's brother would graciously supply them with a temporary remedy for the anthrofusis sickness *out of the kindness of his black heart.*

He watched his brother-king accept gifts and accolades from the foreign ruler. tyr-aPt played his part well, but neither he nor his brother were interested in gold or possessions. They sought power and land.

tyr-aPt conversed with the other ruler and motioned to his brother, the architect of their grand scheme. [grr'Shaalg will set a delivery route through your tunnels if you will set it up with him. I'm sure a prompt schedule will be a high priority for your people.]

qrn'Ke feigned disinterest in the supposed underling, as expected, although grr'Shaalg watched him break protocol and greedily drink down the entire vial of katadoolu as soon as he laid claws upon it. bRraphf bowed to tyr-aPt, and then his king before falling into rank step with grr'Shaalg.

The goblin led his counterpart through the royal corridors and into his own office in order to take care of shipping schedules and routes. Everything moved according to plan except for the time-table of his long game. grr'Shaalg still wished he could produce the necessary mature warriors within a shorter timeframe. Without a vast army, a complete take-over of his enemies would be a difficult gambit. Even given the rapid reproduction rate and comparatively short time it took for goblins to reach adolescence, his projections kept his goal beyond reach for several years yet. Also, attrition due to goblin mischief would certainly factor into the species' headcount.

[Tell me, bRraphf,] grr'Shaalg asked, [have your people been instructed to orgy by the church? Have you increased your breeding stock?]

bRraphf regarded him suspiciously. Under normal circumstances, that was the sort of query asked to determine if an enemy mustered against you. The goblin envoy relaxed and simply shrugged.

[Yes. The Order has asked us to prepare for a great need of troops.]

[And also shamans?]

bRraphf nodded. [Yes. We are excited to send some of our number to be trained as Luciferians.] He looked far off. [Perhaps if we'd had as early of an entry as your Zilke, we'd have been able to head off this anthrofusis on our own.]

grr'Shaalg nodded diplomatically. He knew that there was no chance of that. [The Order can be quite helpful when embraced,] he said, wondering about his maturation problem looming against the near future. Perhaps some Luciferian spells or potion could help speed up the process, grr'Shaalg mused. He quickly dismissed the idea; he did not want to be beholden to Absinthium or the Gathering much beyond the current political intrigue.

Besides, he could always have Zilke search for such a thing and dispatch Griq'nnr to steal it from the Order.

[The Luciferian's have vast resources for the time being,] grr'Shaalg continued. [Just remember your own, when the time comes,] he cautioned. [Devotion to any cause should always come second to racial loyalty.]

The devious shadow-king knew that a time would come when he could break free of the cage Absinthium kept him in. grr'Shaalg had a bigger endgame than the one the arch-mage had planned for him, and it was better for grr'Shaalg if only goblin-kind knew the true strength of their fighting forces. There would undoubtedly come a time when that army might be needed to be brought to bear against his current allies.

bRraphf nodded, agreeing with the sentiment. Goblin loyalties were fickle, but they didn't exist at all beyond kin.

Even if bRraphf did not commit to the ideal with his heart, he would commit with his blood which even now raged with anthrofusis. It demanded fealty to grr'Shaalg who controlled the only remedy—a remedy which took regular doses to combat the deadly symptoms making it the perfect control—something that surpassed even religion.

One way or another grr'Shaalg would raise his army.

***

Rashnir's horse wheezed spittle as he urged it forward. Zeh-Ahbe's lagged behind, clearly tired. Their hooves had kicked up dust as the duo charged across the Nindan tracts of land. They'd ridden for nearly two days now and had only slowed to rest the horses, and even that was limited. At this pace, they would probably kill the horses with exertion within another couple days if the beasts didn't revolt first.

Ahead, Zeh-Ahbe' saw Rashnir pull back on his reigns, stopping the haggard mount. He caught up and found the ranger crouching on the ground, examining a patch of freshly turned dirt. He wore a sour face.

"What is it, Rashnir? And where are we?"

"We just crossed into Adumarr," he said without looking up. "We're getting close."

"Well? What is it, my friend?"

Rashnir turned and held up a child's shoe. As Zeh-Ahbe' scanned the ground he spotted the tell-tale signs of a skirmish. Dark patches of soil blotted the area where the topsoil drank deeply of blood; small personal belongings lay scattered like forgotten flotsam and whitewashed stones formed oblong circles in random areas.

Turning over a stone twice the size of his fist and painted a chalky alabaster, Rashnir drew on his long history with Nindan ritual. "They're graves," he said. "Slaves bury the unknown and unimportant this way. The lords typically let them because the bodies fertilize the ground and the stones ensure nobody plows up a diseased corpse before its decomposed enough to be safe."

They shared a moment of silence. Rashnir broke the quiet and began wildly digging into the loosened dirt with his hands.

"What are you doing?" Zeh-Ahbe' demanded, fearing his friend had lost his mind.

"I have to know!" he yelled.

"But Kevin was in Sprazik!"

"But so many of our other brothers and sisters were not." He stopped and locked eyes with his friend. "You can watch if you like. But I'm going to dig," he stated passive-aggressively.

Zeh-Ahbe' joined Rashnir in the circle and began shoveling the soil with his hands, too. A few minutes later, they disturbed the flesh of the first corpse. It lay cold and turgid in the shallow grave.

Following the body's outline, they quickly unearthed the young woman, dusting her clean. Rashnir cradled her reverently in his arm as he examined her mangled cadaver. "I recognize her," he said.

Zeh-Ahbe' shook his head. "As do I. She was one of our sisters from Driscul." He paused regretfully. "I do not remember her name."

Rashnir nodded his assent. "Someone took her arm."

Quizzically, Zeh-Ahbe's face asked him to elaborate. "Maybe she lost it in whatever battle happened here?"

Holding up her stump arm, he pointed to the joint. "It was cut cleanly here. See the jagged, but clean incisions? It wasn't a severing blow taken in battle—that would have been one crisp cut—and it wouldn't have gone in through the joint so cleanly. That sort of wound would have probably damaged the bone nearby, nicking it at the very least. This was cut as a trophy; someone boned her out like a butcher." Rashnir stood, disgusted as he surveyed the scene. "These people, our people, were hunted and murdered."

"Who would do this?" Zeh-Ahbe' took back his words immediately. He knew who. "Why would they take her arm and then bury her?"

Rashnir kicked a stone from the circumference. "I'm sure local slaves buried them to prevent disease... but this is what the hunters wanted." He pulled up his sleeve and pointed to the sword-like mark of the Lord that had been etched upon his skin. "They were after bounties."

Zeh-Ahbe' helped his friend lower the woman back into her grave and covered her over again with dirt. "This world grows ever more dangerous for us, then."

Rashnir nodded. "We may have been too late to help these ones, but let's pray that we're not too late to rescue Kevin."

"I agree," Zeh-Ahbe' said. "Let us pray!"

But Rashnir was already walking back to his horse. "We'll pray in our saddles, Zeh-Ahbe'! We've got to make haste!"

***

ekerithia descended the secret stair and into the deepest dark where even *his vision* could not pierce the supernatural black without a lantern or torch. However, he had memorized the layout of the dark maze. A torch or lantern could not stay lit for the duration of this journey. He clutched the supernatural orb which he always kept pocketed, letting its slight glow guide his steps.

The new demon walked the labyrinth for a stretch. The angles formed perfect, smooth and straight lines with crystal precision. Amid the stark silence, the only sound in the corridors was the occasional drip of water or a random rattle of chains that bound Tartarus's residents with unbreakable shackles.

So long had ekerithia watched the course of humanity and his supernatural brethren that he had become an expert in deduction over the millennia. With great accuracy, he could predict the next several major events affecting hay-lale's realm. He didn't need to waste his remaining imbuement of heavenly power on prognostic charms which were too subject to change with every new human decision. His deep magics had to be metered and reserved for necessary actions, like this one. Foretelling took only common sense, not magic.

The demon came to the passage he needed, noticing how he no longer felt uncomfortable in Tartarus—not since embracing his destiny as one of the damned. The unnerving quiet had become a comfort to him.

He steeled himself for the rest of the journey. Using bursts of his remaining holy power felt foreign to him but he'd held it in for so long that even small uses felt wasteful to him—though he knew better. The endgame was huge, and it was everything. Winning the coming war necessitated multiple fronts.

Unfurling his leathery wings which hung hooked around his neck like a fine cape, ekerithia exploded into action. He rushed forward at supersonic speed. An echoing boom trailed him and reverberated through the hallways as the sound barrier shattered; the blast elicited a corporate groan from those languishing in their bonds.

The journey took only minutes. ekerithia halted the charge and found the spiraling stair. He began the upward trek and found the secret door. He traced a symbol, which only few had ever known, upon the stone door and it momentarily phased out of reality. The aperture opened onto the top of a mountain peak. ekerithia stepped out and into the cold, thin air as the door reverted to its natural state.

Taking in the mountaintop view, ekerithia congratulated himself on wise decisions made eons ago when he destroyed all recorded knowledge of how to enter Tartarus. Of course, he'd still hoped for some kind of boon from Yahweh in that era, but his foresight had paid off, now.

Slipping outside of the corporeal, ekerithia disappeared from sight. The supernatural state also guarded him against the natural elements and the cold, biting air. He began his trek towards the immense castle perched atop the peak further up the rise. While he preferred to remain in body form, this one had its uses and it required none of his innate magics. For all heavenly-created being, this was a natural ability. It would allow him to approach the queen more quickly and while it would shield him from the eyes of ghouls and wendigo, the Adamic vampires would see him as clearly as ever.

Formerly the Watcher, ekerithia's attuned eyes could see across the vast distances from the trail atop the Noddic mountain peaks. Lush forest and jungle cropped the craggy ridges. From such a height, he could see signs of the distant people that Kevin's troupe had been commissioned to locate.

ekerithia shifted his gaze. He spotted the wide canal that separated the two continents from each other. Troops had amassed upon the shores, waiting for the longboats to ferry them across.

The demon had already guessed Lilth would make such a political play and conscript disposable ghouls to strengthen beh'-tsah's tenuous throne. Soon an army of ghouls would climb the Babel tower and bolster the beleaguered Gathering's troops as they beat back the uprising.

On the opposite side of Nod, ekerithia's eyes could barely make out the twin spires hidden within the misty distance. The shut doorway home was shut to him and ekerithia would never again be welcome.

Grimacing, he pressed forward. Renewed vigor welled up within him and spurred his long legs onward.

***

Absinthium forced an affable smile to form upon his otherwise grim face before he entered the doors. With a welcoming expression, he pushed open the doors to the lectionary chamber where students in the Order collected for their studies.

New initiates beamed with excitement. In this room, Absinthium was the ultimate celebrity. They stirred slightly in their seats as he made the rounds, visiting with as many as he could stomach in the time he'd allotted for it.

"I see that you each have your papers and supplies for copyist work today?"

The students buzzed enthusiastically. Even the professor, a frumpy old Luciferian with curly grey hair and a paunch had been enthralled with his visit. The teacher had hit his glass ceiling decades ago

"Professor. I wonder if I might put your students on a specific task for me this day?"

The teacher nodded vigorously, surrendering his students to whatever the Order's leader desired. He went so far as to take a seat and pull out copyist tools of his own.

"Excellent!" Absinthium said. He procured a short stack of copies of the current bounty flyers for

286

Rashnir and Zeh-Ahbe'. "I need as many of these bills altered as is reasonably possible. We need every old one collected and edited. Some by hand, some by press as able, and all of them distributed."

The class hung on his every word, anxiously awaiting the revisions. "I am increasing their price tenfold, but I want them delivered dead! There is no reward for live capture."

Eagerly springing into action, they moved with the zeal only possible of true believers. The mage sank back, letting the machine move of its own accord, now.

Once they'd begun he slipped away quietly, mulling the tension in the pit of his gut. His recent vision still plagued him: a future where he saw Rashnir and his werewolf minion killed his beloved master. *I must not let this come to pass! By whatever means necessary!*

***

ekerithia walked through the opened gates of the immense chantry as he journeyed to the castle's stony heart. He noticed that it had changed little since he had last been here so long ago; a pall hung over the facility and only shades of grey painted the exterior.

As the demon slipped through the court and into the regal manor, recognizing the posh comforts and elaborate accouterments that appointed the interior. He slipped past a group of wendigo as they engaged in intense conversation. Their pale skin highlighted their manicured appearance and elegant dress.

He walked towards the queen's royal chamber with eager purpose and locked eyes with the majordomo stationed outside the door. ekerithia slipped back into his physical form; clearly, he had been noticed and it would only delay his meeting if her brood thought ekerithia was up to some foul scheme.

The chamberlain maintained eye contact during his entire accession as ekerithia approached the royal door. "Do you have an appointment, Watcher?" The Adamic vampire's words dripped with superiority. They'd met before.

The majordomo scanned ekerithia; his eyebrows rose slightly as he noticed the featherless nature of his wings.

"Tell your queen that EKERITHIA has come to parley."

The vampire's head bobbed eagerly. "I will inform Queen Lilth immediately." He turned his pointy nose up and slipped through a side door, leaving ekerithia in the spacious hall.

Moments later, he returned. "She will visit with you," he only bowed now that the guest had the approval of the queen. "I will announce you." He pushed open the ornate double doors with regal pomp and circumstance that the demon largely ignored.

ekerithia sidestepped the majordomo and approached the queen who lounged upon a comfortable chaise lounge. Her throne sat upon a raised dais at the center of the room, but the remainder of the chamber had been filled with more plush appurtenances.

The polished stone was both decorative and functional for the vampire leader; no matter how many moppings the floor received, the grout lines could not surrender the bloodstains they'd absorbed over the millennia.

Lilth greeted him with a smile that revealed her sharp incisors. "Greetings, EKERITHIA," she acknowledged the creature's final transformation. "It has been far too long."

He'd nearly forgotten how beautiful she was. Her pale skin shone alabaster in the light of the decorative candelabras stationed around the room; raven-hued highlights framed and shot through her platinum hair. She wore only the finest clothing; the vampire aristocracy had their own style—all of it summed up as seductive. Her intense eyes and manicured appearance would prove siren-like to any being, but ekerithia was not bound by the trappings of other creatures.

"Greetings, Queen Lilth. You appear as well as ever."

She smiled. "But you certainly have changed, *Watcher*." She leaned forward and smirked playfully. "Ever have I found you intriguing. You certainly seem to have come into your own. And the only thing I find more appealing than an interesting story is a man with power."

Lilth leaned back and made a show of caressing the buttons which barely held her clothing upon her lithe frame. She gave him a flirtatious look, inviting him to unfasten the hooks of her corset and ravage her.

ekerithia stared at her, stone-faced. This was not what he had come here for and she knew it. The invitation had been a long-standing one and he'd shown no interest in taking advantage of it.

Lilth smiled lasciviously and took a more proper sitting posture regarding him with mock surprise. She only pouted for a second, knowing this was not a game she could engage him with.

"What pressing business finds you in Nod?"

"Long have I watched over the realm. But you have existed in this sphere for even longer than I. While I possess vast knowledge, I am short of omniscience."

"You have come for information, then? Advice?" The demon had surprised her, yet again.

"I have few equals on this field, and I'm sure you know things hidden even from me."

"What, or who, are you looking for?"

"I want to rapidly age a creature."

"Human or ekthro?"

"Does it matter?"

"I'm quite intrigued," she grinned, resting her chin on her fists. "I know a way," she stated, rising to her feet. The vampires reached up to touch his tall shoulder and she walked a circle around him as she examined his new form. "But it may require something of you."

ekerithia glared at her.

"What is this price?"

"Just that you keep an open mind towards a future… alliance. Nothing concrete, even."

The demonic visitor nodded to accept her terms.

"Before you cloistered yourself away within that tower there lived a race of humanoids that lived in Domn."

"The atelís?"

"You know of them?"

"Only by name. They were gone prior to my arrival, as you pointed out."

She fixed him with her brilliant, amethyst eyes. "The atelís were hyper-intelligent, but they were incomplete and they could not procreate. They had already split into several factions when I was still creating the first line of wendigo.

"One faction devoted itself to technological advancement; they harnessed the power of lightning and crafted ghosts who lived within the machines: a consciousness of its own.

"Another devoted itself to self-improvement and perfection. They grafted biological and technological components into their own bodies, hoping to both surpass all others and to live forever.

"The other bloc sought the means to replicate themselves: the core material of their flesh. They developed methods cloning and even transferring and copying memories and knowledge."

"And what happened to them?"

"War. For all their intelligence, their polarized philosophical positions led them to destroy each other. They are not quite extinct, but very nearly so. The atelís live on in a variety of manners, but Domn will never again rise. Her children often harvest humans for spare parts in their vain attempts to live forever."

"Then what good are they to me?"

"Them? None. But one of their creations might be exactly what you desire: a machine which emits an energy that ages the flesh and replicates mental images, memories, personalities. It is how that third faction readied their next generation of bodies and inserted their minds into them." She pursed her lips lustily. "Would you like me to draw you a map?"

ekerithia smiled.

"I will also require the service of a loyal ghoul."

***

Kevin awoke. His throat burned and felt as if it had been stuffed with briars. He gasped for air and looked around. Only a thin shaft of light leaked into the stony well-like chamber. The only entrance to his prison was high overhead.

He crawled around the floor, searching for the first source of available water. He felt that at any given moment he might die, consumed by the burning in his throat.

"You are awake?" a smooth voice asked him.

Kevin looked around the cisternesque prison and realized that he was not alone. "Yes." It hurt to use his ragged voice. "Water?"

"I've saved you some," the other prisoner said. "You've been unconscious since they threw you in here several days ago."

Greedily chugging half of the clay cup's contents, he tried to conserve the other half, taking only tiny sips to wet his throat. He raised the cup and nodded his thanks. Only now did he pause to examine his cellmate. The massive being was clearly blind. "Thank you," he forced the words to come from his aching esophagus.

The angelic being wore scars and permanent marks from the many beatings he had received. He was absent two lower digits of his right hand and wore a ragged strip of cloth across his eyes. Bloody marks had seeped through it long ago staining the blindfold-like bandage where the sockets were. Kevin guessed that his eyes had been plucked out in as a form of torture. The creature's wings hung limp and hadn't been stretched in ages. Many of the feathers had ratted and snarled.

The angel was dirty and obviously in ill health. "You're most welcome," he said. "I'm so glad to finally meet you. My name is Karoz."

Chapter Eleven

Rashnir and Zeh-Ahbe's horses crested a hill. The grade slopped down on the northern side and the mounts uttered ragged grunts and groans. They'd been pushed to the physical brink and could not last much longer before collapsing. From atop their animals, Rashnir and Zeh-Ahbe' could see the destruction that spread for miles.

Smoke still crawled upward in languishing tendrils as the ruins of Sprazik smoldered. The city had somehow been completely wiped off the map; not a single structure stood upon the charred earth. Stone foundations had crumbled and wooden pallet walls had turned to cinder and charcoal.

Its level of destruction took even Rashnir by surprise: a blanket of annihilation so utter and complete. Holes pocked the distant surface; large swaths of soil were absent, carved into black chasms. Corpses of men, goblins, elves, and dwarves littered the vale. Dwarven war carts lay tipped and busted and feathered arrow shafts stuck into every surface, looking like a caricature of pygmy darts at this distance.

Rashnir clicked his tongue and urged his horse onward with a heavy heart. He angled the beast towards the only area with movement. His horse would no longer run and so he trotted forward more slowly than Rashnir wished. The pace forced his heart to take in the macabre view of the devastation. So many friends lay motionless upon the killing field.

Finally, the horses reluctantly arrived to dump their riders at their destination.

Only a few steps away, three of the four resting around the campfire waved them forward. Dri'bu appeared the only one capable of making the stew which they had gathered around the campfire to eat. Kyrius lay upon a pile of bedding, breathing shallowly. Havara wobbled in place; with his leg bound tightly between splint boards he defied the pain and stood to lean upon a crude crutch in order to welcome his friends.

Barely recognizable outside of his assassin's garb, the pale prisoner sat stripped to the waist. His head hung and the long, unkempt white hair hid his face. Prock's unpigmented, white skin nearly shimmered under the midday light, only broken by the dark mark between the man's hunched shoulder blades.

"Curious," Rashnir remarked momentarily, before returning his attention to the urgent matter at hand.

Dri'bu took the horses by the reigns as the riders dismounted. "These animals are on the verge of death," the elf lamented, wasting no time to guide them towards food and water.

"We'll get new ones," Rashnir said. His sense of urgency overrode his compassion. He turned to his remaining friends. Rashnir briefly embraced Havara and then sank next to Kyrius. Zeh-Ahbe' followed close behind. "Will he be alright?" Rashnir asked of the wounded angel.

Havara winced as he pivoted to them. "Dri'bu is certain he will recover."

"Where is Jorge?" Zeh-Ahbe' asked.

"Where do you think?" The acolyte spat from below the thick mop of hair. Prock had somehow worked his gag free. He tipped his head enough to deliver a baleful glare with his reddened eyes. "Your foolish angel is charging headlong into the mouth of the beast."

Zeh-Ahbe' looked to Havara who nodded and confirmed it.

"The Order didn't want this one back?" Rashnir asked.

Nobody responded to the comment. They let it linger for the indictment that it was: the Order left their own to die.

"When did Jorge leave?" Rashnir finally asked as the elf returned.

The horses ate voraciously in the distance. "He left yesterday," Dri'bu replied. "He was on foot. You can overtake him tomorrow."

"We should be able to get to him tonight," Rashnir insisted.

"Your horses will die without rest," he insisted firmly. "And that's if they'll even let you into the saddle."

"We'll find new ones, then."

Dri'bu crossed his thin arms and looked at Rashnir skeptically. "Be my guest and help yourself to any of the remaining livestock." He spread his arms wide for emphasis.

Rashnir looked around at the war-torn battlescape. The only visible creature among the blackened remains of the city was a guinea hen that clucked and pecked the ground for insects. He sighed. "The horses can be ready by morning?"

"Unless we can find a small enough saddle for the poultry it's the only option. But yes, I believe they will be rested enough by then. I have a way with animals; I'll do my best to prepare them."

Havara interjected, "Maybe those three will loan you theirs?" He pointed up towards the hilltop from where his friends had come. "Did they come with you?"

Rashnir and Dri'bu shielded their eyes from the sun and looked. Three women on horseback perched in the distance. They turned their animals and walked out of sight behind the ridge to shield their movements from the Christians.

"Friends of yours?" Havara asked.

Rashnir clenched his jaw. He had hoped that they couldn't follow them through such a hard ride. These horses had not been overly fast, despite pushing them to their limits. They'd been the first mounts available in their moment of need.

"No," he simply said.

***

Zilke sat at the table with grr'Shaalg. His insides roiled with a mixture of excitement and anxiety. Raised in a mostly human environment, the anomalous goblin still felt uncomfortable when immersed entirely amongst his own kind.

[You have secured your appointment within the Temple of Light?] grr'Shaalg asked. Eyeing him up and down, the Shadow King knew that Zilke felt he had something to prove to his species—it was an attitude he felt certain he could manipulate.

Nodding, Zilke replied, [Yes. I've notified my superiors and subordinates in Grinden of my short sabbatical in order to study in the great libraries there. The King is currently searching for a qualified individual to take my post, but I should be cleared to leave shortly.]

[Perfect,] grr'Shaalg said. [I have need of you once again as one of my most trusted friends.] The goblin handed his Luciferian kinsman a rolled up note and grinned while imagining Dyule throw a tantrum at the loss of his newest advisor so soon.

He turned the paper over in his paws. [What is this?]

[I need you to find something like this and secure it for me.]

[I understand my duty to my race,] Zilke said. [Do you fear that continued thievery within the Order will shed suspicion upon us?]

grr'Shaalg shook his head. [Do not worry about that, but don't make any rash choices either. Our race needs this thing, even if it seems like such an irrelevant piece of my grand plan. This list could secure the continued advancement of our people.]

Noticing his reluctance, grr'Shaalg continued. [It is not needed immediately. Take the note with you. If such a thing even exists or can be made, let me know. We cannot tip our hand or our enemies will guess our plot. They must not see us marshaling any forces without direct orders. I want this, *but not at the expense of my inside man.*] grr'Shaalg was an exceptional liar.

[So long as I'm able to perform my actual studies while I am there, too,] Zilke insisted.

grr'Shaalg nodded. *So he is a true believer—Zilke wants to protect his own interests and opportunity to avail himself of the Temple's resources.* [Of course! I need you to be as learned as possible.] He embraced the Luciferian kinsman who had lingered so long in the shadow of his mentor, Frinnig. grr'Shaalg poured on his diplomatic charm. [When our kind rises to dominance over this land, who do you think I would choose to install as ruling arch-mage of The Order except for one of our own?]

Zilke looked up with surprised flattery and desire. He nodded. [I will search for this thing,] he promised and then departed.

***

By late afternoon Rashnir and Zeh-Ahbe' spotted the distant traveler as he slogged forward at a brisk pace. The tall jogger headed straight towards the western tower. Minutes later, they overtook him, even on the legs of such weary horses.

As they caught up, they dismounted and kept pace on foot with the cloaked pilgrim who refused to slow. "Do you have a plan?" Rashnir asked.

"Go back," Jorge insisted from below his disguise as a member of house Horpah. "This mission is suicide."

"So you do have a plan, but it's terrible?" Zeh-Ahbe' offered.

Jorge answered with grim silence and the determined gait he'd set a day previous. Finally, he repeated, "Go back. The others will need you—especially if I fail again."

Rashnir almost chuckled at the order. "No."

Jorge turned to look at him.

"We're not going anywhere but to the tower. This mission is bigger than you," Rashnir insisted.

The angel sighed and relented. He knew that there was no convincing either of them.

Rashnir made his case. "You're going to need help. You'd have just flown to Briganik if it was possible, so you're obviously injured."

Jorge shot him a glance that confirmed his suspicions. "It will heal... in time."

For several minutes they traveled in silence. The horses perked up at the slower pace.

"We're being followed," Jorge said without breaking stride. "They're a long ways off."

"Yeah," Zeh-Ahbe' said. "Three women. One wants to kill him. One wants to marry him to her ward. The other one doesn't really care either way."

Jorge glanced at Rashnir. "That sounds about right," he said dryly.

Rashnir rolled his eyes. "Do you know how long of a journey it is?" he tried to change the subject. "As early as possible, we should get you a horse, or at least ride doubled up. Even overladen, a slow horse is quicker than on foot."

Jorge nodded slowly. "Very well. If you two insist on accompanying me, then we should make all due haste."

***

Absinthium stared into the spicy smoke. His bleary, wide eyes stung with the acrid bite of the curling wisps. He clenched his teeth and pushed through the pain, grabbing at the tangle of ethereal, silver cords nestled within the astral plane. They made up the potential realities of the futures he scried.

His bloodshot eyes blinked against the painful sweat that welled at their corners. He pushed his consciousness into an eldritch strand and looked into the future again.

As before, Zeh-Ahbe's innards hung partly outside his belly, shredded open by the demon lord who bore down upon him. The arch-mage asserted his will upon the cord and manipulated it. Exerting his will into the image, an army of demonic minions burst through the door, but the end result was the same: Rashnir's blade severed the head of his beloved beh'-tsah.

Absinthium pushed his mind back down the cord to Zeh-Ahbe's evisceration. This time he launched a furiously immolating beam into the ranger's chest but the werewolf leaped upon beh'-tsah and tore his surprised throat out as the spell-caster killed the ranger. With a mighty heave and twist, Zeh-Ahbe' ripped the demon's head clear, even at the expense of the krist-chins' lives.

The sorcerer went back. Over and over again he manipulated the vision, but none of the possible fates resulted in beh'-tsah's survival. Only if he went further back along the cord could he reach a satisfactory conclusion: one in which beh'-tsah never encountered the krist-chins.

Absinthium released the silvery cords and pulled out of the potentialities. Wearied by all of his astral searchings he grabbed a dried handful of shialekorik mushrooms and dipped them in a tincture to activate them. Moments later his center refocused and turned back to his work. Absinthium shifted his gaze back into the smoke and looked for what happened now.

He saw Rashnir's approach. The ranger and his two companions pursued them. A disquiet welled up in the archmage's gut again and he verged on vomiting.

If the ranger would not be dissuaded and if his master could not be deterred, then Absinthium was forced to prevent the fateful meeting from occurring. Contingencies had to be laid.

Pulling his face from the smoke, he surrendered the scry spell and grabbed his quill and parchment. He needed allies to make his plan work; the otherwise loyal mage bit his lip and quickly penned a letter to peh'-shah, the demon who had devised the ill-timed coup against the Gathering.

The arch-mage snatched a songbird from its enclosure. He pressed his lips to the confused bird's head and put his thoughts and feelings into the animal— impressing his request into the winged messenger's heart. Absinthium went to the window and sent his first request to one of his master's enemies. "Queen Mother," he whispered and thrust the bird into the air.

He turned to the letter he'd written. Courting peh'-shah was a dangerous gamble… but the Luciferian would risk it all to prevent his vision.

Absinthium sighed heavy-heartedly and stamped his seal upon the hot wax at the page's bottom. In order to save his master, he had to consider all the potential courses, even defecting against his lord in order to save him.

Rolling up the paper, he tied it to the leg of a winged lizard caged in the minor bestiary amongst the other creatures at the far wall. He paced near the open windows of the Babel Keep. Finally, he set his heart on the task and enthralled the reptile with his dark magics. Commanding the animal to deliver the note to only peh'-shah, or otherwise kill itself in strong enough fire to consume the package it carried, he released the lizard into the sky.

It soared above the reaches of the upper firmament and disappeared into the distance. Absinthium exhaled a tense breath. *I must stop this future from happening.*

***

The gate overhead slid open slightly and Kevin craned his neck to get a look at the visitor. Karoz stiffened at the sounds of the gate—traditionally, visitors brought only pain.

This demon was different than the one who'd fed them before, it wore a set of stunted horns as common to lesser demons but one had been broken. He dropped two wet sponges that slapped to the floor and slopped a bucket of table scraps down the side of the wall where it dribbled to the floor; slimy globs and chunks splattered on Karoz who was closest and couldn't see to avoid the spray.

"What is it?" Karoz asked, wiping his face.

"You don't want to know," Kevin said, sniffing a handful and recoiling.

"Many days you have been down there," the creature above them said. "The human must eat or he will die."

Kevin reluctantly shook his head. "So your master can eat me at his table in a few days' time?"

"Stupid human," he said. "Kristchins taste like filth. They are not good for eating."

The angel shrugged and Kevin blithely noted the new information. He took a sponge and cautiously tested it with his cracked lips. It tasted like iron and smelled like piss, but it was wet.

Several moments later he noticed the demon hadn't left. Their captor watched them studiously. "Are you looking for something?"

"I am ELZTCHKEY the Great!"

The demon stared at them as if that should mean something.

"Should I know that?" Kevin whispered to Karoz.

His cellmate shook his head.

"I am the writer of the Book of EIZTCHKEY keeper of all history that matters. I want to know about the kristᵗchins."

"Christians follow the Messiah who redeemed mankind from sin and death," Kevin explained the basic tenets of the faith. The small demon's brow rose as he looked towards the ceiling, searching for information as if he'd known this and forgotten it.

"Mankind's redemption had always been the plan of Yahweh, the Father," Kevin continued. "His Word was established before time and has always existed since the beginning."

"The logos," eiztchkey stated. "The personhood of the logos..."

"Yes. Jesus Christ, the Messiah—"

eiztchkey yelped at the name. A jolt of pain rippled through him and made his skin crawl, resulting in gooseflesh. The fresh excitement surprised and revolted him all at once.

The demon held up a hand to stop the preacher.

"The Book of EIZTCHKEY preserves the things that concern the realm and rule of the Gathering."

A grin tugged at the corner of Kevin's mouth. "You do not like the name of Jesus? Don't you want to record the histories?"

eiztchkey recoiled with only a slight shudder. He grimaced, no longer in pain, but the sounds of the name bothered him like nails on a chalkboard.

"I cannot write the ineffable name. This is not the information I want."

"But it's who we are." Kevin noticed a smile breaking on Karoz's face. "He is central to our being. There is no such thing as a Christian without Jesus."

eiztchkey curled his upper lip, staving off a twitch as the prisoner said the name.

"Perhaps my book needs no mention of your kind. Your time in this realm will be short," eiztchkey stated matter-of-factly. "You shall not remain long."

"No," Kevin said confidently. "No, we will not."

With a scowl, eiztchkey slid the door shut and left.

Karoz nodded, still wearing his warm smile. "Without a doubt that has been my most enjoyable moment in two-thousand years… thank you."

Kevin looked at the emaciated messenger. "How long have you *been* in here?"

***

Werthen, Vil-yay, Shimza, and Fixxer snuck across the rickety framework of the massive mining elevator. They had crept across the rocky ridge and managed to stay out of sight, although the cover of dusk only hampered their maneuvers. The enemies' sight could not be impaired by the dark.

Lying prone on the roof, they peeked over the edge of the facility; a massive operation sprawled before them. The quarry had been ripped open and gutted. Sloping paths rolled around the edges and ended their massive curvature at the bottom of the gaping hole. Pallid ghouls and unturned human slaves pushed handcarts up and down the road as they emptied their loads of broken shale and bedrock before returning for more.

Stations built at the top of the pit burned oil fires and reflected, the light, intensifying it with giant mirrors. The beams illuminated the floor of the dig site so that the slaves could see.

"This is new," Shimza whispered.

Werthen looked at the hunter incredulously. They had only spent a few days in captivity and surely the work below demanded at a year's worth of labor.

At the center of the excavation rested an immense, stone head. Artisans worked on the scaffolding they had built around the house-sized carving. They removed any clay and detritus that still encased it.

Teams of mules and lines of sturdy slaves prepared around the carving where they'd looped giant ropes and chains around the head. Slaves set up rollers between the sculpted figure and the sloped trail. They clearly intended to drag it from the bedrock.

"What is it?" Fixxer asked.

"Whatever it is," Shimza said, "I don't like it." His ears prickled and he whirled around as a hissing creature rushed at them. A vampire clambered up the slope of the mining elevator's rooftop.

Shimza sprang to his feet and drew his curved blade. It flashed in the dim light and he cut through the wendigo.

Shrieking in pain, the vampire bled sand, spilling fine granules across the tiled roof. His cry split the night before Shimza could pierce the soul-orb lodged within his heart with a wooden stake. The vile creature collapsed in a heap of dust and ash.

Swinging rapidly towards the sounds, the nearest light tower flashed its beam of light upon the intruders. Screeches filled the night air as the vampiric battle-cry rose up from all around Granik's overrun High Town.

"Time to go!" Fixxer shouted, scrambling towards the rocky butte the elevator had been built against.

The four rushed through the dark as quickly as they could, returning the way they had come. "We can't go back to the villagers in Low Town!" Fixxer howled.

"I think the point is mute," Shimza yelled, leaning over the cliff face. He yanked out a bow and knocked an arrow, shooting a vampire in the face before it could fully scale the wall to catch them. "I'm not so certain we can make it out of here."

Fixxer followed his friend's lead. He leaned over the ridge and blasted another wendigo. The arbalist erupted with alchemical fury, burning the victim with both flame and jagged pellets. "So what, then? Stay and fight? Cuz I think that's a losing option," he stated as he reloaded with a new cartridge. The wounded wendigo crashed downwards and broke open upon the sharp rocks below. Moments later, it picked itself up off the rocks, albeit at a slower pace.

"Right now, let's just stay alive," Shimza said, slashing a vampire which had made the climb. He rammed the wooden spike into his enemy and kept the pace of the retreat.

More and more vampires made the ascent. Within moments, they were doing more fighting than they were fleeing.

Werthen's flaming blade shone like a beacon in the night as it erupted. The azure edge ripped through the faux flesh of the undead, spilling sand across the blocked path. Slicing his blade in a wide arc, he severed the taloned hands of the wendigo who leapt towards him. Spinning his blade while thrusting, Werthen pierced the heart of the vampire with the holy blade and the creature erupted in a burst of ashen particles.

The swarm kept coming undeterred—even in the face of a new threat.

"You've got to go, Vil-yay!" Werthen screamed. "Get out of here, lead our people away… go around Lol. Take them to find Kevin or Rashnir—just go! Now!"

Vil-yay shot his friend a look like a betrayed dog. "I can't just leave you here!"

"You're the only one of us who can possibly escape!" Werthen yelled as he struck another pale enemy.

Hesitating a moment longer, Vil-yay turned and assumed his lupine form. Using his powerful legs, he sprang into the distant darkness and into the black night.

Seconds later the wave of the vampires crushed around them, forming a solid wall of enemies on all sides. The three remaining spies shrank back to back, weapons held out to ward off any attack against the encircling force.

Another attack did not come. Instead, a row formed within the ranks and two elegantly dressed vampires approached them. They stood in front of Werthen but did not draw any closer than the circle's edge.

They stood there silently, trading looks that ranged from curious to amused. One vampire narrowed his eyes at Werthen's companions. "Our friends are back, Naadine."

"So it would seem, Fayge. But look, this one has a pretty sword."

Fayge squinted at it inquisitively. He grabbed the nearest underling and thrust him forward. The surprised vampire did his best to correct his charge and reached for Werthen with extended claws.

The Christian reacted with precision and split the creature from hip to head. Taking a step to stabilize, he slashed sideways through the wendigo's chest and ruptured the vital heartstone. The wendigo burst into a cloud of sooty loess.

Fayge wore an impressed expression.

"There is no weapon that can overtake this blade," Werthen stated with authority. "This is the blade that easily cut through the hide of the Dragon Impervious! Nothing can stand against it. Let me and my friends go."

"Oh, yes," Naadine said excitedly. "I have heard of that!"

Werthen waved his sword in his enemy's face, "Then you will let us go?"

Naadine laughed. "No." With lightning speed, he threw a swarm of tiny darts at the cornered humans.

Werthen could not block them all and two of the tiny, pointy bullets lodged in his body. He turned in shock and spotted Shimza and Fixxer. Darts pierced their skin, too.

He turned back to the leaders but felt suddenly and overwhelmingly drowsy. He couldn't concentrate and try as he might to hold it, the flaming blade evaporated from his hand. Werthen sank to both knees. Fixxer fell next.

"A toxin," Shimza noted sluggishly before he too took a knee and then slumped to his side.

Naadine walked triumphantly forward and caressed Werthen's chin. The Christian swayed like a drunken man as the vampire tilted his prey's head and exposed the neck. "Let's see just what this krist-chin blood tastes like? Perhaps you will become one of the feeders here, like all the rest?" With a grin and a playful laugh, Naadine bared his fangs and sank them deep into Werthen's flesh.

The vampire drank deeply, and then recoiled, screaming. His face reddened until his eyeballs suddenly popped like ripe berries, rupturing in a bloody mess. Blood! Not sand! Flames shot from Naadine's sockets as he flailed, incinerating from the inside out. He quickly melted into a puddle of viscous slag.

Standing over the putrid pile that just been his brother, Fayge recoiled with wide eyes. "Seize them all! Quarantine them—and nobody dare drink *from any of them*! There is poison in their blood!"

Werthen's eyelids fluttered and he felt his attackers grab him and haul him off the ground. The sleep darts finally took full hold as they pumped venom further into his veins and he lost consciousness.

Hiding just behind a large granite formation, Vil-yay watched the entire encounter. He calculated which of his friends might be the closest. They had left three of Dri'bu's Regal Red-Tail falcons with their companions only a day's travel from Low Town. Raz-aphf and Rondhale shouldn't be too far off near Vigna. Kevin should be in Xorst by now; perhaps Havara could dispatch some of the Gleendish military if things had gone well. Rashnir and Zeh-Ahbe' were perhaps far off, but surely one of the three could send a rescue party.

Vil-yay offered up a quick prayer. He hoped that his friends' travels had led them to greater fortune. Things were certainly not going according to plan in Lol.

Chapter Twelve

She was unmistakable. Rashnir could smell her at this distance… like jasmine and crushed iliac… could reach out and wrap his fingers in her golden hair. His eyes traced Kelsa's form before she turned and met his gaze with her lustrous, green eyes.

Shaking away the buzzing sensation in his forehead, Rashnir reached for her hands. Kelsa clasped them in her own, breathing incredulous and heavy. She kissed him fiercely.

Rashnir pulled away for air and finally recognized the buzz of warning in his mind. Something in his spirit told him that this was not right. A sense of déjà vu washed over him, only the setting was wrong for such an intimate encounter.

He looked up and spotted the backdrop. They stood at the foot of the Babel Spire, the entry to the demonic heavens—the mockery called Paradise.

Rashnir growled. He'd been here before; the wizard had played this game with him and lost. The only thing that changed was the scenery.

Kelsa gave Rashnir an apprehensive look as he stepped back, putting distance between himself and her. She reached for him but remained fixed in her location.

The vision darkened and the sky turned as Rashnir exerted his will upon it, forcing the façade to fall away. The scent of perfume gave way to the odor of wet ashes.

"I know you're here," Rashnir called shouted at the tower. The buzzing in his mind intensified. He locked eyes with her again, and she appeared genuinely frightened. Her hands felt for him as her eyes turned milky and unseeing. Rashnir's gut ached to see her like this—even if it wasn't really her.

"Where are you, wizard? Show yourself!"

"Please," Kelsa pleaded. "Please, it's so dark here. I cannot see."

"Don't you want to save her?" Absinthium's hot breath was so close that it warmed the ranger's ear.

Rashnir whirled as the archmage walked leisurely around him, hands clasped behind his back. "Stop toying with me. I know this is all a lie."

The black-cloaked mage nodded. "Perhaps. Your gut was correct last time… in the glade. That was an illusion. What does your gut tell you this time?"

Rashnir refused to look at her or acknowledge the sorcerer's trickery.

"This time it is no illusion," Absinthium insisted, motioning to Kelsa. He waved a hand and she stiffened as if she could not breathe. She went mute at his mystic command.

Rashnir's eyes glared daggers at the ethereal intruder.

"I have come to you in order to strike a deal, Rashnir."

"You have nothing I want."

"I have *her*."

"Kelsa is dead—and partly because of *your* affairs in Jand! I was there when she died."

Absinthium chuckled. "True, she did die. But *she is not dead.*"

Rashnir's set jaw and hard eyes silently expressed his disbelief.

"As I live and breathe—"

"Which won't be for much longer," Rashnir interrupted him.

Absinthium exhaled his frustration and patiently started again. "I swear upon my master's seat at the Gathering that her body still draws breath."

"That's impossible! You lie."

"As a favor to that twisted fop, Harmarty, I healed her body. She remains as beautiful as ever, ageless in her repose, and forever in my custody."

"You have a shell, and nothing more," Rashnir argued, believing the mage's veracity for some reason.

Absinthium sneered and stalked closer to the blinded woman. "True. Her heart beats red and her lungs take air, but the breath of life, her unique spark, is not inside her—it departed at her death."

"Her soul is gone. Kelsa is no more."

The mage wagged a bony finger at him. "Not true! *What do you know of death, krist-chin?*"

"I know that when the faithful die in this fallen realm our souls escape through the western gate and are ushered into the throne of heaven. Her soul is gone."

Absinthium put a hand on Kelsa's shoulder and she gasped for breath. "Tell me, my dear, where are you?"

"It is so dark. I cannot see!" She groped about the air again.

"Yes, but *where* are you?"

She blindly turned towards the voice and choked on the air. "Tartarus," she finally managed to whisper.

Absinthium withdrew his hand and she began choking again. "She died long before you were taken into Yahweh's fold. So where, then, does her soul go?" His intense eyes challenged Rashnir.

The warrior grimaced and stared at the ground.

"Can she gain admittance through the western gate? Surely not! She does not meet the requirements you so clearly laid out. Her soul remains in bondage—she wanders the abyss, awaiting the great emptying of the Black where after she will be forever damned. Is that not what you believe?"

Rashnir took a deep breath and glared at the Luciferian. "We all make our choices. Life… reality is not fair; I don't expect it to be so, and I don't have to like it for it to be right."

Absinthium cackled. "How noble." He waved away the argument. He knew he'd already won his case. "Regardless, I have her living body. Were it united again with her soul, she could be whole again." The wizard slinked around Rashnir who glowered apprehensively.

"That is impossible."

"Not for me," he smiled with phony, diplomatic warmness. "It may be impossible to accomplish from Earth where the way is barred, but not from *this side*. It's merely difficult; it's never been done, but only because Tartarus remains hidden and few know the way."

Rashnir paused in consternation. "What do you want? What's your angle?"

"Simple. Forget this mad expedition. It will only claim your life. Instead, seek Tartarus and find a way to restore your lost love. Rescue her soul. I will freely give you her body, only turn aside and forsake this quest."

The warrior looked at Kelsa's blind and groping form. His heart cried out for her, but he could not bow to the wicked one. He could not abandon Kevin and his friends—not even for the hope of saving Kelsa.

Rashnir closed his eyes. He stated emphatically, "No." He refused to open them until the vision burned away, finally dissipating and removing his life's greatest temptation. Rashnir finally opened his eyes. It was morning. The sun barely crested the horizon and the stars still shone in the remnants of dusk.

He exhaled, trying to expel the tension in his chest, but he could not. A stroke of insight hit Rashnir: the enemy feared their approach so much that he'd resorted to bargaining.

***

Gans scrambled up the rocky hill, panting for breath. His heart pounded in his ears. The Christians who'd followed him screamed one by one as the enemy picked them off. He continued onward as fast as he could, not stopping for anything since the order had gone out to scatter the group.

One hundred and ten of his fellow refugees from Grinden had passed beyond the Quey and Tribben Forests. They'd gone north towards the hill country surrounding Brohd, where Lake Ruet drained through the mountains. There, things took a disastrous turn.

As Gans climbed higher in the cliffs, his hands grew slippery with mud and sweat. Gans chanced a look over his shoulder and spotted a combined group of barbarians, both men and orcs. They fell upon the last of the men who had split off to follow him; he watched an orc use a battle-axe to hack off his prey's forearm. Hand over hand, Gans kept moving, hauling himself further up the stony face.

From the added elevation he saw the random lines of his peers fleeing, scattering like confused insects—they hadn't planned for this! Occasional blue blades flared up as some turned to fight. They flashed brilliantly against the trained blades of the bounty hunters who had polished their weapons with 'âbêdâh oils. Some found success and continued to flee; others fell under the blades of their pursuit.

Gans kept running. His breath caught in his tightened lungs. They burned and refused to cooperate as Gans demanded that his body continue climbing.

He ignored the crouching blackness in his vision and poured on even more energy. He had to escape—he was this flock's guide and they'd relied on his leadership ever since his group broke with Ersha, Thim, and Drowdan. Surely some of them would survive the well-planned assault against them. They had to survive and regroup.

The pain in his chest suddenly intensified, shooting jolts through his back. He tried to cry out, but there hadn't the oxygen in his lungs to do so. An arrow protruded from his back and bright pink lung-blood leaked out of the wound. He looked down from the steep rise as he kept clawing his way up.

More barbarians level their bows at him again and released. Two more shafts found their mark. Pain shot up his spine, briefly, and then his arms went numb.

Gans looked skyward as the pain suddenly fled. He felt a sense of regret for not having accomplished more: his burden of leadership ended in a massacre by the enemy. A serene peace fell over him and then his fingers slipped away as his grip released. He tumbled backward, sending a prayer up and surrendering his soul to its fate.

His body plummeted to the ground, and Gans saw no more.

***

Jorge and his team skirted the southern border of Lol and made good speed. One horse bore the angel and the other carried Rashnir and Zeh-Ahbe'. The wide open, albeit stony, plains availed themselves to expedient travel. Briganik was not too far off.

In the distance, the trio of travelers continued stalking them. They sometimes slipped into the visible range but they intentionally shadowed them at enough distance to stay beyond concern. Luckily, they left them alone each night as they made camp.

Jorge pointed to the skyline. His keen eyes picked out something not yet visible to the humans. "One of Dri'bu's falcons, coming in from the east."

They watched for a few minutes as their horses continued plodding westward. Finally, the bird began its descent, angling its trajectory.

It suddenly faltered and plunged from the sky.

Rashnir looked behind and spotted the trio of women as they returned their bows and retrieved the bird. It would likely be lunch for them.

The ranger sighed with discouragement. They wouldn't get whatever message had been meant for them. "Focus on the mission," he said aloud, mostly for himself. "The others must take care of themselves for the time being."

***

Absinthium rushed from the central chamber of the Babel Keep. He had received orders from beh'-tsah.

Lilth commissioned ten thousand ghouls as conscripts for his lord and he had to make arrangements to receive the army. beh'-tsah's demonic forces had already mustered at strategic positions; the added forces would help them push the attackers into submission if used wisely.

beh'-tsah's defenses had been erected sufficiently, but war was a risky game, especially given the subterfuge of the players. The demon grudgingly accepted tribute from his opponent on the far-away front.

Absinthium had already sent a message to Mesler, one of his counterparts in The Order's Council of Four; Mesler was a student of the Combat discipline. He would not typically delegate tasks to his arch-mage peers, but his schedule necessitated it. Mesler would ensure that the ghoul conscripts knew their roles in the Master of the Gathering's battle plan. Hopefully, the Order could keep enough eyes on the vampiric units to prevent more than the expected token subterfuge—but all of the units were due in Paradise and wouldn't cross paths with the living.

Ghoul conscripts would begin filtering through the gates and tramp across the Fields of Splendor within the next full day. He'd given orders to keep the army as obfuscated as possible; if anything, Lilth's ilk *were* good at stealth.

Mesler had been given explicit instructions from Absinthium. If he failed at any point in them, Babel could fall to the rebel demons and all his work might be rendered moot. Spells were specific; troop deployments and mission orders had been highly detailed.

The mage did not believe that Mesler was incompetent. But neither did Absinthium trust any person beyond himself.

He glanced back hesitantly and exited the Gathering's primary fortress. Absinthium scrambled up the side of his gryphon; the beast squawked and climbed above the sky of the upper firmament.

From high above, the mage circled the petrified trees jutting high above the stagnant, dead pools. He zeroed in on one tree in particular: the agreed upon meeting place. peh'-shah shimmered slightly as he phased between corporeal and incorporeal forms from his perch in the vacant, skeletal branches.

Absinthium slid off his flying animal and into a tangle of limbs. peh'-shah solidified; he held the letter the arch-mage had sent previously crumpled in his fist.

"Am I to believe you would betray your master, and for what   some misguided ideal?"

The demon's yellow eyes glowed balefully from behind his goat-like face. The letter erupted in pale, yellow fire, like an ill-omened moon. Burned to cinder, the dust of the incriminating note drifted away on the breeze.

Absinthium held the mighty demon's gaze unflinchingly and licked his lips. "If beh'-tsah *was not the Lord of the Gathering*, then I would not be caught in betrayal. I am a servant of The Order and to the one who sits upon the throne of the Babel Keep."

peh'-shah sneered.

"Do you think I can be tricked so easily into surrendering sensitive information to my enemy's lapdog? If you seek to join the side of might and enter into our coup, then you must first prove yourself."

"I expected no less," Absinthium said.

"Then tell me what information you have for me?"

The arch-mage sighed and his heart sank. Crossing the threshold and committing treason could not lightly be undone. "Lilth has sent forces from Nod to aid beh'-tsah. Even now, thousands of conscripted ghouls have begun ascending the stairs to Paradise. In a couple days' time they will be outside the Babel Keep, which you so greatly covet... performing maneuvers and combat exercises."

"How is this beneficial to me?"

"Ghouls are loyal to Lilth, not to the Gathering. Certainly not to beh'-tsah. I have already bought a large number of them. During these maneuvers, if you attack, the ghouls will turn on your enemy."

"And he will retreat within the fortress until his allies arrive."

Absinthium nodded measuredly. "The fortress will be locked. He will find himself trapped beyond his refuge, far from the power of his throne with his entire force caught up in the betrayal. They are just ghouls, anyway, easy enough to forfeit. Even many thousand ghouls could not take him alone—not so close to his home. But if you showed up in force... there would be no tide to turn. You would overrun him."

A devious grin spread across peh'-shah's face as he entertained the idea.

"What is the strength of his armies?"

"The bulk of his army is currently committed to the muster near kah'-as's fortress, but I'm sure you were aware of that. After the ghouls arrive most defenders from beh'-tsah's castle will bolster the offensive campaigns. As you know, the Babel Keep requires very few defenders to staff its impenetrable walls... so long as its master is capable of calling back her troops and making them a hammer and her the anvil. It will be a minimal crew, such is beh'-tsah's hubris."

peh'-shah sneered again. His stained teeth gleamed.

"And what do you require, arch-mage, in order to secure your cooperation?"

"I am loyal to him who sits on the throne. I require only that you prevail. You must make sure to kill beh'-tsah. If he survives, we shall both pay with *more* than our lives."

The demon turned to depart. He looked over his shoulder.

"You had better deliver on your promise, human. Or I will drown you in these very marshes."

peh'-shah shifted beyond the visible spectrum and departed, shaking the branches as he leapt into the sky. Absinthium swallowed the lump in his throat. His desperate plan had been set in motion and he couldn't turn back now.

***

Rondhale sat with his lycanthrope friend Raz-aphf. They shared stories over a hot drink in the morning. Stress had crept in on them after taking in the Vignan refugees.

Reports of race wars and rioting all through Gleend had certainly set them on edge. A few moments peace had been absolutely necessary to keep them centered.

Workers from the Christian community had already begun folding the Vignan humans into their ranks. Some had joined their cause, others merely existed within their number in order to continue living, but the believers were happy to share life with them, conversion or no. They certainly needed protection and the secular humans would not find it with elves or dwarves.

The former blacksmith leaned back. Rondhale shielded his eyes from the sun and stared at the sky. "A bird. Finally, a message from Kevin! It's been too many days and I've been getting nervous."

Spiraling downward, the falcon came to a halt between Rondhale and Raz-aphf. Rondhale picked up the letter and scanned it quickly. All positivity on his face quickly slid away into a worried grimace.

Getting to his feet, Rondhale stroked the stubble at his chin. "It's bad news. Our brothers in Lol have come under attack. They never made it past Granik. Werthen has been taken prisoner by a nest of vampires. The dark dwellers are up to something big—but, as of yet, undetermined."

"What do we do?"

"Vil-yay has requested reinforcements," he said as Robear walked near their fire-pit, attempting to join their morning meeting with his journal of handwritten notes. "Robear, come here," he waved him over. "I desperately need you!"

The young man hopped forward. Rondhale had been mentoring him and he'd made a studious habit of recording as much data as he could in the hopes that someday he could lead another group as their numbers continued growing. "Yes? Is everything alright?"

Rondhale paced the fireside for a bit. "No, in fact. Our friends are in grave danger and have asked for help." He fixed Robear's eyes with his. "I'm going to ask you for something big. Do you feel capable of leading—of protecting our family here at Vigna and carrying the mantle?"

"Yes... but no."

"No?" Rondhale looked bewildered. "What do you mean?"

Robear held his gaze. "You're going to ask me if I will lead so that you can go on a fool's errand and rescue our brothers. I feel capable, but I refuse the call."

Rondhale cocked his head quizzically.

"You are too important to risk losing," Robear insisted.

Rondhale turned to Raz-aphf who nodded in reluctant agreement with the younger warrior.

"Then what do you suggest? Should I leave my friends in their hour of need... even when they have requested my help?"

Robear shook his head. "No. I will go."

Raz-aphf looked at him for a long moment. Then, he nodded.

"I have my own crew of men," Robear promised. I can go in your stead. Please, you are too important to Vigna to risk your life."

Rondhale stared long and hard at his young friend. Finally, he nodded and gave his blessing to Robear. "Please gather them quickly; our brothers at Granik need help as soon as we can send it. When you get there, send my blessings on to Rashnir and whoever Kevin's team has sent." He hurriedly scribbled some warm thoughts and notes down on a piece of paper and rolled it up. "It seems likely that it would be Jorge. We are one of three this letter was copied to and I can only assume they are the other recipients."

He thrust the letter into his hand. "Now quickly. Make haste!"

Chapter Thirteen

grr'Shaalg sprinted up and through his secret entry into Jand's Capitol Castle. Dyule had contacted him via linked qâsam, but something about his demeanor was off-putting. There was something very wrong happening and he could not spare more than a few second's effort to right a toppling Jand.

Post-Rutheir, it had been set up as a well-oiled machine with Dyule at the levers: a job necessitating very little actual input. If that engine faltered, action would have to be swift and decisive. Besides, as far as the Jandish overland was concerned, it had outlived its usefulness. They had been a stepping stone to integrating goblin kind into the Order. If Dyule didn't present new ways to retain his value to the Shadow King, grr'Shaalg wasn't beyond having the man killed outright.

The goblin slipped into the hidden sub-basement and stiffened at an unexpected sight. Dyule was there, slack-jawed and motionless; an accompanying human in a cloak stood adjacent to him.

grr'Shaalg paused to regard him coyly. [So you are pulling Dyule's strings?] He asked in his native tongue, testing the massive intruder who stood at least two full heads taller than the diplomat.

"You might say that," he said as he pulled back the cowl to reveal a fair, almost angelic face. "I apologize for my deception," he said, "though I assume your kind could appreciate such a thing on a nuanced level. It seemed the best way to get a private audience with the true king of all goblins."

Unflinching as stone, grr'Shaalg refused to react with any sort of tell that might verify such a statement. "Many people believe many things about me... some by observation, others by knowledge more intimate."

grr'Shaalg relaxed and struck a genial posture. "I know nothing about you, but observation tells me much. You are something similar to these krist-chins' angels... but you are not one: the eyes are wrong. Your aura is broken."

Removing his cloak's cape, he let the goblin see his angelic form. It was tainted by a pair of leathery wings draped at his back.

"You knew how to find me and you know, or think you know, about certain affairs below ground. You are either highly intelligent or keenly observant."

"Perhaps I am both," he replied and bowed. "My name is EKERITHIA, and I have watched from the shadows since before the countries, both above and below ground even existed. I know what it is that you seek, grr'Shaalg."

"And what do you think it is that I desire?" The creature's wealth of knowledge unnerved the goblin.

"You are searching for a way to mature your growing, larval brood which you are grooming for the greatest military campaign this realm has ever seen."

grr'Shaalg neither flinched nor blinked.

The demon took a step forward.

"I can meet your need. I know of a device which requires neither magic nor potion. It can both age your force and also educate their minds within mere minutes." ekerithia toyed with the goblin, dangled his hopes in front of him.

"But if this artifact does not interest you then I will take my leave."

He feigned a step away as if he meant to depart.

"Yes." grr'Shaalg stated. "Such a device would be valuable to me." He snorted with mild disgust, sure that the price would be higher than he'd hoped to pay. "What are your terms?"

"I will give you this information freely," ekerithia promised. "But you must pledge to answer my call when it is given. Our purposes align, grr'Shaalg—we seek the same end game."

"And what is that?" grr'Shaalg chuffed.

"Seeing the Gathering shattered so that new powers can rise beyond them."

The goblin tapped his chin thoughtfully. "When will this call come?" It was of no value to him to breed an army for someone else's sole advantage.

"Not for some time," ekerithia promised. "Not until after Paradise is ripped from the sky. And I mean this in a literal sense."

grr'Shaalg bobbed his head. Perhaps their goals really did coincide, although he sincerely doubted a physical collapse of Babel was possible. "Secrecy will be paramount," he intoned, glancing at Dyule.

"Absolutely," ekerithia agreed.

He whispered a few words of an old spell and Dyule's nose bled as his eyes jittered and rolled back in his head, erasing anything he may have learned. The king collapsed to the floor in an induced fugue.

"Tell me everything about this device."

***

Werthen, Shimza, and Fixxer stood within the tiny cell that held them. A couple days had passed; they couldn't tell exactly how long they'd languished under the blasting midday heat and the frigid nights from within the sturdy, iron prison. Their captors had been certain to keep them drugged to enough of a degree that Werthen couldn't slice their cage open.

The trio could see outside where a nearby window remained open. Little traffic came and went inside the quarry office where the cage had been assembled specially for them. Vampires had taken Fayge's warning seriously; even deliveries of food and water had come few and far between.

In the last twenty-four hours, the activity at the quarry only intensified. The occasional rumbling underfoot had increased. Over the last several hours they had become a constant, grinding sound—a vibrating, droning noise

With nothing else to do but survey the window, they watched and tried to figure out what caused the constant tremors. Finally, the massive stone head rolled slowly into view dragged over hewn rollers and pulled by teams of mules. The ancient monument was larger than even the building that confined their cage.

The three men traded wide-eyed glances, speculating as to its purpose. The monolithic effigy crawled so close that it completely obscured the window, filling it completely and shading out the light. It moved so slowly that it crawled on for hours, scraping against the building at points, nearly crumpling the walls inwards.

Werthen wondered aloud, "What can we possibly do?" They had already tried any escape plans that came to mind.

"Nothing," Shimza said as stony-faced as the giant head that passed them by. "As a believer in the empirical and in my own ability to affect the world under my own power, I am out of options. But perhaps you can pray to your god on our behalf?"

Werthen considered using his sword to cut his way free, except that he couldn't seem to draw it—his concentration still swam from the toxins in his system. They would also lose any element of surprise and almost certainly be captured again.

As if in response to his thoughts, the rear door of the structure opened and Fayge arrived. He brought water but no food and offered the cup to Werthen first.

The Christian looked at it skeptically. He sniffed it and turned up his nose. It smelled stagnant and vile.

Fayge cocked his head. "You do not wish to drink?"

Werthen stared at him, and then looked back into the cup.

"You probably think that it is poison. You would be right."

Werthen looked back up and Fayge blew a handful of powder into the man's face. Werthen reeled, spitting and sputtering, but the dust already found root in his membranes and absorbed into his system. The Christian slowly collapsed and fell asleep.

"We cannot risk any intervention by meddlers," Fayge stated.

The wendigo smiled wickedly. Shimza and Fixxer stared at the spilled, black water which seeped into the floorboards as they licked their lips.

Not knowing if his other two enemies earned the same abilities as the unconscious Werthen, Fayge threw another handful of enchanted dust into the cage and knocked out the other two men. He turned and departed the way he had come

**

Pinchôt and his companions sat upon the stony overlook. They each pressed a telescopic monocular to an eye and greedily watched the distant riders as their chargers kicked up a trail of dust in the gulch below. "I recognize that one from Grinden," Pinchôt said. "He was an orphaned farm-boy before Kevin brought his plague to the community. I believe his name was Robear."

"But Rashnir is not among them," Krimko hissed. They'd been tasked by the Temple with taking him down. Current intelligence suggested that he was somewhere between the north side of Ninda or the bottom of Gleend just a few days ago. They'd made a strategic guess that the operation near Vigna might have hosted the renowned warrior. The plan had been to lie in wait for him and set a trap where they could isolate and then slay him.

"It's not Rashnir," Pinchôt said, "But it's a bounty that we can take. There are only ten of them; maybe they have some clue as to our Rashnir's movements."

Jandul nodded silently and pointed to the elevating trail on the western side of the gorge. "There is a choke point over there. We can rig it with traps and take them."

Krimko nodded vigorously. He often dabbled with alchemy. "I have just the thing!" He procured several flasks and a paper envelope. He dumped its contents into them and added water then swirled the contents until they turned a ruddy hue.

They took strategic positions and waited for their prey to enter the killing box. As the line of riders bunched up near the mouth of the canyon trail, the massive Grirrg stepped onto the trail, slowing their approach and focusing all attention on him. He shouted wildly as the signal to his peers.

Flaming arrows shot from behind stony outcroppings. The ambushers' arrows struck the hidden flagons triggering massive eruptions. Flame and stone burst at the detonation points; a sickly yellow smog fouled the air with a noxious cloud.

Horses shrieked and toppled, kicking up thick clods as they panicked or died from the choking vapor. Men howled; blue blades flared to life, indicating where the survivors of the blast were. They choked and coughed on the ochre mist.

Wearing scarves pulled over their mouths and noses, Pinchôt and Jandul leapt into the fray. Krimko leveled a crossbow and launched shot after shot from the rear while Grirrg charged forward with his massive battle-hammer.

Jandul's 'ãbêdâh slicked claws found home after home as he blocked and slashed, whirling between two zealous krist-chin youth. He chiseled away their defenses and whittled them down until nothing remained but killing blows.

Pinchôt and Grirrg took on the other three. They hacked and slashed wildly at the barbarian, stupefied as to why their blades did nothing but burn the scarred hide of the abomination. His eyes flashed red with each strike as the 'ãbêdâh flared within his body.

As Grirrg kept them occupied, Pinchôt stepped around his teammate and delivered the killing blows. The final, remaining krist-chin realized Pinchôt's fatal tactic: the smaller man dispatched his brothers while they ducked beneath the mighty pendulum swing of the barbarian. Robear leaped backward and just beyond Pinchôt's reach instead of ducking under the swing.

Grirrg twisted his wrist as he swung the hammer through the air and stepped forward again, spinning his torso and swinging the second arc with even greater distance—well within the reach of his surprised quarry.

Robear's startled eyes dilated with sudden understanding just as the blood-stained mallet end of the hammer smashed through his skull. The krist-chin's body flipped a full spin, flinging gore across the roadside.

Krimko cackled gleefully as they set about the grisly work of taking trophies to verify kills at the Temple. Pinchôt kicked Robear's broken body over and rummaged through his pockets.

Retrieving a journal, Pinchôt leafed through it and smiled, calling the others over to share in his discovery. Unfolding the letter he pointed to the crudely drawn map sketched in his journal. "Young Robear was sent to help his friends up in Granik." He pointed at the map to indicate the probable travel path.

"The letter states that Kevin and Rashnir were also requested to help—but Kevin's entire group was massacred outside of Sprazik," Krimko interrupted, giddy. "I heard it from one of the intelligence officers.

"Right," Pinchôt stated. "I also heard that, but thought it was only a rumor… except that these guys charged through here without Rashnir—if Kevin is being held in Paradise, then where will we find Rashnir at?"

"Paradise—attempting a rescue," Krimko exclaimed.

They all nodded in agreement with the logic. "The Granik cult will be quite dismayed when they learn that

Sprazik is gone, Rashnir is absent, and Robear is dead. Help is not coming," Krimko said with sarcastic disappointment.

"If Rashnir is going to Paradise, then he must travel through the spire," Jandul observed.

"Right," Pinchôt agreed. "We've got to get back to Briganik as fast as we can if we're going to cut him off…he's probably alone or in a tiny group so he doesn't draw suspicion."

Krimko nodded and then commanded the other soldiers that accompanied the hunters to gather the forearms as trophies. "Hurry up! We've got bigger prey to hunt!"

***

Griq'nnr reclined at the king's table. tlaFFr scratched absentmindedly at the thick scrofula hanging from his neck and tore another limb from the sizzling beast at the table. The scirrhous tumors had begun forming at his armpits as well and they flapped as he struggled with the oversized helping.

[The tlaFFr kingdom must give up the tunnels under Drindak,] Griq'nnr insisted, eyeing the tooled, smooth bore of the stonework in the great hall.

[I should have you executed for suggesting it!] tlaFFr spat the mouthful with disgust. [Do you know the lengths our ancestors went to drive the dwarves out from the mountains?]

Griq'nnr shrugged.

[What's to stop those dirty kreeches from moving back in if we leave?] the king cursed.

[That is kind of the point,] Griq'nnr said. [There are many grottos below Gleend that are perfectly suited to home the royal city of the tlaFFr Kingdom.]

[And only one that was taken from the dwarves!]

Griq'nnr nodded. [True, but is it worth the lives of your subjects to…]

[I'd kill every dwarf with my own claws if I could,] tlaFFr howled. [I don't think you understand how much I hate those dirty…] the King rambled on a tirade of subterranean profanity, spitting and flinging his engorged jowls with vigor.

[As a race, this is an important move for us,] Griq'nnr insisted. [I'd hate to see your obstinance result in possible slowness in delivering the katadoolu.]

tlaFFr fixed Griq'nnr with a murderous glare. [You would risk open war with the tlaFFr?]

[No! No,] he held up his hands to calm the king. [I simply know that you are due another shipment tomorrow and our convoy is at a crossroads—there is a schedule conflict and other of our kin also need a dose.]

[I would rather die than see this hall back in the hands of the dwarves!] tlaFFr stood as he screamed the edict, stabbing his utensils into the singed cadaver to punctuate his point.

Griq'nnr sized up the belligerent king and tossed him a scrap of cloth to wipe away the spittle that oozed down his thick neck. [Think about our request,] he said, rising to his feet. [Perhaps we can revisit this discussion in a few days.] The Shadow King's envoy turned his back on tlaFFr and left, letting the king glare at his backside, tight-lipped and grim.

Grinning, he turned the corner beyond the door and heard a whisper that caught his attention.

[Psst… Griq'nnr?] gLarmng leaned out of a nearby gallery where he kept out of sight.

Griq'nnr grinned and tiptoed over to the current king's majordomo.

[Yes? gLarmng, is it?]

The King's chief servant nodded. [Yes… I'd like a word before you leave?]

***

Havara and Dri'bu argued polarized positions across the campfire. Kyrius faded in and out of consciousness, trying to rest his injuries as much as possible and speed his recovery.

Rest was something Havara had a difficult time doing given the circumstances. The deposed prince was eager to form the next step in his plan, to formulate something actionable.

"None of this speculation does you any good," the elf insisted. "There are too many variables to consider. There's no way that you can plan your triumphant reemergence to the kingdom from the rubble of Sprazik."

"I suppose you're going to tell me that my time would be better spent resting?"

"Yes! Again, yes!"

Havara rolled his eyes. "I just can't do that! My mind won't let me." He disgustedly threw a hollow bone into the embers. He knew the elf's council was wise, but his thoughts refused to let go the notion that he needed to act.

"I promise you, my friend, we can work on this problem together… as soon as you have regained your health and gathered some credible information."

Havara finally lay on his back, stirring with agitation as he tried to relax. "I just can't take this waiting."

"For Rashnir and Kevin to return, or regarding the status of your country?"

"Either."

They had traded barbed words since the day after Rashnir and Zeh-Ahbe' left to pursue Jorge. "Keep it down, would you?" Kyrius groaned from his bed. "Some of us are trying to sleep."

"Sorry. I just find it difficult to sit idly... even when injured," Havara motioned to his splinted leg and crutch. It had improved significantly but was still far from fully functional.

"Perhaps this bird bears news that can take your mind off our current problem." Dri'bu pointed skyward where one of the Red Tail falcons started a spiraling descent. The elf took the letter and looked around for a secure cage to hold the bird.

All their cages had been destroyed in the acolyte's attack; their birds were destroyed in the onslaught. Dri'bu let the bird perch upon his shoulder while he scanned the letter and then set it aside.

"Well?" Havara asked from his fireside position.

"It is nothing," the elf said.

"Seriously? It can't be *nothing*! Oh no. It's bad news," Havara concluded. "If it were good news you would have told me to put my mind at ease."

Dri'bu sighed. The ruse had been too transparent for the prince. He handed it over. While Havara read it, Kyrius sat up, wincing. The intrigue had gotten the better of him as well. He took it and read it in turn.

"This is bad."

"Yes, very bad."

"We'll have to go right away."

The three talked amongst themselves and over each other. Finally, the fourth man, their prisoner, shouted out—curiosity finally took hold of him, too. "Would somebody tell me what's so bleeding terrible," Prock yelled from the post he'd been bound to.

They had nearly forgotten about their prisoner. Each one stared at the other, dumbfounded for a moment.

Rising to their feet, the threesome began securing any supplies that would make the journey easier. Kyrius, weary and bleary-eyed, finally pulled his friends aside. "I will follow, truly, but may seem to be in a trance. Don't rouse me. I will be praying—deeply—shielding Jorge, Rashnir, and Zeh-Ahbe' from prying eyes or divinations. The enemy probably expects them, but I believe I can at least confuse the seers from pinpointing an exact location. It is perhaps how I can help best in my current condition."

Havara and Dri'bu nodded, clapping him into a firm, but gentle embrace. "We will defend you if need be and will keep your path straight."

Kyrius returned Havara's gesture as the elf tended to their prisoner.

"We have to go to Granik," Dri'bu told him. "You're a human and unless you want my people to burn you at that stake, then you will have to come with us."

Chapter Fourteen

Far below the Babel Spire, the tower's forgotten roots bubbled and churned in a dark and ethereal pool. ekerithia hastily stalked the narrows, the forgotten and restricted corridors one level below the tower's surface level where a passage leading further below remained concealed.

His descent plunged him further than the upper tunnels where the goblins had made occasional forays since before the Order welcomed their ekthroic brothers. It spiraled deeper, down beyond the precise grid-work of the massive labyrinth which stretched the length of the continents, drawing perilously close to the oceans. He delved deeper yet, down, down, to the sub level of Tartarus.

The demon wandered around the rim of the massive, domed chamber and kept close to the wall. Moisture seeped through crumbling, musty stonework with its smell of wet earth and worm. Even ekerithia felt trepidation here. He steeled himself and walked down the final set of steps and into the basin-like recess at the center of the ancient room.

He was in heart of the mysterious, hidden Tartarus.

The pool at the center bubbled with a greyish, smoky fluid: not quite liquid, but not mist, either. Encircling the pit stood a circular, brick wall like the guard around a well-house; the top boiled with the inky froth that threatened to spill over.

336

He approached by the light of his soul orb; it burned even more brilliantly here as the agitated spirit trapped within responded to the place's dark energies with increased anxiety. Unlike his demonic brethren, ekerithia did not see himself as malicious; he felt a sense of pity for the woman whose soul he could feel weeping in the black void.

Sensing the soul's thoughts, the consciousness within realized where it was and despaired. *I was not destined for here! For the abyss! Please do not leave me here!*

ekerithia sent his thoughts to the soul orb, *I have come to collect another. One who has spent the days of her afterlife in the darkness until now.* He shifted his thoughts to the pool and listened. Finally, he heard her again, crying in the dark. *I am here.*

I burn, she sent, asking for release. *Please, free me from this hell.*

You are mistaken. You are not in hell, nor in Tartarus... you burn because you remain as you were in death. But it will not always be so. And neither will your new companion remain trapped forever.

The orb dimmed slightly as the disembodied spirit calmed some at his reassurance. ekerithia approached the pool and traced his finger around its perimeter.

Words had been chiseled into the raised rim. ekerithia's eyebrows raised as his eyes scanned them, remembering. It was written in the old language, the tongue of creation. He was unsure if members of the Gathering would even have remembered how to read it... but ekerithia remembered.

Ancient letters formed a simple warning to any who dared breach the abyss. The bubbling blackness was one of two doors. The heavenly side remained firmly secure, no doubt, and would until the time of the great emptying. This backdoor could be exploited, but surely not without consequence. One simple phrase embodied hinted an unspoken threat of action if meddlers intervened in the heavenly order. He interpreted the phrase.

THOU SHALL NOT STEAL.

ekerithia swallowed hard… the original language was more concise than the text below and more accurately said *thy will not be stolen from*. The possible repercussions would undoubtedly be severe. The demon withdrew a second orb, this sphere empty, from the leather pouch at his waist. He weighed the risks and blew the fine ash and silica from his empty spheroid to polish it.

Bending over the dark liquid, ekerithia held his breath plunged the orb below the surface. His consciousness went with it, breaching the surface of the void as if some load dragged him to the depths of the ocean. Breathless and cold, his skin burned in the darkness. The souls of the condemned swirled around him, moaning in blind torment as they cried for release.

ekerithia reached out with his mind, locating the one that he sought. Her spirit smelled of the life that she betrayed: the regret and the lost joy. The soul screamed with loss as it drifted derelict through the murk, moaning one name over and over again. *Rashnir.*

The demon reached out with the orb and used the mystic device to scoop up the spirit, trapping her within the globe. ekerithia reeled back from the pool on uneasy legs and caught his breath.

Anger rolled off of the pool like a fog. The thief could sense the abyss crying out at its loss and screamed with rage; it felt almost alive.

A flash erupted from the pool, flaring upward all the way through the upper firmament like a lightning bolt. The shockwave shook the Spire, enveloping it in a beam of eldritch light. High above, denizens of the Temple of Light inventing sudden prophecies and declared omens as the ground vibrated around the tower, intensifying at its center. With an audible groan, the force sent a final push from base to peak of the Babel Spire. It shifted on its foundation and separated slightly, gaping the winding steps that otherwise aligned with the lengthy crack.

Retreating back to the other side of the breach the angry presence retreated back to the void; the waters roiled more fiercely than ever. ekerithia gasped for air, knowing that something else far worse than an earthquake would follow.

But it was done. He'd acquired the next piece of his game.

ekerithia fled the chamber, ascending the secret stairs. He stepped over the chasmatic split as necessary. The two trapped souls rode at his hip. ekerithia grinned, knowing that his time grew ever nearer.

Plunged back into darkness, the chamber below the central hub of Tartarus continued to buzz with anger and wrath. Black smoke crept from the pool of the Deep Well. Something had been taken from it and for that, judgment was owed.

For the first time since creation, the thing within the Deep Well awoke.

***

Jorge, Rashnir, and Zeh-Ahbe' shielded their eyes from the intense light that erupted skyward. The blast of energy sheathed the distant, barely visible tower. A sonic boom cracked the sky, echoing a peal across the landscape.

"I hope that's not a welcoming party anticipating our arrival," Zeh-Ahbe' said.

"I daresay it is," Jorge stated. "It's not too late for you to turn aside and leave the burden on my shoulders."

Rashnir and Zeh-Ahbe' both gave him looks of defiance. They continued riding in silence for some time. The elevation continued to climb as they neared the mountains. Glances backward revealed the trio of warrior women, ever on their tail, kept pace with them.

They kept their heads down and drew ever nearer the Luciferian pilgrimage site; other travelers became more and more frequent. The Christians gave them silent nods or brief waves as they passed, trying to maintain an affable front so that their cover remained intact.

Looking behind, the women stopped a group of travelers for a brief conversation. "We might have a potential problem, here," Rashnir noted.

He stopped the next traveler who came near and asked for a favor. The young Luciferian monk was happy to oblige. "Can you ask the three woman some distance below to come up and speak with me? I will remain here, awaiting their company."

Rashnir noticed the sigil of tah-av-aw' tattooed on the monk's neck. "Right away, my friend," he winked with the desire to help feed the hunger of his demonic lord who consumed lust.

A short while later, Ly'Orra, Shi'Nala, and Ri'Aqua joined the company under a temporary truce.

They stood in talking distance but kept enough of a buffer that they could draw their weapons if they encountered any foul play. Zeh-Ahbe' sniffed with his sensitive nostrils; he detected trace scents of 'âbêdâh, even over the smell of their sweaty horses.

"You summoned us?" Ly'Orra asked.

Rashnir nodded and stepped forward. The hands' of the female crew dropped to their hilts in response.

"Yes," he sighed. "I am prepared to strike a deal with you. You wish to fight me to the death in order to claim your honor… to complete your Pawar."

"I must fight until I die, correct. You have been named and so only one of us may survive."

"I would still rather that you come with us to Zipha so you could meet our queen as a potential mate," Shi'Nala said, casting a sidelong glare at Ly'Orra. "Your sister deserves an honorable counterpart."

"Whatever," Rashnir held up his hands to stop what was some obvious infighting. "You two work it out between you. I'm here to offer myself—in whatever role you desire of me—but you must help me uphold my end of an honorable mission, first."

The women returned skeptical looks.

"I only need for you to do *nothing*. I just need you to guarantee that you will not give away our position. My friends and I have traveled all this way to rescue my mentor who was taken prisoner by one of the arch-mages."

"After this, you will accompany us to Zipha?"

Rashnir sighed and looked at his companions. "Yes. But I'll not abandon my friends until they have escaped the clutches of the Order."

The three women huddled and began arguing intensely in hushed tones. "It is an honorable mission," Ri'Aqua's voice rose above the others. "This only increases the desire for him by either party." Ly'Orra and Shi'Nala were both silenced by that statement and nodded with tacit agreement.

"We have an accord," Ly'Orra said. "On our honor, we will not disrupt your mission. And on *your* honor, you will join us afterward."

Rashnir bowed. The women bowed in return; the deal was struck.

***

Elo'misce disappeared from the qâsam stone in Elo'wiind's hand, she had passed on vital information for his campaign. He grinned, reassured of a successful venture, this time.

Through his telescopic monocular he spotted worry on the faces of the Vignans who the krist-chins protected within their encampment. The heretics seemed less worried, even in the face of the distant, growing line of elven and dwarven fighters that had begun mustering against them these past couple days.

Elo'wiind added another lens in front of the primary spectacle, increasing its range, and shifted it into focus. He spotted raiders in the distance kicking up trails of dust. Their formation began to split off into flanking groups.

The elven general looked back to the lockbox his sister had sent from the Xorst treasury. He reassured himself that it still remained in his possession; the mercenaries would do them no good if they couldn't be paid at the end.

He scanned their number, counting them, and fixed his gaze on a couple wagons that trailed after the team. The group was far smaller than the Gleendish forces arrayed on the hillside which had been set up in an intimidating row against the krist-chins.

Elo'wiind memorized the blood-red logo painted on the side of the mercenaries' wagon: a bright logo boasting a winged fist in the middle of a fire. This team contracted from Briganik by Elo'misce, claimed to have already slain a group of these cultists. They possessed the 'ãbêdâh potion which allowed them to fight against these abominations against the Order.

The elven general didn't care for religion. It was benign as far as he was concerned, but if these two opposites wished to kill each other, then so be it. He only desired the power to overcome the terrible weapons of this rogue sect so that they would remain beneath his feet.

At least the Order could be manipulated, used. These krist-chins had to be eliminated.

He stared at the wagons again. One of them contained a shipment of the stuff, sent along for Gleend's armory as part of the deal the elven diplomat had brokered.

The army encircled the Vignan encampment and began to squeeze them from all sides simultaneously. Chaos ensued. Blue, flaming blades sprang to life and a number of the defenders transformed into bestial werewolves.

Strange alliances, Elo'wiind thought, ironically noting that the mercenary force was almost exclusively composed of humans. He pressed the lens tighter against his eye as the battle intensified. Blades flashed and sparked as the weapons of the enemies met with force. Blood spilled and distant wails tickled his ears.

Elo'wiind gave the signal to his troops and they began to march towards the chaos at a reserved pace. They'd hoped the skirmish concluded by the time they reached the embroiled area. Better to pay someone else to fight on their behalf in this instance.

The battle remained fairly one-sided as the mercenaries charged unexpectedly from the flanks. Elo'wiind's presence on the slope had distracted the force enough that they'd been caught unprepared from the rear and sides. Still, several Vignans and krist-chins managed to scramble free from the net and flee into the distance. The mercenaries let most of them go in order to focus on the battle at hand.

Arriving just as the turmoil subsided, Elo'wiind's carriage rolled into the middle of the gruesome carnage. Barbarians followed with an empty rickshaw. It stopped as the mercenaries turned over bodies, searched them for markings, and hewed arms from the corpses they could get bounties on.

A large man rode his horse up to Elo'wiind. "Do you have our payment?"

The haughty elf stared at the man, a Mankran by the looks of him, but did not surrender his treasure quite yet. "You let some of them get away."

He turned a half smile through the grizzled beard. "A few harmless humans. Maybe a krist-chin or two... and some werewolves. Surely you can find a few lost humans; the werewolves are practically worthless to us to take a bounty on, save their leader... we'd have to skin them whole to take a bounty, anyway... they don't have the same mark as the rest."

Elo'wiind nodded, pretending that he understood everything that the bounty hunter had told him. "You have our potions?"

"As long as you've got our gold." He waved over a wagon laden with sealed flagons.

The elf bobbed his head in the affirmative and pointed to the chest behind him. "Gleend thanks you for your services. I'll give you something of further value: information."

The barbarian cocked his ear.

"Leave Gleend as soon as possible, and don't return. All human and ekthroic alliances have dissolved. Any day now there will be bounties posted upon any humans found within our borders. I suggest a hasty departure."

He only grinned in response as his partners rode up behind him. They weren't all human—some were so much *more*.

***

Tall bastion walls rose from the mountain slopes ahead of Jorge, Rashnir, and Zeh-Ahbe'. The line of bricks only broke with intermittent, curved apertures where the roads came and went to form the edges of the immense Temple of Light. Urban rooftops jutted into the sky and a shimmering haze wafted above the city as the smog of several hundred thousand people and their tandoori fires burnt trash, cooked food, and warmed homes.

Beyond them, the Babel Spire towered over the sprawling monastery-city. Pilgrims and monks wandered in and out of its gates. City noises roared dully within the lower threshold of their ears, barely masking the sounds of their horses' hoof steps.

The trio halted their weary mounts when they heard their names called from the steep, rocky slope that bordered the beaten road.

"Up here," the cloaked figure called. "Join me!" it insisted.

Reluctantly, the three dismounted and scaled the steep grade. As they drew nearer, they found a figure that looked very much like Jorge's duplicate. He also wore a Horpahthian disguise.

ekerithia pulled back his hood and scanned the horizon to ensure that they remained beyond earshot. He'd cleared a flat space of dirt and drawn a circle where he wrote sigils upon the ring to block any shama' spells and ensure their privacy

"Do not disturb the ring."

The travelers stepped inside the warding circle. "What is it? Is Kevin still alive?"

"For a while longer, yet. But my spy tells me that beh'tsah plans to kill him in celebration of his next victory over his enemies in the Paradise War. He's also increased his army with a large force of Noddic ghouls, so time draws short."

"Then why stop us?" Rashnir asked.

"I've been busy since we parted many days ago. And in that time, much has developed. I have information critical to your success, but you must trade for it with a favor."

Jorge looked hesitant to comply. "What is this favor?" He understood the high price demons were wont to extract.

ekerithia only looked at the two mortals. He ignored the angel.

"I need for you to retrieve something from the Babel Keep. There is a key within the central chamber: beh'tsah's throne room. It is a dangerous mission, but one that makes your friend's rescue easier."

"That doesn't sound so hard," Rashnir stated.

"If it's the key I think he's referring to," Jorge said, "it's what gives beh'-tsah the authority to rule over the Gathering."

"It is not that key." The demon shook his head. "That key is made of enchanted material and appears gold in color. The key I seek is with it, but of no known value to the demons. I seek the silver key."

Jorge was about to turn ekerithia down when Rashnir stepped forward. "I will get you this key if your information is as good as you promise."

"I know which of the temple guards are corrupt. I can give you a list if you like—you will find it easy enough to enter Paradise unmolested."

The demon handed him a weighty pouch of gold coins.

"You will meet my spy at the servant gate of the Babel Keep. Search out Cheska the ghoul; he will be your guide through the fortress. But there must not be the faintest hint of my involvement. As soon as he leads you to Kevin, you must kill him. Ghouls are notoriously untrustworthy. My existence cannot be known to the Gathering before my appointed time."

The demon looked at the position of the sun. From their current elevation they could see beyond the Temple of Light. A field separated the temple from the tower: the Fields of Splendor. A green blanket dressed in yellow and white flowers and studded with boulders. The massive stones had been set to mark the hours as the sun passed overhead, casting the tower's shadows over the appropriate time.

"The guards will change shifts soon. You must hurry if you hope to access Paradise this evening. It is no small journey."

***

Sim-khaw' paced back and forth through the encampment. His mind weighed heavy. It had been about a week since Rashnir and Zeh-Ahbe' departed. The Zaw-nawb' leader was on his sixth circuit through the grounds, muttering to himself, wondering at how gloriously Zeh-Ahbe's higher transformation had been after he'd gained this new power from the krist-chins. If the Say-awr' had gained such an impressive form, surely the Zaw-nawb's would be something greater.

His frustration ebbed slightly when he spotted the children again. They followed him, barely visible in his peripheral vision, walking in his footsteps like it was some kind of game.

A few days ago the children noticed his frequent pacing and started following him—part of the game being that they didn't want to be spotted playing it. Jibbin, Rashnir's ward, started it and the handful of other children followed suit. Whenever Sim-khaw' would turn around, or potentially notice them, the children would scatter or pretend to be involved in any number of ordinary tasks to avoid discovery.

Sim-khaw' smiled. Their children were just the same as his kin's. His grin soured; the children of Zaw-nawb' deserved the kind of life that Zeh-Ahbe's transformation could afford them. *He had to have it.*

The lycan continued his route, waving at those who he'd come to know, or at least recognize from his walks. Finally, he spotted Haisauce who made preparations to begin their play for the second time—they expected a bigger crowd this time. Much as Grinden was the example, he assumed they would draw a crowd from the friends and family surrounding the farming village and pull in those who hadn't seen it the first time.

Sim-khaw' glanced at him. It was time to make a decision. "Haisauce," Sim-khaw' called. "Do you have a few minutes?" He glanced over his shoulder and the children scattered like roaches in the light.

"Sure. I can spare time for a chat."

Sim-khaw' sighed. "My life demands my attention," he said. "My people need me, much like Zeh-Ahbe's need him—more so, probably."

Haisauce nodded, understanding that this was an important moment in the werewolf's life. "What can I help you with?"

Sim-khaw' leveled his gaze at him. "I must have this power that you possess, that you wield. I need it for my people; surely you understand that my motivation is pure, and good, and right!"

Haisauce continued to nod, validating Sim-khaw's request. "You do speak truly, my friend. But you have to understand that the path to this power *does not come by seeking the power*. It comes from the very person of God. We've had some conversations to this end. I know you've had them with Zeh-Ahbe' as well."

Sim-khaw' growled with discouragement. "You will not give me this power?"

"I wish that I could," the human stated. "But it is not for me to decide what God will do, who God will bless."

"Fine. Then I accept this god. I will bow before this Jesus. Only give me the greater transformation!"

Haisauce chuckled. "I cannot. I am not its keeper, and you cannot give a pledge to God in exchange for His power."

"Do you want gold, then? I will give you all I have, and I can get more."

"My friend," Haisauce looked into his eyes. "I would give it to you freely. *God gives it freely,* but you are still bound up in your own world. Your eyes are still clouded."

Sim-khaw' sat for a long moment in silence. Stoic and introspective he sat at the crossroads of his heart. Haisauce sat with him… waiting for whatever would come next.

Finally, Sim-khaw' stood to his feet. "My people need me. I have tarried too long away from them."

Haisauce nodded. It hurt his heart, but he had to let the lycan make his own decisions. "Until we met again, then, my friend. I truly do hope that you find what you are looking for."

Sim-khaw' nodded but did not turn to look at him. Something in the distance had fixed in his mind. "I do not think that such a day will come," he said with sadness in his voice. Finally, he began one last walk through the camp.

He came to the western edge and whirled around to look at the kids who followed him, neither knowing or understanding the heaviness of his heart. The children scattered with a gleeful squeal. Sim-khaw' bowed with a little smile and then took his leave. Jibbin crept out from behind a nearby table and gave a little wave before the lycan left.

Sim-khaw' waved back and then turned and began walking.

Chapter Fifteen

Absinthium stood shoulder to shoulder with Mesler, another member of the Council of Four who had helped set up the impromptu army's training exercises. Absinthium and his peer stood in the high tower above the Babel Keep.

The ghoul forces underwent a brief training and drilled. It was now a matter of waiting.

Absinthium had attempted to locate the approaching krist-chins but could not discern their location—something seemed to be blocking the spell caster's vision. For the moment, he could only focus on this front of the battle and work the plan. Trusting in the strength of others had never been his strong suit and frequently disappointed him.

Mesler, on the other hand, seemed almost giddy. It had been many years since the Order had any significant input on large-scale military operations and he was pleased to be a part of it. Absinthium rolled his eyes—he had experience in this area as beh'-tsah's hands and feet, but he'd carried it out so well that no others knew of any direct Luciferian involvement.

Far below the overlook, they watched beh'-tsah address the divisions of ghoulish conscripts. They had dressed for war and wore the armor as if battle-ready, carrying different weapons depending on their role in the force.

The demon champion spread his massive wings as his growling voice carried across the wind. He explained in gory detail what fate failures would meet.

Absinthium glared at Mesler who drew sketches of battle formations on his personal tablet. Some of his strategic ideas were good, but if his plans didn't work, Absinthium would see to it that Mesler met with the same fate as any of the failed ghouls.

For now, he had to rely on the ability of untried, untested, and unloyal minions of his master's sometimes enemy. He stared across the blasted, barren valley where his battle-plan would soon unfold, so long as peh'-shah performed as expected. He stared and sighed promising himself that if even one ghoul messed up he would pitch Mesler out the window.

***

Elo'misce and Bwar sat opposite of grr'Shaalg, the Shadow King. Naked but for the standard goblin loincloth, his simple amulet swung at his neck while he paced. grr'Shaalg dusted off his purple fez as he stopped to look beyond the exterior porch and survey Xorst. Rust-hued blood smears stained the sunbaked walls and sidewalks of the city on the canyon.

Buildings had been torched leaving blackened husks dotting the liberated city. Ekthroic residents had exterminated the humans, burning them out where necessary. Bodies hung upon trellises and pergolas where the executioners lacked sufficient trajectory to fling the corpse all the way into the Drindak rift which split the city into two halves. The skolaxis would feed well, far below, increasing their strength and numbers enough to accommodate the growing forces below the crust.

grr'Shaalg smiled. "You have done well in maintaining the anti-human fervor we initiated."

"It was surprisingly easy, with Lo-sonom out of the way," Elo'misce admitted.

The dwarf, as blunt as ever, demanded grr'Shaalg's attention. "The throne sits open, at the moment. What are we going to do about that?" His tone carried the weight of consequence if the answer didn't meet his approval.

grr'Shaalg merely looked at him. He sidestepped Bwar's play for power, "Who is the king, here?" He locked eyes with the dwarf and his voice dripped with such vitriolic power, that even Bwar nearly shuddered when he heard it.

"Y-you?"

"Do not forget that!" The goblin smoothed his tone and responded to Bwar's initial inquiry. "I will make good on my promise to give you each your own kingdom. Elo'misce will sit on the throne and I will return to your race the ancestral homelands of Under-Gleend which my people took from you so many generations ago."

Bwar nodded. His gumption returned to him. "Just so long as she is not crowned before my people are returned to our halls. That would insult my people and I might lose control—they are already in a fighting mood."

grr'Shaalg looked at the elf. Elo'misce shrugged off the minutia.

"So be it," the goblin decreed. "My race will clear out of the tunnels below the eastern mountains where the royal halls stretch for miles and miles. There will be an enormous celebration, a coronation, and you will be crowned King over your entire people, Bwar. Do you find this acceptable?"

Bwar stiffened regally and nodded his bearded head. His moment of fleeting humility behind him, he asked after the timeline.

"It will be soon," grr'Shaalg promised. "Very soon."

***

A horn blasted in the distance, startling Absinthium from his reverie. It split the sky with an announcement of war and echoed supernaturally loud.

He turned his gaze to the valley where his master stood amongst his troops… his *new* troops whom he had little rapport with. beh'-tsah's prize regular forces were currently capturing a prize from his enemies.

The demon whirled around to see the war banners flapping above peh'-shah's army. They shimmered as they came out from an invisibility spell that had allowed them to come so close without early detection.

With at least four-thousand of peh'-shah's blooded warriors, the coup leader outnumber him two to one. Many of the ghouls quaked with fear, turning to look back at the safety of the fortress.

Absinthium glared at the trembling cowards, ready to pitch Mesler from the parapet. Finally, peh'-shah howled with rage and rushed ahead, holding his massive sword high above his head. He led the charge as his enemies snarled with rage, making a beeline for the Gathering's lord.

beh'-tsah's ghoulish force rushed around him to provide a buffer as the enemy poured through the funnel that was the valley floor. The massing armies seemed to carom off of the raised bluffs as they pushed ahead for the choke point—where beh'-tsah stood.

Slowly, beh'-tsah's army backpedaled towards the large doors on this side of the fortress. They moved slower in retreat than the attackers who would soon be upon them.

Suddenly, Absinthium blew a horn from the tower. He locked eyes with peh'-shah, and then with beh'-tsah. Both looked confused; neither was aware of the mage's plan.

Absinthium bristled under their piercing stares and released a dispelling wave that pulsed outward from the keep. Camped upon the hills was another army on either side, each five-thousand ghouls strong. The secret legions rushed down the slopes, both flanking and surrounding the invaders to prevent any escape.

Snipers from the hillocks launched volleys of arrows at peh'-shah's surprised army. The demons in his ranks phased out and were unaffected, but the other conscripted troops scrambled to get under cover.

peh'-shah roared with defiant rage. He'd been baited into the trap and overextended his current forces, committing them to a losing hand. The demon snarled at the tower where Absinthium watched, and then charged into the fray, whirling his massive, flaming blade as he devoted himself to burning through as many of his enemy's forces as possible, though they outnumbered him three to one.

Flashes of concussive magic and eldritch bursts erupted as the demons hurled elemental forces at each other. Detonating bursts of arcana deflected around them, kicking up dirt as it blew craters open across the ground, flinging the charred bodies of each other's minions skyward. The air which sizzled and buzzed with the raw energies that two embattled demons commanded.

"And so it begins," Absinthium stated, knowing that this battle would pitch for hours, perhaps a day or more before peh'-shah could flee or would fall in battle.

"Keep watch for me, Mesler. I have other tasks I must attend at this particular moment."

***

Jorge, Rashnir, and Zeh-Ahbe' slipped through the Temple grounds with relative ease under the pretense of travelers on pilgrimage. Many of the nearby monks yelled dark omens on one side of the street; on the opposite edge, others proclaimed positive portents.

Rashnir and Zeh-Ahbe' stiffened when an actual Anakim crossed their path. He stopped to converse with Jorge for a moment.

To his friends' amazement, Jorge responded in the giant's tongue and spoke it well enough pass and receive an invitation to stay amongst other friends of his supposed ilk—the Horpahns. The angel did a good job of keeping his hands concealed beneath his cloak to avoid any giveaway.

"What did he say?" Zeh-Ahbe' asked as they hurried along.

"He spoke of the sign—the omen. The end is at hand, he said, 'the Nephilim will rise.'"

They kept their heads down in the midst of the bickering and pressed onward through the dusty streets. Ahead they spotted the gates which exited further onto the pilgrim's path. Nobody paid any attention as they spilled through the curved aperture in the wall, just as any sojourners might.

When they hit the Fields of Splendor they almost broke into a sprint but maintained enough composure to keep the contrite gait expected of a Luciferian pilgrim. At the final checkpoint, the trio arrived at a tollhouse where a small troop of guards expected a donation for the Order's coffers before they were allowed to ascend the massive, spiraling tower. Jorge reached into his pocket for the coins which Dri'bu had given him.

Rashnir put a hand on top of his. "No, my friend. Let me pay for this visit."

Jorge looked at him interrogatively. Rashnir wiggled his fingers in front of the angel as he reached for the pouch of coins that ekerithia had given them.

[Thank you,] Jorge bowed and said in the tongue of the anakim, knowing Rashnir would understand it by context.

Rashnir dumped the purse into the coffer, and receiving a nod from the attendants, the group began moving up the massive tower, stepping gingerly over the large crack that ran vertically through its form.

***

Minor skirmishes flared up over the past couple days in the tlaFFr realm, far below the crust of Gleend. grr'Shaalg sent a number of low-level emissaries from the tyr-aPt kingdom to try and smooth things over, but tlaFFr encouraged his denizens to riot against any of their neighbor's manipulation.

The resistance had grown so weary as the anthrofusis ravaged their bodies that they knew it safe to pass. tlaFFr's rebels could hardly raise their swords anymore.

grr'Shaalg and his company rode through the wide tunnels towards the grand halls of tlaFFr on the backs of their most vicious skolaxis. They towed several carts behind them, covered to conceal their contents. grr'Shaalg held his head high as the giant worms entered the massive subterranean kingdom that had been hewn from the stone by the dwarves who crafted it so many eons ago.

The powerful goblin hissed at the crowds who threw rotten vegetation and roots at his company in protest. They posed little threat; most had insufficient strength remaining to send a projectile more than a few feet without bursting the sores and seeping pustules that covered their bodies.

As grr'Shaalg's skolax reached the middle of the great, cavernous hall, the milling crowd parted, clearing the way for him to meet with tlaFFr. The king sat slouched upon an impressive dais at the central narthex.

The shadow king watched as his warriors and nawchash empowered shamans took point at the edges of the immense cavern. They began setting up their carts and yanked the sheets away to reveal rows and rows of glass vials—but until the time was right they kept the crowds away with pikes and falchions.

grr'Shaalg ascended the steps and could see that King tlaFFr was on the edge of death. His cracked sores leaked dark ichor that discolored the king's robes; his eyes had begun to bleed and verged on rupturing.

The sickly king's envoy, gLarmng, leaned against a desk nearby. His condition appeared similar.

Producing a vial of the katadoolu, grr'Shaalg waved it in front of the ruler. [Swear fealty to me,] he whispered into his ear.

tlaFFr regarded him with slight confusion. He stared vacantly at first before recognizing that grr'Shaalg held the antidote to the anthrofusis disease. The king weakly nodded and grr'Shaalg poured the contents down his throat. He handed gLarmng a different ampoule filled with katadoolu, which he greedily quaffed.

gLarmng stepped to the stage where the hold-outs had gathered and motioned the emissary over.

[Brothers and sisters,] grr'Shaalg shouted from his side, [we have discovered the source of this sickness! It is a disease caused by the very existence of mankind! It has taken hold in this geographic location and the great hall has become so toxic that goblin kind cannot survive here any longer! I urge you to abandon these holes. I have arranged for others to assist your relocation.]

The crowd booed and hissed, not caring if grr'Shaalg spoke truth or lies. They cared only to remain in their homes.

gLarmng already felt better mere seconds after ingesting the dose. He looked back at the king—sure that his vial had contained something else other than a remedy. tlaFFr's face turned a deeper hue of purple. He listed to one side and his engorged scrofula suddenly burst below his neck spilling puss and thickened blood all down the king's side and his throne.

tlaFFr fell off the chair and thrashed momentarily upon the floor as he expired. The royal crown, a crude construction of bone and teeth wrapped together with dried sinew, clattered across the stage.

gLarmng bowed, pretending to mourn. Finally, he made a proclamation, [The King was too far gone— tlaFFr is dead. Any kin with a claim to the crown should come now and take it!]

Only two contenders moved to the front. They glared at each other and drew blades in challenge. Charging for each other in wearied slow motion, they traded blows like battle-wearied warriors with one foot already in the grave. Finally, the older of the two scored a slashing blow across his cousin's artery and killed the contender.

gLarmng cried in celebration of the victory and beckoned for the new king to take his position. The blooded warrior shambled up the steps and then fell stone dead upon the dais—the anthrofusis coursed unchecked through his veins as his excited heart pumped him full of poison with each beat.

[Are there any others?] gLarmng called. None stepped forward. Finally, gLarmng retrieved the crown and set it upon his own head.

grr'Shaalg gave the new king a respectful bow to follow protocol. The audience followed suit out of habit and acknowledged his rule.

[My first decree,] the invigorated gLarmng shouted, [is that we shall evacuate the great hall for our peoples' preservation!]

grr'Shaalg nodded spoke in a harsher tone, addressing the crowd. [Hear me and hear me good,] he spat as he took out another vial of the potion. [Goblin kind is alive by my grace and lives by my pleasure.]

The impotent crowd surged with anger at being addressed by a foreigner mid-coronation but they were too weak to do anything more than shake their fists. They fell starkly silent as grr'Shaalg handed the unstopped vial to gLarmng.

The new king held it out for show.

[Any who do not abandon these halls with me will find only death.] gLarmng tipped the ampoule upside down, spilling the contents to the floor. A collective gasp ran through the horde. [There will be no more katadoolu in this cursed place. The gLarmng kingdom will clear these halls.]

grr'Shaalg nodded to his guards who began smashing and destroying the rows of glass bottles. Broken shards of glass coated in sticky antidote splashed across the floor. Sick goblins nearest the chaos flung themselves to the ground and gobbled up the jagged debris. Broken glass cut their mouths and throats as they swallowed it in desperation. A shrill wail went up from the throng.

gLarmng began a confident walk towards the exit. [Follow and live! I will lead the way to our new kingdom, the gLarmng Kingdom,] he promised. [There is a large cache of katadoolu waiting at the great hall's doors.]

As quickly as the invalid creatures could move they followed the king in a mass exodus.

Mounting his skolax grr'Shaalg locked eyes with gLarmng at the front of an enormous parade and then he rode towards the main exit ahead of the procession. The majority of the shambling horde slowly followed suit, surrendering the long-held hole.

***

Rashnir was the first of his group to finish climbing the heights. He exited the stairs into a brick structure that capped the spire. His steps faltered at the edge of the rotunda. His heart, bound up in the urgency of the situation, insisted he sprint all the way to beh'-tsah's fortress and take it by force. His mind, however, locked his steps at the edge of the building.

The closer they got, the smarter they needed to be in order to rescue their friend.

Looking at his feet, he could see the sheer drop to the surface below. His heart leaped into his throat as the clouds blew lazily across the sky below his perch.

Jorge and Zeh-Ahbe' caught up and approached from behind. "Why have we stopped?"

Rashnir pointed down to the drop. A walking path led away but appeared to be no more than a wisp of smoke.

Zeh-Ahbe' cocked an eyebrow. "The firmament should be solid," he said. "The monk, Minstra, told me about this during one conversation."

Jorge's face soured at the mention of the name. Minstra had abandoned them during the battle where the acolytes had taken their friend.

"He said that the upper firmament was composed of a crystalline type of substance. It allows the light to wrap around much of it, allowing the sun's rays to still shine below, albeit perhaps a little dulled by the pollution."

Across the surface of the upper firmament, patches were crystal clear, like drop-holes. Further away, mounds of dirt, hills, land, even bodies of water could be seen. Through some kind of magic, the firmament acted like an invisibility shield and the land did not block the sky beyond

Except for large crystalline formations which occasionally jutted upwards, the landscape resembled more of what they were used to on the ground below, though cancerous patches of tar and baked mud littered the grounds with increasing frequency. Efforts to clean and shape the land near the pilgrimage point remained evident. In the distance, they easily spotted a large castle.

"By all means, then," Rashnir said. "You should take the first step."

Zeh-Ahbe' looked at him apprehensively.

"I've got wings," Jorge said, taking a step to go.

"Wings that are broken," Rashnir put up a hand to halt him.

Zeh-Ahbe' leaped forward and onto the invisible ground. He stumbled as his feet caught the unexpected plane. "Let us hurry," he said, and his two peers stepped out as well.

They crept forward as quickly as possible along the "Pilgrims' Road." The dusty trail featured a number of monuments with donation boxes affixed. Signs informed the loyal Luciferians of historical events and possible facts about the realm and history of the demonic council.

Paradise is composed of thirteen floating islands, each with a castle ruled by a member of the Gathering. They are connected by wide highways. It is very difficult to see the upper firmament from the ground below. If it was not for their benevolent interventions, we might never know of their existence or efforts on our behalf. Which demons do you pledge to?

Rashnir scoffed as he read it.

Below the sign was a collection of steel, locked coffers with coin-shaped slots intended to take donations, as if travelers could purchase a boon from such a pledge. The trio looked up as a loud horn blasted in the distance.

The Babel Keep captured their attention as troop movements could be seen in the distance. Brilliant flashes strobed from the far side of the fortress where some opposing force had obviously met with resistance.

"Quickly!" Jorge insisted. The trio sprinted along the road, hoping that the cover of the nearby conflict would provide enough concealment for them to arrive unmolested.

They darted across a parched hummock. The gentle rise afforded them just enough view of the battle to see the two giant demons, each towering over their respective armies, trying to kill each other. Each whittled away at the others' forces. Insignificant as the three spies were, Jorge and company pulled their hoods closer for good measure.

Any ekthro they found out in the open had secured a relatively defendable position where they could watch the skirmish unfold in gory detail. None of them paid attention to the three invaders that skirted the edge of the scene, taking as wide of a berth as possible until they arrived at the rear of the Babel Keep.

A nervous-looking ghoul fidgeted near the refuse containers.

"You there!" Rashnir called.

The ghoul whirled anxiously and pointed at his own chest. "Me?"

With the serendipitous distraction raging beyond the walls, they didn't have a moment to lose. "Are you Cheska?"

The revenant shifted his eyes from side to side to check for spies. "I am Cheska. You are here for the prisoner?"

Jorge nodded solemnly, acknowledging their mission.

The sallow-skinned, hairless man looked sickly, as if on the verge of death—but that was the state of all ghouls. They subsisted on the whims of the master who had turned them. Ghouls were lost; they had already surrendered their souls to another power.

"Quickly. We must not be seen," Cheska hissed. He took the large key-ring from his belt hook and led them to a small servant port. Just before he could fit the key into the lock, the door flung open.

Another ghoul darted from the door. He clutched an enormous, gilded book to his chest. He locked eyes with Cheska momentarily and the two broke eye contact. Each acted as if the encounter had never happened. Two more ghouls who skulked near the refuse pit crawled up to meet the burglar. The trio of thieves turned away as a unit and scampered off in the direction of the tower. Clearly, there were more angles at play than anyone suspected.

"Do not be seen," Cheska repeated as if covering up the encounter they'd just had. He pushed his way through the door and led them down a winding path. They slipped past kitchen scullions and maintenance workers—the hidden, the outcast, and the lowly members of Paradise's servile caste. Even *they* failed to see each other as anything more than shadows.

Jorge memorized the turns and twists, planning the quickest exit possible, should they need to escape without their guide. Cheska took out his keys again and unlocked a door in the wider part of the hall where the ceilings grew to nearly ten feet tall; it led steeply downward and into the bowls of the keep.

At the bottom, a number of locked doors lay closed upon the floor. Each opened to a pit within the dungeon. "He is *here*." Cheska pointed to a closed and barricaded gate.

Rashnir pulled the ghoul aside for a moment and questioned him as Jorge and Zeh-Ahbe' banged on the door."

"Kevin? Kevin, are you there?" Jorge asked, raising his voice only slightly.

"I am here!" Kevin replied. "And so is my friend!"

Zeh-Ahbe' tried to pry the door open, but the lock held. Jorge's flaming weapon flared to life in his hand and he sliced through the lock; Zeh-Ahbe' pulled open the doors, flinging it wide open and exposing the recessed pit where the preacher had been dumped.

Rashnir joined them at their side a moment later. Cheska's blood covered his forearms.

"Karoz?" Jorge exclaimed. "By the rood, is that you?"

"It is I," the blind angel spoke into the air. "Who is it, friend? Your voice is familiar!"

"Jorge!" the angel said, hopping down into the hole. He hoisted Kevin up to Zeh-Ahbe' who waited with open arms.

"My friend! My friend!" Karoz exclaimed. Though he was bling, his ducts still worked and hot tears rolled down his cheeks, spilling beyond his crusty blindfold. "I can hardly believe it's really you," he said, taking Jorge's face in his hands. "Quickly, you must go— get Kevin Johnson to safety. You must leave me! My bonds are unbreakable; they come from the same chains as those binding the ones kept under the darkness of Tartarus."

"Nonsense," Jorge said. "You're coming with." The angel's azure blade warmed the blind one's face, and he heard the crackle as the blade spit and hissed against a heavenly metal that it could not cut.

"I told you," Karoz insisted. "You must flee— leave me!"

Jorge slashed again, and this time Karoz felt himself falling out of his taught bonds. Karoz grabbed at the brazen links which had held him for so many centuries.

"But how?"

"Your chains and the manacles they connected to were not made of the same stuff. I assume they blinded you before they trapped you here?"

Karoz nodded. "I kept cutting myself free. I slashed at those chains for years before I gave in to my fate."

"There is only *One* who controls fate."

Karoz nodded as Jorge clasped his badly atrophied arm and helped haul him to the surface level of the detention block.

"And now, we're all getting out of here!" Jorge insisted.

Rashnir embraced Kevin. "I'm so glad you are safe!"

A rumbling explosion rocked the fortress from beyond. Dust shook from the ceiling.

"Who knows how much longer the battle outside will keep those juggernauts distracted?" Zeh-Ahbe' urged them to haste.

Jorge helped Karoz find his footing and one by one they stepped over Cheska's corpse. Rashnir handed the ghoul's keychain to Jorge as they came to the top of the stairs.

Rashnir embraced them each in turn. "I have to go deeper," he insisted. "I have to keep my word and retrieve the key for ekerithia."

Jorge shot him a look as if to warn him away from his task. His grimace finally broke into resignation. The angel knew that the warrior intended to keep his word and preserve his honor—even to a demon.

"I won't be gone long," he promised. "Besides, if I don't make it, I won't have to marry the queen *or* fight her sister."

Kevin shot his friends a questioning look. They couldn't spare a moment to explain it to him.

"I'm coming with you," Zeh-Ahbe' insisted. He looked to Jorge to give his blessing.

The angel scowled but nodded. "I will see them safely out," he promised. "Godspeed, and blessings on you!"

The fellowship parted company. Two angels and the preacher went towards the exit. A ranger and a werewolf followed the directions Rashnir received from Cheska before Rashnir silenced him. They plunged ahead further into the dark heart of the Babel Keep.

Chapter Sixteen

Minstra stared down into the empty cup made of baked, glazed clay. The strong liquor caused his eyes and thoughts to swim.

The disgraced monk's heart hurt as he thought of his failure, his act of cowardice. He wasn't quite sure why he even ran during the invasion which claimed so many lives at Sprazik. Minstra tried to convince himself some higher power had compelled him... but he knew better. Deep down he'd always been afraid.

He'd traveled to Briganik in hopes of finding information on the outcome. The word on the street is what drove him to the bottle: *they'd captured the krist-chin leader*. He stared at it his cup, emptied it, and angrily chucked it out the terrace which overlooked the Fields of Splendor. The cup sailed over the second story veranda.

"Hey! You're gonna pay for that," the bartender scolded.

Minstra nodded mockingly. His cheeks glowed drunkenly.

The monk had been desperate in his hope that Kevin might truly possess the answers to all his life's biggest questions, but he had been taken captive by the Gathering. And nothing escaped the Babel Keep unless the demon lords let him or her or it go freely.

His head pounded almost as much as his heart. He laid it down on the countertop and turned his head. Minstra squinted to see if his eyes had betrayed him.

Minstra thought he recognized the man walking through the door.

He rubbed his eyes, head still on the table. *It can't be... can it?*

***

Rashnir crept silently through the massive corridors. Zeh-Ahbe' followed closely behind. The activity outside the keep captivated the attention everyone within the structure. The distraction allowed them to move mostly unchecked as they drew ever closer to the throne room. They'd only been forced to eliminate a small handful of under-demons. They melted under the azure flames of Rashnir's blade before they could alert anyone of the intruders.

The two invaders slinked along the wall, stalking right up to the edge of a massive, stone archway which opened to the main throne room of the castle. Rashnir poked his head around the casement and peered inside.

At the far end, a wrought iron throne sat upon a raised podium. It glowed faintly from below where a luminous line etched through upon the floor. The blazing seam connected the seat of power to a slightly recessed well at the chamber's center. Twelve more radiant lines connected to the central hub. Each emblazoned within the surface. Some shimmered, others glowed strong and steady.

Rashnir spotted the key jutting out from the mystical hub. The pulsing illumination glinted off the burnished gold. A type of brazen chain connected the key. The mystic links looked the same as the ones that had held down Karoz and the ranger knew his sword would be useless against it. The other end of the fetter connected to a silvery key which lay on the floor, slightly corroded, as if it were an afterthought compared to its more valuable counterpart.

Neither Rashnir nor Zeh-Ahbe' had any idea what each key was for. They only knew that they had to claim it.

Ducking inside, Rashnir and Zeh-Ahbe' clung to the safety of the wall. Their eyes searched intently for any signs of observation. The room had so many places an ambush might lurk that entering it felt foolish.

Twelve pillars supported the tall ceiling of the domed chamber; hooks upon the walls held long banners stretching floor to rafter. Each one displayed the sigils of the lesser and greater demon houses: the thirteen castles located in Paradise.

Zeh-Ahbe' shifted into his lycan form. His hair bristled under the palpable tension in the air.

Rashnir steeled himself, slapped his friend on the shoulder, and stepped out beyond the row of pillars. He compromised between a crouch and run as he stalked towards the central key.

Suddenly the air crackled and Rashnir flung himself forward into a tumbling roll, barely evading the bolt of lightning that zapped just past his ears.

"Intruders!" Absinthium screamed, even as the castle's foundations shook under the kinetic force of a blast beyond the fortress walls. One of the blazing lines that cut across the floor flickered violently as it erupted.

The arch-mage stepped forward from behind the throne as Rashnir scrambled to the far side of the room opposite of Zeh-Ahbe'. Absinthium wore a strange, scaly sort of tunic which neither of the Christians had ever seen him in before. "I knew you would come," he spat. "I have foreseen it, and yet I have protected my dread lord from your deadly plot. He is not here—murderers!"

Zeh-Ahbe' shot Rashnir a look of befuddlement. Rashnir returned it in kind.

"You will not leave this chamber alive!" The sorcerer blasted a fiery burst into the pillar where Rashnir hid. Flames washed over the cylinder, heating the warrior's face.

Rashnir tried to form a plan, but little came to mind except to face the mage in open combat. That did not strike him as a wise idea.

Absinthium slowly stepped down the steps of the dais as he flung another blast of eldritch energy at the pillar. "Tell me, Rashnir the krist-chin, where is your friend—the werewolf. I have foreseen his death. In every future I've seen, he dies in this room. I will kill him today!"

Rashnir glanced worriedly to Zeh-Ahbe's position, but he was gone, creeping up the edge of the room while the mage focused on the ranger. "I don't know what you're talking about!" Rashnir yelled, praying that the Luciferian's visions weren't a matter of fate. He fled his post and jumped behind the next pillar which afforded him a better angle of approach to the room's center.

His movement elicited a trio of blasts. They scarred the floors and walls as Rashnir barely evaded the projectiles. Behind him, against the wall, the blood-red banner of raw-tsakh' caught fire and vented an oily, cloying smoke into the chamber.

Blasting the new pillar with enough force to chip away at the nigh-indestructible material, Absinthium remarked, "But if you are not here lying in wait for assassination…" His eyes widened as he trailed off and stared at the key.

Rashnir seized the momentary distraction and sprinted from his protection, heading straight to the keys as his sword burst to life in holy glory. The mage's fists lit with flaming bombs.

Absinthium threw the first one just behind Rashnir, leading him and using it to calculate a second throw that would tear the warrior to pieces when the werewolf suddenly clawed at him like a feral animal.

The sorcerer's flaming bullet dissipated in a puff of acrid smoke and he reeled backwards. Absinthium spun and grabbed his toqeph, just slipping under the sharp claws of the furry mountain of muscle.

The mage spun his magically imbued staff with expert precision, blocking three strikes from the powerful lycan even as Rashnir hacked vainly at the chain which connected the keys. Absinthium caught Zeh-Ahbe' in the chest with such strength that it seemed to defy the old man's wiry frame.

Zeh-Ahbe' was flung backwards several feet and landed on his rear as Absinthium hurled a crackling blast at Rashnir. The ranger leaped to the side as the raw power washed harmlessly over the indestructible keys.

The mage followed the blast with a second one intending to fry the helpless Zeh-Ahbe'. The lycan scrambled to the side and sidestepped the deadly burst just in time.

Rashnir jumped back into the central hub, sliding to the keys on his belly. He seized the large, golden key even as Zeh-Ahbe' leapt, claws extended, and slashed at the wizard's face.

"Nooooo!" Rashnir screamed. Time seemed to slow as he watched Absinthium duck low, and grab his toqeph with both fists. The sorcerer blasted Zeh-Ahbe' as he sailed overhead.

Like an arrow, the lycan shot beyond and crashed through the throne, ripping it from its base mounts and breaking the metal fixture. The mangled seat toppled, hiding the werewolf's position.

The sorcerer whirled to face with Rashnir. A look of terror plastered itself upon Absinthium's face—without even realizing it, Rashnir had turned the large, golden key within its mechanism. All the glowing lines flickered with a panicked kind of strobe effect.

Absinthium leveled his staff at the prone warrior. The glowing end of his toqeph vibrated and whirred as it blazed brilliant, about to discharge a lethal dose of eldritch energy into the sprawled ranger.

Rashnir gulped helplessly, and suddenly the energy bolt shot upward into the ceiling, breaking a hole open overhead. The arch-mage howled and collapsed to the floor beneath the weight of the blood-soaked werewolf who'd dug his claws into Absinthium's shoulders.

Zeh-Ahbe' scrambled off their wounded opponent and sprinted towards his friend, kicking the toqeph into the distance. "Quickly, we must flee!"

Getting to his feet, Rashnir whole-heartedly agreed with his friend. He yanked the golden key from its socket and slung the chain over his neck. All the luminous, shimmering lines went dark in an instant. "I couldn't agree more!"

They sprinted as fast as they could from the darkened chamber even as Absinthium clutched for his staff, spitting vitriol and hate as they fled.

***

All of the sudden, both beh'-tsah and peh'-shah staggered under the wave that pulsed out from the Babel Keep. They each stumbled like something had struck them dizzy.

They stood there, glaring at each other as the ghoul army held their own against the lurching advance of the under-demons pledged to the rebel. Neither lord moved. Each one's thoughts caught up in the sudden turn of events.

peh'-shah leveled a finger at his counterpart. His accusation boomed across the sky.

"What vile treason is this? Are you this desperate to beat me in combat? You have committed the unthinkable!"

The Lord of the Gathering merely stared at him. He refused to answer the question, completely unsure of exactly how this had happened. Foul play had certainly been afoot. First, a secret army lay hidden from him by his most loyal worshipper, and then the leylines which empowered the members of the Gathering beyond the other demons suddenly fell silent.

beh'-tsah turned his head to the keep's tower. Only Mesler remained at his perch, watching the battle by himself. The demon grimaced and turned back to the rebel. He roared in defiance, bellowing a challenge to peh'-shah, taunting him into further attack.

Neither beh'-tsah nor peh'-shah was willing to tap into their innate power and press the battle further—not until the sudden blockage of power was vetted.

peh'-shah glowered, stabbing his enemy with his malevolent eyes. The demon stepped a few paces back, and then pulled out in full retreat, concentrating all of his forces on breaking the line of ghouls meant to prevent stragglers from a route. They wouldn't stand up against a concentrated force in withdrawal—not since they still had measurable strength in his army.

Eager to get to the bottom of it, beh'-tsah snarled at him but let the invader go. He turned and flew towards the Babel Keep.

***

On the northwest slopes of the Briganik Mountains, Wynn and his troop of acolytes laid in concealment. Using intricate telescopes and shama' spells they silently waited, collecting data as they stalked their prey. His master had given them this special task.

Wynn basked in the glory of his master's praise following the capture of the enemy leader at Sprazik. Unlike his predecessor, Wynn had proved capable of standing toe to toe with the krist-chin threats and emerging victorious. He allowed himself this token vice and reveled in the vanity.

He assumed the threat of heretics would greatly diminish with the capture of the cult's figurehead. It seemed likely, then, that another mission would come up so quickly: a sensitive mission requiring great stealth.

Following Sprazik, Absinthium commissioned him to locate the source of the sudden influx of qâsamai. While the Order dabbled in many aspects of their trade, the sales of seeing stones had been wrecked by the suddenly high volume of the devices, the reasoning felt more sinister than economic warfare. Absinthium suspected that some nefarious source had ulterior motives other than mere profit—why else flood the market?

The mage suspected that whoever sent these stones abroad was using them to build an unsuspecting spy network by eavesdropping upon any qâsamai with a parent stone secretly bound this new generation.

Using a series of hand signals to communicate with his brothers who hid across the slope in deep camouflage, he verified what he was seeing. A large mud and stone warehouse set back off the main path appeared to be the target they'd been searching for. Traders had come and gone, mostly hired hands—paid traders and movers delivered orders and received shipments.

Occasionally the door swung open. Magic gave them access to the conversations but only revealed info on business contracts and shipping schedules. Little had been identified beyond the local source. The true supplier still remained a mystery—one that his men were tasked with solving.

Suddenly, the shama' faded and faltered. Wynn raised his eyebrow in ire and flashed some signs to his peers. They experienced the same thing. Their tie-in to their master's power had been severed.

Incredulous as to its meaning, the door swung open again and Wynn's keen eyes caught a glimpse of something new. The creature visible through the door was clearly an Anakim—a massive, first-generation offspring of a human woman and a Nephilim.

Wynn desperately wished he could hear the giant's conversation. More than that, he hoped that the sudden block of his access to magic was not in any way connected to whatever plot had urged an Anakim to journey to the opposite side of the mountain range as their community.

***

Jibbin felt the heat rolling off the raging fire nearby. On short legs, he fearfully fled the skirmish line where he heard his fellow actors shriek in terror. Mercenaries had joined the Luciferian adherents from the city before they could do their play again. They showed no mercy.

"Kantror must be cleansed!" a voice rose above the din. Jibbin recognized it from the town: it was the tainted voice of the demon-possessed man from their first performance, the same one that Zeh-Ahbe' had freed from supernatural control. *He must have gone back to him!*

Looking back momentarily, the boy spotted Haisauce. The temporary leader in Rashnir's absence tried to escape the two armor-clad warriors who pursued him carrying blades slicked red from both blood and 'ābêdâh fluid. He turned and ordered Jibbin to run, ignoring the two arrows that protruded from his back.

Haisauce turned back and crossed swords with his pursuit. The Christian chopped one of the men down, but the other struck him from his weak side. As Jibbin watched in terror, the enemy stood over his friend and delivered a killing blow.

Pandemonium gripped the camp as tents nearest the flaming trees began catching fire and the violent intruders pressed hard against the overmatched defenders. Jibbin tearfully watched one of the other children, a boy his age, run across the rocky soil and drop to his knees, wailing over the body of his dead mother.

Jibbin screamed as a helmeted mercenary walked up to the child and swung his bloody scimitar, cutting down the boy who suddenly joined his parent in eternity. The mercenary looked up and saw Jibbin shrieking in terror. A horrible grin crawled across the villain's mouth.

Turning to flee, Jibbin raised his hands against the wall of flame, shielding his face as much as possible. He couldn't see anymore living Christian adults. Nothing but death remained behind him—nothing but death appeared before him.

His heart clamored for rescue. *God help me! Where are you, Rashnir?*

The line of burly, bloody mercenaries crept towards him. There was nowhere to go, but let his spirit fly to the western gate.

Where are you, Rashnir?

The boy turned and dashed as quickly as possible towards the line of flaming tents where the dead mother had been washing clothes earlier. He had to find help! He ran through a sheet that had been hung to dry—*still soaked!*—and somersaulted through the flames.

***

Bwar stepped over the putrefied bodies of dead goblins that had lain exposed to the air for several days before his arrival. He considered sending a crew of his dwarves in to clean out the carcasses. It would have been easy to pile them high and push them out of the broken tunnels where they emptied into the depths of the Drindak Canyons. Bwar decided against it—he thought it an important token of the dwarves' triumphal re-entry to their rightful home.

He grinned as he spun, taking in the glory and grandeur of the view. His greedy eyes drank in the scenery as he and his dwarven brethren filtered into the immense halls. The dwarves tore down obscene goblin contraptions and rickety construction which had been erected throughout the place. Goblin huts populated the great hall which had been converted to their grandest city; Dwarven brothers and sisters set them on fire, smashed them to pieces, or otherwise annihilated them.

A massive flood of his species spilled in from the myriad entrances, answering the call he had sent out across Gleend. Bwar demanded their presence at his coronation and the installment of a new dwarven empire under his rule.

Bards sang rousing songs which got their hackles up as he ascended the raised platform with great pomp and circumstance. At the summit, he raised a ceremonial battle hammer above his head and howled victoriously. The hammer elicited a chorus of cheers.

A servant helped him don the old kingly robes which his people had preserved for millennia. Bwar scanned the audience, looking for Elo'misce. She had promised her presence to make a political statement. Her absence did not much to wound his pride, but he had hoped she would make it.

Feasting and celebrations stretched out through the day. Evening drew nigh with the wine running strong and long, immense drums began booming at the far end of the hall announcing the arrival of an important goblin. The crowd scowled and bared their teeth at him as he approached. He approached holding the unmistakable mithril crown that his ancestors had wrested from the dwarven progenitors so long ago.

As the crowd parted in the distance, Bwar could make out grr'Shaalg's dark form, topped by his purple fez. He held the crown high for all to see and the crowd began cheering his arrival as he meandered ever closer to the throne.

He crawled up the platform and Bwar winked at him with his wine-warmed cheeks. The raucous mob applauded as he bent low for the goblin to set the precious crown upon his brow. grr'Shaalg's blockish metal amulet swung in front of his eyes and Bwar stared at it as it swayed. This amulet boasted a number of carvings and decorative engravings.

Even through his wine-buzzed vision, he realized the deception far too late. Like the rest of his kind, he had a far better eye for metalwork and crafted art than he did for the faces of other species.

The Shadow-King's amulet was plain and unadorned! Bwar looked into the goblin's eyes. "Yer not grr'Shaalg," he stated as he stood to his feet, standing a full head higher than the imposter.

As he stood, the dwarves announced him as their official king with a thunderous blast of their loud horns. The fake grr'Shaalg laughed as the signal went up. And Bwar instinctively understood his betrayal. "But I had a speech prepared," he lamented as the instruments' blast echoed through the chamber.

All the pillars throughout the hall simultaneously exploded at top and bottom, blasting with alchemical fury. Chemical fire broke the supports carved throughout the massive gallery, shattering every stone column that held up the ceiling…and the Drindak mountains.

Standing upon the mountain path high overhead, the ground faltered under grr'Shaalg's feet where he stood with Elo'misce. The entire mountain range shuddered and the nearby massif collection sank and lurched. The sky above cracked and boomed with sickening, crunching sounds and the shrieking moan of tectonic movement.

After several long moments, hot blasts of air blew dust out of the portals and vented into the Drindak Canyon. It finally settled and the air grew calm again.

Breaking the newly dawned silence Elo'misce giggled with pleasure. "Is it finished?"

grr'Shaalg laughed. "The dwarven empire is no more. Gleend is now an elven nation. It will be your responsibility to mop up any aboveground stragglers. The new goblin kingdom of gLarmng has been warned against trespassing aboveground without a treaty."

Elo'misce smiled. "Our deal is struck, and you have upheld your end beautifully." She smiled at her goblin counterpart who parted company.

The goblin slid down a hole in the earth that none other than a goblin could recognize as such. The elf walked a little ways down the trail and found a simple shack in the foothills of the Drindak range. She kicked in the door.

Bre of Lars sat at the foot of a bed in the middle of the flat.

"You're a long way from Lars, aren't you, elf?"

He grinned as she approached seductively. "I felt the ground rumble."

"You haven't felt anything, yet," she winked.

**

Rashnir trailed only slightly behind Zeh-Ahbe' as they sprinted for the demon realm's only exit. Even nursing a limp, the lycan could run faster. The keys jangled around Rashnir's neck as he ran for his life. The heads of all ekthro who resided in Paradise turned their heads inquisitively as the duo dashed past.

Looking behind, the intruders saw the old man in pursuit as the Babel Keep shrank with the distance. Absinthium seethed with rage; his speed surprised them as he kept the pace. He obviously had no intention of letting them leave alive.

The arch-mage screamed curses and rallied any nearby troops and fiends loyal to his master. They turned to join the pursuit as Absinthium screeched, demanding the murder of the krist-chin fugitives. Over the course of a mile, an entire throng filled in behind the sprinting arch-mage.

Rashnir poured on more speed, praying he would not stumble and hoping that a second wind would kick in any second. He cast his gaze forward; Rashnir didn't have any plan of escape past reaching the top of the Babel Spire first. He could only pray that some opportunity presented itself.

Zeh-Ahbe' pointed ahead and shouted something at him. Rashnir could not understand the words that his pounding heart muted but he saw what he pointed to. Much further ahead moved three figures: Jorge, Karoz, and Kevin. They limped ahead at a much slower pace. Jorge and Kevin were both injured and Karoz was weak and blind from eons in captivity. Rashnir guessed that they would arrive at the exit from Paradise at approximately the same time… only a few short minutes.

Drooping his head, the warrior stared at his feet while they continued the retreat; almost a mile separated him from their escape point. Foot after foot, step after step. The cries of the swelling horde in pursuit grew louder in his ears as he pushed his body, demanded his lungs to continue sucking down breaths.

The mile passed quickly—too quickly for any plans to come to mind! Rashnir spat out the thick wad of phlegm that his lungs pushed to the surface of his throat. They needed a miracle.

***

"No. It can't be," Jaker groaned incredulously.

The drunken monk, Minstra, waved awkwardly from the countertop he'd slumped over. He pushed himself up and staggered over to the former ranger.

Jaker got one smell of him and winced at the overpowering scent of alcohol. He took a few steps out and onto the dining terrace so that the air could dispel the overwhelming scent of pickled monk.

Minstra slung his arm over Jaker's shoulder. Clearly uncomfortable with that, he shrugged it off.

"You know, you're maybe the only friend I got right now?" the monk slurred.

"Oh great," Jaker said with an eye roll. He turned to look at the tower, instead, hoping that the drunk man would get the hint and move on.

"Hey." Minstra looked suddenly very serious and tapping the ranger on the chest. "Hey, we should go up it."

Jaker sighed. "I can't believe it. I leave Grinden to try and find my next big thing and you all follow me here." He disgustedly picked up a menu and continued venting. "I had to dodge Pinchôt and his Luciferian buddies earlier when I spotted them out in the square, too. The next thing I know, I'm gonna see Rashnir and Kevin come walking outta the Babel Spire over there."

"Pssshh," Minstra hissed. "That'd be impossible."

Something about the way he said it suddenly worried Jaker. "What do you mean by *impossible*?"

He looked around for something to drink. Minstra shrugged when he couldn't find anything.

"*Minstra*. What did you mean by that?"

"I mean *impossible*. Rashnir is far away and Kevin's dead er captured up'n Par'dise."

Jaker stared at him wide-eyed for a moment. The monk's half-shut eyes opened and closed as he bobbed his head, trying to keep it upright.

Suddenly, Minstra bent over and heaved the contents of his guts over the edge of the porch. Jaker recoiled in disgust as Minstra turned with a slight smile. "I think I almost hit someone down there."

CHAPTER SEVENTEEN

Jibbin slapped the hot embers that still clung to his clothes from the fiery escape until they quieted and then crawled onto a supply cart in order to gain a better view. He was only four—but turning five soon. In his mind, he was practically a man. Rashnir could verify that. He was Rashnir's sidekick; nothing bad could ever happen because of that fact. But this new thing scared him, and Jibbin hadn't truly been scared since the alley—when his parents were murdered and he was forced to watch… the alley replayed in his dreams every night. This scene would, too.

He saw the ring of enemies that flew the flag of the Order as it formed a semicircle around their group. A smell floated on the wind: a spicy smell that reminded the child of death… the red stuff they put on their swords.

The wind shifted as he overlooked the gypsy-village that made up the Christian collection of tents and persons. Smoke burned in his nose and eyes and he looked west to the copse of trees behind them. They were further up the hillock in the only direction where Luciferians couldn't be seen barring their path. A murder of nearby crows screeched and leaped into the sky with hearty complaints as they fled the black smoke.

To the east, a billow of dust rose, kicked up by the hooves of the horses. A large drove cut a clear line across the Himnp district, obviously angled for the town owned by Kantror's freedmen.

Jibbin almost cried again as his diaphragm tightened with fear. His thoughts turned to his parents: killed by the hate of Luciferians. He pushed it back and thought of Rashnir. *Rashnir will save me*, he insisted, imposing his own thoughts upon the fear. *Rashnir is a hero! He can do anything?*

***

Krimko led the Deathsquad near the edges of Temple of Light. He guided his horse through the meandering mountainside approach when he heard the booming thunder and the vertical eruption of light enveloped the temple's centerpiece.

The members of his party traded confused glances and then pressed in through the crowded streets where monks and criers shouted omens of either doom or triumph. The team picked their way through the crowds as best as possible as they attempted to make it back to Herang's station where they could collect their bounty and perhaps gather new data on the mission to kill Rashnir.

They steered around a couple sons of anak, both mendicants. Finally arriving, they found the booth unattended. Pinchôt drummed his fingers on the table as the minutes stretched long.

"Was Sheech a member of house Horpah?" Krimko asked his companions, thinking of the two that they passed in the streets. That had been nearly an hour, now.

Jandul, always direct, departed for the intelligence and bounty office where they had previously gotten their assignment. A few minutes later he reappeared practically dragging a young adherent. The low-ranking Luciferian apologized for the absent attendant. An important meeting had been called to try and discern the meaning of the quake that shook the Babel Spire earlier today.

The Deathsquad promised to return later for new leads. For now, they demanded payment so they could take in the sights and smells.

They ordered lunch at a tiny, high profile bistro known for its kaboshalged. Krimko contended they let it be his treat. They chatted over the stew.

"You've never seen the view from the Babel Spire?" he exclaimed to Pinchôt. He understood if Grirrg cared little for such things—he literally had no soul. Jandul had been required to take the pilgrimage as a matter of rank acquisition long ago, but Krimko felt Pinchôt had missed out on one of life's pivotal opportunities.

"I insist that you let me take you up!" Krimko raised his hand, calling for the attendant to deliver the check.

"Now?" Pinchôt asked with surprise.

"Absolutely! We have time."

A short while later, Krimko excitedly led the way past the primary gate which yawned open onto the Fields of Splendor. He looked up, taking in the sights, and immediately leapt to the side, shouting his ire and disgust as some patron in one of the two-story booze-joints vomited over the hand-rail of the parapet above. He spat curses at the drunkard overhead and continued ahead.

He pushed the inconvenience from his mind and happily led this party across the Fields of Splendor. Krimko breathed in the scent of the yellow and white flowers as they intermingled with the musky odor of traveling pilgrims.

Suddenly, a loud kra-boom! exploded high overhead. They turned their gaze up to see a large section of the firmament break away and begin to fall.

***

Shimza and Fixxer regained consciousness long before their Christian counterpart did. Dosed with a far less potent mix of the drug, they groggily came to their senses and waited out the day.

The vampires' prized monolith slowly passed into the distance as the day ebbed into night. Nobody had come to deliver food or drink; the intruders had become an afterthought with the flurry of concentrated activity.

Faded into an afterthought was the rumbling of movement as the giant stone barely grumbled in the distance. Granik High Town calmed significantly. The evening insects began to chirp and buzz, but no lights illuminated what remained of the town as far as they could tell from within the cell.

Shimza prodded Werthen but their companion did not stir. In fact, he barely breathed. A cursory check revealed that his body still maintained a pulse.

"I say we give him a day and then we eat him," Fixxer said coldly.

Shimza replied with an incredulous look. "I'm not looking to become a blood sucker myself anytime soon."

"It's about survival," Fixxer sighed. "It's totally different." Thirst burned his throat and his lips had cracked.

"What if his blood does the same thing to us as that it did to them? Maybe he *is* poison inside." He stared out the window knowing that the vampiric travelers were far gone by now.

Fixxer looked at the unconscious warrior. Clearly, he hadn't entertained that thought.

"I figure we have about two more days before dehydration kills us," he stated, still staring. A long silence followed before either spoke… perhaps an hour.

"Shimza?"

"Yeah?"

"If I die before you… you can eat me." Fixxer slumped against the corner of the cell. They didn't even have a device to catch and store urine for drinking.

Shimza shook his head with a mixture of disgust and amusement. "I just wish I knew what that thing was that they hauled out of here. I understand leaving us to die… but at least tell us why. I thought the bad guys were supposed to bore you with a monologue."

Fixxer shrugged. "I guess being a bad guy is a matter of perspective."

***

Rashnir knew he could only sprint a few more steps before his lungs would burst or his legs betrayed him. Turning his gaze, he saw his friends just arriving at the topmost structure of the tower. They were a couple hundred feet away when Jorge spun, casting off his cloak.

The flaming blue weapon split the air with a crackle of power. Zeh-Ahbe' howled to Rashnir, urging him to greater speed as the throng seemed to gain ground against him even while his weary legs protested.

A swelling crowd of enemies seemed to peek into his peripheral vision and he demanded one final burst out of his failing feet.

Jorge stood before the door like a defiant guardian. He shouted against the swarming horde, "You shall not have them!" His voice boomed across the sky with adamant resolve even as Rashnir's knees buckled and he tumbled forward. The ranger skidded across the crystalline flooring which he'd so recently feared was nothing more than air.

Rashnir slid underneath the angelic defender and flopped to his side, twisting to catch sight of the Jorge who brandished his sword high overhead, ready to strike any who came near. The mob pressed in right up to the angel—as close as they could safely come without stepping into striking distance. Absinthium stood at the front, hissing.

The ranger gasped for air. They must have been right on top Rashnir's heels!

He turned, winded and clutched his aching side. Hurrying to his feet he tried to catch his breath. Zeh-Ahbe' and Kevin helped Karoz as they attempted to navigate the top of the spire's entry.

Rashnir brandished his own blade and the rotunda filled with a soft blue light as he struggled to take those few steps toward his angelic friend.

Just beyond, the sneering, raging, sorcerer waved his toqeph through the air and chanted. His staff traced a slow series of arcs, drawing upon what limited power he had remaining to him. The air seemed to rush into the void that he had created out of sheer force of will; his words spat vitriol and the mage's scaled shoulder mantle grew red hot. It burst into flames as an orb of pure nothingness burst into existence, sucking inward like an imploding star a foot above the sorcerer.

Rashnir turned into the wind that rushed past him only to find his friends clinging to the Babel stair, trying to keep from being thrown down the shaft or off the steps.

Absinthium growled, screaming with worry. "It's not enough!"

Rashnir turned back to the spell caster, ready to try something crazy.

Jorge put out a hand to warn his friends to stay back.

Absinthium dropped his toqeph to the floor and urged more power into the nether sphere which shimmered and spun above his gnarled hands that clutched at the air. With a howl of rage, his burning garment crept up the wizard's wispy hair and melted his neck skin. All of his forces gathered behind him suddenly collapsed as the void pulled a shadowy essence from their bodies like steam escaping into the atmosphere. The black orb absorbed them and grew and grew, crackling with lightning and taking greater form and color, looming out of control.

With a mighty yell, the arch-mage hurled the sphere at his enemies with incredible speed. The globe of destruction hit the angel with cosmic force and detonated like a volcanic eruption.

Jorge groaned as he tried to shoulder the explosive load—tried to shield his friends from the eldritch bomb, but his defiant growl turned to a shriek of pain. Everything exploded, incinerating the angel and shattering the top of the Babel Spire. A chunk of the firmament itself snapped and shifted.

Beginning with an awful groan, the fractured shard slid against itself with cataclysmic force, and then it fell, hurtled to the ground with unrelenting fury. The wave of power washed over the Christians, who hid behind whatever protection they could find.

Rashnir dropped the keys as he dove out of the way. The force of the blast tore apart even the mystic links that held them together.

The concussion bomb flung shrapnel, ash, fire, and bodies in every direction. Rashnir tumbled through the sky. Hurtling towards the ground even as stones and broken bricks smashed into him, he angled a vector to reach the tumbling keys. He spotted the glint of precious metal but a plummeting chunk of crystalline firmament smashed the golden and silver keys, fling them out of sight and beyond his reach.

Above, Zeh-Ahbe' tumbled through the air; limp and knocked unconscious he slowly shrank down in size, returning to his slightly smaller-than-average human shape. The blind angel had one hand around his waist. Karoz's other arm grabbed a hold of Kevin. The preacher, too, had been knocked out cold.

Rashnir groaned as he fell, pelted by debris. The top of the tower smoked far overhead; he suddenly realized Karoz streaked towards him, following the sound of the warrior's yell.

Karoz wrapped his arms around the warrior, squeezing Zeh-Ahbe' and Kevin up against his body before locking his hands around the trio. Throwing his weak and weary wings outward, the air caught under them and their descent came to a jarring, momentary halt. The angel fell in an uneasy, controlled fall. Chunks of debris continued smashing into them and the angel grunted in pain as he tried to slow their still-too-rapid descent.

Rashnir put his hands to his face and tried to shield himself from the ground as it rushed up to meet them. The promised painful impact rushed forward to greet them.

***

ekerithia watched the scene from the edge of the Fields of Splendor. He saw the arcane blast explode far above them just as the trio of ghouls exited the final rungs of the tower. They darted to safety just as the firmament cracked and ripped apart.

The concussive blast obliterated the topmost section of the Babel Spire—vaporizing his original post. Nothing remained of the hidden alcove where he'd spent millennia observing the realm.

A huge part of the upper deck collapsed and crumbled and an enormous part of the crystalline upper-ground fell with tremendous speed. It shifted color to something like shale when it separated from its parent plane and tipped downward like a jagged spear, lodging into the yellow-dotted fields and kicking up geysers of dirt on impact.

The demon watched as the angel was atomized by the sorcerous blast and the humans tumbled and plummeted towards the mountainside. ekerithia saw the blind angel scoop up the spinning, falling Rashnir as he tried to slow their fall.

But the demon's eyes were primarily drawn to the metallic glimmer of the keys which flung wide as they plunged to the field far below. The two ghoulish accomplices to the book holder also saw them. Ducking beneath the hail of deadly stones they each sprinted through the debris and snatched a gold or silver key.

ekerithia patted his leather pouch and set his eyes upon the ekthro which slinked away and into the shadows

394

as quickly as possible. He purred to the two trapped souls within.

"Soon. Very soon."

***

Rashnir hit the ground with a fleshy *Whap!* The wind left his lungs and he gasped for air, feeling every inch of the several-mile sprint he'd just run as well the force of the impact. He turned over and groaned. A hail of stone and brick continued raining around them.

Groaning and wincing, he scrambled to his knees and began to drag Kevin to safety. Rashnir shouted to Karoz for direction. He dragged Zeh-Ahbe'. They crawled up against the fallen chunk of firmament which had buried itself in the soil, creating an immense bastion for them to hide behind.

Rashnir peeked over a jagged edge, praying for some kind of help. He glanced across the field, past the combat monks who rushed into the shin-deep fields, ready to act as damage control. Rashnir spotted ekerithia turn and walk away, completely consumed by some other person or thing and disinterested in their plight.

Looking back at the enemies rushing to the scene he continued his whispered, desperate prayer. His heart sank further when he spotted the Luciferian Deathsquad. He made eye contact with the insidious, little man, Krimko, who narrowed his eyes to slits with recognition.

"What do you see?" asked Karoz.

He worriedly looked in the other direction, keenly aware that the Deathsquad would be on its way shortly. On the other side, he spotted another threat: the trio of warrior women rushing towards them with 'ābêdâh oiled weapons brandished and held high. They looked ready for a fight and Ly'Orra scowled at Rashnir—her honor demanded first blood against the former-ranger.

Rashnir spat and bit his lip. His heart raced and adrenaline pounded in his ears. *She must've finally convinced them this was the setting for her Pawar!*

"What do you see?" repeated Karoz.

"Only trouble," the exasperated Rashnir lamented.

Epilogue

ekerithia followed the creature into the shadows.

A ghoul hissed and yipped short notes to his companions. They thought they had the upper hand in the blackness after the sun had gone down. Creatures of vampiric power only strengthened in the absence of light.

The ghoul grew confident in the dark. It knew something followed it but remained unsure of its pursuer's origin as it cast pale, yellow eyes back and forth through the darkness, watching the creature through a wood of ebon tree trunks. Lilth's agent had no idea that its stalker was so much higher on the food chain.

Carrying the massive tome it had stolen from Paradise, the one creature refused to slow for anything. He was of no interest to the demon.

Shifting into his invisible form, ekerithia slid through the rows of trees and over-matched the strides of the ghoul he pursued until he found himself in the lead. Running ahead, the vampiric minion crashed into the invisible hunter and tumbled to the ground.

It thrashed and flailed, failing to understand as ekerithia bent over the thief. He seized it by the throat and squeezed with his hands, pressing until the soft neck in his hands collapsed and cracked. The demon squeezing until a liquid, gurgling noise bubbled up from the body.

Smiling with satisfaction, ekerithia slipped his hands into the pockets of the fiend. He grasped the cold metal and pulled out the key. It flashed silver in the moonlight.

The prize had fallen to him. The plan was in motion. Soon it would all burn, and just as before, he would watch.

***

Crashing through the massive double doors of the demonic fortress where his peers had gathered, peh'-shah spat curses as he strode forward. A defeat had been bad enough, but the final insult had been levied. He scanned the room and deep satisfaction welled up within him.

More than just the original demons of the coup had arrived at the council. Other powerful demons who held lesser seats not on the Gathering had joined them. He nodded to ter-aw-feme', rem-ee-yaw', ked-ay-shaw', nid-daw', moot-teh', and eesh shek-o'-beth eesh. He'd been unsuccessful in courting these demons to his side earlier in his campaign to overthrow of the Gathering's leader.

peh'-shah looked up and recognized one face which he did not expect.

"TXAPOREH'-GMAHEE? I had not expected to see you at this meeting."

The slender, graying demon merely nodded his head and acknowledged his presence among their number.

"I only seek the same answers as my counterparts here."

He waved his hand to indicate the other six, vile figures who suddenly threw their weight behind the other side of the conflict.

"I will tell you what happened. I was there with beh'-tsah when it happened. Someone pulled the key from the

leyline nexus—he must have had his minion do it just as I
began to assert my dominance on the field of battle!"

The demons nodded. Some still appeared
cautiously skeptical, but they certainly understood that
the source of their power had suddenly switched off—this
was the only answer. gay-ooth' appeared more ready than
others and he stepped up to speak.

"What does this mean for us?"

Nodding, they others threw their voices behind
the question, crying for an answer.

"It means exactly what you think it means, brothers.
This is no longer a coup or some mere power struggle. Forces
of Babel, we are at war."

***

Deep below the crust, an angry black smoke
gathered above the roiling pool of souls. A singular
consciousness awoke in the heart of Tartarus. Only
vaguely was it aware of itself, so preoccupied with its
primary thought. The mind was raw, churning with
animal instinct.

*Something has been stolen from me. It must be
reclaimed.*

Having no body, it reached out with ethereal
tendrils of power. The feelers first found an underground
aqueduct which teemed with subterranean life. It seized
the living beings dwelling there. Shredding their ichthyic
flesh, he called them to himself and built himself a body
so that he could walk amongst the world. The guardian
pulled the husk of a blind squid into his new form; it
voided its excretory organs in terror as the invisible arm
snatched it—the terror brought pleasure to the entity.

Flesh knit itself together in a terrifying cacophony
of piecemeal fragments. But it was still naked. With a

pulse of energy, ethereal tentacles of smoke latched onto a number of those angelic creatures bound above in the long hallways of Tartarus. It clutched them with a cold, vise-like grip and tore their skin from their bodies.

Barely aware of their pained shrieks, the mind paid them little attention. It called the pieces together and stitched the gruesome patchwork cloak together. It dragged the ratty flesh coat over the newly created body, staining the cape an iodine yellow with viscous and fishy entrail fluid.

Enveloping his body, the consciousness crawled in through the nostrils and found its home, sparking the form into life. It drew ragged breaths and looked through the darkness with new eyes.

The tentacled face twitched and the guardian caught the smell of his coveted item. He sensed that which he desired—tracked it.

He took his first two steps, leaving behind sticky, inky footprints upon the bare stone of the Tartarus floor. It sniffed again, ascertaining clear direction.

I smell what has been stolen from me. It will be returned. Thou shall not steal.

Forward the guardian walked.

***

Absinthium groaned as he blinked into the vacant sky. Pain like deep arthritis lodged in his joints and his head radiated torment from neck to scalp where meh'-red's draconic mantle had immolated his head in an exchange for dark power.

The arch-mage pulled his dangling feet back from the hole that had cracked open over the top of the Babel Spire. He dragged himself back from the brink and stood over the corpses of a thousand of beh'-tsah loyal followers whose life forces he'd sucked dry in order to pursue the escapees—the mage had drained them like Domnish batteries in order to fuel the potent spell he'd blasted the angel with.

Standing on uncertain legs, Absinthium stared at the massive damages Paradise had sustained. The crater formed by the detonation had blasted all the way through the tower's exit and destroyed the top third of the vertical passage. The top gate of the ascension had cracked and fallen off leaving a gaping hole where the crystalline flooring had once been.

He grimaced when he heard the sound of massive feet behind him. The talons made a distinct, faint skritching sound as they clutched at the dirty ground between he and the fallen bodies. The arch-mage knew the sounds of his master.

Absinthium turned to face the fifteen-foot-tall demon lord. beh'-tsah took a moment to survey the scene and then stared at his servant. His hollow, yellow eyes stared at his servant and his bovine tail twitched as he waited for an explanation.

So many things demanded answers. The hidden army beyond the Babel Keep, the betrayal, the escape of the demon's prize, the deaths of a thousand minions, but most importantly—the sudden unfettering of the leylines which imbued the ranking demons with additional, supernatural energies.

"What I did, I did to protect you," Absinthium stated weakly.

The demon only stared at him, searching his minion's face.

"We have much to discuss, you and I," he said with a hint of threat.

beh'-tsah stared at his man standing in the middle of the smoking rubble. His chief prophet had much to answer for… much that demanded atonement.

Appendice A
Dramatis Personae

The Christians:

Kevin	Werthen
Rashnir	Ersha
Jibbin	Gans
Jorge*	Thim
Kyrius*	Thaadim
Lo-sonom	Erki
Havara	Katerna
Zeh-Ahbe'	Kadoz
Rah'-be	Naphta
Sil-tarn	Dri'Bu**
Nipanka	Minstra***
Drowdan	Jaker***
Rondhale	

(* angel)
(** ekthro)
(*** undecided)

The Luciferian Alliances:

Absinthium
grr'Shaalg**
tyr-aPt**
Prock
Wynn
Pinchôt
Shimza the Greater
Jandul
Krimko
Zilke
Dyule

The Demons:

[† denotates a demon seated on the Gathering]

[‡ denotates a demonic rebel involved in the coup]

hay-lale' – deception (Lucifer, Satan)

meh'-red – (previous Gathering leader, slain by beh'-tsah)

beh'-tsah – bitterness †

exaporeh'-omahee – despondency †

raw-tsakh' – murder †

zaw-lal' – glutton, worthless †

gaw-law' –naked †

shik-kore' –drunkard †

makh-al-o'-keth -division †

tah-av-aw' –greedily lusting †‡

gay-ooth' –pride †‡

keh'-sem –witchcraft †‡

peh'-shah –revolt, rebellion †‡

sheh'-ker –untruthful †‡

kes-eel' –stupid, fool †‡

gaw-nab' –stealing ‡

khaw-nab' –covet ‡

kah'-as –wrath, rage ‡

kin-aw' –envy ‡

ter-aw-feme' –idolatry

rem-ee-yaw' –slothful

ked-ay-shaw' –prostitute

nid-daw' –incestuous filth

moot-teh' –perverseness

eesh shek-o'-beth eesh –homosexual relations

eiztchkey

The Werewolves:

> Zeh-Ahbe' (Say-awr')
> Rah'-be (Say-awr')
> Sil-tarn (Say-awr')
> Mil-khaw-mah' (Kaw-bade')
> Sehkel-saykel (Ahee-sthay-tay'-ree-on)
> Sim-khaw' (Zaw-nawb')
> Khad-dood' (Tsip-po'-ren)

Appendice B
Key Terms

Lexicon

'ābêdâh – Luciferians' weapon protection serum, magic potion

Acolyte – mindless devotees, assassin disciples of Absinthium

anakim - also called the "sons of Anak" these men are giants

caisson – a small wooden box with filled with shrapnel and protruding spikes, contains some form of ignition (explosives or magical)

ceroscopy – a divination where the user observes wax drips falling into water

ekthro – term for all sentient beings (all nonhumans) created by Lucifer

Gathering – the governing body of demonic activity that was established after a time of war that followed the great flood; this body oversees the Luciferian religion.

kama – a sickle-type weapon like a miniature scythe, wielded by the Acolytes.

kil-yaw' – the governing body of werewolf clans

Logos – the word of the Lord

lupine – the altered beast form of the werewolves

scald – magical ancient amulet, a devotee takes it in hand when red hot to burn a mark of alliance upon themselves, gaining shapeshifting powers

to-ay-baw' – cursed, excommunicated from the kil-yaw'

toqeph – staff of power, usually magically imbued

qâsam – a magically linked seeing stone

vrykolakas – a type of shambling zombie, only stopped by fire or lightning, feed on the living

The Kil-yaw'

Shaw-than' – urine (to-ay-baw')

Say-awr' – hair

Zaw-nawb' – tail

Ore – hide

Tsip-po'-ren – claw

Shane' – fang

Dawm – blood

Eh'-tsem – bone

Gheed – sinew

Kaw-bade' – viscera/internals

Ahee-sthay-tay'-ree-on – senses

Appendice C

Geography of continents and mentioned countries

Continent 1:

Jeena- Very little fresh water is present here. It is flanked by ocean and wasteland, buffered by mountains. Here, people obey a strict code of honor and discipline.

Continent 2:

Briganik- This country is very feudal. Monarchy Anakin (sons of Anak: giants) live on the western half; the eastern half is low mountains. The mountains of Briganik are home to the Temple of Light, also called the Monastery of Light, and the first Babel tower.

Zipha- This country is basically closed off. It is ruled by tyrannical, trollish ekthro. It deals primarily in slaves and has a heavy military, run and policed by orcs and half-ogres. Also home to a rogue band of humans.

Jand- Allied with Ninda, it is a monarchy. Western Jand lives in constant fear of abduction by orcs and their troll masters for their slave trade; many of these slaves are sold in Briganik. Jand's commerce and agriculture is based mostly on its large system of forests and mountains/hills. Much of its produce is gathered from the forests or can grow in hilly/mountainous areas or on vines. Goblin kingdom of the southeastern region is located just under the mountains of Arnak, north of Capital City.

Ninda- Allied with Jand, aristocrats control their own lands and make up a council which democratically dictates rule. The country is mostly flatland and primarily agricultural, doing a great deal of business in its ag trade.

Ninda and Gleend were once a single monarchy, until Nindan nobles rebelled and formed their own country.

Lol- Composed of mining communities, it is rich in various metals. The terrain is almost entirely made of rocky badlands.

Gleend- A monarchy north of Ninda, Gleend has a large mixture of the races, (moreso than any other country,) and contains a working social system combining elves, dwarves, men etc. It is run by a human king, though he has advisors from each sentient group. Their King is revered as the wisest anywhere (Kevin's Earth experience has identified him as having Down syndrome and thus sees things more readily as black and white than as shades of grey. His handicap is not enough of a hindrance to make him easily manipulated, and is looked upon as a gift.) The capital city of Xorst.

Mankra- Composed primarily of thieves and warlords, Mankra is broken up into districts owned by warring factions. These constantly try to expand their territory, fighting each other, and sometimes their neighbors. They are subject to an over-warlord who rules the country; tribes pay him a yearly tribute, etc.

Screep- a caste-based society ruled by the neighboring Anakim

Continent 3:

Very few human settlements exist in this region; those that exist are aboriginal in nature, jungle dwellers. The people here have been twisted through occult magics and many are cyclopses. Their children are born as men but wear a brace that off-centers one of their eyes as they develop; the other eye is later plucked out. Many of these people are cannibals. It is often known as the Land of Nod.

Vampire aristocrats live in the mountain peaks. Other subordinate vampire sects live abroad.

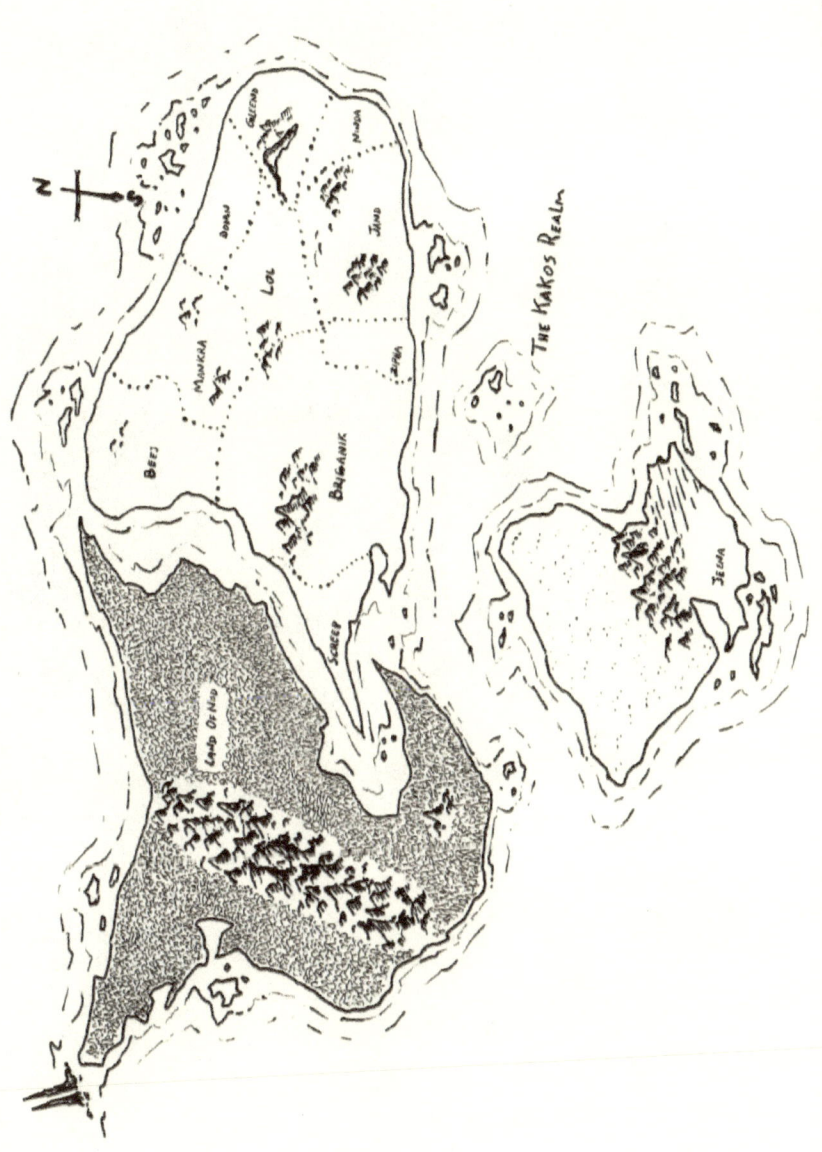

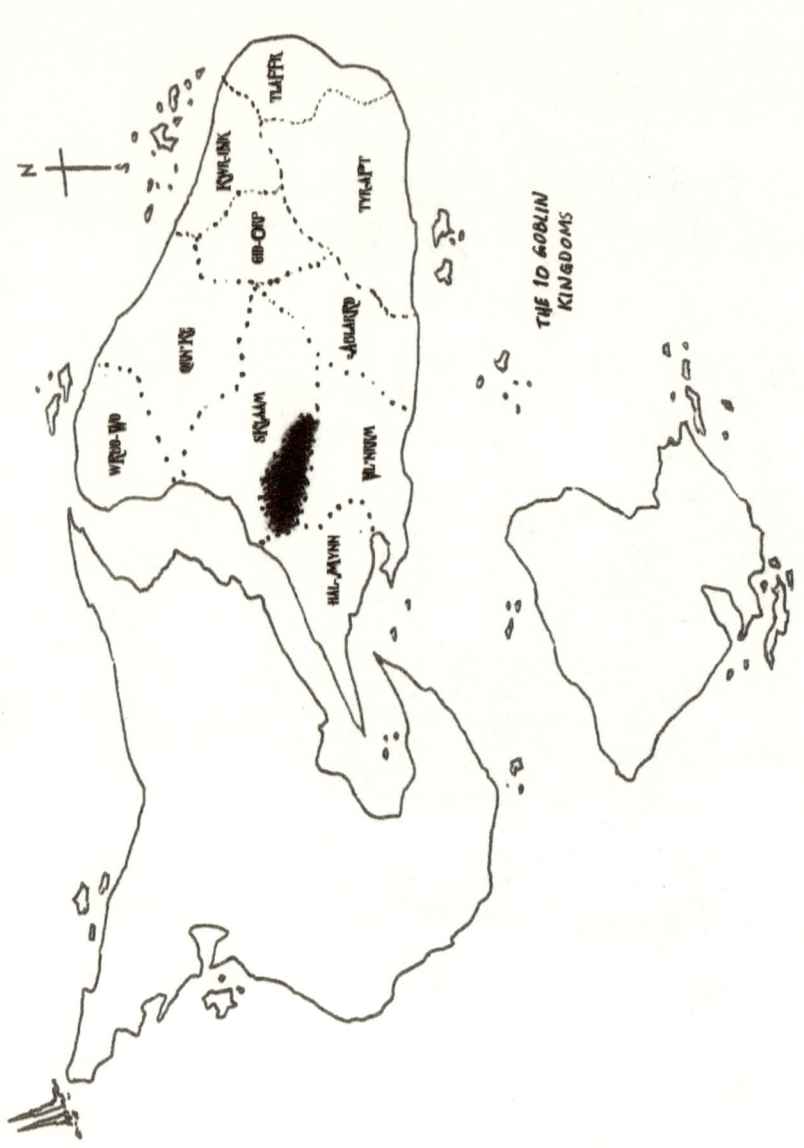

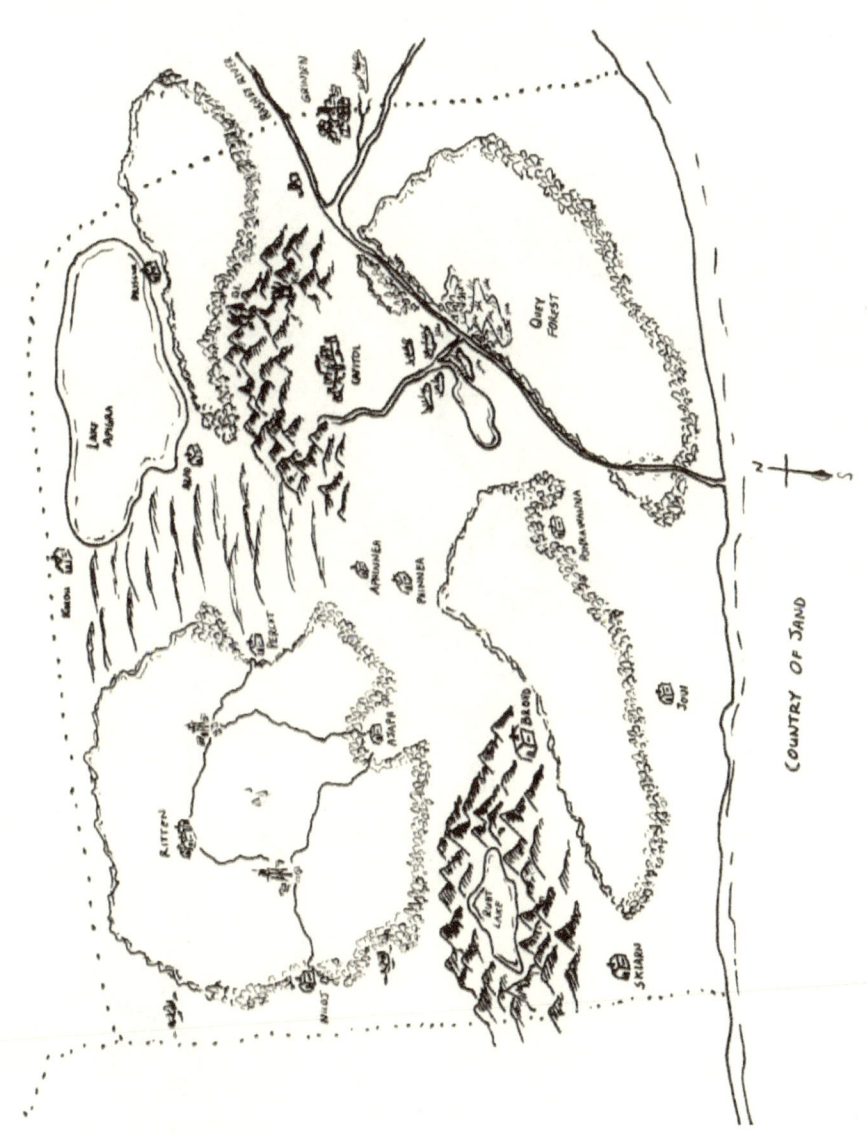

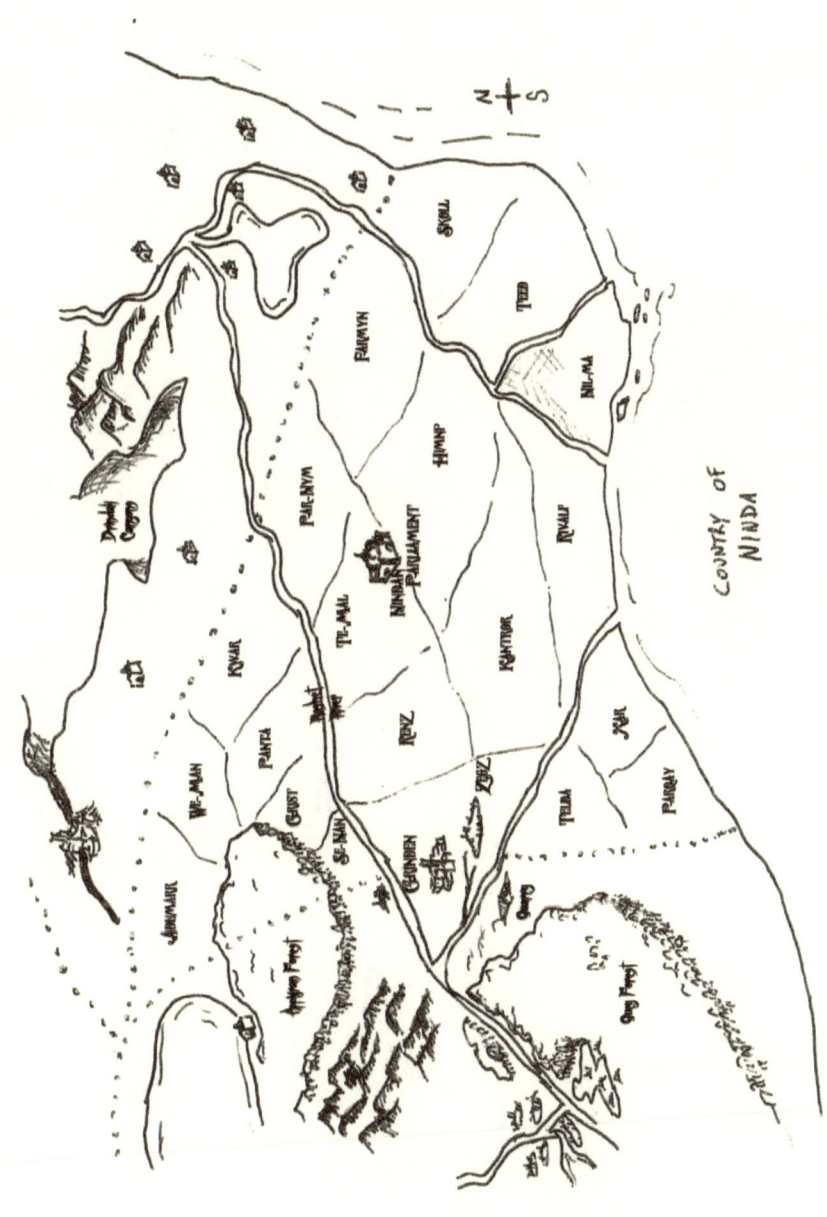

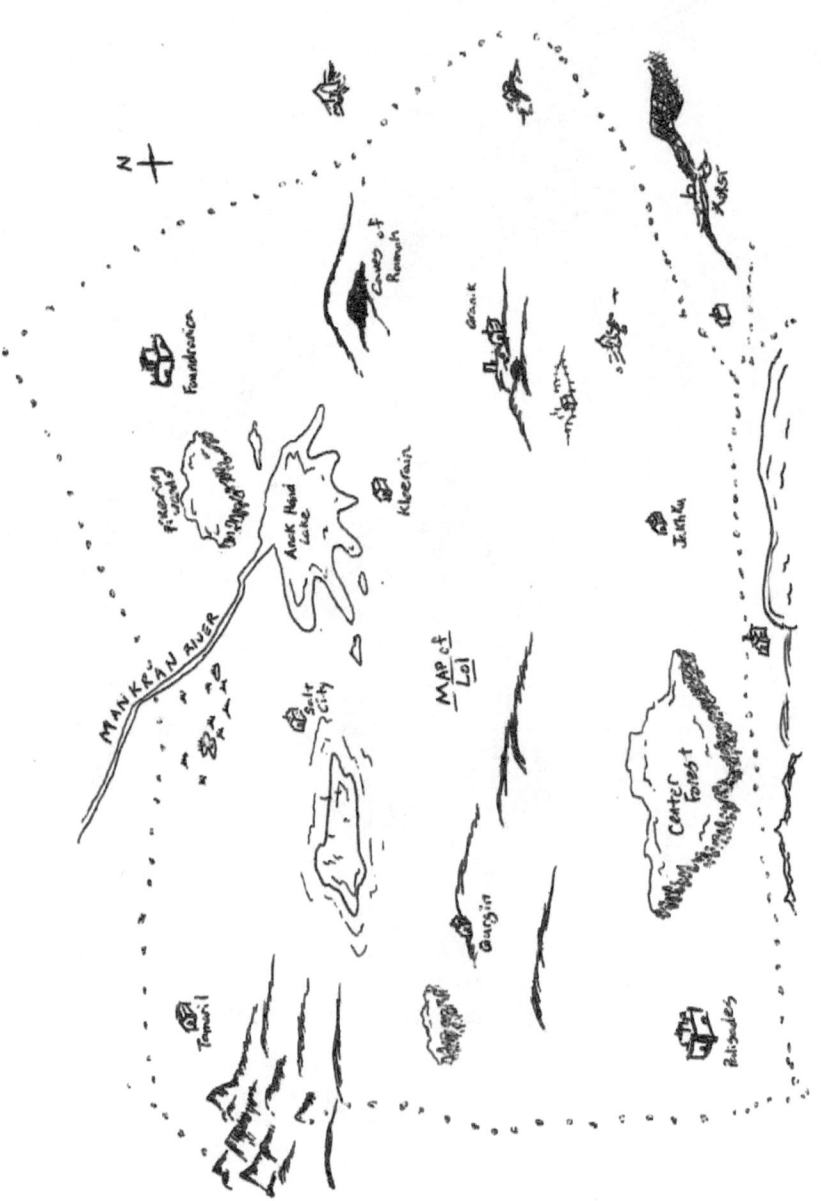

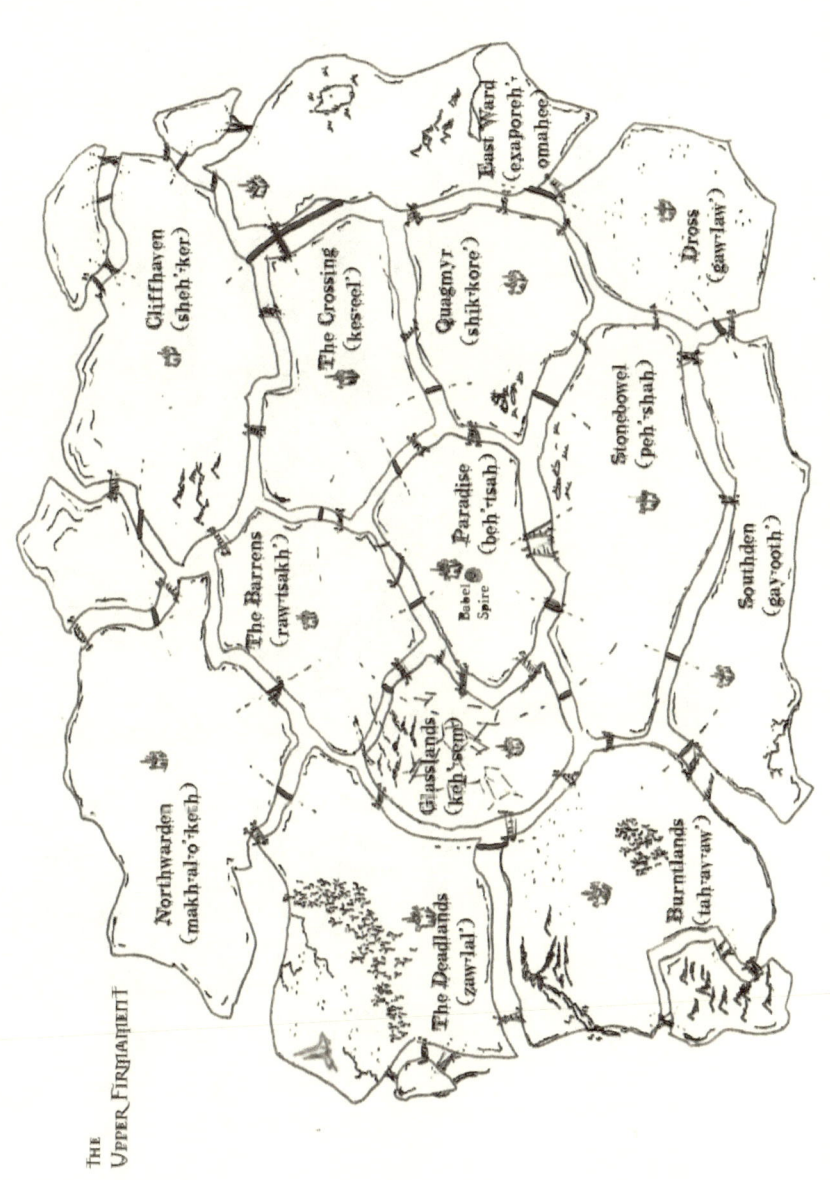

The Upper Firmament

Cliffhaven (sheh'ker)

The Crossing (kes'eel)

Quagmyr (shik'kore')

East Ward (exaporeh' omahee)

Dross (gawr'law')

Stonebowel (peh'shah)

Paradise (beh'tisah)

Babel Spire

The Barrens (rawr'tsakh')

Southden (gayrooth')

Northwarden (makh-ul-o'keeh)

Glasslands (keh'eem')

Burntlands (tah'ray'aw')

The Deadlands (zaw'lal')

417

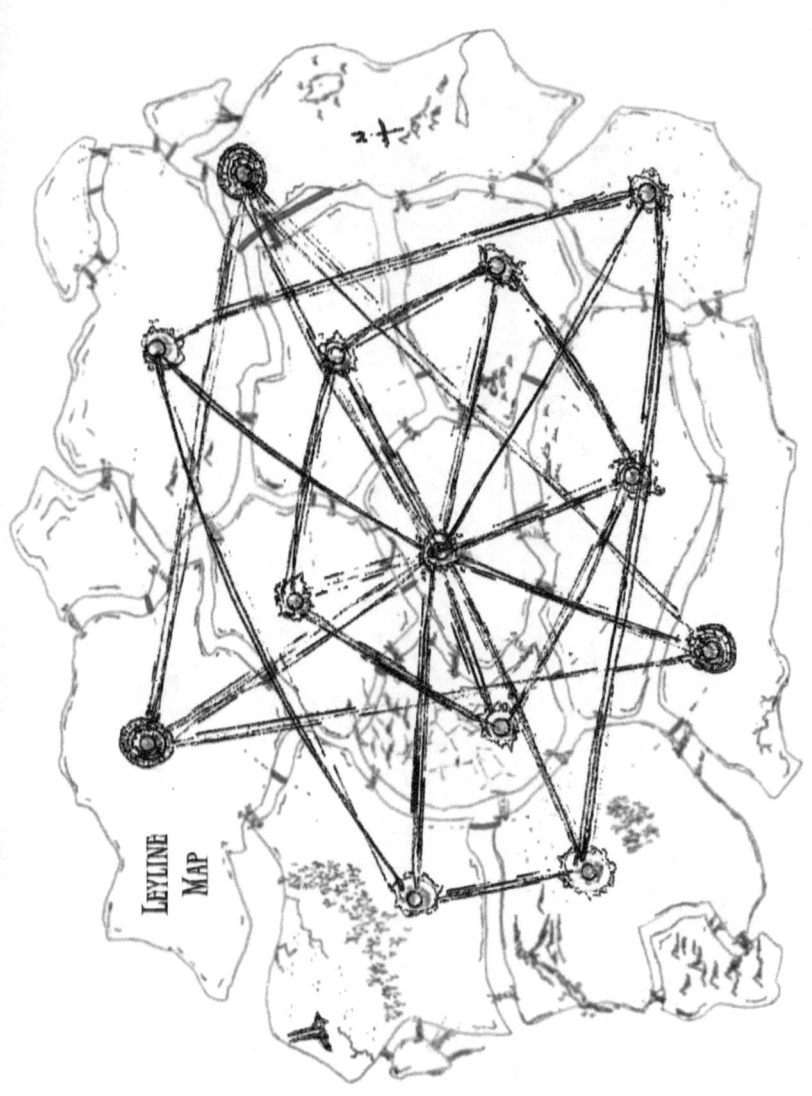

LEYLINE
MAP

Dear reader,

Thank you for reading my book. If you enjoyed it, won't you please take a moment to leave me a review at your favorite retailer (or on Amazon.com as a safe default) and share this title with your friends on social media? Discoverability is the lifeblood of success for authors and we can't continue writing without your help! Internet pirates have literally made more money off of my stories than I have and I'd certainly love to make a career out of my passion!

I also hope you will keep tabs on me by joining my mailing list. You can get free books and other updates by signing up for the list at:
www.AuthorChristopherDSchmitz.com.

Thanks for reading and sharing!

Christopher D Schmitz

About the author:

Christopher D. Schmitz is the traditionally published and self-published author of both fiction and nonfiction. When he is not writing or working with teenagers he might be found at comic conventions as a panelist or guest. He has been featured on cable access television broadcasts, metro area podcasts, and runs a blog for indie authors.

Always interested in stories, media such as comic books, movies, 80s cartoons, and books called to him at a young age—especially sci-fi and fantasy. He lives in rural Minnesota with his family where he drinks unsafe amounts of coffee. The caffeine shakes keeps the cold from killing them.

Schmitz also holds a Master's Degree in Religion and freelances for local newspapers. He is available for speaking engagements, interviews, etc. via the contact form and links on his website or via social media.

Discover other titles by Christopher D Schmitz

The Last Black Eye of Antigo Vale
Burning the God of Thunder
Piano of the Damned
Shadows of a Superhero
The TGSPGoSSP 2-Part Trilogy
Dekker's Dozen: A Waxing Arbolean Moon
Dekker's Dozen: The Last Watchmen
Wolf of the Tesseract
Wolves of the Tesseract: Taking of the Prime
Wolves of the Tesseract: Through the Darque Gates of Koth
Warrior: Gift of Sight
The Kakos Realm: Grinden Proselyte
The Kakos Realm: Rise of the Dragon Impervious
The Kakos Realm: Death Upon the Fields of Splendor
The Kakos Realm Collection Alpha
Anthologies No.1

Why Your Pastor Left
John In the John
Gospels In the John
The Indie Author's Bible

Please Visit
http://www.authorchristopherdschmitz.com
Sign-up on the mailing list for exclusives and extras

other ways to connect with me:
Follow me on Twitter:
https://twitter.com/cylonbagpiper

Follow me on Goodreads:
www.goodreads.com/author/show/
129258.Christopher_Schmitz

Like/Friend me on Facebook:
https://www.facebook.com/authorchristopherdschmitz

Subscribe to my blog:
https://authorchristopherdschmitz.wordpress.com

Favorite me at Smashwords:
www.smashwords.com/profile/view/
authorchristopherdschmitz